To J.

Gluck Art!

11/09

OTHER BOOKS BY C.D. BAKER

THE JOURNEY OF SOULS SERIES

Crusade of Tears

Quest of Hope

Pilgrims of Promise

BOOKENDS OF LIBERTY

The List

Swords of Heaven

CHRISTIAN LIVING

101 Cups of Water

40 Loaves

for more information about C. D. Baker

visit

www.cdbaker.com

The Seduction of Eva Volk

A Novel of Hitler's Christians

by

C. D. Baker

FOR ARNOLD LAUX (1925-1945)
AND THOSE WHO LOVED HIM.

PrestonSpeed Publications

PENNSYLVANIA

A note about the name PrestonSpeed Publications:
The name PrestonSpeed Publications was chosen in loving memory of our fathers, Preston Louis Schmitt and Lester Herbert Maynard (nicknamed "Speed" for his prowess in baseball).

The Seduction of Eva Volk: A Novel of Hitler's Christians
by C. D. Baker

Published by PrestonSpeed Publications,
51 Ridge Road, Mill Hall, Pennsylvania 17751.

This book is printed on acid-free paper, and its binding materials have been chosen for strength and durability.

ISBN 978-1-931587-50-1

PRINTED IN THE UNITED STATES OF AMERICA

PrestonSpeed Publications
51 Ridge Road
Mill Hall, Pennsylvania 17751
(570) 726-7844
www.prestonspeed.com

SEPTEMBER 2009

ACKNOWLEDGMENTS

I would like to briefly note a few of the many persons who assisted in my research. These include Dr. Manfred Rommel, son of Fieldmarshal Rommel, and Johann Voss, former Waffen-SS soldier and author of *Black Edelweiss.* I also thank: Friederich Haenssler—a veteran of the war and founder of the Christian publishing company Haenssler-Verlag, Dr. Claude Foster—author of *Paul Schneider, Buchenwald Apostle*, the curators of the Koblenz Archives, Ulrich Helsper –my Mosel Valley guide, and Joseph and Elizabeth Christ—my patient German language instructors.

I also owe a great debt to the extensive historical research done by others and I recommend the following sampling of books for the reader's further interest: *Ordinary Men* by C. Browning, *Betrayal* by R. Ericksen & S.Heschel, *The Soul of the People* by V. Barnett, *Theologians under Hitler* by R. Erickson, *The Nazi Conscience* by C. Koontz, *The Holy Reich* by R. Steigmann-Gall, and *Black Edelweiss* by J.Voss.

Finally, I extend my deep gratitude to those many German military and home-front veterans, shop keepers, and even passers-by who shared their painful past with patience and with hope for a better tomorrow.

PREFACE

I am quite certain that most readers of this novel would agree that Nazism stands opposed to all things they consider to be decent and moral. The story to follow, however, presents a disturbing reality: Adolf Hitler was able to draw enthusiastic support from the overwhelming majority of Germans who—like most readers of this novel—also considered their world view to be decent and moral.

The hard truth is that sane, reasonable—even 'good'—people approved Hitler's policies by referendum margins of 95% or more. By the end of Hitler's first year, 75% of Germany's public school teachers had rushed to join the Nazi Teacher's League. Most Protestant ministers willingly took the oath of loyalty to Hitler. Tens of millions of other citizens took personal oaths of loyalty by radio.

Why?

Wouldn't only monsters support Nazism?

Perhaps it would be better if that were true...for then we would only need to fear monsters. However, the story to follow is not about monsters.

It's about human beings.

It's a story about ordinary people in Hitler's Germany who were so seduced by evil that they became blind to truth.

But it's also story about us. For if we dare to look, we will find in them what lies within us all when fear, shame, confusion, and pain become desperation. Indeed, blindness is not exclusively a German condition—it is a human condition, and as St. Paul put it, "we (all of us) see the mirror dimly."

Still, blindness may be opposed and history can help do just that, particularly when we use her as a mirror. If we dare, we can learn much by looking at ourselves in the reflection of 'the other,' whether she be German or Jewish, Palestinian or Israeli, Christian or Muslim, American...or not.

The truth is, but for our providential place in time and space we *are* the other.

The characters you are about to meet are created out of years of research. I hope that you will understand these people but in understanding them I do not ask you to excuse them, forgive them, love them or hate them. I only ask you to know them and in the knowing find something of yourself in them. For if any among us denies our common humanity we have already taken the first step along the path that led the Germans into the abyss.

PART I
GROANING FOR SALVATION
1929-1932

"There are twenty million Germans too many."

Prime Minister Georges Clemenceau of France

"I'm for peace but that gang should be given a bayonet peace...It is a shame we can't go in and devastate Germany and cut off a few of the Dutch kid's hands and feet, and scalp a few of their old men."

Future American President, Harry S. Truman

CHAPTER ONE

EVEN A CHILD may be judged harshly from the safe distance of time. After all, the passing decades prove what should have been. And what should have been was not, not for Eva Volk.

In truth, little was ever as it should have been for the girl. On this cold night her heart was breaking. But Eva wanted to be brave. She wiped the tears from her brown eyes and settled deeper into her hand-me-down robe as she stared into the silent streets below her grandfather's bedroom window. She sniffled. Eva's Opa was very sick.

And so it was with her world.

Eva's village was not unlike others scattered across the broken Germany. A decade of defeat had shrouded them all within a murky haze of despair. For most, hope had become the faded afterglow of a former time. Even now the stars struggling over Weinhausen flickered dimly as a lackluster moon yielded to the slow gathering of unseen clouds.

But Eva was not one to yield to clouds.

Not easily.

Perhaps it was because she was only thirteen.

A distant steam train whistled. Eva smiled. She liked the trains. They were loyal companions who never failed to return home. She liked their determined chugging and their husky, defiant snorts. And she liked the way the steam swirled furiously around their panting black engines. For her the sounds of trains, like the gentler sounds of church bells, were sounds of comfort—sounds of belonging.

And belonging helped the girl feel whole.

But her world was far from whole.

Chasing a chill, Eva gathered her well-worn robe close to her throat and watched a lonely figure trudge through the snow into the foreboding darkness of nowhere. She wondered who he was, if he was sad, hungry or sick. Did he have a wife? Did he have children? Were they scared, too?

Her grandfather called from his bed and she answered. "I love you too, Opa." Eva did love her grandfather. But she wished she didn't have to return to his side just yet. She was frightened by his hollow eyes and his breath was stale. So she tarried a bit longer by the window that faced the wider world. She exhaled lightly to steam the cold glass and drew a heart with her fingertip.

"Come, child, come close." Opa Volk held a small wooden box on his belly and waited as Eva finally came to his bedside. She fussed with his quilt. The room was cold and draughty—coal was expensive and hard to find, even for the family of a pastor. "I took your Oma to Salzburg...for our wedding trip..." Opa closed his eyes for a few moments. His fingers tapped the box, lightly. "She loved music so..."

"Yes, Opa." Eva took a seat on the bedside stool as she had done so faithfully for these past few weeks. Her father, the reverend Paul Volk, took a turn when he could but her mother, Gerde, had grown weary of the sponge baths and the feedings.

Opa unfastened the brass latch of the box with a trembling hand and lifted the lid, then retrieved two items: a tarnished key and a smooth-worn necklace. He placed the key on his chest and lifted the gold chain with two spread fingers. It suspended an onyx, Teutonic cross that was fashioned with a golden ring encircling the intersection of its slender arms. "I bought this for Oma...from an antiquities dealer near the Mozart house. It was made to honor the Irish monks who saved Salzburg from the pagans."

Eva stared at the black and gold cross. It swung hypnotically in the dull light of the room's single yellow bulb. She thought it was the most beautiful thing she had ever seen.

"Oma's dream was to wear it to America." Opa took a slow breath. "She collected postcards from there..."

"It's so...so..." Eva had no words.

"Take it my Schätzen, now it is for your journey."

Astonished, Eva obediently extended her hand and let the chain pour into her palm. It felt warm and heavy like the comforting weight of an old blanket; it assured her like the expectant hope of a new friend. She closed her hand around her treasure and pressed it tightly to her heart. She kissed her grandfather's cheek.

Opa laid his hand lightly on Eva's head. "May it bless you, child."

A hall clock chimed seven o'clock. The old man then handed Eva the key. "Now this: find Hans Bieber...tonight. He'll be at a river inn. Show him the key and tell him it is time."

The slate-roofed village of Weinhausen squatted atop the north bank of the winding Mosel River from which it rambled uphill about a quarter of the distance to a high ridge which separated the narrow river valley from the rolling countryside beyond. Along the curving riverbank, a double set of shiny steel tracks guided slow-moving trains on their timely jaunts between Koblenz in the east and Trier in the west. These trains, like the shallow barges docked nearby, were an important lifeline to a village otherwise dependant on two poorly maintained gravel roads.

By this year of 1929 the village had evolved into an eclectic collection of buildings that were strung along narrow, haphazard cobblestone streets dating from medieval times. Some were of local brown stone and some were centuries-old half-timbered buildings, many of these tilted like the pictures in fairy tales. In the south-eastern quadrant a market square offered a variety of poorly stocked small shops. Scattered throughout were any number of work sheds and a few inns. The village was as well-kept as one might expect from a people renown for order, though a decade of depression had clearly taken its toll.

The gray years since the Great World War had made life difficult for everyone who called themselves German. Eva's parents had lost what savings they had to the terrible post-war inflation, making Eva's early years in the city of Weimar ones of extreme shortages. Now unemployment had become the great fear.

That and chaos and immorality and Bolshevism.

Eva pulled a hand-me-down coat tight to her throat in the dampness of the December night, then hurried across her street, Lutherweg—a small street running parallel to the river a ten minute walk below—and to the brick sidewalk bordering her father's Evangelical Church which lay just opposite her house. Typical to the season a heavy mist had fallen over the village providing cover from the French soldiers who had patrolled her village for a decade.

As she approached the riverside inn some silent shadows caught her eye. They were slumping their way under the train trestle, no doubt heading for the docks. She thought one of them walked like Hans Bieber. Eva followed and crouched in the cold fog near the dock where she could smell the mud and the fish scent of the river. A passing hint of sweet pipe tobacco drew her closer. She cocked her ears to the sound of men's voices. She moved closer. Suddenly, a truck engine started directly behind her and headlights stabbed through the fog just long enough to expose her squatting form.

"Who's that?" snapped a man.

Eva wanted to run but her legs went wobbly. "Please...I..."

"Eva? Eva Volk?" The first to arrive was young Wolf Kaiser, a classmate of the girl and one of the village schoolmaster's two sons. A small group of others hurried from behind.

Eva peered through the dark mist. "Wolf?"

"What are you doing here?"

"I...I..."

Hans Bieber waved for the truck driver to turn off his engine. "Eva Volk?"

She recognized the voice. "Herr Bieber, I am sorry...I..."

"What are you doing here? It's dangerous."

Eva strained to see the circle of faces now pressing close to her under the fog-filtered moonlight. "Well...I need to talk to you."

Bieber stared from under the brown leather cap he always wore. It was a short-brimmed Dutch fisherman's cap that he had bought years before while marching through Belgium. "Then talk."

Eva reached inside her coat where she dug in a sweater pocket for the key. "Opa told me to show you this and tell you that it's time."

Hans said nothing. He stared at the key and then took it from the girl, slowly.

Eva looked carefully at the weary faces pressing close. She recognized Adolf Schneider, a river pilot. "Why are you loading your boat now?" she asked.

Andreas Bauer, the soft-spoken older step-brother of Wolf, answered. "Eva, no one needs to know about this."

The girl nodded. She liked Andreas—especially his watery blue eyes that she squinted to see. "I understand..."

Bieber held the key tightly in his hand. "Go home, Eva, and tell my friend that I am on my way."

⌖

"She's only a girl in braids." The bald vintner closed the bedroom door and set his cap on a table. He was a wiry man with kind, hazel eyes set deeply under bushy white eyebrows that dominated his face along with a wide, white mustache.

"But she can be trusted." Opa Volk rallied his fast-fading strength and raised himself on one elbow. "Promise me, Bieber...you old..."

Hans laid an arthritic hand on his friend's chest. "Of course I will."

Old Volk relaxed.

"It will all be over by July anyway."

Opa Volk did not answer.

"Did you hear me?"

"Ja. I did. I am so tired, Hans..."

Too sad to answer, Bieber could only nod. At sixty-three he was younger than old Volk—thirteen years younger to be exact—but having lost his two sons to American guns and a wife to cancer, Hans had been happy for a friend of any age when the Volk family arrived in Weinhausen.

"How are the vines?" Volk mumbled.

Bieber lowered his eyes. "It is December, my friend. They are sleeping."

⌖

Two days later, on Friday, 5th December 1929, Eva's Opa Volk went to his eternal rest. On the cold gray Monday to follow he was buried in the graveyard of his son's church surrounded by his family and a village who loved him. Because the man had served the young nation of Germany against the French in 1870, a group of veterans ceremoniously placed a ribboned wreath by his grave. The chilled mourners then gathered at Paul Volk's manse for a pitiful meal of thin soup and dark bread. Few spoke and all were still hungry when they left. Most had hoped for better from the Volk family. After all, the reverend Paul Volk was employed by the government.

Later that day Eva arrived at Hans Bieber's door and knocked, anxiously.

"Ah, Eva, come in." Hans' eyes were red and his bushy white brows were standing in all directions. Eva knew he had been crying. "Thank you for coming, Fräulein."

"Ja, of course," said Eva. She slipped into a narrow foyer that was cold and dimly lit by a single yellow bulb. A black and white photograph hung on one wall. It was of a company of soldiers standing proudly under spiked helmets.

"1915," said Hans. "By '19 all but three of us were dead." He looked at the picture as if he hadn't for a long time. "They were like brothers to me." He took Eva's coat. "Follow me."

Eva followed Hans into his sparsely furnished living room and sat on an old stuffed chair. The room was clean but lacking of everything except efficiency and order. Age-yellowed lace curtains hung limply over well-washed windows. The air smelled of musty upholstery and pine oil soap. A wooden chair was placed to one side, a crudely repaired velvet sofa to another. A pearl-framed picture sat atop a poorly mended lace doily which lay on a small mahogany table. "Your wife and sons?"

"Yes." Bieber took the picture in his hand. "My Elsie, Otto, and Johann. You would have liked them."

Eva waited for the man.

"But, this is not why you've come." He put his picture down and walked into the adjoining dining room where he stooped to reach inside the bottom drawer of an old hutch. He dug under a few table linens and took hold of a green metal box which he retrieved and handed to Eva with the key. "Here. Your Opa wanted me to bring you in to our business. Open it with your key."

Eva was confused as she slowly pushed the brass key into the hole in the metal box and gave it a twist. The lid released and she raised it with a gasp. "It is eight hundred twenty-six Reichmarks." No one had this kind of money except the bankers in Koblenz. Eva lifted the bills from the box carefully as if they might dissolve like precious gold-leaf in her fingers.

Bieber reached for a half-drunk mug of beer. "Now, you must listen carefully." He took a long, deliberate swallow. "Your grandfather was pushed out of German Sudetenland after the war. The Czechs burned his business and your Oma was even attacked for wearing her Dirndl to a concert. So, he knew he needed to keep his money out of Prague. He also knew that inflation would soon ruin everybody so he converted his money to gold and kept it in Dresden.

"Times were very hard, like now, only different. People worked but money meant nothing. Prices went up by the hour. In those days it was cheaper to blow your nose with a handful of Papiermarks than to buy a kerchief. Well, when we met he said he had a plan to save my vineyards and help the poor of Weinhausen at the same time." Bieber took another drink. His mood became serious. "Now, you must swear on his memory that you'll not tell another."

Eva nodded. "I swear."The man took a deep breath. "Opa and are...were...smugglers."

Eva stared at him, blankly.

"As you know, the French don't allow us to sell our wine anywhere but to each other in the valley. If they could stop that they would. They say that their own vintners need to recover from the war we supposedly started..."

"But..."

"Anyway, your grandfather reasoned that we could avoid the embargo by smuggling wine through brokers that he knew along the Rhein. So, for the past six years we've made wine in a secret cellar and have been shipping barrels of it on Adolf Schneider's barge...that's what we were doing the other night."

Eva stared at the money again.

"One more thing: your grandfather and I split the profits seventy-thirty. You're holding what's left of his thirty percent."

"What about my parents?"

"Your Opa left your father a decent bank account in Koblenz with some conditions that withdrawals be limited. He didn't want your father to take it all out at once and lose it. He also left you and your little brother an account. The rest he hoped you'd give to the poor."

That sounded like her Opa.

"Now, if you agree, your job is to do what he did: every week you will put some of our money into the church's alms box. That way no one knows where help has come from...and rumors don't stir up the French"

"But I'll be seen."

Hans shook his head. "No, my dear. You don't do it on Sunday. You need to do it when no one can see you. That's the whole point. You can come and go into the church whenever you want."

"Treat her as the dangerous lunatic of Europe, take every precaution against her, and one day Germany will break out of her cell with the demoniac force of the lunatic."

'Social-Demokraten,' Swedish periodical

CHAPTER TWO

LATE ON A COLD February afternoon the wind whistled outside as Eva poured coffee for the workmen in Bieber's secret winery, a cellar hidden under a low, run-down stone barn in a mountain hollow high above Weinhausen. A year's worth of hard labor had transformed it into a cavernous winery complete with proper ventilation, vats, bottling equipment, and the other magic necessary to make a reasonable wine from good grapes. The room was shadowy and damp, however, lit only by the irregular light of generator powered bulbs.

Eva carried her pot and a mug toward Andreas Bauer. Over her shoulder hung a netted bag filled with black bread. The lad was holding his stiff hands toward the warmth of an iron stove. As she approached she fixed her earth-brown eyes on the almost fifteen-year old. She liked Andreas' broad shoulders and lean body; she thought he was becoming handsome. Of course, ever since his father made him move into the attic bedroom his clothes smelled of moth balls. "Coffee?"

Andreas turned. "Please." He reached for the mug and when his fingers touched hers Eva could feel her heart flutter.

She hoped his did too.

"Thank you, Eva." Andreas watched her carefully as she poured the coffee. "Lindie tells me you had a birthday...let me think...January the 18th."

The girl smiled. *He knows my birthday*! She understood why Hans Bieber—and nearly everyone else for that matter—liked him so much. Andreas was caring, honest and hardworking, decent, loyal, earnest and fair-minded. But some did say he was a hopeless romantic. From the very first day they met Eva had never forgotten how she felt whenever she looked at him. She once told Lindie that looking into Andreas' wet, blue eyes was 'like having your soul drawn into a well.' "Isn't the coffee wonderful?"

Andreas nodded as he swallowed. "Here we are, hiding in a mountain cellar drinking real coffee while everyone else has to drink that chicory crap."

Eva laughed. "Would you like some bread?"

Andreas grabbed a large chunk and gnawed away a large bite. "Thank you. I swear, Offenbacher bakes the best bread in the valley." He let his gaze linger.

Blushing, Eva moved away to serve others until she came to Andreas' half-brother, Wolf. Something about the blonde almost fourteen-year old had always drawn her—maybe his forcefulness; perhaps his boldness? "Are you cold, Wolf?"

"Me? Uh, no, not me." Wolf's blue eyes were as piercing as Andreas' were soft. "I like it in here." He sucked a long breath through his nose. "Smell that."

Eva obediently drew a deep breath. The warm air of the winery was heady with the thick smell of pressed grapes. The aroma was intoxicating and delicious; it was the stuff of dreams and she suddenly wanted to get lost in it.

Wolf reached for a piece of bread. Eva liked serving him; she liked nourishing him like this. When he stopped chewing to stare at her she looked down, submissively. Her heart beat a little faster. She wasn't exactly sure why she liked being near the boy, but there was something about the way he seized her with a single look.

Wolf was one of those whom people either loved or despised. He was loyal to his friends and cruel to his enemies. He worked hard—a high virtue, to be sure—but he was also one to conspire. His passion lay in extremes. Like Andreas, he too was a dreamer, but his dreams were more like wild fantasies.

Grumbling voices summoned Eva and her coffee pot to others. One of them, an unemployed engineer named Richard Klempner, was animated. He had recently joined the National Socialist Party and had lots to say about being German. He was speaking passionately about the special virtues of the German Volk and of their grand history. Eva paused to listen as he rambled on about the Germans' love for the land and for things decent. He stared right at her as he explained that 'National' meant all German-speaking peoples and that 'Socialist' meant the common good.

Eva wished she could feel better about being German. Her father had certainly encouraged patriotism but the films she had seen and the things she read made her feel somehow ashamed. Living under French occupation had given her little reason to be proud. For her, being German meant that she and her friends were nothing more than 'Huns,' '*Boches*', or 'Krauts'. And her flag certainly meant nothing to her or to anyone else for that matter. For most, the black, red, and gold paneled banner represented the weakness and corruption of the Weimar Republic that her people's conquerors had given them.

Bieber cleared his throat and pushed his cap back on his bald head. "We've less than twenty weeks to go before they leave."

A voice answered. "Ja, that's if they keep the treaty." A few grumbles followed.

Bieber nodded. "They will. The French have money troubles of their own now." He sipped his coffee.

"Will they give back the houses to our folk in the Ruhr!" A few years prior, the French had dispossessed 150,000 German residents from their homes in Germany's nearby Ruhr region. The German government had done nothing.

Bieber shook his head. "Let's not get into that. Yesterday the poorhouse used the last of its coal. The deacons are calling an emergency meeting to raise some money but the village is bankrupt. They'll appeal to Weimar but the politicians don't care. Besides, the children are cold *now*."

"The government is sinking fast," grumbled a voice. "I hope it collapses."

"There are riots in Berlin again," added another.

"Bolsheviks." The room murmured. Rural Germans like these wanted nothing to do with an international movement of unionists, especially one known for its ruthlessness.

Bieber lifted his hand. "Forget politics for a minute. We have a few more shipments to make but we need more money than that to get folks through the winter. If we pay for the poorhouse coal in advance we can get a better price." He looked at Richard Klempner. "And doesn't your little boy still need his medicine?"

"I have a little left."

"Do you have enough money for medicine *and* coal?"

The man hung his head. "The Party's trying to help."

"You should have come to me."

"So, are we going to sell the good wine?" Wolf blurted.

Hans Bieber had been saving a selection of spectacular white Riesling wines but he had never planned to risk a single cork until it was safe to do so. "No. Absolutely not. Not until the French leave. That wine is for the future. We can take our chances shipping the lesser stuff, but no, not my best. But I do have an idea." He lit his pipe and released a cloud of smoke. "I've decided to mortgage my vineyard. That should give us enough to buy the coal. I'll repay the bank when it's safe to ship the good stuff."

The men shifted, uneasily.

"I know what you're thinking but I don't see any other way. This very night children are sick and dying in the cold. I just can't wait and do nothing."

⌖

Through the rest of that winter Bieber's charity kept the poorhouse warm, the hungry fed and provided medicines to some. Through it all Eva Volk had never felt such joy. With every midnight trip to the alms box of her father's church the happy youth had experienced the power of belonging to something greater than herself. She felt secure and important—she felt whole.

But on an awful evening in April, all that changed.

CHAPTER TWO

Weinhausen had fallen strangely quiet under the rise of the early stars. The air was damp and a light breeze scratched a few brown leaves across the bricked courtyard of the empty market square. The faint whistle of a distant train drifted lightly atop the still waters of the nearby Mosel and Eva walked arm in arm with her giggling friend, Lindie Krause. Crossing the market square Eva paused by the ancient village well and whispered, "I saw him looking at you, you know, like..."

Lindie tittered. She, too, was fourteen. Round-faced and big-boned, the girl was kindly and gentle. She was a little clumsy and not terribly bright, but she had been a loyal friend to Eva.

"You know he did," teased Eva. "Gunther Landes likes you and I can prove it."

Lindie rocked on her feet, still giggling. "But you're the pretty one."

Eva didn't answer. She *was* the pretty one even though the idea of it embarrassed her. Even-featured and fair, the girl had the early makings of a true beauty. Uncomfortable with the comment, she turned her attention to the dull light marking the margins of closed shutters. "It's past curfew. We're going to have to hurry."

Eva had barely finished the sentence when her ears suddenly piqued to the chilling sounds of hobnailed boots on bricks. She and Lindie looked at one another with a start. A company of soldiers rounded the corner. Frenchmen! Eva's heart began to pound. "Lindie, r..."

"Halt!" A surprised, drunken officer pointed his finger at the two German girls.

The pair froze and turned, wide-eyed.

The man mumbled something to his fellows and they laughed, wickedly. "You Mädels, stand still. Do not move." His German was fluent. He pulled his shoulders back and tightened his face in feigned fury. With his men in tow he swaggered toward the girls. The officer approached and removed the embroidered kepi from his head with a mocking flourish and bowed. He took Eva's hand and kissed it, lightly. "*Oui*? Such a pretty thing standing under starlight."

"We were going home, sir. We are very sorry to be late."

"*Oui*?"

Eva's mouth felt dry as she nodded. She took Lindie's hand and stared nervously at the soldiers now encircling them. Seven were French and three were Senegalese. Her eyes fixed on the unfamiliar features of the Africans.

The officer turned to Lindie and scowled. "Do you speak?"

Lindie lowered her face.

The officer spat, then studied the steep-roofed houses and shops lining the market square. He pointed his finger at a few villagers now peering from darkened windows. "Mind your own business," he shouted. He drew his revolver—a six-shot, 8mm Lebel—and squared his shoulders in the direction of one lingering silhouette watching from the half-opened doorway of the grocery. "You, too, Jew." The door closed.

The officer holstered his pistol. "We should have slaughtered the whole of your stubborn race." The man staggered slightly. "So now I find two little braided *Boches* disrespecting my curfew. What am I to do?" He twisted his black mustache and then set his finger by his nose. "*Non*, this cannot go unpunished." Turning his face toward the shuttered houses he lifted a flask from his belt and swallowed a long swig of Russian vodka. He belched. "They think that I am a fool. I know they are still watching. I want them to be watching."

Eva's body was tense. She felt her heart racing and her breathing became shallow. Her mouth was dry, her mind whirling. *Oh dear God, what will they do to us*?

"You, pretty one, undress." The startling order was matter of fact and cold.

Shocked, Eva could not move.

"Now!" roared the officer.

Eva hesitated. "But sir, p...please..."

The officer slapped Eva with the back of his hand. "Do as I say or this whole stinking village will pay a price."

With a submissive whine Eva lifted her trembling fingers slowly toward the buttons of her thin spring coat. She then pulled one arm from each sleeve. Removed, she held the coat in her hand for a lingering moment before letting it fall silently to her feet.

"Go on, *Boche*."

Beneath was a green blouse her mother had bought from a seamstress in the poorhouse just months before. She balked and cast a terrified glance at whimpering Lindie. A rough hand struck Eva across the back of her head and she flinched to meet the leering gaze of one of the Africans. Her mind immediately filled with images of things her mother had told her about men. She felt faint.

"So, little German pig, how about this," said the officer. "Either you hurry or we will do it for you."

Eva nodded. Her fingers found the top button of her blouse, then dropped to the next and the next. To the lascivious delight of the men she then released her blouse to the ground, exposing an undershirt. *Oh, God, please...*

From one side a door suddenly slammed shut and leather soles could be heard flying along the cobblestones at the edge of the square. All heads turned and the officer yanked his pistol from his hip. He fired three wild shots in the direction of a dashing shadow. "*Vous, allez*!"

The figure vanished but in the momentary distraction Lindie burst from the ring with a shriek. Like a panicked filly she sprinted across the courtyard with two of the soldiers in immediate pursuit.

A firm hand gripped Eva's elbow. "Steady, Mädel. You're not going anywhere."

Eva cried out in pain and her face contorted. She offered a quick prayer for her friend. "Oh, please, sirs ...can't I just go home?"

"Shut up and undress."

With tears sliding down her face Eva loosed her shin-length skirt and let it fall into a pile atop her shoes. She stepped out of the skirt, removed her shoes, then her socks. Trembling in only her cotton panties and her undershirt she began to plead for mercy. Her pleas quickly turned to uncontrollable, halting sobs until Lindie's woeful cry from a distant alleyway startled her. She knew her friend had been caught and horrible things were surely happening. Eva fell silent and she tensed. Clutching her hands at her heart her eyes flew from one captor to the next.

"All the way!"

Eva clenched her eyes shut. *This cannot be real.* She drew cold air through her nostrils and tried to envision herself floating on a wooden raft along the beautiful Mosel on a summer's day.

But it was not a summer's day.

With a quaking whimper she slowly lifted her undershirt over her head, exposing her budding womanhood to the lustful murmurs of her captors. It was then that an odd but charitable numbness began to cover her, mercifully distancing her from the moment. She removed her panties and dropped them at her feet. Now utterly exposed in the moonlight, Eva lifted her quivering chin and covered her breasts with folded arms. She pressed her thighs tightly together and waited, very much alone.

"What do you want, Jew?" grumbled an unshaven man at the door of the nearly bankrupt inn known as Weinstube Krause, owned by Max Krause, Lindie's father.

"The French have Lindie and the Volk girl...in the market...they're drunk and they're going to rape them." Samuel Silbermann was gasping for breath.

The news was cried to the men meeting inside. Max Krause was also the local leader of the Nazi Party and commander of the village the SA—the Party's paramilitary storm troopers known as the Sturmabteilung. He roared for all to be quiet.

"My Lindie?"

Samuel Silbermann nodded. "Ja, ja. And the Volk girl, too."

Standing wide-legged in his high black boots, Krause was stunned. He glanced momentarily at the armbands on the sleeves of his fellows' starched brown shirts. They were red with white discs that boasted black swastikas—the ancient sun sign of good fortune. With a roar he raised his fist. "Brothers, follow me!"

The blanket of numbness that had shielded Eva was quickly removed by a hard slap on her bottom. Wincing, the painful sting tingled in the cold of the night air. The Frenchmen surrounding her began to taunt and poke. One snatched away her necklace and wrapped it around his wrist. "No, oh please, no," begged the girl. "Please, not that."

The officer's face was flushed. He had tasted of such delicious spoils before but he would not release himself or his men upon this prize too quickly.

"On your hands and knees, little gilt, and root like the German pig you are."

Eva's whole body was trembling.

"On your hands and knees, pig."

Weeping, the helpless maiden slowly collapsed her body, folding herself together as she moved downward until she squatted on the balls of her feet.

"Hands and knees!"

Wrapped tightly within herself, Eva could not move. She was punched in the back, driving her to the ground. Crying out she obediently set her knees on the hard bricks and then slowly stretched her body forward as she placed her palms before her. Her braids fell from either side of her face and she squeezed her eyes closed.

"Now, pig, let's see you root."

Eva could barely move. *Oh God, where are you*?

"Not good enough."

She couldn't. Tears dripped atop the bricks beneath her face.

"Then at least grunt!"

Eva struggled to project some deep, throaty rumbles from her belly.

"Now, root."

Eva dipped her head slightly.

"Root deeper and grunt!"

Shamed and degraded, the poor girl submitted.

"Root, you filthy swine, root!"

The officer then commanded something in French and the men fell quiet. Eva stared blankly at the blurred bricks beneath her face. Frozen in fear she remained on her hands and knees and waited in dread as she heard rifles being laid on the ground.

Her breathing quickened.

Then, worse, she heard a belt buckle open and a low, bestial murmur potent with lust.

She whimpered.

The officer suddenly snapped his head to one side. "What?" From around a corner a giant emerged leading a raging tide of men from the shadows of the unlit streets.

"Lindie!" cried the giant. "Papa comes!"

"Weapons!" shouted the officer as he fumbled with his pants. His pistol fell from its holster and he lunged for it. The others scrambled for their rifles—old bolt-action Berthiers from the war years. If they could chamber their rounds fast enough they'd have six shots each before reloading.

Several rounds were hastily fired at the village men, two flying into empty air, one striking a Brown Shirt in the leg. The stampede roared closer. More shots rang out, this time dropping two others.

Then shouts came from behind.

The officer whirled about with his pistol and emptied it at a new group, missing Wolf Kaiser by inches, ringing a lamp post by Andreas' head and nipping Bieber's arm.

The Frenchmen had mere moments. They fired a few final rounds in both directions, one striking Max Krause in the throat. The man arched backward with his hands grasping at his wound in disbelief. Gasping, he staggered to one side and then the other before careening wildly into a wall and tumbling over a cart, dead.

Krause had barely hit the ground when the angry swarm of his fellows swallowed the Frenchmen. Cursing and venting the rage of a decade's suffering, the men of Weinhausen began to beat them mercilessly.

Wolf skirted the *mêlée* and outran Andreas to Eva's side. The girl was trembling and desperately trying to cover herself. "You're safe now," Wolf panted.

"Find Lindie!" Eva pointed. "That way, hurry!"

"We Germans must become a pious Volk, a Volk in which the gospel has power over our consciences."

Emanuel Hirsch, Protestant theologian

CHAPTER THREE

A WEEK LATER, Andreas Bauer stood in front of Rev. Volk's parsonage holding a small bunch of yellow daffodils in the darkness. The brown stone house was located conveniently across from the church and at the end of a short row of houses. The young man self-consciously re-fastened the top button of his blue shirt and wiped a hand through his combed-back brown hair. Inside he could hear the pastor's gramophone playing the sounds of an orchestra recording.

Andreas raised his knuckles to the door but shrank back to gather his courage. The fifteen-year old had always adored Eva. In fact, he had spent the last week thinking of nothing other than her and the wonderful times they had shared. He remembered how he and Eva would hide behind wine barrels and laugh at Frau Kneckle's terrible voice during the village hymn sings; he remembered picking wildflowers for her on one Pentecost Sunday.

Andreas licked his lips.

He wanted to tell Eva that he had prayed for her every morning and every evening since that night. He wanted her to lean on him in her time of crisis. He especially wanted to tell her that he did not believe the rumors. Village gossip was insisting that both girls had been raped and were now forever spoiled. And some, it seemed, wondered if the naïve pair may have enticed the men in the first place. Such talk made him angry.

Ready, Andreas knocked.

Rev. Volk answered the door with a newspaper in his hand. He was one of two pastors serving the spiritual needs of Weinhausen's predominantly Protestant population. Wearing a white shirt and pleated pants held up with suspenders, he removed a pipe from his mouth. "Ja, lad?"

"I...I wondered if I might see Eva, sir?" Andreas glanced into the lamp-lit living room.

Rev. Volk looked at him kindly. He had liked Andreas from the first day he met him.

"Who's there, Paul?" It was Eva's mother, Gerde, calling from the rear of the house.

"Andreas."

"What does he want?"

Andreas thought her speech to be a little slurred. He had heard plenty of rumors about Gerde Volk.

"He wants to see Eva."

"I don't think she'll see him. She's upset."

The reverend was inclined to agree. "Well, son, Lindie's mother was here earlier to see her and I think the conversation was difficult for them both."

Disappointed, the lad politely suggested that his friendship might be a comfort to her.

Paul hesitated. "Well...we could at least ask her. Come in, please."

Andreas stepped through the front door and into the living room. The room was modest but comfortably furnished with a small desk, a stuffed chair, two fringe-shaded table lamps and a sofa. A few watercolors of Rhein castles and rural landscapes hung against faded floral wallpaper. An embroidery of the Lord's Prayer was displayed on the wall behind the gramophone.

Rev. Volk lifted the needle off his record and called through the dining room and into the yellow kitchen where Frau Volk was cutting onions. "Gerde, tell Eva that Andreas has come to see her. We'll be in my study."

"But..."

"Please, Gerde." Paul Volk was a soft-spoken man and even timid, but he could be stubborn.

Annoyed, Frau Volk set her knife down hard on the cutting board and wiped her hands on her apron. "As you wish."

The minister bade Andreas follow him up a flight of stairs which rose from the left side of the living room. At the top of the stairs the two crossed a narrow hallway, past a print of Martin Luther and stepped into the pastor's study which overlooked the church and its gardens. The office was generally tidy with the exception of a tower of newspapers in one corner. The room smelled of pipe smoke and gasoline—a small storage garage being directly below. Shelves lining one wall were well-stocked with books. Andreas scanned the names of Schiller and Goethe, Nietzsche, Luther and Calvin, Freud, and even Charles Darwin. On another wall hung a print of *The Peaceable Kingdom* by the American artist, Edward Hicks. Andreas fixed his eyes on the painting.

"You like that one?" asked Volk.

Andreas nodded. "I do. But I like my father's better. It's the one thing he left me."

Paul Volk nodded. "Yes, I've seen it...very enigmatic."

Andreas took a seat in a curved Windsor chair to one side of the man's roll-top desk.

"Eva has suffered greatly," said Paul.

"Indeed, sir."

The reverend took a long draw on his pipe. "She cries a lot of the time. She says that she feels like something has been taken from her. She's right about that."

Andreas waited.

"She says she feels like a different person now. These things are complicated."

Andreas nodded.

Paul drew a deep breath. "Those are nice flowers."

"Thank you sir."

"I haven't seen you in church lately. You've grown taller since your confirmation. You look fit and strong." The man sucked on his pipe. "I'm told that you are getting more like your real father every year. Apparently, he was a bit melancholy like you. He was an artist?"

"Yes."

"Professor Kaiser says that you inherited many of the man's traits, including a high intelligence and a good attitude about work. These are things to be thankful for."

Andreas shifted in his chair.

The reverend studied him. "You are not like your brother, Wolf, though, are you?"

"My half-brother." Andreas' correction belied a growing distance between the two boys. They were close in age—almost exactly one year apart, both having birthdays in April. But they shared little more than a common mother who had been married to Andreas' father before the man was killed during the first battle of Champagne in 1914. The woman immediately married another soldier, a professor of history named Ernst Kaiser with whom she bore Wolf. Soon afterwards she died of tuberculosis.

"Yes, of course, your half-brother. He's quite an...enthusiastic...fellow." Rev. Volk harbored unspoken concerns about Wolf.

"So, how are the French going to punish the village?" asked Andreas.

"Well, I had hoped that the death of Max Krause would have satisfied them. By the way, have you seen Herr Bieber?"

Andreas nodded. "Dr. Krebel says the bullet missed the bone. He'll be fine but he needs to keep in hiding or else the police could prove he was there that night."

"Of course, good." Paul tapped his finger lightly on his desk. "Four of the French were killed..."

"They deserved it." The lad's soft eyes were suddenly steely.

"Ja, ja, I suppose so. The French, of course, see it quite differently. So, for starters they are clamoring to arrest and execute every known SA man in Weinhausen. I think the Reds in Koblenz are pushing that idea." Paul drew on his pipe, now unlit. He tapped it hard on his palm and dumped black ashes into a waste basket. "But that's beside the point. To answer your question, on Monday Bürgermeister Beck and we pastors will be appealing to the French governor for restraint. I only wish the Americans were still here to be a voice of reason."

"The Americans seem to be more even than anybody else."

Rev. Volk nodded. "I fear we Germans are the most immoderate people of all. We tend toward excess in nearly everything. Some have called us a people of Grenzenlösigkeit—boundlessness. Our orderliness becomes perfectionism, our loyalty becomes blind obedience, our goals become obsessions, our love of community becomes intolerance..."

"Why?"

"I don't know, though I suppose our history has shaped us to some extent. I also know it's difficult to expect moderation with over six million war casualties and an unjust treaty."

Andreas thought for a moment. "The Americans only lost five percent of the men we did. They should be more moderate." He looked about the study then cast an impatient eye into the hallway. "My father tells me that the German Reich was supposed to be God's special guardians of Europe. Now he doubts God even exists."

Volk nodded. "Ja, he and many others. But God has his purposes...even for our sacred calling." The minister leaned forward. "Our defeat must be understood as a rod of learning. Over the centuries this kind of struggling has forged us into a superior people." He sat back. "When we are ready God will restore us to greatness once again. He must; the Christian world depends on it."

"But some say we weren't really defeated since not a single enemy soldier crossed our border. They say the Jews stabbed us in the back, and that the armistice was supposed to be a truce but that Jews betrayed us into surrender so they could profit by the treaty."

Rev. Volk shook his head. "Well, I'm not so sure about the Jews stabbing us in the back. As far as I'm concerned the Jews died in the trenches just like we Germans did..."

Frau Volk appeared at the door of the study. "And what would you know about the trenches?"

Andreas watched the reverend's face draw tight.

"Have you spoken to Eva?" he answered.

Frau Volk turned to Andreas. "I'm sorry, but she's not willing to see you. I believe she said, 'especially not Andreas Bauer.'" The woman's tone was matter-of-fact but not hard.

The lad was crushed. *Especially not Andreas Bauer*? "And do you know why?"

"You are a young man and not a young woman. You have no way to understand how humiliated and ashamed she is. If you did you would know why she is unable to face anyone, least of all someone she cares about."

Cares about? The words helped ease the youth's disappointment. He handed Frau Volk the daffodils and reached into his pocket to retrieve Eva's beloved necklace. "Then would you see that she gets this?"

⌖

"Eva, you said were going today. Now hurry or you'll be late." Gerde Volk was relieved that her daughter would finally be returning to school. In the three weeks since the assault the girl had been too distraught to do anything but cry in her room. She had reluctantly agreed to see Frau Krause but only once, and that had been a matter of pity for a grieving widow.

Dressed for school, she lay on her bed and stared at the ceiling. A lump filled her throat as she thought about Lindie. The day that the girl's father was buried she had tried to puncture her insides with a skewer from the Weinstube kitchen. Now the frantic teenager was in restraints in a Koblenz hospital where she was expected to stay for a long time.

Anxious about the day ahead, Eva ignored her mother's voice now echoing loudly from the bottom of the stairs. She rolled to her side. With her knees tucked close to her breast she stared at a faded painting of the Good Shepherd on a far wall. She whispered to her Savior, asking Him to show her mercy—to erase that awful moment from her life. She only wanted to be the happy girl that she once knew, the one who she could barely now remember. That former Eva Volk had felt secure and welcome; *that* Eva Volk had felt whole and happy. This Eva's mind was spinning and her belly was filled with anxiety. This Eva felt fractured; she felt only holes in her spirit, ones punctured by shame and humiliation. *How can I face them at school...how can I face anyone*?

The girl wiped her eyes and blew her nose, then sat on the edge of her bed and took a deep breath. She touched fingers to her Oma's necklace; Eva would need to be brave. Her little brother appeared at her door with a flower. "Thank you, Daniel," she said as she stood. "Tell mother that I'm coming."

Eva followed her mother uphill along Strauss Str. until she arrived at the two-storey, brown-stoned schoolhouse. It had been a Protestant school before the war but had been released to state control in the years following Germany's defeat. This would be Eva's last year in the building. She was considering continuing her education at the Handelsschule in Koblenz where she would spend two years concentrating on clerical skills.

Her mother took the girl's face in her hands, firmly. "Now, no more tears."

"Yes, Mutti." As Eva's mother turned away her friend, Anna Keller, took her hand. Anna was similar to Eva in a number of ways. She was strong, daring, and compassionate. But Anna had her differences as well. She was more flamboyant than the oft' modest Eva and was petite and red-headed. "I'll be with you."

Eva squeezed Anna's hand and walked with her toward the door before shrinking back. She removed her book-heavy rucksack and leaned against the stone wall. "I'm not sure."

Anna looked at her, sympathetically.

"No, you go. I'm not ready."

Eva shuffled to a place beneath the half-open windows of her classroom. Overhead, the school's bell rang loudly. In a few moments she heard the students rising from their double-seated slanted desks to greet Professor Kaiser, a decorated veteran of the Great War who had once taught history at the university at Marburg. She then listened to the man's morning prayer and his rhythmic reading of a Bible passage. She heard his wooden leg click atop the oak floor boards.

Emboldened, Eva took a deep breath. "Enough of this." She entered the building and hung her coat on a hallway peg, smoothed her dress, secured the button at her neck and pushed her braids behind her shoulders. She then knocked, boldly, and inhaled.

Professor Kaiser opened the door with a smile. "Ah, Eva! Now this is a good day." He leaned close to the girl. "I like your spirit, Mädel."

Eva's mouth went dry as she stepped tentatively into the quiet classroom. She faced the floor and followed the bald-headed professor through the room and across the painted line that divided the handful of Catholics from the Protestants.

Professor Kaiser put a hand on the edges of his wide lapels and stared at his classroom with eyes fixed like rivets on a steel beam. There would be no doubts about Eva's welcome. "All rise to receive our friend, Fräulein Eva Volk."

The pupils stood and applauded.

Pleased, the large-bellied professor directed Eva to her seat. He leaned on his cane and addressed the class. "Our Eva has suffered oppression, as have you. She has suffered because she is German, just like you. Her enemies are your enemies." He turned his face to Eva. "You surely belong with us, my dear."

The morning lessons were familiar; Eva listened politely as Professor Kaiser banged his cane on the floor, reminding the class again that the World War had been fought to protect Germany from Russian aggression and the jealousies of the French and English. Eva stared at her desk. *How many times does he have to tell us*! Before breaking for lunch he read the class a newspaper article which announced the rising unemployment rate for Germany to be at fourteen percent—almost twice that of America. He finished with a warning about the spread of godless Bolshevism in both Germany and America. Eva wondered if her American cousins knew.

"Hallo, Vati," Eva said as she entered the front door for her two hour lunch.

CHAPTER THREE

Paul Volk had just returned from giving devotions to the ladies' sewing circle gathered in the church auxiliary building next to the graveyard. The man looked weary but he gave his daughter a hug. "By your smile I'd say you had a good morning. I'm so proud of you."

Eva let her father's arms enfold her. She closed her eyes.

"Good, she's home. I need her help in the kitchen." Gerde Volk's speech was slurred again. Against her husband's objections, Gerde kept bottles of plum schnapps and vodka at the ready. "Come in here and slice the Wurst."

Eva threw her rucksack on a table, then hurried into the kitchen and wrapped an apron around her waist. She reached for a short roll of souse.

Paul Volk ambled into the room with a freshly lit pipe. He leaned on the door jam and looked at Gerde's three stacked pots of boiling water. Weinhausen's housewives had concocted every conceivable means of efficiency.

"I guess you want coffee?" asked his wife.

"Real coffee?" he teased.

"You know what I mean." The woman shook her head.

Eva smiled to herself, then raced upstairs and returned with a small brown bag. "Here, Papa." She beamed.

Curious, Paul reached for the bag and stuck his nose inside. He breathed, deeply. "Oh, the smell of heaven!"

Gerde snatched the bag and stared into it. "Coffee? Real coffee? Who has real coffee in this village?" She smelled the beans slowly, letting the delicious aroma fill her nose. Her eyes fluttered.

"I thought you'd like it and..."

"Where did you get this?" Gerde's tone was now laced with suspicion.

Eva began to flush. "I... bought it from...Herr Silbermann at the grocery. I wanted to thank him for . . ."

"With what money?"

"Uh...uh...I sold my doll."

"Your doll? The doll your grandmother sent from Danzig!" Frau Volk was now furious. She glared at the girl for a long moment and narrowed her eyes. "Wait. You're lying . . . again, I can feel it. I just saw your doll . . ."

Paul interrupted. "Now, Gerde, leave the girl be. Just believe her for once."

Eva stared blankly at her father, and then turned to her mother. "Lying again? Believe me for once?" Tears began to well. "You don't believe me about that night?"

Gerde tossed the bag of coffee atop the table. "Both of us have tried very hard to believe you . . . but now this. You're lying about coffee so why not about that other wicked business?"

Eva's mind whirled. Speechless, she stared blankly into the fast blurring face of her mother. Yes, she had lied about the doll but that didn't matter to her now. Her fears had just been confirmed—her mother had never been her advocate to the gossips after all.

Yet that was not the half of it.

Another question now stabbed at her heart. What about her father? Eva turned to the man, not wanting to believe the thing she now feared most of all. "And you, Papa? You believe me, don't you?"

Uncomfortable, the man answered awkwardly. "I believe you sold your doll..."

"The doll? No, not the doll!" she cried. "What about that night?"

Paul looked away.

Eva gasped. Her father, her Papa, didn't believe her. If he wouldn't defend her who would? She followed his evasive eyes. "Why, Papa, why?"

"You were naked in the market," blurted her mother. "And you hid in your room for three weeks. What else could have happened? You act like you're hiding something."

"Gerde..." Paul Volk was shifting on his feet.

"No. I'm talking to Eva...Eva, come back here!"

"In Christ, the embodiment of all manliness, we find all that we need."

Dietrich Eckart, mentor to Adolf Hitler

CHAPTER FOUR

ON A WARM, mid-May Saturday morning, Eva moved stiffly toward the storage garage with a paper bag tucked inside her blouse. She had not recovered from her father's silent abandonment so she hurried past him as he feigned interest in a failing grapevine that climbed the front of the house.

"Eva, here, have you looked at this vine?" Paul said. He feared he had lost his little angel and the thought of it pressed heavy on him.

Eva kept walking.

The minister tried again. "Look, the leaves on these branches are healthy, but those are yellow, those are black...some others are wilted. Even Herr Bieber can't figure out if the problem is in the roots or the branches."

"I'm sure you'll get it eventually," offered Eva sarcastically. Her cold tone felt oddly good to her.

"You think so?" Paul's throat swelled. "Well, you're probably right. Hans is the best vintner in the Rheinland."

Eva said nothing.

"Do you know how I know that?"

The girl opened the door to the garage with a shrug.

"Look at his legs. You only get legs like that from spending sixty-three years on the side of a mountain!" The girl didn't laugh.

Eva had decided to visit Lindie who had been released from the hospital just a few days before. Ignoring her father, she stepped through the blue frame of her Wanderer bicycle and put her foot on the wide pedal. She emerged quickly from the garage and rode by the church yard, quickly turning away from the hard eyes of three women mulching the rose garden. She knew they were angry about the penalties the village had suffered on account of that night.

Eva took the first right which took her along a row of half-timbered houses and past a woman washing windows. The woman spotted her and threw down her sponge. "You! My husband is still in jail because of you." The woman's face was red, her nose lifted by a curled upper lip. "You and that Krause girl are little whores. No decent man will ever want you now!"

Eva stood on her pedals and aimed her bicycle uphill. She wanted to cry but she also felt anger heating her at the edges. Wolf Kaiser's panting voice suddenly came from behind. "Eva!"

The girl turned her head.

"You're hard to catch!" said Wolf as he pedaled close.

Eva dismounted and the two dropped their bikes atop the sidewalk.

"What's the matter?"

Eva plopped herself on the curb.

"What happened?" Wolf's voice reflected genuine concern.

Eva shook her head. "I hate it here."

Wolf sat next to her. "Because of that old cow?"

Eva shrugged. "I'd like to slap them all."

Wolf laughed.

"Shut up."

"So where are you going?" asked Wolf.

"Lindie's." Eva blew her nose into a kerchief.

"I heard your Uncle Rudi is coming for the confirmation service."

"Ja." Eva relaxed a little. She liked her uncle. Rudolf von Landeck was a worldly, confident man who came and went from time to time with a wealth of news and a few laughs. He had a soft spot for Eva.

"He's your mother's brother, right?"

Eva nodded.

"And he's your only uncle?"

"My only uncle in Germany. My father has a brother, Uncle Alfred, but he moved to America when the war started. He even changed his name from 'Volk' to 'Folk' so it would be more American. My mother thinks he's a coward."

"Me too," Wolf said. "I hear Rudi's rich."

"He works for an ink company in Berlin...Rosenstein Tinte...and he travels all over Europe selling to newspaper companies. He even gets to New York sometimes. He sends my father newspapers from everywhere."

"Rosenstein sounds like a Jew. I wouldn't work for a Jew."

"Why not?"

"Why should I make a Jew rich? They stabbed us in the back and now they feed off our misery."

"I bet Richard Klempner told you that," Eva said.

"The Party has all the proof. You really should consider joining the other girls in the BDM. They'll teach you about Jewish Bolshevism and how to be a good German mother. You could get a magazine like *Youth and Homeland*."

Eva stood and lifted her bike. "The only Jews I know are the ones that live here and they never bothered me. Herr Silbermann's the one that ran for help that night."

Wolf spat and threw his leg over the bar of his bike. "Yeah? Well you should read what Henry Ford has to say."

"The car maker?"

"The National Socialists aren't the only ones who understand the problem with the Jews."

Eva wasn't interested.

"What's under your blouse?"

Eva reddened. "You shouldn't be looking there."

Eva slowly turned at Professor Kaiser's two-bedroom corner house where she noticed Andreas and his step-father in the side yard. Andreas was facing their vegetable garden with his fists on his hips. Professor Kaiser was pointing with his cane and shouting.

"Tear out the whole row!" roared the professor.

"But, I..."

"Do as I say. That's the end of it." The man stormed away.

Eva got off her bike and quickly removed the bag from her inside her blouse. "Andreas?"

The young man turned and brightened. He was beginning to broaden in the shoulders and his face was becoming more angular. Eva thought he was getting more handsome with each passing month. "Eva! Hello. I was just tending the garden."

"Maybe you should keep tending then," said Wolf as he arrived behind Eva. He set the kickstand of his bike.

Andreas walked close to the girl. "I'm glad to see you, Eva. I'm..."

"Thank you for the flowers and for getting back my necklace."

"You're welcome. Klempner got your necklace off a dead Frenchman and Hans had the jeweler fix the clasp."

"That was so nice. Really." She lifted her necklace from inside her blouse. "It means so much to me." Sudden memories prompted her to change the subject. "Why was Professor Kaiser yelling at you?"

"See the cabbages?"

Eva nodded.

"Well, that row came up with a couple out of line."

"So?"

"He says that the row is out of order so I'm to tear it out and plant cucumbers."

"Why don't you just move the odd ones into place?"

"Yes, that's exactly what I said. But he says if one is out of place the whole row is out and he won't have it."

"But he's right," blurted Wolf. "Tell me your row's straight."

Andreas threw his hoe. "Tearing out the row isn't the way to fix it! He's just trying to make some bigger point but I have to do the work!"

"Well, I'm late," said Eva. "I'm supposed to see Lindie."

Andreas wiped his face with a rag. "I hear she's doing better now?"

"Yes, much."

He looked at the bag in Eva's hand. "What's in there?"

"Oh, I'm giving her something."

"What?"

"A doll."

Pentecost Sunday fell on 8 June in this year of 1930. The day was dreary and wet; a steady rain had begun to fall at daybreak. As with every Sunday, Rev. Volk had routinely rung the church bell at 7:00 a.m. to remind the village of the Sabbath. He had rung it again at one hour before the service to remind his people to keep moving. Then, like always, he would ring it one more time at precisely ten minutes before the start of the service so they'd hurry.

Eva left the breakfast table as her father made his move toward the front door for the second bell. Today would be her confirmation, the day she would confirm her personal belief in the doctrines of the Christian church into which she had been baptized as an infant. She climbed the stairs to what had been her room—what was once her Opa's room—and exchanged her robe for a traditional black dress that the traveling seamstress had refitted for her. It had a delicate white collar, was gathered slightly at her waist and fell nearly to her ankles. She then reached for the shiny new pair of black pumps that her uncle Rudi had given her. She slid them over her feet, anxiously.

With the tip of her forefinger she quickly dabbed some of her mother's cologne on her neck. It was Echt Kölnish Wasser 4711—the very same cologne that Napoleon had bought for his second wife, Marie-Letizia, or so she had been told. Actually, the fragrance could also be drunk to cure all manner of ailments including a nervous stomach. Eva swallowed a thimble full and then ran a brush through her hair one last time. Usually in braids, today it was loose and fell to her shoulders in a long, page boy style—straight bangs and blunt cut on the ends. She hesitated, but finally pinned on the small lily-of-the-valley corsage that her father had bought her. She had not yet forgiven him.

Eva held her mirror at arm's length and studied herself. The fourteen-year old was blooming as quickly as the pansies in her window box. She had a symmetrical face with high cheekbones and wide-set brown eyes framed by soft, arching brows. Her nose was straight and in perfect proportion to her face. She had stopped growing, but at 5'4" she was taller than most. No longer gangly, she was now taking the shape of a young woman.

As she stared at her reflection the words of the window-washing woman whispered within. *No decent man will want you now*. Eva's throat swelled. She wondered if that might be true. The girl closed her eyes and tried to pray the whispers away.

Eva was more pious than some. She sometimes prayed along the river, especially when the Mosel's spring meadows boasted yellow flowers and when white apple blossoms bloomed brightly against green grass. Other days she would walk or ride her bicycle along the river road a short distance west toward the Catholic village of Kobern where she climbed the hill to the ruins of Niederberg Castle. There she would sit on the edge of the ancient stone well and read her Bible. So for Eva this day was important; it meant something. She would receive her first Communion and be welcomed into the holy Christian Church as an adult.

But she wasn't excited.

In fact, since the incident with her father she had let herself feel little, except the persistent abrasions of shame, anger, and fear.

As the pipe organ played Johann Heermann's, *O Gott, du frommer Gott*, the female confirmands entered the side door of the church ahead of the boys and took their places in the front pew. To one side of Eva sat her red-headed friend, Anna Keller. To the other sat a very uncomfortable and very self-conscious Lindie Krause. Lindie had continued to suffer much since her recent release from the hospital, not the least of which was her mother's shame. But Eva had been a stubborn friend and Rev. Volk had graciously traveled to Koblenz many times to provide the girl with her confirmation lessons. His selfless kindness had inspired Lindie to risk venturing into public.

Volk was pleased to see so many of his people in attendance. Since the war, many had become discouraged with a God who seemingly abandoned them to an unjust defeat and cruel humiliation. That, coupled with modern science's half-century of ridicule for the Bible had taken a toll.

After offering a loud and heartfelt prayer, Volk motioned to the upstairs organist who played the hymn, *Commit Thou All Thy Griefs*. He then read from the New Testament book of The Acts, chapter two, which related the story of the Holy Spirit's descending upon the people of God. Finally, he delivered an impassioned sermon from Ezekiel 14 in which he reminded his flock that idols draw men close before crushing them.

The minister then turned to his sixteen candidates. He looked at each one carefully. He had examined them individually during the week before and found them all to be satisfactory in their knowledge of the *Heidelberg Catechism*. To prove it he would ask them two random questions of the one hundred twenty-nine they had attempted to memorize. With a voice loud enough for the quiet church to hear, he asked the whole group, "From question number one: What is your only comfort in life and death?"

The sixteen answered in unison: "'That I with body and soul, both in life and death, am not my own but belong unto my faithful Savior Jesus Christ who with his precious blood has fully satisfied for all my sins and delivered me from all the power of the devil.'"

Volk nodded. He then looked directly at Wolf. The minister was not pleased to see the boy wearing his Hitler Youth uniform. "And, now, from question number ninety-two, what is the First Commandment?"

Relieved, the group answered, "'Thou shalt have no other God before me.'"

Eva held Lindie's hand securely as the sixteen finished by reciting the *Apostle's Creed* and the *Lord's Prayer*. She watched her father walk to his place behind the Lord's Table and raise a hand over the sacraments as he read, "Beloved in the Lord Jesus Christ, attend to the words of the institution of the Holy Supper of our Lord Jesus Christ, as they are delivered..."

A grumble was heard near the center of the church. Eva turned to look as her father cast a casual glance over his glasses. Volk continued. "But let a man examine himself and so let him eat of that bread and drink of that cup; for he that eateth and drinketh unworthily..."

Another mumble was heard. Eva squeezed Lindie's hand.

The minister finished his reading without interruption and the chorister led the congregation in singing, *Oh, Sacred Head, Now Wounded*. Rev. Volk then opened his arms and invited the confirmands to stand and form their line. They would then come forward to the table individually to receive their first Communion and a prayer of blessing.

The black-dressed girls were first in line and the last of theirs was Eva who took her place just behind Lindie. The first girl stepped forward and kneeled as the minister laid a wafer on her opened palms for her to eat before holding the chalice of wine for her to sip.

Eva's eyes remained on her father as she shuffled forward. Tears began to well. Hearing his gentle voice and watching him smile so kindly over each kneeling girl suddenly reminded her of how much she really did want to forgive him despite how badly he had hurt her. After all, her love for him had never been extinguished. And he had surely been sorry. How could she not forgive him here, under the ancient wooden cross and at the very table where grace is found?

Eva inched closer to the table, ignoring a few snide remarks whispered into her ear from behind by Wolf. The congregation began singing another hymn. Hearing the voices fill the corners of the church restored the girl to some sense of welcome, to some assurance of hope.

And then it was Lindie's turn.

Lindie knelt before the pastor, awkwardly, and opened her palms just as the second stanza of the hymn ended. In the untimely pause, a voice abruptly grumbled, "Not her."

Whispers hissed through the front half of the sanctuary. Rev. Volk looked up briefly and stared blankly at his congregation as the third stanza began. He then laid a wafer onto Lindie's sweated palms. "The body of Christ..."

"Not her," growled the voice again. This time it came over the singing. The organist stopped, the church fell silent.

Shocked, Eva turned her head and stared into the congregation.

"Now, please," began Rev. Volk. "Please..."

"Make them stop, father," Eva whispered.

"Well..."

Frau Scharf stood, defiantly. "Herr Pfarrer, we've heard of no confession from your daughter or the Krause girl. This is not right for them to receive Holy Communion."

Rev. Volk faltered.

"Confession?" blurted Wolf. He stepped in front of Eva as if to shield her. "What are you, Catholic? They've nothing to confess."

Eva felt the blood rush to her face.

"Not so. They brought us all our troubles!" cried Frau Scharf as she turned to the congregation. "They had no business flaunting themselves to the French..."

Lindie nearly fainted. Eva threw her arm around her shoulders and she and Anna seated her in a pew. Other voices stirred as a confused Rev. Volk floundered.

Wolf thrust out his chest. "That's a lie! Why don't *you* confess, Helga Scharf, you and your husband?"

The surprised congregation murmured as Volk tried to restore order.

"No, Herr Pfarrer," snapped Wolf. "I want to hear that old sow tell us the names she gave the French."

The people fell silent, waiting.

Andreas' voice sounded from the balcony. "Tell us!"

"Enough, please," pleaded Rev. Volk. "This is the house of God. Please, no more."

Eva stared at her hand-wringing father incredulously. "Father, tell the Scharf's to leave."

"I...I...I don't know anything about the French, I..."

"Oh, Papa!" cried Eva. She turned to Wolf. "Take us out of here."

The next morning Eva stared listlessly into the bare sheen of her breakfast plate. The debacle of her confirmation had returned her to those dark, lonely places within herself. She hated those places but where else might she find refuge? Her father's love was suspect, again; Lindie was a mess; her church felt dangerous. She wondered how many in the village thought the same way that Frau Scharf did. The question kept the tortuous memories of that night very much alive.

Then again, there was always Wolf and Andreas, and Bieber's little band of smugglers. But could they be enough?

Disheartened, the girl was not enjoying her Uncle Rudi's visit. He usually told fascinating stories and he almost always managed to spend a little time with just her. But on this trip he had taken only one brief walk with her on which he had seemed distracted. She wondered if he no longer loved her like he used to do. This visit was actually depressing her. He had spent every table talk discouraging everyone with dreary news of national and international conditions. Eva was quite certain this morning's breakfast would be no different.

"I know the Germans, their tendencies and their methods. Thus I understand perfectly well that every German that we can somehow get rid of must leave Poland.

Future Polish Interior Minister, Cyryl Ratajski

CHAPTER FIVE

RUDI ARRIVED AT the table already speaking of trouble brewing in the Orient. Apparently the Japanese military had recently assassinated their nation's prime minister. Eva feigned interest as he went on with new reports of Joseph Stalin's brutality in Russia, but soon her eyes returned to her empty plate. She just wanted to get to Anna Keller's house to hear the new jazz record just arrived from Berlin. *Let's just eat and let me get out of here.*

"So, Gerde, I'm sorry to leave this morning but I've an appointment in Frankfurt." The thirty-nine year old Rudi watched his sister deliver a basket of bread to the table.

"We've been happy to have you." Paul Volk pulled up a chair. "And thank you for the groceries."

"Yes, of course, and thank you for your hospitality," Rudi said. "But this place has become so grim. It's worse than ever. Are you going to be alright?"

Paul nodded. "Yes, God is good."

Rudi leaned forward. "Are you sure?"

"Yes. I have a salary..."

"A pittance," growled Gerde. She turned to her four-year old. "Daniel, drink your milk."

"And my parishioners provide us with a pig every year, vegetables in summertime, and plenty of wine and beer."

"If you ever need..."

"Thank you, but we're fine." Anxious to change the subject, the minister bade everyone to bow for the morning's prayer. When finished, he passed the basket of bread to his guest first. Rudi quietly reached for a hard roll, then took one boiled egg and a half-slice of ham. Gerde helped herself to a rye roll on which she spread a thin smear of black Johannisbeermarmelade.

Rudi cut the top off his boiled egg with a flare and quickly reminded everyone of another concern. His and Gerde's mother (Eva's maternal grandmother, Helga von Landeck) was enduring much hardship. She lived in East Prussia which, though still part of Germany, had been separated geographically from the rest of the nation by the Versailles Treaty. "Mother had a cold winter," said Rudi. "She claims the Poles blocked the coal trains from Germany. The devils won't let us have a corridor to our own countrymen, you know."

Gerde set down her knife, angrily. "This can't go on. How can they leave a part of Germany cut off from the rest of us like this? It's un-Christian."

Rudi nodded. "She says the Poles have slogans scrawled on her building like, '*Co Niemiec, to pies*...Whoever is German is a dog.'"

"Their day will come," Gerde said. She lit a cigarette. "What about the others?"

Rudi bit off a piece of his roll and swallowed. "Mother says she gets letters from Helmut sometimes. The whole family's suffering. Some have been run off their farms; others have lost their jobs to the Poles." He took another bite. "It's bad."

Paul reached for a slice of cheese. "I've read that the Poles are pretty hard on the Jews."

Rudi shrugged. "So? The Jews make enemies everywhere they go...always have. Most of them keep to themselves like they're better than the rest of us, and they make their money on the hard work of others. Did you ever see a Jew with calluses?" He drew on his cigarette and released a cloud of smoke, laughing. "It's funny. In one way they're all the same, in another they're different. In Poland they keep the old customs, wear hats and beards, dark clothing and the like. The boys wear side-locks." He looked at

Daniel with a scary face. "And they all have black eyes and big noses!"

Daniel squealed with laughter. "I saw pictures. They look like monsters."

Paul looked at his son, sternly. "You're not to talk at the table." He finished his coffee. "And that's not nice to say about anyone. Drink your milk."

Rudi bounced the ash off his cigarette. "Actually, most German Jews don't want the eastern Jews here but they keep coming to escape the Poles. My boss wishes they'd all go back."

"What do you think?" Eva asked.

"I don't care much either way. German Jew, Polish Jew...a Jew's a Jew to me, side-locks or not." He reached for some cheese. "I read where that American flyer, Lindbergh, says that too many Jews create chaos in a country.'"

Paul nodded. "They seen to disproportionately influence money, politics, and the arts..."

"Of course," interrupted Rudi. "And as long as they can muddle the identity of their host nation, they prosper."

"If that's true, who can blame them? That would make them less likely to suffer the persecution we Christians have inflicted on them over the centuries."

"Read your Bible. The Jews started the whole business by killing Christ and then his followers. They hunted down the early Church without mercy." Rudi sipped his coffee. "However, don't get me wrong. I don't think they deserve some of the vulgar actions of the National Socialists, either. Not every Jew should be blamed for the actions of a few. You know, my boss is a Jew and he pays me well. To his credit he gives a lot of money to the poor...Christian poor."

Paul reached for another roll. Changing the subject he said, "I appreciate the newspapers you're sending, Rudi. I read them all but I have to say the more I read the more troubled I become."

Rudi squashed the end of his cigarette. "You should be. The cities would shock you. Prostitutes are everywhere and homosexuals flaunt themselves in public. Abortionists are busy. I tell you, Berlin seems more like New York or Paris. The Jews have the cabarets and cinemas filled with immoral filth. Somebody had better come up with some answers."

"I'm afraid we'll soon have to choose between the Communists and the National Socialists; the parties in the center are shriveling up." Paul ripped his bread. "The Reds are no choice but I'm not thrilled with Hitler and his Party. Some of their ideas are good but some seem very extreme."

"I confess a certain fascination with this Hitler fellow. Something about him reminds me of Napoleon. But, I wouldn't worry too much, Paul. You know what they say, 'the soup is never served as hot as it's cooked.' Rudi took his suit coat off the back of his chair and shoved his arms into its sleeves. "Besides, most of the theologians I've read see National Socialism as having a solid Christian core." He reached for Paul's hand. "So, enough of all that. I need to get on the road." He looked at Daniel. "You haven't drunk your milk, boy."

Daniel stared at the yellowish goat's milk waiting in his glass. "It tastes like zoo."

Rudi roared and lifted the glass to his nose. "Phew. Gerde, have some mercy on the imp and find a parishioner with a cow." He put his straw hat smartly atop his head. "Now, time to go."

The family followed Rudi out the door. His car was parked across the street. It was a green, two-door, 1924 Opel Laubfrosch. A few unemployed men had gathered around it. "Many thanks." Rudi shook Paul's hand. "I'll come back and check on you." He then squatted and handed Daniel a brass compass. "Maybe you can find the right path for Germany." The two laughed.

Rudi turned to Eva. "So, young lady. Congratulations on your confirmation...such as it was. I guess you'll get your sacraments eventually?"

Eva shrugged. She didn't care anymore.

⌖

Eva was hopeful and even happy as she stood on the bow of Adolf Schneider's barge. She liked being with Bieber and his smugglers; they had never abandoned her.

CHAPTER FIVE

Today was a special day. It was the day that Bieber's prized wine would be shipped to the broker's warehouse in Koblenz without any fear of the departed French who had finally ended their occupation about a week prior. Beginning in the earliest hours of the morning Eva had helped her friends load the barge with truckloads of their precious cargo. Now, she, Wolf, and Richard Klempner were waiting for the last load to arrive from Bieber's mountaintop cellar.

The July morning was hazy and humid. Wolf sat in short pants and a loose shirt on the stern of the barge. He swallowed a large draught of cool water that Eva handed him. Richard Klempner was staring westward as if French patrol boats would be rounding a bend at any moment.

"You worry a lot, Herr Klempner," said Eva.

"Say what you want, I still have a bad feeling about this. I just want to see Bieber get his money and pay off that Jew banker." The twenty-six year old Party chairman was agitated.

Eva handed him a drink of water.

"Klempner," added Wolf. "You're like the old man. He's been fretting over this stuff like a mother hen. Just relax; it's going to be alright."

"When's the last time anything was alright?"

Wolf shrugged. "Well, you're not in jail anymore."

Eva wanted to change the subject. "How's your son?"

"He's breathing badly today and coughing more than ever. Dr. Krebel said he might have tuberculosis." The man's voice tightened.

"Too bad," Wolf said casually. He spat into the river and watched the foam float away. "Eva, don't you wish we could have gone to the parade in Koblenz?"

Richard interrupted. "We can celebrate the end of the occupation all we want, but without a German army in the Rheinland the French can come back any time they please."

Eva shook her head. "The treaty won't allow our soldiers here."

"Burn the blasted treaty."

Wolf spat over the side of the boat again. "Can you imagine the politicians in Weimar saying that?"

Klempner cursed. "Weaklings. Corrupt, pocket-lining democrats is what they are, nothing more. Give me a strong man who knows his duty and we'll all live better than under these wheeler-dealers with their big cigars and fancy clothes." He tossed his cigarette into the river. "Stinking Americans."

"What?" Eva was always curious about the Americans.

"Those meddlers jumped into the war to 'make the world safe for democracy.'" He cursed. "The democracy they forced on us is nothing more than corruption, and now all Europe is soft and vulnerable to the Jew Reds. It's easy for the Americans to be idealists. They don't have Stalin's armies a two day march from their border, and they don't have the world's largest Communist Party trying to take them over!"

Wolf yawned. "I saw a big, black car drive to Bieber's house on Tuesday."

"That was the Jew banker and his homo clerk. You'd think he'd take his foot off the old man's neck," said Richard.

"Is he after Herr Bieber?" The girl's brow furrowed.

Klempner nodded. "He foreclosed on two farms in Horchfeld, and then told Bieber that he was in the area so he thought he'd stop by and ask why he was behind." The unemployed engineer lit another cigarette. "I want to be there the day Bieber dumps his cash on that moneylender's desk, and then I'd like to burn the bank."

"Do you think this sale will cover his mortgage?" asked Eva.

"Bieber says it should pay most of it but the next harvest should take care of any left over. I just hope it satisfies that bug-eyed Jew." Klempner stared into the green water. "But I think Hans is in deeper than he lets on. Besides taking care of the poorhouse, I know he made loans to more than a few families over the past couple of years. His wine is good but it's not gold."

Wolf grunted. "You heard that Lindie's pregnant?"

"Do we have to talk about that?" Eva said.

"Yeah. Bad news for her," said Richard.

"Another Rheinbastard," said Wolf.

Klempner cursed. "Just what Germany needs, another half-ape."

"That's an awful thing to say," said Eva. "Why don't you two just leave it alone."

"Lindie swears a white man did her but Frau Krause thinks she's lying," said Wolf.

Klempner thought for a moment. "Volk shouldn't baptize a half-breed. He always taught that God intended the races to be separate." Klempner wiped his face. "Even in America it's illegal for races to intermarry."

Eva was pretending not to listen.

"I thought you said the Americans are idiots," Wolf said with a sarcastic grin.

Eva had enough. She walked atop the wooden crates now filling the barge's open hold and watched Wolf jabbing playfully at Klempner with a stick. She quickly remembered how the boy had charged toward her from the *mêlée* in the market. She liked Wolf, a lot, even though she really didn't know why. Her brain told her to stay away; her heart yearned to be close. Both head and heart agreed that Wolf could be a confusing blend of contradictions. On one hand he could be a passionate protector of the downtrodden, yet he could be calculating and cruel. He could be a dreamer in the extreme, yet a calculating pragmatist. Furthermore, village gossip still spun the story of how he once robbed a blind woman in Trier and set her hair on fire for fun.

Eva also knew that the word most often strung in the same sentence as Wolf's name was 'arrogant.' The title was sometimes blurted when the lad swaggered through the marketplace in his Hitler Youth uniform. It was a well known fact that his father had indulged him beyond all reason and some believed that such spoiling had added fuel to a disposition already shaped genetically by the impulsive, high-strung mother the boy had barely known.

Adolf Schneider's three white-haired boys arrived at the dock, shouting and wrestling with one another. Eva groaned. The Schneider boys were the village hellcats. Otto, almost twelve, was the oldest. Spirited but sometimes mean, he was always game for adventure. The often sickly ten-year old Udo was a bony imp who could sing like an angel in children's choir yet bite like a devil on the playground. The youngest Schneider was Heri, eight. To survive, this little fellow had learned to be cunning and quick.

The girl's head was then turned by the familiar purring of Oskar Offenbacher's 1918 Ford delivery truck. *Finally. Let's hope this is the last of it.* Relieved, she jumped on shore and climbed the wide cement steps leading to the top of the bank where she met Bieber, Andreas, and four men climbing stiffly out of the canvas-topped truck. "Last load?"

Andreas answered. "Ja. Good thing. I'm tired."

"Are you coming with us?" asked Eva.

"No. I'm supposed to help your father fix his gramophone after lunch."

Eva was disappointed.

Smiling, Bieber reached for a pry-bar and opened a crate. He lifted two green bottles high overhead. They were distinctively labeled with the name, "Bieber" in black gothic letters printed over a cream-colored background. Alongside the name was the sketch of a muscular vintner shouldering a large basket filled with grapes. "What say we have our last taste before these bottles are on tables in Berlin or Frankfurt...or maybe New York!"

⌖

"Who are you? My deal was with Peter Kleppinger." Hans Bieber was confused. Cap in hand, he stood alongside Eva with his men in the wine broker's office at Koblenz.

"As I said, Herr Kleppinger does not work here now."

"I just talked to him Wednesday." Hans' tone was respectful, but firm.

Standing, the middle-aged broker tapped his left hand along the bottom hem of his pin-striped suit coat. He narrowed his dark eyes at Bieber. "Peter Kleppinger is in police custody. He was caught smuggling a shipment of handguns to the SA in Bonn."

Hans cast a sideways glance at Richard Klempner. He held his receipt forward. "We unloaded just an hour ago and your warehouseman told me to bring this receipt for payment. I would like my money."

The broker took the receipt and then checked the pocket watch in his vest pocket. "Well, we're ready to close the office." He took two cigars from inside his jacket and offered one to Bieber. "As I said, we are about to close but for you we will stay open a little longer. Please, come with me."

"And my friends?"

"Of course." The businessman led the vintner and his party through the half-staffed office. To a person, Bieber's friends were uncomfortable. They didn't trust this 'suit' and they didn't like the way they felt in his office. Dressed in overalls and clumsy work shoes Bieber's men felt dirty and inferior to the spectacled clerks gawking at them from behind their desks.

Bieber was directed to a low, wooden chair in front of the broker's desk. The others stood behind him.

"My name is Jakob Gercowski and I am the owner of this firm." He sat down in a leather executive rocker and eased back to scan Bieber's receipt.

Anxious, Hans rolled the edges of his cap in his knotty fingers.

"Ja, ja. All is in order." Gercowski removed his glasses and lit his cigar. "So, Herr Bieber, you are sure your wine is good?"

"Yes." Hans relaxed.

"I see. And I should just take your word for it?"

Bieber did not like the unexpected inference. "Sir, are you a relative of Shmuel Gercowski, the banker?"

"Does that matter?"

Bieber nodded. "It may."

"I see. Yes, he is my father."

A look of relief came over Bieber's face. "Good. I owe him a mortgage. Pay me and I'll see that my debt to your father is addressed within the hour. That should please him."

"Well, that would be a good thing except I can't pay you today. Even if I could, it's Saturday afternoon and my father's bank is closed. You do realize this is our Sabbath?"

Bieber hadn't thought of that.

"I'm only here because Kleppinger had you on his calendar and I wanted to honor the obligation he left us with."

"Sir, I would like my money." Hans squeezed his hat again. "If you really want to honor his obligation, pay me now and pay me his price."

Richard Klempner leaned over the broker's desk. "Pay him now, Jew, or you'll be missing more Sabbaths than this one."

"Is that a threat?" Gercowski stood. He looked narrowly at Klempner. "You sound like an SA man. Perhaps Kleppinger had some business with you."

Klempner paused. He had secretly bought one handgun from the man on a nighttime delivery the month prior. "No, but if he did I'd blow your Oriental head off!"

Jakob Gercowski' lip twitched. He cast an eye beyond his office door and tilted his head for one of his employees to come in.

A young man scurried from behind a desk and lifted a visor from his head. "Ja?"

"Herr Beck, you are a Christian, not a Jew?"

The man looked puzzled. "Yes, but..."

"Then please explain to these Aryan gentlemen why we cannot pay them for this delivery today."

Beck looked at the receipt through the small lenses of his spectacles and then handed it back to Bieber. "Well, sir, it is very simple. This receipt is your proof of delivery to our warehouse. We will truck your product to our wholesaler who will inspect and grade your wine. We will negotiate a price with him, deduct our commission, and then pay you the balance."

Bieber knew he was out of his water. Like most Germans he was inclined to take people at their word—which was exactly why he was stubbornly fixed on his deal with Kleppinger. "But that's not what I was told."

Beck looked to his boss for help.

"No, you answer the man, Herr Beck. I'm a Jew and they don't believe anything I say."

The clerk tried again. "Herr Bieber, Peter Kleppinger is a criminal. Unless he gave you something in writing from our company we cannot stand by anything he might have said. I assure you that this is customary business practice. You'll get a copy of the wholesaler's bill of sale so you can see all the steps. By the way, you should consider buying our cargo insurance..."

"Man overcomes his doubts and anxiety, not by seeing himself as absolutely good, but by knowing where he belongs."

Ernst Beumler, Nazi intellectual

CHAPTER SIX

TWO WEEKS LATER on Tuesday, the 22nd of July news of a disaster in Koblenz was broadcast on the radio. The few who still owned working sets quickly informed the others. A bridge in had collapsed, drowning an undetermined number of persons and sending trucks and automobiles to the bottom of the river.

But the next morning worse news arrived in the village and it fell to the postman, Fritz Schmidt, to make a delivery. Riding his exhaust-belching motorcycle, Schmidt rumbled uphill from the Post Office and past Eva.

Since Schmidt only used his motorcycle for urgent matters, Eva's curiosity was aroused. She grabbed her bicycle and followed the distinctive sound of Schmidt's NSA until she saw the postman exiting Hans Bieber's home. She stopped at Hans' door perspired and panting. Wiping her face with a kerchief, she caught her breath.

The summer air was pungent with the smell of manure and she could hear pigs snorting from the rented pens in the alleys. A baby cried—a reminder that homeless people from the countryside were now overcrowding the village garden sheds. Hans' door suddenly opened and the old man emerged holding two telegrams limply in his hands. "Herr Bieber, what's wrong?" Eva drew close.

Saying nothing, the man handed her the telegrams. Eva's eyes flew along the first lines of the first one:

23 July 1930
Koblenz

To: Herr Hans Bieber
Weinhausen, Rheinland

Regret to inform you of wine shipment
believed lost to bridge accident.
Phone at once.
Jakob Gercowski 45 32 10

"Oh, God." Eva took hold of Hans' forearm. "So you think..." She stared into the broken man's face and tears welled. She hastily read the second.

23 July 1930
Koblenz

To Herr Hans Bieber
Weinhausen, Rheinland

Your wine assets are confirmed as lost.
Phone at once.
Shmuel Gercowski 45 47 53

At lunch Hans Bieber mustered his courage over a bowl of sausage soup and some dark bread, and in the late afternoon he walked slowly to the post office where the only public phone was available. By now the postman had whispered the contents of Bieber's telegrams all over Weinhausen and Richard Klempner had summoned those he could to stand by the old fellow as he made his call. With a grateful hand to his friends, Hans lifted the black receiver from its cradle and placed it against his ear with one hand. With his other hand he tapped his fingers nervously on the small table. Frau Schmidt made the connection and, at last, Jakob Gercowski answered.

Bieber exchanged courtesies and then listened carefully as the broker confirmed the details of the telegram. Apparently, Bieber's wines had been loaded onto three large transport trucks which followed one another onto the bridge. According to the solemn businessman, his warehouse manager had informed him that the trucks were near the very center when the collapse occurred. All three trucks sank to the bottom of the river along with their drivers and over thirty other persons now believed to be drowned. Salvage was impossible.

"Of course, I am sorry for your drivers, very sorry." Bieber took a breath. He listened, nervously. "I see. And no cargo insurance, you say? I remember."

All color drained from Hans' face as he strained to comprehend every detail. "And...and...but...oh, I see. Ja, I see...Uh, yes, I shall call him...yes, yes..." He wiped his forehead. "And...well...So, there is nothing that can be done?" He listened to a long answer and then his voice trembled. "Of course, Herr Gercowski. Ja, ja. But..." Hans pressed the receiver hard to his ear as if waiting for some final word of hope.

Beaten, Bieber finally hung up and turned toward his friends to confirm the worst. Drawn and gray, the man looked as if he had aged a hundred years. His hands were now shaking. "All is lost. Perhaps the bank will be patient."

Richard Klempner and Herr Offenbacher exchanged worried glances. Klempner was convinced the banks wanted to foreclose on worthwhile properties while conditions allowed. Unfortunately, Bieber had not put a single RM against his account since the loan was made in February. He had unwisely ignored the bank's regular requests out of stubborn anger for their foreclosure of a friend's farm in nearby Horchheim. In fact, overly confident in the expected sale of his prized wine, he had uncharacteristically rebuffed the bank's president twice.

"I need to make another call, Frau Schmidt. Please, here is the number." Hans handed a slip to the postman's wife. He assured Eva that he was confident that the bank would not be rash. Again, courtesies were exchanged. Then Bieber explained why he had nothing with which to pay his debt until the coming harvest. He listened, biting his lip, and then answered. "But Herr Gercowski, the vines are healthy this year. I expect a strong harvest." The anxious man then listened again. "But...but...with respect, sir, Mosel wines will be in demand soon enough...But...no, I don't think that is...but..." Hans stopped to listen again. His face was taught and his body slowly turning in on itself. "If you could please consider...I have...yes, Herr Gercowski, but..."

Klempner, Wolf, and Andreas had begun to pace. Klempner was grumbling about 'Jew moneylenders,' and Wolf was slamming his fist into his hand. At long last Hans Bieber set the receiver into its cradle as Eva laid a gentle hand on his hardened shoulder. Tears welled under his eyes and he wiped his hand over his bald head. All knew that the worst had happened. Embarrassed, Bieber blew his nose. "Because I am already delinquent the bank will not extend the terms. I have forty-five days to pay him in full."

"Outrageous!" cried Klempner. "He could wait another few months. That Jew wants to sell your vineyards and your winery to a friend of his in some Frankfurt synagogue."

Hans shook his head. "He's within his rights. And I would need more than one good harvest to cover the debt. The arrangements were clear enough and I am in default according to the law."

Oskar Offenbacher surprised everyone with a growl; Oskar was not a man who growled easily. He had returned from the Great War determined to honor the wish of a dying comrade who begged him to survive so that he could live out joy for the sake of the fallen. So the soft-faced baker was more apt to chortle, to crow, to guffaw or to giggle—but now he growled. "The laws are not just anymore. They're being used against you...against us all."

Samuel Silbermann abruptly appeared. At the sight of him, Eva's cheeks flushed. *Another Jew*, she thought.

"Herr Bieber...my wife and I have just heard of your loss. If we can help you in any way, tell us." He leaned close and whispered. "We know how you've helped others. Let us help you."

Klempner grabbed the gray-haired grocer by the shoulder and spun him around. "Let me guess. You've come to offer credit in your shop!"

"My rabbi probably knows the banker and he might be able to soften the terms."

Hans set his jaw. "I have forty-five days."

Despite every effort by sympathetic villagers and Silbermann's rabbi, no one was able to help Hans Bieber. On Monday, 25 August a police car and a long, black Maybach Zeppelin cruised slowly through Weinhausen and parked in front of the old man's house. From the Maybach stepped the banker, his attorney and an appraiser all dressed in dark suits and sporting summer hats. The banker, Shmuel Gercowski, drew a deep breath of village air and coughed.

Bieber was abruptly served a writ demanding that he vacate his house, remove all furnishings, and present free access to his land, his hillside sheds and his winery by noon on Monday, 15 September. The attorney spoke for Shmuel. "My client has heard of your kindness to the poor and wishes he could help. But he is beholden to his investors."

The gathering crowd grumbled. The attorney continued. "We have been patient, Herr Bieber, and we are not pleased to do this. But we need to put everything on auction before the harvest is in earnest. This way you'll have the advantage of the most credit to your account."

Hans stood stiffly, knowing that the man was right about the timing. And he knew that the bank's position was certainly legal. This all would just have to do. "So I now have until the fifteenth of September?"

"Ja."

"If I can find a way to pay you by then we'd be square on account?"

The lawyer gawked at the stubborn vintner. "Ja, of course."

Hans looked into Gercowski' eyes. He thought for a long moment. "The matter cannot be negotiated any further?"

The banker's attorney answered. "We've been through this. No. Now, how many times do we have to say it?"

Hans lifted his shoulders, proudly. "I am not a fool, sir. I understand."

Shmuel Gercowski spoke with a sympathetic tone. "Why don't you take a collection from the village? If everyone gave five..."

"I am no beggar, sir, and others have greater need than me. No one has a mark to spare. Besides, I'd sooner see hungry children fed than see your impatient bank get a collection from the poor of Weinhausen."

"Impatient?" The attorney scowled. "You haven't seen impatient. Our business here is done."

⌖

"Don't you dare leave this house!" scolded Frau Volk. The day was Monday, 15 September.

"Stop me if you can." Eva brushed past her mother and headed down the stairs on her way to help Hans Bieber face the bankers.

"Paul!" shouted Gerde. "Stop your daughter. She's going to the rally."

Rev. Volk emerged from his study and trotted down the stairs with a grim expression. He called after his daughter. "Please, Eva..."

"I'm going."

Paul took deep breath. "You are being disobedient."

"Herr Bieber deserves my help...if you were a man you'd help him, too."

The words stung. "I have tried to help, within the law. This protest will not turn out well, Eva. The police are not going to be gentle with some village rabble."

"'Village rabble'. Is that what we are to you? Is that what *I* am to you?"

Gerde Volk untied her apron and threw it on the floor. "You are acting like disorderly criminals."

Eva sneered. "My friends are not rabble." She flung the door open.

"Eva, dear, you must think about this."

The girl turned. "Father, Herr Bieber has a good harvest coming in just a few months. The Jew could have worked something out if he wanted..."

"You'll not be using that tone in my home." Paul's voice was strained.

"Then I'll use it out there!"

The morning was humid and gray. A thunderstorm had washed the sidewalks during the night. Eva splashed through puddles as she ran past groups of determined villagers pressing their way quickly toward Bieber's house. She hurried uphill past Professor Kaiser's house, and sprinted by groups of others. But when she turned right on Weinstrasse she stopped and stared, open-mouthed. Chills ran up her spine and her scalp tingled. The street was jammed with the angry folk of Weinhausen. Faces that had once looked at her with secret contempt now welcomed her as one of their own.

Eva greeted this one and that until she came across Anna and finally Andreas. She thought he looked distressed. "What's the matter?"

The young man shrugged.

"No, tell me. What's the matter?"

Andreas leaned close. "I'm not sure about all this."

Anna interrupted. "About all what?"

"This."

"I don't understand," said Eva. "What's there to not be sure about?" She felt a twinge of anger.

"Well, I...uh...I don't know if the banker is really wrong."

Eva and Anna stared at one another in disbelief. "You're kidding, right?" asked Anna.

"No. Herr Bieber didn't pay his debt. The bank waited for months and then even added a couple of extra weeks. What else are they supposed to do?"

"You really believe that?" said Eva. She put her fists on her hips. "They could wait a few more months for starters!"

The lad sheepishly followed the two girls as they pressed their way toward the Weinstube which had become the unofficial headquarters of the day's resistance. "Look!" said Eva. The whole block from the Weinstube to Bieber's house was awash with National Socialist flags. Some flew from windows, others had been draped over the grapevine canopy shading the street. Eva was beginning to like the sight of them. "Klempner's been busy."

"And Wolf," added Anna. "He's Klempner's recruiter for the HJ now. He's telling everyone that the Hitler Youth is just like the American Boy Scouts...but I doubt the Americans have their fingernails checked for dirt! He says they have Hitler Youth for girls, too."

"Yeah, the BDM. He's worked on all of us. I'm thinking about it." Eva pointed to a second story window in the Weinstube. "Look, there's Lindie."

Eva waved as Lindie stared forlornly down from her second floor window. The girl was now five months pregnant and had remained inside her mother's apartment since the terrible confirmation service. Eva had visited her faithfully but she had not been able to coax the girl outside. Even gracious letters from Gunther Landes, the farm boy who liked her, had not helped.

A thumping drum could be heard coming from around a corner. The crowd hushed. Snares snapped and the sound of tramping feet falling in regular marching rhythm stirred the moment. Eva held her breath. The excitement of it all was exhilarating. The village band emerged from a side street dressed in their blue uniforms and defiantly heralding the banished red, white, and black flag of the Second Reich.

Eva cheered with the roaring villagers as Postman Schmidt led his proud band toward the Weinstube Krause in a deliberate stride until they were positioned just outside its doors. Chills rode Eva's spine again. She watched the jolly baker, Oskar Offenbacher, blast his tuba from ballooned cheeks. Eva laughed. It was the first laugh in a very long time. The butcher's young apprentice, Ulrich Obermann, struck his bass drum in perfect meter; the station's baggage-man played his clarinet. Eva Volk clapped for them all.

Schmidt raised his baton and the music ended to loud applause. He nodded to Obermann. Then, with an impassioned down stroke, Schmidt directed his band in a commanding rendition of Martin Luther's, *A Mighty Fortress is our God.*

To this, Eva found herself near tears. She joined as the entire crowd sang the great reformer's mighty hymn:

Eine feste Burg ist unsere Gott
Ein' gute Wehr und Waffen...

As the words of faith and justice echoed through the streets of Weinhausen, Eva felt as though no force on earth could penetrate the wall of righteousness now guarding Hans Bieber. The girl paused during the second verse to watch her neighbors. Despite their own hardships and their differences they had chosen to rally together in defense of one of their own. Her own embarrassment notwithstanding, Eva now believed that her people might actually stand by her against the wider world, after all.

Eva's eyes then fell on the children of the poorhouse, however, and when they did she choked. A line of threadbare waifs had formed a little human barrier of held hands and dirty faces. They stood from curb to curb across Weinstrasse and stared downhill, waiting—daring—the wicked men from Koblenz to drive over them on their way to seize their beloved Herr Bieber's house.

The poorhouse children didn't have long to wait. A line of police cars on either end of a black Audi appeared turning right at the bottom of the hill. As the crowd fell silent the column drove slowly toward them, gliding uphill like a segmented serpent. The band stopped playing. Men clenched their fists.

Eva turned to see Father Steffen raise his hands over the people. Though only a few in the village were Roman Catholic, the rest appreciated any man of God willing to stand with them. Rev. Hahn, the squat young pastor of Weinhausen's smaller Protestant church and now a uniformed member of the SA was there as well. He quickly took a position by Father Steffen as the priest prayed.

Most wondered why Paul Volk was nowhere to be seen.

The police vehicles drew closer. Sensing trouble, the matron of the poorhouse quickly ran to her children and tried to drag them from the street. The children protested and stubbornly squeezed one another's hands. Eva ran to help. The police cars came closer.

Eva had barely dragged one child to the curb before the bumper of the first police car slid between her and the now scampering legs of the fast dividing crowd. Shouts and curses were directed at the police as their column then crept past the Weinstube and neared Bieber's front door. A shower of eggs splattered the windshields. Inside their cars, helmeted policemen looked grim; their nightsticks were at the ready.

"To us, Christianity is not an empty phrase but a glowing life. It lives through us and in us and thus is the strength of the nation gathered under the sign of the Cross. When the red beast sneers at us we look up to the Cross and receive the doctrine of struggle."

SA (Storm Trooper) Journal

CHAPTER SEVEN

IN THE FACE of authority and without leadership, the shouting folk of Weinhausen quickly began to lose heart. Eggs and curses were simply not going to stop helmeted police. Eva's heart sank. She watched the village band split hastily to either side of the street. She thought that they must now feel foolish; the bravado of their music and their march had proven to be impotent.

A forest of nightsticks protected the bank's attorney as he stepped smugly from his car and followed an officer to Bieber's door. Hans answered and stepped on to his stoop. As he did the muttering crowd fell quiet. The man was wearing the smart uniform that he had worn during the Great World War. His green-gray tunic was spotless and freshly pressed, and boasted an Iron Cross First Class medal pinned to the center of the left breast pocket. The old fellow seemed calm under his spiked helmet. With a grateful nod to those who loved him, he bravely received his eviction notice with a gentleman's bow and signed it, obediently.

Eva watched in awe. The dignity of this man was a quality that Germany's enemies had tried to strip from them all. Witnessing the self-respect and stiff-backed courage of the Reich's old veteran restored a taste of pride for Eva. The crowd began to cheer.

Not moved in the least by the poise of the decent man, the attorney then blundered. With a contemptuous grunt he ordered the police to seize Hans by the arms and drag him off his "former" door-sill. Two overzealous officers, apparently grubbing for the favor of the city lawyer, grabbed Bieber roughly, causing the man to stumble and fall to his knees atop the brick sidewalk.

The crowd roared its disapproval.

Police lines tightened.

Then suddenly, rising from a side street, a chorus of men's voices could be heard singing the *The Song of the Germans*, the newly declared national anthem that so many German boys had died singing during the war. Weinstrasse fell silent as a hypnotic rhythm of tramping feet drew closer and closer.

Eva clutched her heart as two well-ordered rows of Brown Shirts emerged at the head of additional ranks of Party members. The hard-faced SA men sang loudly from under their chin-strapped caps. As they marched toward the police line their swastika armbands rocked in unison and their jack boots rose and fell in perfect order. The crowd cheered wildly and joined them in their song:

Deutschland, Deutschland über alles,
Above all else in the world,
When, united for protection
We stand together in brotherhood...

Eva felt the chills again. Standing next to Anna she sang loudly as her eyes flew from the Brown Shirts to the people. With a rush of excitement her eyes fell on Wolf Kaiser who was leading a column Hitler Youth. Like Wolf, each boy wore a smart cap, brown shirts with ties, armbands, black shorts and calf-high socks. Eva's heart fluttered.

Richard Klempner motioned for silence and faced the attorney. "We demand you return this man's property."

The lawyer laughed from a safe distance behind the police. "Ha! Storm Troopers, eh? Stupid farmers is more like it. Listen you fools, the law is the law!"

A Party man from the rear called out, bitterly. "The law is wrong. Tell that to your Jew boss."

Eva smiled and the crowd cheered.

"We are going to take that notice from your thieving hand and shove it down your throat. Then we are going to escort Herr Bieber back into his own house."

The police line shifted, nervously. They had not failed to notice that the SA men were armed with clubs. The officer, however, had his orders and his pride. "I will have you arrested for threatening government officials. Now, disband at once."

"Government officials?" mocked Klempner. "You're puppets. Traitors, every one of you."

"This is your final warning!"

Eva held her breath. The Brown Shirts held their ground and Weinhausen became still as death under the gray September sky. Faces drew taught.

Hans Bieber quickly squeezed out from behind the police line. Raising his hands over the SA, he pleaded with them. "Please. Calm yourselves. Order must be supreme."

"Our anger is all we have left, Hans," answered Adolf Schneider from the ranks. "They've taken everything else from us."

It was then when Eva heard the sounds of engines roaring from one side. Three large trucks rumbled around a corner and accelerated toward the confrontation. Eva's heart began to race, nervously. "More police?"

The trucks screeched to a halt and from within their canvassed beds a small army of men leapt out led by a man waving a large red flag that bore the feared hammer and sickle. Andreas cried out from behind Eva. "Reds!"

In moments, three dozen city toughs dressed in worker's overalls and wearing solid red armbands charged the Party men with sticks and clubs. Andreas paled. "It's Otto Wagner and his men, Eva. They've come for the SA. Run, Eva, run away!"

Eva could not run. Her legs felt like heavy weights. She simply gaped at the sight of real, live Bolsheviks charging across the streets of Weinhausen under their terrible flag.

"Eva!" cried Andreas. "Eva... Anna, run." He grabbed each girl by the arm and dragged them out of harm's way as the Reds stormed closer.

Eva stumbled alongside Andreas and fell against a corner as

Andreas turned to join the coming fray. She held her breath as the SA, some Party men and Hans Bieber quickly formed ranks in front of the Hitler Youth.

With the police busy rushing the terrified attorney to safety, the Reds clawed through the parting crowd knocking many to the ground including Father Steffen. At last they were within striking distance of the Brown Shirts.

The outnumbered SA men braced themselves as the red wave rolled into them. Hans was instantly dropped to the bricks by a stick swung hard against his shoulder. Clubs rose and fell as men from both sides bloodied one another in a furious riot. Rev. Hahn took a terrible beating to one side while Adolf Schneider knocked three Reds over with three mighty roundhouses.

The Bolshevik's commander, Otto Wagner, sought the smaller Richard Klempner and broke the Storm Trooper's nose with a club. Tumbling to the ground, Klempner surprised his opponent by jerking his contraband pistol from beneath his shirt. Pointing it squarely at Wagner's face, he growled, "Call your men off." Klempner cocked the hammer and climbed to his feet.

Wagner hesitated. "You'd hang."

"I don't care."

"Then shoot me."

A stick fell across Klempner's arm. The pistol flew from his hand and spun wildly onto the cobblestones of the street. Both men lunged for it and the pair rolled around in a desperate life and death struggle.

Eva watched the riot in terror. She had heard of such violence on the streets of German cities; she knew that Germany was being torn apart.

But it was different to be a witness.

Andreas flew toward his half-brother now being beaten badly by a well-muscled man. With a shriek the lad crashed atop the man and toppled him onto the cobblestones. Rescued, Wolf clubbed the fellow hard across the face as Andreas turned toward another.

Andreas was no match for bigger men but he gave a good accounting of himself, so much so that his one-legged step-father was cheering him on from the edges. Battered and bleeding, the fifteen-year old reeled from fist to fist until he was finally knocked hard against a stone wall where he collapsed to one side.

The fight drew in others. Villagers who had previously listened to the National Socialists with some reserve felt suddenly forced to make a decision. Actually seeing the red flag carried across their village streets was a shock. With all that they had heard about godless Bolsheviks and their treasonous labor unions, could they simply stand by and do nothing? The decision became easy for most. With angry cries men left their wives' sides and rallied behind the SA.

Suddenly, a shot rang out and immediately the combat sputtered. The police made a mad dash toward the sound and found a gasping Otto Wagner lying at Richard Klempner's feet. They rolled the man over and found him bleeding badly from his chest. "He had a gun," wheezed Klempner. "He tried to shoot me but I turned it on him."

Wagner struggled to speak but he expired while whispering something unintelligible. Klempner's pistol lay in the man's opened hand.

As the police restored order, Andreas craned his neck to find Eva but it was plain to see that she was not looking at him, or even at Hans Bieber who was now being tended by Dr. Krebel. Nor had she noticed her father who had finally come running. Instead, she had fixed her gaze on the object of her true concern—on Wolf.

Over the weeks that followed, news of Weinhausen's riot added weight to the grim mood which hung over the whole Rheinland like an ever thickening river fog. Disorder to a German, of course, was like witchcraft to a priest. Their aversion to chaos rivaled the American antipathy toward tyranny. The villagers had been troubled enough to read about German cities boiling with partisan violence, but such disorder in a sleepy hamlet along the Mosel was startling evidence of systemic peril. Furthermore, the idea of a Communist riot in a place like

Weinhausen was frightening. Had Western liberalism really weakened German order this badly? If so, wouldn't the nation be easy prey for Stalin's gathering hordes? The teachers in Eva Volk's trade school feared it could be so.

Eva's classes ended in the mid-afternoon and she reluctantly walked the quarter-hour jaunt down Marktstrasse to meet her father at Werrmann's delicatessen before going with him to the serve the soup-line at the mission. She still had not forgiven the man, not completely. She kept trying to forgive him because she knew that was what she was supposed to do. But something new was in the way—possibly disrespect. With every crisis the man proved to be timid. He had never stood up to defend her and had not even come to Bieber's defense until the very last...when the fighting was over.

Nevertheless, given the choice between this and going home to her mother she supposed she was satisfied to be here at Werrmann's. But the truth was that she no longer felt good about either of her parents—or about much else for that matter. Now that the short-lived glory of Bieber's resistance had faded, no purpose had united anyone other than that of simple survival. She was feeling isolated again, and as haunted by shame as ever.

Walking beneath her umbrella, she coughed and snuggled in her coat. The damp city was sooty and the air was heavy with coal smoke. At the end of the street Eva could see a long line of hanging heads waiting for free bread. It seemed to her that folks in the city were either rich or poor; the few that were rich seemed very rich and the many poor were very poor. She supposed that she must look a little rich to some since beggars had asked her for money. Yet, snobbish businessmen had brushed by her as if she was nothing. Her conclusion was that she must be one of those few left in the middle.

"Ah, Eva, my dear." Rev. Volk leapt over a puddle and crossed the sidewalk jammed with a throng of gray-coated men.

"Hello, Father."

Paul longed for the days when Eva called him 'Papa.' "So, some Wurst and soup?"

Eva followed her father into the warmth of the small deli and took a seat at a wooden table.

"I'd like to catch the four o'clock ferry." Paul took his chair.

Eva nodded.

"You're coming to the funeral tomorrow?" asked Paul.

"Ten o'clock."

"Right. I feel terrible for the Klempner's. I've spent two days with them and I've no more words. Richard will not grieve. He's turned everything to rage."

Eva's eyes flashed. "I'd hope you'd be angry if it was Daniel who died from lack of medicine. The French are hoarding all sorts of medicines but won't spare a single vile to help a little German boy. The politicians wring their hands like helpless dolts."

Paul faced his watery soup. "Richard and his SA men are all so angry...everyone is angry and everyone is exhausted...You, too."

The cross-Rhein ferry was launched at the mouth of the Mosel, directly opposite the imposing, brown stone fortress of Ehrenbreinstein. As it neared the far dock it made a wide arc around a low-sided laundry ship where shivering women were crowded along slanting chutes to scrub their clothing in the river water. Eva felt for them.

Arriving on the eastern shore of the Rhein, the pair took a bus to the center of the small town. Like most of Germany, Ehrenbreinstein had become drab over the past decade. Dreary homes lined streets paved with gray blocks. The trees were bare, of course, and on this late afternoon their lifeless October branches disappeared into the barrenness of the darkening sky. Rain-slicked streets reflected the blur of the few passing tail lights.

Eva then followed her father on a brisk walk through what was left of the shopping district. The surviving shops were closing early. Eva looked into their windows and wondered why any stayed open at all; shelves were nearly empty of merchandise.

"Look, Eva." Paul pointed farther down the street to a

brightly lit department store. "That one's open. Shall we have a look?"

"Jewish. All the department stores are Jewish and they're driving German shops out of business."

Paul Volk released a long breath. "Listen to me. First, stores aren't Jewish or Christian...their owners are, and second, who cares? Scripture teaches us that there is neither Jew nor Greek."

"The verse says, '*in Christ,* there is neither Jew nor Greek.' That, father, is a very different matter."

The minister grumbled. "Well, you get my point. Hatred is a sin. I can't make it any simpler than that."

"I don't hate them. I just don't like them."

"You never used to talk like this..."

"You don't like the French."

The pair entered the well-stocked store. Like the Colonial Stores of the past, it offered bananas and cane sugar, pineapples and Belgian lace. Paul rounded an aisle where he paused to survey a small wine assortment. Curious, he bent over to lift a wine bottle from its rack, only to put it down, hastily.

"Father? What is it?"

"Nothing, my dear. Time to go." He took his daughter's elbow.

"Father?" Eva was curious. Something was very odd, indeed.

"Eva, don't bother with that...Come with me." His voice was uncharacteristically commanding.

Eva pulled away and took hold of a green bottle with a cream-colored label sporting the name, "Bieber." She fixed her gaze on the label's muscular vintner shouldering a large basket filled with grapes. "Gott in Himmel!"

"No, Eva, I repeat: you cannot tell him." Paul Volk was pleading with his daughter on the train ride home from Koblenz.

"Someone defrauded Herr Bieber...and me, your own daughter, and you want me to keep quiet about it?"

"You'll never know who. My God, it could have been the broker, the shipper, a wholesaler, or anyone with a clever, wicked mind that had any contact with the stuff...even the warehousemen."

"Somebody needs to pay." Eva was furious. "I knew something was wrong with the whole bridge collapse from the very beginning."

"But the bridge did collapse."

"Yes. What a wonderful opportunity for the broker and his father! Think about it. The broker claims that the wine is lost, then sells it on the sly. That makes Bieber default and the bank—his father—gets Herr Bieber's vineyards, winery, and house. They are the ones who stand to gain from this. The Jews are parasites just like Richard Klempner says; they live for profit and for each other and no one else." She folded her arms and set her jaw.

Paul closed his eyes. "I suppose it could have been them. That much I'll give you. But being Jewish does not automatically make one a criminal. Besides, such a deed could ruin those two forever if they were caught. Nothing of Bieber's would be worth the risk." Paul took a breath. "Think about this logically. If I were to guess, I'd say it was the warehousemen. Lots of the dock workers are Communists. They could have easily conspired in this with very little risk. Imagine the profit..."

Eva's face tightened. "Jews, Communists...politicians, I don't care. Besides, they're all the same. I'm going to tell Herr Bieber and Wolf and Richard. They all deserve to know."

"You especially cannot tell Richard Klempner this, not now, not while he's grieving his son."

Eva thought for a moment. Her father was probably right about that. "Soon, then."

Paul was exasperated. "Eva, you saw violence and death come to Weinhausen...you saw it with your own eyes. If you tell anyone of this they will think of nothing but revenge. But they'll never prove who did it. Their hatred will spill over to people undeserving. Do you understand?" He reached for Eva's hand.

She pulled away and stared into her reflection on the inside of the train's window.

"Listen to me. Imagine if Herr Bieber ever knew. It would drive him insane...it would kill him. Eva, you can't tell him. You can't tell anyone."

Eva pursed her lips. Her father might be right but she'd not admit that now. She stared mutely through the glass. Outside, all was dark. Inside, all was dingy. Everything felt disconnected and fractured. The world was so unfair and so very cruel. She so desperately wanted revenge for Bieber—she wanted the same for herself.

The girl wanted to scream.

⌖

The next cold weeks were bitterly frustrating for Eva. She had charitably said nothing about the wine to her dear Hans Bieber, nor had she breathed a single word to Wolf or even to the trustworthy Andreas. But on Saturday, 24 January 1931 she had something else to think about.

Eva rushed through the dining hall of the Weinstube. The hall was filled with unemployed men sitting slump-shouldered along the bar and at the wooden tables. The air was heavy with cigarette smoke and the smell of beer.

"Good thing you're here," grumbled a patron.

Eva hurried up the wooden stairway and into Lindie's room. "Oh, Lindie, where's your mother!" She wiped her friend's brow and cried for Frau Krause.

The woman ambled into the room with a pan of steaming water. Eva quickly immersed her towels and began to wash the blood from Lindie's body.

"She wanted an abortion, you know," said Frau Krause. "She begged for one. Your father talked me out of it and made her feel ashamed to think of it. But it's not against the law anymore."

Eva didn't answer. She heard a truck wheel up outside. Its brakes screeched and two doors slammed. She ran to the window. "Herr Offenbacher?" She was confused.

Boots thundered up the steps and Oskar Offenbacher burst into the room followed by a trio of other men. Offenbacher was firing orders. The baker had been a cook in the Great War but only after he had been badly wounded as a combat sergeant.

Eva protested.

"Quiet, girl. You and I are taking her to Koblenz in my truck."

Lindie groaned. Her mother faded away.

"But...where's Dr. Krebel?"

"Horchfeld. And the ambulance is broken down. Bring extra blankets; it'll be cold."

"No people may be denied the right to maintain, undisturbed, their previous racial stock and to enact safeguards for this purpose. The Christian religion merely demands that the means used do not offend against the moral law and natural justice."

Archbishop Gröber, Roman Catholic

CHAPTER EIGHT

KOBLENZ LAY ABOUT ten kilometers from Weinhausen but the road leading to it was in terrible disrepair. The times had left it pocked with potholes and edged with broken shoulders making it a slow, treacherous ride. It took a little more than a half-hour for Offenbacher's Ford to lurch its way to the ferry where the baker jerked on his hand brake. He roared for the ferryman to hurry. Fortunately, the ice breakers had been through earlier that morning.

Offenbacher bounced his truck on board and within a quarter hour the baker's truck was climbing up the far bank onto Koblenzer Strasse, then past clusters of dilapidated brick sheds and broken down factories before entering the gray downtown of Koblenz proper. Honking his horn and shouting, Offenbacher raced past beggars, cripples and relief lines. Finally, ignoring angry police whistles he wheeled up to the front door of St. Josef's hospital. He barked at a passer-by who helped him lift Lindie from the truck's bed. Panting and wheezing, the pair carried her up the steps and into a tiled corridor where two nuns ran for help.

Eva waited with Oskar in a cold, scantily furnished room. In the draughty hallway beyond, clicking leather soles could be heard hurrying from duty to duty. An occasional gurney rolled by on squeaky wheels.

"Do you think she lost too much blood?" asked Eva.

"She's young and strong."

Eva also had other concerns. Secret ones.

The door opened and a doctor entered with a nun. His face was grim. The sister next to him looked exhausted. "Are you the girl's father?" the doctor asked Oskar. "Me? No, heavens no. I am her baker."

The doctor raised a brow. "I see. Are you a sister?"

Eva answered. "No. We're friends."

The doctor nodded. "Well, first, the Fräulein is as well as can be expected and can go home in a few days. The child is a girl."

The nun spoke. Her voice was sharp but not unkind. "The mother does not want the child so we'll be sending her to our orphanage in Limburg."

"Is there anything else about the baby?" pressed Offenbacher. His wife had suspicions.

Eva held her breath. She wished he hadn't asked.

"She's a half-Negroe."

Eva stifled a groan. She had feared as much.

"Another Rheinbastard." The baker sighed and turned to Eva. "Poor little thing."

"Ja," the doctor answered. "The Rheinland has hundreds of them now. The French laugh about them as their farewell insult."

"If Frau Krause finds out she'll throw Lindie out of her house. We can never tell anyone."

The baker scratched his head. "Well, I'd feel funny lying to my wife..."

"You'd feel funnier if you ruined Lindie's life!"

Oskar shook his head. "I don't know... I'm not good at keeping secrets."

"You'll learn."

"There's no shame in this for Lindie; she was attacked."

"But she kept saying that no African had her. Do you know any boys who'll want her after an African?"

"Well, I...I suppose..."

"We'll tell the village that we know nothing about the child other than that she was born healthy and Lindie gave her up for adoption. Right?"

"My God, I remember days without these kinds of problems," grumbled Oskar. He released his hand brake and rolled the truck on to the ferry. "Yes, yes. I agree."

The months and seasons that followed passed slowly for the folk of Weinhausen and for the whole of Germany. Nearly two years crawled by—two gray years of relief lines and increasing violence, and two years of deepening unemployment. In fact, while unemployment in America's Great Depression stood at twenty percent, by the closing months of 1932 Germany's unemployment had reached thirty percent and was still climbing. Hunger had become a familiar companion; farms and homes were being foreclosed in record numbers and the government's retirement system was nearing bankruptcy. Crime had risen dramatically and labor unrest disrupted cities now littered with prostitutes and panhandlers.

For the folk of the German heartland—folk like those in Weinhausen—fear was being driven by other events as well. The German Communist Party had made gains in recent elections and now comprised sixteen percent of the Reichstag. Not far away Joseph Stalin was deliberately starving millions in the Ukraine—the papers estimated over seven million deaths so far. And he was also starving thousands of ethnic Germans who had long ago been invited to settle along the Volga.

In addition to these terrors, the Soviet military—like Germany's other neighbors'—was ever-enlarging. Poland's armed services alone were larger than America's—a fact that had emboldened them to threaten an invasion of German territory and expand their de-Germanization policies. All the while the Versailles Treaty still limited Germany to an army of 100,000 men. Germans were uneasy.

However there was some good news for most in Weinhausen. The Americans had elected a perceived socialist strongman—Franklin Roosevelt—as president, suggesting an aggressive model of security and economic order that their own nation might follow. To that end many began to listen more seriously to Germany's own rising socialist, an Austrian-born war veteran named Adolf Hitler. He had recently been defeated in his bid for president but had become a comforting voice for justice and order, nonetheless. His National Socialist Party had gained seats in the Reichstag, reassuring some as a formidable block against the ever-mounting threat of Bolshevism.

In the midst of such national and international drama the secrets of Weinhausen had been preserved. Eva had not slipped a single word about Bieber's wine, though the subject had become a source of unrequited anger for her. And Lindie had been spared, leaving her to enjoy the shy attentions of Gunther Landes.

On Christmas Eve of 1932 Eva stared about her room longing to feel the magic of the season once again. For the blossoming nearly-seventeen-year old the warmth of the Advent was the last tie to a former time when she was very young and happy. Despite the nagging shame of that night, the young woman smiled as a flood of pleasant memories filled her mind. She toyed with the necklace her Opa had given her, convinced that Christmas could keep her tethered to things whole.

The young woman pulled a stool close to her window and wrapped herself in an old blanket. The moon hanging over Weinhausen had slowly given way to eastern clouds as the hushed quiet of Christmas Eve descended like a securing blanket atop the village crushed by hardship. A few light bulbs cast a modest glow from windows not yet shuttered. The cobblestone streets were covered by a well-packed coat of week-old snow and Eva watched a group of chilled carolers pad softly by as they hurried to another doorway. The last of the village shops locked their doors; a small truck dashed downhill toward the river road.

CHAPTER EIGHT

Soon all was still.

Weinhausen was no different than a thousand other hamlets spread across Germany. Each was tucked neatly within its own snowy nook and bathed in Christmas candlelight. But for each, this Christmas would be harder than the one before. And Eva knew hers would be different, too; it would have to be and for lots of reasons. Her mother had told her to expect far less than ever since so many were unemployed. She said that it wouldn't be right for a pastor's family—one paid however meagerly by the government—to enjoy what many did not have.

However, just knowing that she would still find a Christmas tree, even a scant one, waiting green and glorious in the living room was all Eva really wanted. Admittedly, she had been disappointed for her little brother's sake. Three weeks earlier he had set his boot out for St. Nikolaus with high expectations, only to bravely feign gratitude for the rather plain wooden whistle that he found in the morning. He had told Eva that the Christmas saint shouldn't be blamed because the Reds had probably robbed him along his way.

The girl shifted on her stool and snuggled within her blanket. She smiled at the wooden gnomes a neighbor had placed in the church gardens. She imagined them coming alive and dancing happily through the streets with merry Christmas elves. She drew a deep breath through her nose to smell the comforting aroma of butter Stollen and fresh-baked Pfeffernüsse floating upward from the kitchen.

With her face pressed to the glass she watched the first flakes of a coming storm; they would keep the wider world at bay. She looked sideways at the row of homes lining the street which bordered the far end of the church. They were the medieval, half-timbered buildings decorated modestly with greens stripped from the north-slope forests; she wondered how many Christmases they had seen.

The smells, the village candle-glow, the stately beauty of the church bedecked in green finery, and the snowflakes floating lightly by her window made her feel warm and safe, just as she had hoped. The sounds of Christmas music on the downstairs gramophone filled the house with comfort. She unconsciously let her fingers toy with her Oma's necklace; She looked at her Good Shepherd print and He felt near.

Eva took a deep breath and dared to hope.

A few minutes before six o'clock Rev. Volk made his annual journey to the church for the ringing of the bell. He prayed that the words of the Gospel he would preach later that evening would make the hearths of Christmas day burn just a little brighter for his suffering people.

Three icy snowballs struck the surprised minister from behind and the man whirled about, only to slip on the snow and crash atop a hedge with a howl. "Schneiders!" he cried. "Will they never grow up!"

Dusting the snow off his overcoat and putting his hat back on his head, the minister hurried to the safety of his church. Inside, Rev. Volk switched on one row of lights and walked down the side aisle of his eight-hundred year old nave, then made his way up the cold curved stairway to the base of the belfry. He looked at his watch and waited. Last year he had rung the bell two minutes late and he had been soundly reprimanded by Frau Wicker and her ladies' sewing club. This year he was determined to avoid that encounter at all costs!

At precisely six o'clock he wrapped his hands around the thick rope and pulled. The bell above swung smoothly and answered with a deep, rich tone which filled both the church and the village with the sureness of heaven. Paul Volk closed his eyes and smiled. He could picture the women of Weinhausen responding to his signal by ringing tiny bells of their own. Their children would then scramble from their bedrooms to find their Christmas trees waiting.

Duty done, Rev. Volk emerged from the church, slyly. He bent as if to tie his shoe but packed three snowballs, instead. He rose, pulled the brim of his hat over his eyes and walked toward his front door. Then, when the Schneiders emerged from the shadows with a few more snowballs of their own, the minister let his fly.

"Ha!" cried the pastor gleefully as the boys scampered away. "I was ready this time." Laughing, he entered his home and shook the snow off his coat.

"Don't make a mess!" slurred his wife. "I've enough to do." The woman had been drinking, heavily.

Paul ignored her condition and caught her by the arm. "Frohe Weihnachten," he said as he pulled her close.

The woman submitted to a gentle kiss.

Humming, the man hung his coat in the closet and then began to sing *Ihr Kinderlein Kommet*. He walked to his gramophone, a Victor II with an oak, spear tip horn which Rudi had given the family as a gift a few years before when the family piano fell into disrepair. Paul set another 78 rpm record on its felt turntable. Still singing, he cranked the handle and held the needle just above the spinning vinyl. "Ready, Gerde?"

Frau Volk nodded. She reached for a tiny silver bell setting on a table and rang it, loudly. "Kinder!"

Eva and Daniel raced down the stairs and burst into the living room. With a happy, "Wunderbar, Mutti," Eva stood before the family Christmas tree and clapped. It was chubby and covered with old painted balls, lead tinsel, tin cutouts, some ribbon, and a paper chain. A dozen tiny white candles burned brightly.

Excited, Rev. Volk dropped his badly worn needle lightly on the vinyl. "Everyone, hold hands and sing!"

O Tannenbaum, o Tannenbaum,
Wie treu sind deine Blätter.
Du grünst nicht nur zur Sommerzeit,
Nein, auch im Winter, wenn es schneit.
O Tannenbaum, o Tannenbaum,
Wie treu sind deine Blätter.

Eva glowed like the little candles on the tree. The room was warm and the world was shut away. She sang the song, then another, and then took a seat as her father reached for the Volk family Bible.

The leather bound book dated from the late seventeenth century and was kept on a special table for use only on Christmas and Easter. Paul pulled on his wire-rimmed glasses and cleared his throat. "Dear family, God's blessings to you all. Now, lest we lose sight of the purpose of the season let me read to you from Luke, chapter two." The man carefully turned the dry, yellowed pages and read the story of Christ's birth.

"Es begab sich aber zu der Zeit, dass ein Gebot von dem Kaiser Augustus ausging, dass alle Welt geschätzt würde..."

When the reading was over, the man set a new needle on a Victor Herbert recording of *Babes in Toyland*. He lit his pipe and then reached under his chair for a gift. "For you, Gerde." Paul Volk smiled, hopefully. He had sold some books from his library to the Church Superintendent in Koblenz in order to raise a little extra money.

Gerde Volk muffled a belch and stared at the nicely wrapped box, lost in a past that was no more. She had been born into German aristocracy and had grown up in luxury in the now troubled city of Danzig. She had met Paul Volk while she was a singer in a respectable cabaret in Berlin but had never imagined herself in a little village like Weinhausen as the wife of a poor minister.

"Open it, Mutti," said Daniel. His eyes were on something else.

Eva watched her mother slowly remove the brown butcher wrap and she cast a glance at her anxious father.

"I think it's a hat." Gerde discarded the paper, and then removed the lid of the box, indifferently. "Ja, as I thought." She lifted a brown, felt hat from the box. It was a brimless, camel-colored cloche hat with a bright green feather fanned on one side. "Where am I supposed to wear this?"

"I...I bought it in Koblenz. It's all the fashion and I thought you'd like it for church." He pointed to the stitching. "See, they call that 'art-deco'..."

"I know what art deco is." Gerde rolled the domed hat in her hands. "Who told you these are the fashion? They *were* all the fashion."

"The saleswoman at Kaufmann's."

"Try it on," said Eva. "I bet you'll look beautiful in it."

"What good is it for me to look beautiful here in an out-of-date hat?" Gerde answered with a slurred bite. She shook her head. "Oh, if I must." She pulled the hat over her hair and rested it near her eyes. Clearly, she knew exactly how such a hat should be worn.

"You look beautiful in it, my dear."

"It is very out of fashion. I'd bet the saleswoman was a Jewess and happy to have this off her shelf." The woman removed the hat quickly.

Paul masked his disappointment the best he could, then reached beneath the tree and handed Eva a small box. "Merry Christmas from your mother and me."

"Danke," Eva answered. She kissed both her parents and then opened her present. "Oh, a Christmas bell of my own! It is wonderful. I can ring it for my own children someday."

Daniel was given a brown box, too big to be wrapped. With glee the little boy tore the lid off and he squealed with delight as he lifted a used metal toy airplane overhead. Holding it high he ran about the room rumbling his lips like they were engines.

Eva then waited for a moment. She wasn't sure if her mother had intended to give her father a gift or not. Despite her mother's distance from the man she hoped she wouldn't hurt him, not on Christmas. Frau Volk's hands remained folded tightly on her lap. Eva sighed and nodded to Daniel.

"Here Papa, here Mama," he cried. The just-turned six year old set down his plane and handed his father a handmade slingshot, then gave his mother a wooden spoon. Both were a bit rough but the lad had tried.

"Ah, Daniel, danke sehr. I can chase pigeons from the belfry." Paul gave his son a hug.

Gerde Volk looked at the spoon and smiled. She loved her little boy—favored him over Eva according to village gossip. "Come here, Daniel, my Daniel." She hugged the white-haired imp and kissed him.

Eva reached behind the sofa and retrieved two oranges which

she had hidden. Beaming, she handed one to each parent. "Frohe Weihnachten."

"But how..."

"I bought them from the grocer."

"With what money?" Gerde was immediately suspicious.

"I...I had a way." Bad memories quickly returned. She really had sold her doll this time.

"A way?" Gerde staggered toward Eva. "A way?" She belched. "I've had enough of your secrets. You've been a selfish brat since those Africans had their way." The woman tilted to one side. "You treat us like we're nothing. Then on Christmas you want to be the perfect little princess in a story book kingdom..."

"Gerde," interrupted Paul. "Please, not..."

"Shut up. She treats you like dirt, too." Frau Volk fell into a chair.

Daniel began to cry.

Eva was shocked; she suddenly sat upright on her chair, tense and hardening as her mother railed against her. With every biting word the girl clenched her jaw tighter. Three times she looked to her father. Each time he looked away. Her hopes for Christmas had just been suffocated like the snuffing of a struggling flame on a fresh candle. But that was only the half of it. She was fast losing more than Christmas.

Gerde pressed harder; Paul faced the floor.

Eva had enough.

Saying nothing, the girl stood. She bent to kiss her frightened little brother now standing beside her and as she did her eyes fell briefly upon her woeful father once more. This time his eyes were mournful, pleading. Unmoved, Eva set her silver bell atop a table reached behind her neck to unclasp Oma's necklace.

It had failed her in the market square and it had failed her again.

She held the chain in her open palm for a moment and stared at the cross that she had wanted to love. The necklace was familiar enough and felt warm in her hand like the night Opa had given it to her. But now it seemed so terribly impotent and even irrelevant.

Like her father and his church.

She squeezed her hand tightly around it. After all, it had been Oma's.

But she needed something else.

Eva looked past her parents' faces and coldly scanned the room and its furnishings. No spark of warm feeling was kindled, no affection aroused. Her house was no longer her home. She stuffed her necklace in a pocket, removed a coat from the closet, and shoved her arms into its sleeves.

It felt heavy on her shoulders.

Then, without a word, the broken-hearted young woman flung open the door and stormed into the night.

PART II
AS AN ANGEL OF LIGHT
1933-1939

"If positive Christianity means the clothing of the poor and the feeding of the hungry, then we are the more positive Christian. For in these spheres, National Socialist Germany has accomplished prodigious work.
May God Almighty grant us peace so that we might complete the mighty work begun in Him."

Adolf Hitler

"The National Socialists have shown both by their program and their practical deportment that they will have a firm, positive relationship to Christianity."

Rev. Otto Debelius, General Superintendent of Protestant churches in Kurmark, Germany

CHAPTER NINE

1 FEBRUARY 1933.

"Well, you can shrug if you like but the times are encouraging." Professor Kaiser was leaning over a frustrated Paul Volk at the fore of the crowded schoolhouse.

"Not now, I'm trying to find the signal." Paul was carefully dialing the knob of his radio to locate the broadcast of the nation's newly appointed chancellor, Adolf Hitler.

"Well, I think President Hindenburg made a good choice. This is the only way to keep the Bolsheviks at bay."

"But we didn't elect him," grumbled Paul. "He got less than 40% of the vote. Hindenburg *appointed* him."

"You're splitting hairs again, Herr Pfarrer. We elected Hindenburg who then appointed Hitler on our behalf. The people's will is still being represented. Besides, our National Socialist Party has a plurality in the Reichstag."

"That may be, but they don't have a majority." Rev. Volk turned his radio dial slowly past buzzing static, to broken sound and then to static again. Richard Klempner appeared and breathed over his shoulder. "Come on, Herr Pfarrer, everybody's waiting."

Volk nodded and fingered the dial again. He loved his new radio—it was an RCA Model 121 Midget sent just weeks before as a Christmas gift from his brother in America. "There." From Berlin an orchestra was playing German marches in anticipation of the new chancellor's speech.

Hoping to see his daughter from his vantage along the wall, Paul Volk searched the many faces which filled the school. Eva had left home over a month ago and was now living and working at the Weinstube. She had not spoken to him since that night. Disappointed, Paul forced a smile at the small youth group from his church. The broad-faced Gunther Landes was the leader and next to him was Lindie Krause. Lindie had finally yielded to the awkward boy's attentions and the two were considered a couple. Volk was worried about Lindie, though. She had been especially despondent since last week's second birthday of her estranged daughter. He had tried to assure her that the Catholics would be taking wonderful care of the child but his encouragement seemed fruitless. All she would say was that if the new chancellor had been in power on *that nigh*t, nothing bad would have happened.

The minister turned his attention to the back of the room and felt a sudden twinge of discomfort. The rear seats were filled with Brown Shirts and one of them had placed the pole of a furled flag upright in the corner. It was true that the minister agreed with National Socialist concerns over the corrupting influence of liberalism from the West. Like them, he was deeply troubled by cubist art, incoherent jazz, abortions and advertisements for immoral entertainment. Instead of rampant materialism he, too, wanted to see the traditional values of the rural German folk restored—values like decency and morality, motherhood and family, social order and economic justice. Furthermore, Paul shared National Socialist concerns over the looming threat of Bolshevism in the East; pictures of slaughter, collectivist farms, and gulags were terrifying.

Yet despite Rev. Volk's agreement with much of National Socialism, he sensed something was wrong at its 'fringes.' Arrogant notions of Aryan racial supremacy and obsessions with Jewish conspiracies discomforted him. The vulgarity of the street toughs disgusted him.

All he could do was to trust his bishop's optimism.

The minister took a deep breath and spotted Wolf Kaiser with his squad of Hitler Youth which included a dozen well-dressed boys and four braided girls in their white BDM blouses. A little girl waved and Volk returned the gesture with a smile. Professor Kaiser had assured him that the Hitler Youth was supportive of Christian values. He hoped it was so.

From the radio, a man in Berlin could now be heard introducing Chancellor Hitler to an enthusiastic Reichstag. The folk in Weinhausen's school clapped. Though only a third of the village had actually voted for the National Socialists in the last election, most were content that Chancellor Hitler was taking the nation's reins. In fact, the majority had come to believe that their own bickering centrist parties had become useless; that Germany had only two real choices for the future—the National Socialists or the Communists; a vote for any other was a wasted vote.

Rev. Volk clapped politely. Settling into his chair he scanned the room one more time. A smile spread across his face. *She's come*!

Eva was suddenly uncomfortable. She saw her father looking at her and she turned her face away. Andreas took a seat beside her. She folded her arms.

"Did you say something?" asked Andreas.

"I don't want my parents expecting me to come home, that's all." Her tone was bitter.

"Oh." Andreas offered the minister a polite wave. "Did you see your mother?"

"No. She's probably drunk." The young woman looked over the audience. "This is ridiculous. Who cares what he says anyway?"

"Who?"

"Hitler."

"I know what you mean."

"So why did you come?"

Andreas blushed. "I…I thought you might be here."

The girl feigned disinterest. She liked Andreas and respected him greatly. Sometimes when he brushed against her she felt tingly and light. She loved his smile. But feeling eyes on her from another side she turned to see Wolf waving from the back of the room. She smiled. She wondered what it was about Wolf. "Lindie told me that Wolf is going to race motorcycles this spring."

"So he says." Andreas wanted to tell Eva that Wolf would be spending the money *he* had earned. "So what do you think of this Hitler business, anyway?"

"Shh," came a voice from behind. "It's starting."

Adolf Hitler's first words came through the radio.

"More than fourteen years have passed since the unhappy day when the German people, blinded by promises from foes at home and abroad, lost touch with honor and freedom, thereby losing everything. Since that day of treachery, Almighty God has withheld his blessings from our people. Dissension and hatred have descended upon us..."

Eva listened. She had heard him on the radio during the presidential campaign but he sounded different to her tonight. His voice was strong and confidant—not angry and strained as she had remembered.

"...We are firmly convinced that the German nation entered the fight in 1914 without the slightest feeling of guilt on its part and filled only with the desire to defend the Fatherland and to preserve the freedom, no, the very existence, of the German people. But now we can only see the disastrous fate which has overtaken us since those November days of 1918 as the result of our collapse at home..."

Murmurs of assent rumbled through the school. Eva remembered her Uncle Rudi saying the same.

"...Bolshevism with its method of madness is making a powerful and insidious attack upon our confused and shattered nation. It seeks to poison and disrupt in order to hurl us into an era of chaos.... Beginning with the family, it has undermined the very foundations of morality and faith, and scoffs at culture and business, nation and Fatherland, justice and honor..."

Eva's attention was now riveted. Hitler was condensing her world into something she could understand.

"The National Government will preserve those basic principles on which our nation has been built. It regards Christianity as the foundation of our national morality and the family as the basis of national life..."

Eva sneaked a look at her father. He was sitting with legs crossed and arms folded, one finger set thoughtfully over his lips. He seemed surprised, even encouraged, especially when the chancellor went on to speak of a four year plan that would finally set things right for the suffering German people.

"...May God Almighty give our work His blessing, strengthen our purpose, and fill us with wisdom and the trust of our people, for we are not fighting for ourselves, but for Germany."

A chill crawled over Eva's skin as the audience leapt to its feet with a thundering ovation. Eva stood and began to clap, first lightly and then with enthusiasm. The SA began to sing its *Horst Wessel Song*. Eva turned her face to a National Socialist flag now suspended just below the old, wooden Cross fixed on the schoolhouse wall. She thought the flag to seem suddenly the more potent of the two symbols. The sight of it brought back powerful memories of the Brown Shirts roaring to her rescue and their brave stand to defend Herr Bieber.

The chancellor's speech, the music, the thunder of applause—whatever the miraculous source, Eva was intoxicated by the sense of hope now filling the school like a font of fresh water bursting from the depths of a dry well. A mysterious sensation washed over her leaving her feeling suddenly safe and whole. She looked at Andreas. The young man, too, was moved.

The villagers began to sing *A Mighty Fortress is our God*. Their grey past was surely over; ahead lay a future filled with promise and dreams, a future far beyond themselves. At last Eva could restrain herself no more. She opened her mouth to pour herself into the stirring song. And when the song ended, she joined with her village in raising her arm, shouting, "Heil Hitler!"

⌖

Andreas would have rather spent the February Sunday afternoon with Eva but she had turned down his offer in favor of a cold ride with Wolf to the new motorcycle track near Horchfeld. The whole idea of Wolf's racing had angered Andreas from the moment he had heard of it. After all, he, Andreas, had been the good son—the hard-working, never-complaining son who had been denied an education so the family would have enough money in these difficult times. Watching Wolf run off to school while he headed for work each day had been bad enough. But watching him roar away on his motorcycle with Eva's arms wrapped tightly around his waist was infuriating.

He kicked at the ground and stared at the grey sky wondering how his love of the landscape and of books could ever compete with the thrill of a cycle race. Gunther had told him of Wolf's latest angle—volunteering in Chancellor Hitler's new Winter Relief program. That move had quickly caught Eva's attention and now the two were feeding Koblenz' poor together.

"Andreas?" a girl's voice turned the nearly-eighteen-year-old's head.

"Anna?"

Anna Keller set her kickstand, giggling. She had curled her red hair and looked nothing like the pig-tailed German Fräulein of just weeks before. "What do you think?"

"I don't know what to say. Lipstick, too. Wow."

"That's right, Ole-Hot Boy, call me Swing-Puppe!"

Andreas stared, blankly.

"What's the prob, just jitterbug jive." Anna threw her right arm forward. "Heil Hottler." She laughed.

"I...I..."

"Don't be icky, you gotta get hep."

"I really don't know what you're talking about."

Anna sighed. "Fine. I thought you knew about Swing."

"But..."

"I have some friends coming over to hear a Duke Ellington record that my father just brought back from Berlin."

Andreas liked American boogie and he used to listen to a ragtime record at Herr Bieber's. He had heard one Swing dance song recently on a crystal set that a fellow in the neighboring village of Kobern had loaned him. He loved the big band sound and all the brass. "The Party hates that music."

"Who cares? I hate braids and little ties. And I hate seeing seventeen-year old boys in short pants." Anna giggled. "Oh, man, the Hitler Youth is really off the cob, unhep if you know what I mean."

"Not really." Andreas offered a half-smile. Anna was always for what others were against. A year ago she had been a rabid National Socialist. "So, you learned this foreign language at school?"

"Hey, you got your boots on!"

"Huh?" Andreas checked his feet.

Anna squealed with laughter. "I mean, you know what's going on!"

Andreas blushed.

"Fine, I'll stop. So, would you like to come?"

"Will the others talk like you?"

"No, this Swing thing is pretty new. But I have two friends at school who really love it. You should see their clothes. One's from Berlin, the other one is from New York...that's in America."

"I know." Andreas thought about the invitation. "Why not? Good, I'll see you later...Swing-Puppe."

Anna Keller's fledgling Swing Club of Weinhausen quickly experienced better success than Wolf Kaiser's Hitler Youth but everywhere else the National Socialists were making tremendous strides. Since Hitler's appointment as chancellor less than a month before, the German nation had, indeed, been propelled on a rapid course of change. Vagrants, prostitutes, beggars and petty criminals were being swept from the streets of Berlin. Abortion was outlawed and order was being restored.

But the most dramatic event occurred on 27 February 1933, for on that night the Reichstag was burned, supposedly by Communists now bent on overthrowing the new government. Riding a wave of public outrage and deep-seated fear, the elected members of the German parliament quickly gave their chancellor sweeping emergency powers to rule as he saw fit. Communists were now being arrested and concentrated into work camps like the new one in Dachau, near München, where they would be re-educated.

By late March, however, Weinhausen's Party members were staring into their beer at their Friday night meeting in Weinstube Krause. The men had learned that their Führer's cabinet minister, Hermann Göring, had apologized to German Jews for the persecution they had endured in the past. The men also learned that the Economic Ministry was grumbling about attacks on Jewish businesses, and rumors had begun to circulate about complaints within the Interior Ministry over articles in the Party's newspaper, *Der Stürmer*, that were suddenly deemed as radical. Furthermore, the New York Times had published an article suggesting that Chancellor Hitler might soon abandon his extreme views on the "Jewish problem" after all.

Round-faced Oskar Offenbacher entered the solemn inn beaming. Unlike most of the others at the meeting the baker was delighted at the apparent easing of Party policy. He delivered a basket of pretzels to Frau Krause and then took a seat by Wolf. "You look miserable."

"He's going soft like your pretzels," groused Wolf.

"The Führer?"

"Maybe not soft but...different."

"Well, with the Communists pretty well beaten the Party was bound to moderate. The Chancellor knows that order and decency are the way for us now. No more street brawls and crazy talk."

Richard Klempner stood, scowling, and raised a newspaper over his head as he addressed the hall. "Listen, everyone. I brought a copy of the *Völkischer Beobachter*. It says that the streets of New York are crammed with thousands of God's Chosen demanding that Americans boycott Germany."

The Weinstube's mood changed.

Klempner looked squarely at Offenbacher. "Yes, even now, when we are just about to get off our knees, those hook-nosed devils want to knock us over again. I tell you, they will goad us and goad us until Hitler has no choice but to harden...whether he wants to or not."

Postman Schmidt suddenly burst through the door. "Herr Klempner?"

All heads turned.

"You have a special delivery letter from Party headquarters in Koblenz." He handed an envelope to Klempner.

The Party chairman quickly scanned the letter and a large, self-congratulatory grin spread across his face. "Well, it seems that Chancellor Hitler has finally run out of patience. He's declared this coming Saturday to be a day of national boycott against the Jews and their endless lies!"

A loud cheer echoed through the room.

With his fist in the air, Klempner read from the dispatch. "It's to begin at 10:00 AM sharp..." His voice abruptly fell. "But all Woolworths and Hollywood cinemas are to be spared?" He lowered his arm and the hall became quiet again. "And I am instructed to read you this," Klempner grumbled. "It is forbidden to harm a hair of a Jewish head."

Offenbacher leaned his elbows on the table. He thought that the Führer's decision seemed supremely reasonable. But he wondered if any boycott was fair to the Jewish shopkeepers of Weinhausen. None of them were Communists, none owned pornographic bookstores; none had contributed to Germany's troubles in any way that he could imagine.

"So, is this decent enough for you, Herr Offenbacher?" asked Wolf, sarcastically.

"Yes, I suppose, though I don't think Silbermann or the others deserve a boycott at all."

"You worry me a little," Wolf said. "You do know that Silbermann is selling cakes from a Jew baker in Koblenz?"

"Yes, and they're very good."

"Are you sure you're not a Jew-lover?"

The baker gnawed a bite off his pretzel. He knew that he was certainly no 'Jew lover'...but he was no Jew hater either. Like most, he thought they could be unpleasant at times but were generally tolerable, and he had always treated them with civility. Actually, until the last few years he hadn't really thought about them at all. Oskar swallowed. "Well, I suppose I really don't care much one way or the other. I just want things to be orderly."

"Without a doubt the Jewish question is one of the historical problems with which the state must deal, and without a doubt the state is justified in blazing new trails here."

Rev. Dietrich Bonhoeffer, future resistance pastor

CHAPTER TEN

WHEN THE MEETING ended Eva began cleaning the tables and Wolf stayed to help. "So, Eva, ready for another motorcycle ride?"

Eva brightened. "Of course, but let's not get caught in the rain this time."

Wolf laughed. "You know, you're pretty when your hair's all wet."

The young woman blushed.

"So, you were listening to the meeting?"

Eva wiped a loose strand of hair off her forehead with the back of her hand and then plunged her rag into a soapy bucket. "A little. Politics bores me."

"And what do you think about the boycott?"

"Maybe some other Jews deserve it but I don't think the Jews we know do. Especially not Herr Silbermann; I haven't forgot how he saved me."

Wolf nodded. "I'll give you that. But don't worry, no one's going to hurt Silbermann, or Baum, or Goldmann for that matter. We just need to make our point."

Eva shook her head. "Well, I do think we're being a little hypocritical. On one hand we don't want the world boycotting all of us for a few loudmouths in the Party, but we do want to punish all the Jews for a few of theirs."

Wolf was quiet.

"Do you know what I mean?"

"You think too much. There's no other way to do it. They want to boycott us, we boycott them. It's that simple."

"Not really."

Wolf put his fists on his hips. He felt suddenly exposed as a man without a good answer. "You women need to have babies and let us do the thinking."

Eva bristled. "A minute ago you asked me what I thought! Make up your mind."

Wolf kicked over her bucket, sending a tide of suds across the wooden floor. He slammed his hand on a table-top. "Don't scold me like I'm some little boy!"

Fear suddenly washed over Eva. She had never felt that around Wolf before. "You...you really don't have to get mad."

Wolf's neck pulsed. He took a deep breath through his nose and closed his eyes, dismissing his fury as quickly as he had summoned it. "You're right, I'm sorry." He bent over to pick up her bucket.

Eva relaxed, but only a little. She fumbled with the rag held tightly in her hands. "I...I need to finish now."

Wolf took her arm, gently. "I really am sorry. You mean a lot to me and I didn't mean to say what I did. And I didn't mean to yell." He reached into his back pocket and retrieved a small envelope. "Oh, I almost forgot. Here."

Eva took the envelope and opened it slowly. Inside was a carefully pressed daffodil.

The young man smiled, proudly. "I spotted it yesterday from the train as it pulled into Güls. I was able to jump off, pick it, then jump back on just in time."

Eva softened. She lifted the yellow bloom to her nose. "It smells good, thank you."

⌖

The meadows along the sleepy Mosel River were delightful in three seasons, if not four. Eva's favorite was summer and by late

August 1933 she had stolen many hours along the grassy banks. She especially liked to wade with Lindie in the river's warm eddies where she would listen to secrets about Gunther's courtship. Eva was sure the pair would eventually marry and she wondered if Lindie would ever tell the gentle boy the whole truth.

Her times with Anna had been fun, as well, but less frequent. Eva had not been as interested in the whole jazz scene as Anna had hoped, so the two had begun to lose touch. Anna had quickly become the "Swing Doll" of the Mosel and was the unofficial leader of the valley's Swing Youth. She had the latest records from America and even a brand new phonograph, all thanks to her father's improved position made possible by laws which had forced Jews out of Civil Service jobs.

Of course, Andreas and Wolf remained as Eva's opposing desires. On one hand she loved the gentle decency of the handsome Andreas. This summer she had attended a number of village walks and hymn sings with him, and would probably be going to the coming wine festival as his date. When she was with him she felt like she was his treasure. She enjoyed his poetic conversations and the way that he loved the land. She was able to share her thoughts with him freely and without shame, and when she spoke to him he really listened.

On the other hand, she found her passions aroused whenever the fiery Wolf was near, especially when she pressed herself against his back as they rumbled through the countryside on his motorcycle. His intemperance sometimes bothered her, to be sure, but his virile confidence and his strength made her feel safe. She was surprised at how much she enjoyed feeling like his possession, and when his anger was aimed at her she felt oddly drawn all the more.

However, as of late Eva's primary concern had become her brother Daniel. The six-year old was often unsupervised and it seemed to Eva that he was being improperly influenced by the Schneider boys, particularly Heri. Frau Volk was often not home. The woman's responsibilities for the Party now took her to meetings in Bonn, Frankfurt and sometimes Köln, and today she was in Rüdesheim along with thousands hearing the Führer's speech.

Rev. Volk had done his best to monitor Daniel but the man was busy with his church. The 'reawakening' of Germany had begun to fill his pews and with that had come increased duties for the pastor. That, plus emergency meetings called by concerned pastors in the region had drawn him away from home until the late hours. So it had fallen to Hans Bieber to care for the lad.

But Eva was also worried about her old friend, Hans. Despite being properly fed and sheltered by the Volks, the light had never returned to the man's eyes nor had the gray left his face. His gait had slowed and his shoulders now slumped; he spent hours tending the grave of his long departed wife. Eva knew that the man's spirit had flown away the day the banker foreclosed on his beloved vineyards. She often saw the pain in his eyes when they lingered on the green terraces overlooking the river.

"They call it 'Führer weather,'" said Eva. Laying back in the green meadow she stared into a blue sky. The summer evening was warm. She, Hans Bieber, and Daniel had just finished a Sunday supper of cheese, ham slices, and day old bread.

Hans Bieber pushed his cap back on his head and forced a chuckle. "It never fails. No matter where he flies or when, the sun always shines." The old man tapped burnt tobacco from his pipe. "It's like our church celebrations. Father Steffen complains that whenever your father schedules a Fest or a village song walk, the weather is perfect. He calls them 'Protestant Highs.'"

Eva laughed. She sat up and picked some grass out of her braids. After a few quiet moments passed, she said, "I'm thinking of moving back."

Hans looked at her carefully. "Back to the house?"

Eva hesitated. She tossed a pebble into the water. "Daniel needs me. I think you all could use some help. I can cook and sew, clean the house..."

"I don't want you coming home," blurted Daniel. "All you do is make Mama cry, and Papa, too."

Thinking, the man took a wine bottle from his basket, slowly. "You wouldn't want to come back only to have to leave again." He poured them both some white wine. "We really are surviving. When your mother is away, I cook. Your father says my Sauerbraten is very good and ministers don't lie...I think."

Eva looked at Daniel. "You really don't want me coming home?"

The boy sat down. "Well, maybe you could. Uncle Rudi came by last week and wanted to see you."

"You didn't tell me."

Daniel shrugged. "I think you were with Wolf on his motorcycle. He bought me some marbles—a big cat's eye shooter. And he bought you a camera from New York."

"A camera? Where is it?"

"I keep forgetting to give it to you. It's called a 'Brownie.' He had film for it, too. He went to visit Oma. He says he needs to stay with her for a while because of the Poles."

Eva tossed a twig aimlessly toward the water and turned to Hans. "I've heard mother is...different."

Hans lit his pipe. He released a sweet cloud of smoke from his mouth. "Ja, well, the Party has been good for her." He leaned forward. "She doesn't drink as much, or smoke...unless her nerves are bad. And she's stopped wearing make-up."

"Why?"

"The Chancellor thinks German women should be modest and temperate."

"So does my father but she never listened to him."

Hans shrugged. "Well, he's not the Führer. People are saying that Hitler is God's choice for us so what he says, goes. They see his successes as evidence of Divine support...God wouldn't bless what He doesn't like."

"Is that true?"

"Well, I couldn't say. That would mean God was against the Fatherland in the Great War and that is impossible."

Eva sat quietly, watching her little brother dash about in his shorts and suspenders. "So, should I come home or not?"

"I don't know. Do you want to, or do you just think you should?"

Eva thought, carefully. She had no answer.

"Hello?" said a voice from behind.

Eva and Hans turned to see Andreas approaching. "I've been looking for you."

"Me?" Hans smiled.

"Well..."

"Ach, I'm joking. I need to take Daniel home now." The old man called for Daniel. "Auf Wiedersehen, you two." He winked.

"So, what are you doing today?"

"I went to the winery after church," Andreas said. "My boss says that we can make it a dance hall for the weekends if we like."

Eva looked at one of the rounded mountains overlooking the village. She could just make out the roof of Bieber's former winery. She hadn't been inside since the auction. "You really don't mind working the vines for those Frankfurt Jews, do you." Her tone had turned abruptly judgmental. Her lips pursed.

Andreas fell silent.

"If I were Hans, I'd be hurt. They own what should be his and you help them."

The eighteen-year old stared into the hills. He hadn't really thought of it like that. "I know every one of those vines. I love working the slopes and looking down on the river. It's beautiful up there."

Eva waited.

"But I did ask Bieber about it. He told me he didn't care...that he was glad I had a job."

"What else would he say? You needed work. But new jobs are coming fast. You could work on the highways. I hear Hitler's planning to build a new bridge in Limburg...you could get a job there. You don't have to work for those people now."

Andreas thought for a long moment. "I never meant to hurt Bieber."

"I thought you would have known better."

"I guess I thought they had nothing to do with any of it, but who knows?" The young man turned his face toward the staked terraces and slopes again. The vineyards were green, lush, and well-ordered. Since he was ten years old he had clambered about the slate mountainsides nurturing wonderful Riesling grapes from vine to bottle. Often alone on the terraces and working high above the river fog, he had easily felt one with his green mountains.

Eva saw the sudden emotion in Andreas' face and remembered how very much he loved the land. He had once asked her what gave her joy. She said she didn't know. 'Probably being loved,' had been her answer. He said that a person could learn a lot about another by what gave them joy. So she had asked him. And he answered, 'Being in the center of a circle where everything connects.' She hadn't known what he had meant until just then. She felt a stab of guilt for trying to shame her friend out of his circle.

The two stood and began walking toward the village. They crossed under the train trestle and began climbing a street. "You know, the foreman for the Roth Vineyard quit for a job on a lock project in Koblenz," said Andreas.

Eva brightened. "I hear the Roth's are good to work for."

Andreas thought for a moment. "You're right. I think I'll talk to them." The pair walked on in silence until Andreas said, "The university in Heidelberg fired all their Jews. My father's been offered a professorship. And Wolf is thinking about quitting school to take a job with the motor works in Koblenz. Maybe I could go to school now."

"What would you study?"

"Botany."

The two walked on and finally arrived at Andreas' door where the young man hesitated. "I bought a few records...would you like to hear them?"

"Swing?"

"Yes."

"Oh. Well, okay." Eva followed Andreas into his living room where she sat in a badly worn velvet chair. She looked around and found the house to be clean, though it smelled of musty furniture and cigarettes. The windows were covered by heavy drapes which kept both summer's heat and winter's cold at bay, but made the room feel gloomy. She threw them apart and let the August sunshine wash the room in bright, dusty shafts of light.

She spotted the professor's brand new Volksempfänger— the radio that the government was distributing to nearly everyone. It could receive broadcasts from three government channels. Richard Klempner had recently reminded her father that he would need to alter his American RCA so it wouldn't be able to receive foreign propaganda from broadcasts like Radio Luxemburg or the BBC.

Eva was then drawn to a host of books on the professor's desk—books by Darwin, Chamberlain, and Gobineau. She picked up one of Gobineau's four volumes titled, *Essai sur L'Ingalit'é des Races Humaines*.

"One of the professor's favorites," said Andreas.

"Huh?"

"I said those books are my father's favorites. They're by a Frenchman as you can see, and about seventy-five years old."

"What are they about?"

"How the races are unequal and how our Aryan peoples are the superior race, and how the Jews are inferior overachievers who want to tear us down." He shrugged. "Wolf has father translate chapters at dinner."

"Sounds like National Socialist stuff."

"Yeah. The Nazis want to make the Jewish problem a race problem instead of a religious one, so they use this Frenchman and some Englishman named Chamberlain. I get bored with the science stuff." Andreas pointed to some other books, mostly peasant novels by authors such as Eckardt and Wilhelm von Polenz. "I like those." He then pointed past a mound of Wolf's Nazi magazines to numerous, dusty editions of *Die Tat*, a publication of the romantic Völkisch movement—an old movement that honored the traditions of Germany's rural past. "In one of those, Otto Gemlin wrote that every people has its own landscape. Ours is endless forests. We Germans are not made for cities, you know."

Eva smiled at the poetic youth's passion.

Suddenly embarrassed, Andreas quickly reached his hand toward a short stack of albums. "Well, anyway, here are my records." Andreas handed Eva a recording by Snooks Friedman and his Memphis Stompers, and another by the Chocolate Dandies. She took a seat near the gramophone and listened as Andreas set a badly worn needle on the first vinyl.

"I have to keep the volume down. The neighbors hate this almost as much as my father," said Andreas as the *Goofer Feathers Blues* began. "They call it Judeo-Negroid music." They both laughed.

"My father told the youth group that this music promotes drunken living and immorality," said Eva.

Andreas shrugged. "I know. Gunther told me. I think he's overreacting."

Eva wasn't so sure. She had heard enough from the Party to believe that music and art could be used to undermine a whole culture. She was actually glad that the government was banning many of the films that the traveling cinema's used to show on the wall at the Weinstube. She remembered how they had made her blush while she was waiting tables.

Andreas hurried into the kitchen and returned with white wine and some mild cheese before dashing to his attic bedroom. He came down carrying a large picture—a framed print by the German artist, Caspar David Friedrich. "My blood father left this for me when he died."

Eva left her chair and studied the painting. It featured the back of a lone man in a black waist coat standing on a mountain peak and facing a world of clouds that crowded a range of jagged mountains.

"It's called *Man above a Sea of Fog.*"

"It's hard to know if the clouds are gathering or parting."

Andreas smiled. He was excited. "I've stared at this all my life. It's a perfect picture of German enigma...something the professor says our people are famous for. Look, the man's posture seems confident but is he content or looking to the next summit?"

"Yes, and see the sun. It may be rising on a new day or setting on an old one."

"Why did the artist hide the man's face?"

"What's he really looking at?" Eva stared at every corner and as she did she saw more and more ambiguity. "The artist leads our eye upward, toward heaven, but..."

"Yes. I say he's facing the glory of a sunrise and basking in his glory..." Andreas took Eva gently by the arm and turned her slowly toward him.

Eva began to swim in the young man's eyes as if drawn into a watery pool of wonder—into a warm, soothing bath somewhere in Paradise. Her legs felt weak and her heart began to race. She released herself to Andreas' strong hands as he gently pulled her against him. She could see him hesitate, shyly. She closed her eyes and waited, hoping. Then, after the slow passing of an infinite moment, she felt his breath on her face and finally felt him press his lips softly upon hers.

"We will restore the unity of spirit and purpose of our Volk. We will take Christianity as the basis for our collective morality and the family as the nucleus of our Volk and State, under its firm protection."

Adolf Hitler

CHAPTER ELEVEN

EVA'S MIND WHIRLED at the succession of events that she and her world experienced over the next twelve months. Despite their kiss, she and Andreas had not become a couple—at least not formally. To the young man's great distress, Eva had decided to keep their relationship civil, even warm, but her unspoken heart-tug toward Wolf had prevented the girl from being totally swept away by Andreas' generous affection. Nevertheless, she had accompanied the young suitor to a number of the past year's events including several hymn sings and village walks. She had even gone with him to the November celebrations of Martin Luther's 450th birthday in Koblenz, and her parents had invited him to at least a dozen Sunday coffees.

However, as kind and as attentive as Andreas always was, Eva found herself thinking about Wolf day and night. Even with Andreas at her arm she pictured Wolf hurtling around the motorcycle track in his handsome leather suit. Her mind drifted to the thrill of leaning through the curves of country roads atop his red, rumbling machine with her arms wrapped around his waist. It was as if his speed and power could carry her away from past pain and toward things new.

So Eva also made time to walk with Wolf, and when she did, she found herself wanting to follow him. When Wolf spoke, Eva wanted to obey. And when Wolf urged Eva to return to her father's home like a proper German girl should, she found herself at her father's door with suitcase in hand.

The next months proved to be ones of reluctant healing. Eva served her father more than one cup of real coffee as he read to her from the many newspapers Uncle Rudi had sent. It seemed that the nation had become a proud community again, united in a common effort against immorality, Bolshevism, crime, and class hatred. The mind-dizzying flurry of news had left Eva barely able to keep up.

Employment was rising at breathtaking rates; all political parties had been united under one National Socialist Party; people now expected to greet one another with the Hitler salute; university students had burned thousands of books that were considered corrupting to the nation; the government had passed laws to sterilize the severely handicapped—like in America as Paul had been quick to say. The poor were being clothed and fed, newlyweds given assistance in marrying. Jews had been deprived of citizenship rights, and political opponents like the Communists had been detained in concentration camps for re-education. The chancellor had withdrawn the Fatherland from the League of Nations because of its antipathy toward Germany.

To these policies and others, the Führer had submitted himself to a referendum of public opinion. The result was an approval rate of 95%, including overwhelming support for his foreign policy from a national Jewish community desperate to prove its loyalty. Germany was further unified by the pope's recent Concordat with the Führer—an agreement which paved the way for German Roman Catholics to support their government with the Church's blessing.

The 'Hitler Miracle' had inspired a number of surprises as well, including government loans to a Jewish department store to protect the jobs of 14,000 workers, and the Gestapo's raising of money to support pastors in foreign missions. Furthermore, Hitler had once again reassured the nation that he would never interfere with the teachings or the religious freedoms of the churches—a point not lost on Paul Volk.

"I kept telling you, 'the soup is never served as hot as it is cooked.'" Gerde hurried to clear the table of a light evening's supper. It was Monday, 27 August 1934. "Paul, you and some of your preacher friends worry too much. And I'm sure your brother's going to have a lot to say."

Eva watched her mother tilt lightly to one side. She was glad that the woman had been drinking less but the prospect of her soon-to-arrive American brother-in-law had wreaked havoc with her nerves. So Hitler's expectations notwithstanding, Gerde Volk again returned to a former lover—schnapps.

Paul ignored his wife's condition, turning instead to answer Eva's question about the complaints of some pastors. "You're speaking of the Bekennende Kirche movement led by Bonhoeffer and Niemöller. You must understand that the vast majority of the BK pastors still support the government even though they don't agree with everything about Nazi ideology. The primary issue for the BK is the 'Aryan Clause' in the law which forbids non-Aryans from all sorts of connections to German institutions. It seems that the State considers baptized Jews to still be Jews and therefore they no longer belong in our churches. So, most of the complaining pastors are objecting to State interference in Church matters."

"But you haven't joined them."

"No. Some of their radicals—especially Bonhoeffer—are beginning to go too far; they don't give the Führer any room at all. We can't expect the State to act without error. Our job is to patiently guide the State toward righteousness." Paul reached for his paper. "I will say this, the chancellor hasn't said the word 'Jew' for more than a year and he's shown remarkable restraint with the Poles, even after their Palm Sunday attacks on their German population..."

A heavy knock on the door turned all heads.

Paul Volk took a deep breath and stood up slowly, casting an uneasy eye at his wife. He hadn't seen his brother Alfred for a long time and based on the tone of recent letters he really wasn't enthused to see him now. However, he was looking forward to reacquainting himself with his niece and nephew. Paul reached for the knob and opened the door. "Ah, wilkommen alle."

Alfred took Paul's hand. "Wonderful to see you."

"And you, Alfred. Please, come in. Let me help with the luggage."

The American led his children through the door and into the living room where he presented Gerde a customary bouquet of fresh flowers.

"Very nice. Thank you."

Alfred looked around the room and removed a tailored suit coat. He was a Baptist minister from a wealthy neighborhood in Richmond, Virginia and had been at an international Baptist convention in Berlin. He brought along his daughter, Jenny—a sixteen year-old brunette, and his ten year old son, Bobby. His German-born wife had died from cancer two years before.

Eva and Daniel stood politely as they met their cousins for the first time, quite relieved that they spoke fluent German. But before the cousins had a chance to start a conversation, Alfred reached into a large bag and promptly began presenting gifts. He handed Gerde an attractive embroidery of the twenty-third Psalm, then handed Paul an envelope with sheet music. "I hope your organist approves."

"Thank you."

Uncle Alfred presented Daniel with a book of Bible stories in English. The boy offered a polite 'danke.' He'd be sure to put the book in the drawer alongside his other disappointment, the Christmas whistle.

Alfred then motioned to Jenny. The girl reached into the bag and retrieved a gift wrapped in brown paper and handed it to Eva. "I hope you don't already have one."

Excited, Eva hurried to open it. "A diary!" Eva opened the brown leather book and stared happily at its empty pages. She wondered what words the future would fill it with. "Thank you, Jenny, thank you Onkel Alfred...thank you very much." She gave them each a hug. "And thank you, too, Bobby."

In the minutes to follow the Volk house filled with a clutter of suitcases and a chatter of voices until Gerde invited everyone into the kitchen for coffee and cake. Eva and Jenny tarried in the living room for a few moments.

Jenny was a rather homely, large girl with a bad case of acne. She was more shy than Eva had expected from her letters, and she seemed uncomfortable. Eva took her hand and was about to ask Jenny of her mother's passing when she heard a knock on the front door. Eva quickly answered.

Andreas was standing at the door with a silly smile and a bouquet of flowers. Eva almost laughed out loud. "What in the world?

Andreas blushed. He was wearing striped pants and an oversized sport coat. A long lock of hair hung over his forehead. "Your Americans are here?"

Eva nodded. "But why are you dressed like that?"

"I got a little pay raise so I thought I'd surprise you." He raised his hand in a Hitler salute. "Swing Heil." He laughed, self-consciously.

"You look...you look...so different. And those shoes." At first amused, Eva was now embarrassed. She looked at Jenny who was staring at Andreas, wide-eyed.

"Who's there?" Gerde Volk came into the room wiping her hands on her apron. She took one look at Andreas and muffled a belch. "Do you need a comb?"

The young man quickly pushed the long lock off his forehead. "I...I was wondering if the Americans would like to come to the club tonight...with Eva and me?"

Gerde tittered. "Are you kidding? They're Baptists. Baptists are worse than the Nazis about that stuff." She looked at Andreas' shoes. "Baptists don't laugh much, either, but those may help." Gerde belched again, loudly. "You know, the Americans banned alcohol...and they think we tolerate tyranny!"

The three youths followed Gerde into the kitchen and as Andreas entered, Paul stood, gaping. "What are you wearing, son?"

"Uh, some new clothes, sir." He watched the color come to the minister's cheeks.

Alfred Folk shook his head instead of Andreas' outstretched hand. "I'd never allow my daughter to date a Swing Kid. You know what goes on, Paul. I'm surprised."

Eva bristled. She hadn't seen her uncle in over ten years and she was suddenly glad he lived far away. "You're surprised, Onkel Alfred?"

The American was portly, self-important, and very opinionated. "My dear," he began. His tone was condescending and unnecessarily loud. Eva knew that he was about to deliver a sermon. "I am surprised that my brother has a daughter involved in such depravity as this."

"But..."

"I've just come from our convention in Berlin. I expected this Hitler fellow to be a puffed up toady, what with his National Socialist flags hanging all over the convention floor. Imagine, Adolf Hitler's banner next to a picture of the great Charles Spurgeon! But, I came away impressed. He doesn't smoke, drink, curse, or carouse. He expects German women to be sober, modest and committed to their families." Alfred fired a haughty gaze at Gerde. "And, he's opposed to the godless Reds, to abortion, and to homosexuals. I believe he may have Germany going in the right direction, after all." He leaned toward Eva. "But now I see Devil Jazz show up in a little village like Weinhausen. I tell you, his cause for German decency may be lost already."

Eva protested. "Our dances are harmless. We're just having fun..."

"Dancing is never harmless, young lady...lustful gyrations...a playground for sin. The dance floor is nothing more than Lucifer's stage. Alcohol, vile language, jungle rhythms...your father should have taught you better."

Still standing, Paul was restlessly tapping his pipe against his thigh. "She's able to make her own decisions."

Alfred turned on his younger brother, angrily. "You Christians in Germany have lost your way. Too many liberals, not enough sound Bible teaching."

Paul said nothing but Gerde had enough. "Is that so? Maybe if you could have restrained your Allies after the war we wouldn't be such lost sheep."

"If you are going to encourage my children to dance and to wear costumes like...like his, we're leaving!"

Gerde narrowed her eyes. "Would you like some Mosel wine, Alfred? It would calm you down. I have a very good Riesling here..."

"No! And by the smell of your breath, you shouldn't either."

"Get out of my kitchen." Gerde lifted the wine bottle to her lips and gulped a few swallows, defiantly.

"Now, Gerde, please..."

"Shut up, Paul. If you were a man you'd throw this Pharisee out the door yourself."

"Pharisee? Well then." Alfred's ears became red as heated iron. "Paul, can't you control your wife?"

Eva watched her flushed-faced father fumble for words.

Gerde answered for him. "No, actually, he can't control me, or his daughter, or his son, or his congregation. The man's almost as pitiful as you, you coward."

"Woman!" Alfred slammed his fist on the table.

"You heard me. My brothers died in the trenches while you ran off to America to change your name. That makes you a coward..."

Andreas and Eva never went to the dance that evening—the mood had been ruined. Instead, Eva and Paul helped Alfred Folk's family carry their luggage to a room in the Weinstube. In the morning to follow, Paul greeted his brother in the inn's dining hall with a plethora of apologies and a pitiful plea for him to remain the week, as planned. Alfred reluctantly agreed to stay on Paul's account but refused any contact with Gerde. So while the two brothers spent the next days visiting with local pastors, Eva was charged with entertaining her two cousins.

Saturday broke warm and fair, and Eva borrowed some bikes to take Andreas, Jenny, Daniel, and Bobby along the sleepy, meandering Mosel toward the village of Kobern which lay a short distance to the west. After pedaling through the village the group was soon laying its bikes at the northern base of a steep, partially wooded hillside. Above, the ruins of Niederburg Castle stood where they had for centuries.

"Follow me," said Eva.

The climb was a strain but not severe. The narrow trail wound its way upward in switchbacks toward the brown stone ruins. The five emerged from behind some scrubby pines and entered the broken walls of the castle's outer curtain. The American children gaped in awe as Eva told them that castle had been built eight hundred years prior, and that nearby were more than a thousand Roman graves. The two boys dashed ahead as Eva, Jenny, and Andreas walked up a set of smooth-worn stone stairs to the next level and then to the next where they stood by an ancient well to enjoy the warm sun. The girls picked small bunches of tiny flowers that were rooted weakly in the time-cracked mortar. Above, a flock of birds swooped close.

Eva smiled.

She loved the Niederburg as much as any place on earth. And the well was a place of comfort for her; it was a circle of stone that drew her eye to the refreshment of its quiet depths. Just a few paces away the towering castle-keep rose smooth-weathered and proud; it made her feel somehow safe and connected to her homeland in ways the Americans could not understand.

The young woman moved to an outer wall and climbed into a nook. From there she peered through one of the windows at the meandering Mosel flowing calmly below. She closed her eyes and imagined herself floating into some wonderful future in the new world now dawning. She opened them to enjoy the green, mountainous panorama of well-tended vineyards and hardwood forests spreading before her in all directions.

"I see why you love it here," said Jenny.

Andreas pulled pen and paper from his pocket and faded away as Eva and Jenny sat against the strong wall of the well. They had grown close in the past few days and both were sorry to see the visit coming to an end. The pair began to share deep feelings of things they feared and things they were confused about. Jenny revealed how frightened she was of her father's anger; Eva how embarrassed she was of her father's timidity. Jenny told of her fear of boys; Eva of Wolf and Andreas. Jenny talked about church and there Eva found things in common.

But then Jenny complained about how Germans were said to be treating the Jews; Eva countered with how Americans treated Negroes. Jenny asked if Germany would try to take back the land it had lost in the War; Eva asked if America would ever return the land it took from the Indians.

Rising emotions quickly subsided and Eva listened to Jenny sympathetically as the girl expressed her problems of 'Germanness' in America. Apparently Jenny was actually glad that her father had changed the family name. Eva felt sorry for her cousin. To her, the girl seemed unsure of who she was or where she belonged. She thought Jenny had been deprived of roots—of blood and soil. And she pitied her for other reasons—like living in fear of a monstrous father.

So Eva decided to go through with it.

She reached her hands into a pocket. "Jenny, do you remember Opa?"

"A little. He used to write to me and always wrote my name as Jennifer *V*olk."

"He missed seeing you and Bobby."

"He did?"

"Yes." Eva opened her hand and looked at the black and gold necklace now lying in her open palm. Everything about it represented the things her cousin and she shared: Christian faith, German blood, family ties. Her father had described these things as parts of 'wholeness' in a conversation the two had a few years ago. She hesitated, suddenly unsure. "Uh...Opa gave this to Oma when they were first married. He bought it in Salzburg."

Jenny took the necklace from Eva's hand carefully, and held it to the sun. "It's so beautiful."

Eva nodded. "It's really old." She watched the necklace spin brightly in the sunshine. She remembered the night Opa had given it to her and the night it had been ripped off her neck by the Frenchman. She also remembered the Christmas that she had taken it off in anger, and the Sunday that Andreas had urged her to put it back on. The simple thing had been her companion through much. She had loved it and hated it; she had needed it and had abandoned it.

But at this moment she felt that she had grown beyond it.

"Oma always wanted to take it to America." Eva could see the love for it in her cousin's eyes. "Why...why don't you take it there, Jenny...as my gift."

If Eva had any reservations about surrendering her golden

companion they were quickly dispelled. Jenny threw her arms around her. "Oh, thank you!" she sobbed. "Thank you."

"Eva?" Wolf was smiling as he marched into the castle at the head of a column of his Hitler Youth.

Eva waved. "Your boys look a little worn out." Eva toyed with her hair. "And you…I thought eighteen was too old for the Hitler Youth."

"No, nineteen is. Then I'll enlist in the SS."

Eva was impressed. The black-uniformed Schutzstaffel was well-known as Hitler's personal guard—an elite competitor of sorts to the regular army, the Wehrmacht. "Are…you tall enough?"

Wolf reddened and didn't answer. Instead, he barked at the youths now standing shoulder to shoulder in front of him. "Form up!" The boys were dressed in their summer uniforms—brown caps, brown shirts with armbands, black corduroy shorts, long socks, and heavy shoes. A black, rolled scarf was wrapped round their necks and tied at the throat into a knot.

"They look like Boy Scouts," whispered Jenny to Eva.

"Something like that, I guess. The younger boys are the Deutsches Jungvolk, the Boys of Germany. Those fifteen through eighteen are the official Hitler Jugend, the Hitler Youth."

Eva was happy that Daniel was still too young to join. The whole Hitler Youth movement seemed a little over-the-top to her, though she did respect the order and discipline the boys were learning. She thought boys should be allowed to play sometimes rather than spending their Saturday's in marching formation or practicing war maneuvers. Their instructors' emphasis on Aryan superiority seemed unnecessary but she did appreciate the fact that their songbook started with a whole section of songs about God. She had grown quite fond of hearing columns of HJ and their female counterparts, the Bund Deutscher Mädel—the BDM—marching along the river singing about God, country, family, and freedom.

Andreas reappeared and as he sat by Eva a scrap of paper fell from his pocket. A breeze tumbled it against the girl's shoe. "What's this?" asked Eva. Her eyes rode lightly over the words before she began to read aloud:

Für Eva,

Mein Liebchen vom Brunnen	(My Darling of the Well
Meine Königin des Tales,	My Queen of the Valleys
Du machst mich so glücklich,	You make me so happy
Du bist jetzt mein alles.	You are now my all.
Mögen Sonne und Blumen	May sunshine and flowers
Und Musik und Wein,	And music and wine,
Dich allezeit begleiten,	Be always your companions
Bis du für immer mein.	Until you are forever mine.)

"It's...it's beautiful. But..."

Wolf's booming voice turned all heads. "For the Fatherland!" The snare drums snapped.

Eva touched Andreas' hand. "Thank you," she whispered.

""We as believing Christians thank God that he has given to our Volk in its time of need the Führer as a pious and faithful sovereign, and that he wants to prepare for us in the National Socialist system a government with discipline and honor."

Paul Althaus, Protestant theologian

CHAPTER TWELVE

"TAKE THE HEM of the flag in your left hand and raise the first three fingers of your right." Wolf's candidates encircled a National Socialist flag and took hold of its edge. The drums were still rolling in the castle yard.

Seven boys answered their commander in unison: "In the presence of this banner representing our Führer I swear to devote all my strength to the savior of our Fatherland, Adolf Hitler. I am willing to serve him to death, so help me God. One People, one Reich, one Führer."

Looking well-pleased, Wolf exchanged the Hitler salute with his new recruits. "Sieg Heil!" He then welcomed his new members one at a time. "Remember these two things: First, God made the Aryan race to be supreme. Second, your allegiance is to your Führer. Our duty is to him as his is to us. Our oath is sacred; our sacrifice is the Fatherland's honor."

The whole castle echoed the cheers. Wolf nodded to the band and they struck up the Hitler Youth Anthem:

"*Forward, forward, call the bright fanfares...we march with Hitler through the night, suffering with the banner of freedom and bread. Our banner means far more to us than death*!"

Jenny looked at Eva, wide-eyed. "This is nothing like the Scouts."

"Well, your country isn't surrounded by enemies."

Bobby Folk was intrigued. Had his father never moved to America the blond-haired, blue-eyed ten-year old knew he'd be standing shoulder to shoulder with these boys. He turned to Eva. "Daniel told me that I'm an Aryan, too."

"Well, don't get carried away with it."

Wolf led his group in the first melody in the HJ songbook, *God is my Song*. Eva turned toward her cousins once again and found herself feeling oddly pleased at their astonished faces. The flags, the drums and the uniforms had made her feel proud to belong to the new Germany. "Let's take a picture." She summoned the two Americans and handed Andreas her Brownie. "Could you take it of us by the well?"

The four cousins gathered close to one another. Eva draped one arm around Jenny and rested one hand on Bobby's shoulder. Daniel puffed his chest and offered a cheerful smile. Andreas squeezed one eye against the small viewfinder. "Everyone's ready? Let's see some..."

Wolf came from behind and took the camera from Andreas. "How about we take a real German picture? How about one good "Heil Hitler!"

The Americans hesitated, and then tittered before obediently straight-arming the air. "Heil Hitler!"

Wolf pressed the shutter.

In the months that followed, the 'Hitler Miracle' continued unabated. But no matter how inspiring the Führer's speeches, nor how solicitous the HJ and the BDM were for the youth of the Mosel Valley, Anna Keller's Swing Club at the former Bieber winery continued to draw members.

"Go, Andreas, go!" Anna Keller laughed as she watched Andreas and Lindie dance to The Chick Webb Orchestra playing *Got the Jitters*.

Eva clapped. The dancers in the room spun and whirled about with rubber band limbs, pulling close to one another, then pushing away. Their legs skipped atop the clay floor like marionettes gone mad. "Go, Lindie, go!"

Twenty-two couples were competing in a Saturday night dance marathon and the couple who could dance the longest would be awarded a new record by the German jazz band, Stefan Weintraub's Syncopators. Eva had tried a few dances. She liked Ben Pollack's *If I Could Be with You*. Of course, that was a slow-tempo song that she could dance to without risking her skirt flying over her hips! Otherwise, she was content to cheer on Andreas as he flew about the dance floor in his baggy, cuffed pants and wide-open double-breasted sport coat.

Andreas and Lindie were dancing the Lindy Hop though they were equally adept at the Balboa. The pair seemed to move well together—a fact not particularly well-received by the normally jolly Gunther. The young farm lad was sulking in a corner with a bottle of schnapps. Like Andreas and the other boys, a long lock of hair hung over his eyes. He and Lindie were engaged to be married and hoped to tie the knot in the spring to come.

The rules allowed for one five-minute break every hour, so when the fellow by the phonograph lifted the needle a great sigh sounded. "Man, I grooved this platter from the first lick," panted Andreas. He cast a disinterested look at a few quarreling boys from Kobern.

"Whatever you say," said Eva.

Lindie reached for a tall beer. "This hep cat is mellow as they come." She giggled and burped.

Eva laughed. "Well, I'm, uh…off the cob."

Lindie and Andreas roared. Gunther quickly added, "And I'm…no wise jive…or something." He scratched his head.

No one understood. The three stared at him blank-faced and the fellow's protruding ears turned red as summer roses.

"Anyway," said Eva. "Did you see Anna's fingernails?"

"Purple on one hand, yellow on the other," said Andreas. "And she must have used a trowel to put her make-up on."

Anna walked over to the group. "You're talking about me?"

Andreas pushed his hair off his sweated forehead. "One hep jitterbug is you. Your front has blew their wigs."

Anna laughed and took his arm. "Wrong riff, you zoot."

Eva didn't like the way Anna held Andreas' arm. She looked away and into the smoky shadows of the dimly lit cellar. Overdressed girls were draped atop slouching boys. Beer mugs were strewn about and flasks were being tipped into nearly every mouth not already fixed around a cigarette.

The spinner was about to set another record on his phonograph. "Achtung, Achtung!" he shouted while standing at mock attention. "Everyone, form up." The room sniggered and fell into ranks. Satisfied, the boy cried a sarcastic "Heil Hotler!" He faced his drunken audience with a mock Hitler moustache. He folded his arms over his chest and looked as fierce as he could. "Jew music! Nigger music! Shall we burn it all and save the Fatherland?"

The laughing crowd answered, "No!"

"Hmm. Well then. Don't get salty. Time for me to cut out!" The winery rollicked and the spinner dropped his needle atop a Josephine Baker record.

Eva watched Andreas run out on the dance floor with Lindie. She was glad that he was enjoying himself. After all, the nineteen-year old was a hard worker. But this room full of drunken, slump-shouldered sloppy boys and frivolous, immoderate girls bothered her. Maybe the National Socialists were saving Germany just in time.

She watched Lindie laughing uproariously at something that Andreas said. She was happy for the girl. Decadence and excess notwithstanding, Eva believed that Lindie had suffered enough to be entitled to nearly any extravagance. Gunther, of course, was just tagging along. She was sure that a farm boy like him would not be drawn into hedonism. On the other hand, Anna seemed different lately. Her father's meteoric rise in the very government these Swing Kids secretly mocked had provided Anna with the means to exercise a defiant attitude that Eva had never seen in her before.

The dance went until Sunday's first light. Andreas and Lindie had long since given up and had fallen asleep with their respective dates near the warmth of the winery's coal stove. "Drunken idiots," grumbled a waking Andreas as he rubbed his bloodshot eyes. "Look at them."

Eva yawned and turned toward Andreas. "How do you feel?"

"Not great."

"Well, no wonder." Eva stood and smoothed her skirt to her legs.

"Will your father be angry?"

"Probably. He's worried that I'm going the way of my mother. She was in the Wandervögel."

"Yeah, they were an odd bunch. Guitars and camping in the woods...unmarried!"

"Odd? Look around."

Andreas noticed the Kobern bunch stumbling through the door toward one of their cars. "That's not a good idea."

Eva grabbed her coat and followed Andreas out the door and into the cold of the January morning. A misty drizzle had left the ground icy. Church bells were ringing below. "Fritz, you shouldn't drive," shouted Andreas. "You can hardly walk...and the road's slippery."

"What...?" Fritz Huber was so drunk he could hardly stand. Another leaned over the fender of the car to vomit.

After a few minutes of bickering it was agreed that Andreas would take the Kobern group home in Huber's father's car—a beautiful 1929 Mercedes 460 Nurburg. Andreas bit his lips nervously as his eight passengers crowded into the vehicle; he had only ever driven a few rusty trucks. He squinted through a tiny patch of windshield cleared of ice, then eased the vehicle into gear. The sleek Mercedes started to glide swiftly down the hill and into the village.

"Slow down, Bauer," grumbled Fritz.

Andreas didn't answer. He braked lightly. The rear of the car slipped to one side.

"Slow down."

Andreas gripped the wheel. He braked again; the car slid to the right and then abruptly to the left.

"Bauer!"

The car gained speed; Andreas tried pumping his brakes but the car began to swing from one side to the other like a pendulum gaining momentum. Midst the rising cries of his passengers, the panicked Andreas finally stood on his brake pedal, throwing the heavy automobile into a hard skid to one side until it careened through a final intersection and turned a full 180 degrees over a curb. A sickening thud followed before the car finally crashed against the corner of a house.

'Did you see that!' cried Gunther. He, Eva, and Lindie started running down the hill. By the time they neared the scene of the accident a group of villagers had already gathered around the car. A neighbor took Eva's arm, firmly. "No, no, just stay here. Dr. Krebel's coming."

"What?" Eva was confused and panting. "What is it? Is Andreas hurt?" She pulled her arm loose and pushed her way between the shoulders of others until she spotted a woman kneeling by someone lying on the street. A pool of blood encircled a head of white hair.

Heart pounding, the girl burst from the circle.

She recognized the woman; she was a nurse who lived a few doors away. "Frau Hoffmann?"

"Oh, my dear. Oh, poor girl, I'm so sorry."

Eva pressed closer, desperately. She gasped. Lying before her was her little brother, Daniel. "Is he...is he..." She staggered and fell to her knees.

Her world went away.

⊕

Diary entry: 27 January 1935

It has been one week since Daniel was killed and I cannot stop crying. I miss him so much. The blood was so red on the snow. I feel sick when I think about it. I hated the ambulance men who took him away. I wanted to scream at them but I could only stare. Everything was blurry.

I saw my father walking to Daniel's grave this morning and he looked like an old man. Mother won't talk to me because she thinks I'm to blame. She told me I should never have been a part of the Swing Club in the first place. For once she's right.

I hate Andreas now. I can't look at him without seeing Daniel's body in the street. I wish he'd stop coming to the house.

How can I tell Daniel how much I loved him?

Lindie tells me that she and Gunther are never going back to the Swing Club and I'm glad. She understands. Anna may move to Frankfurt with her father. I hope she takes all of her records and her Swing junk with her. The sight of anyone in those stupid outfits makes me want to vomit.

⌖

"Fire!"

Weinhausen's fire company siren screamed over the sleeping village during the early morning of Saturday, 2 February. The woeful whine drew Eva to her window where she saw numbers of volunteer firemen sprinting up Kirchstrasse toward the small Fire Department garage located next to the schoolhouse. She dressed hastily and flew down the stairs and out the front door where she stood alongside her parents.

"There." Paul Volk pointed his finger to a column of thick, black smoke rising toward the gray sky from the ridge overlooking the village.

"The winery!" exclaimed Eva.

Paul jerked open the garage door and directed his family into the 1926 Morris Oxford they had been recently given as a gift from a group of parishioners. In moments, the three were rumbling behind others in a mad rush to the scene of the fire.

When the family arrived at Bieber's former winery the whole building was being consumed by ferocious, boiling flames. Smoke rolled upward as fat, folding, black clouds. They had barely abandoned their car when the roof collapsed, sending a volcanic plume of red cinders and hot ash high into the sky.

However, what turned the Volks' attention was a row of SA men and Hitler Youth strung in a perimeter line with their backs to the blaze. Two drummers snapped their snares as a bass drum thumped slowly; a full dozen Nazi flags were angled forward from the belts of flag-bearers. They forbade the fire department access and a brief scuffle ensued.

Eva scanned the conflict until she spotted Wolf. He was in full winter uniform atop a bay gelding. Her admiring gaze must have drawn him, for he abruptly turned his face toward hers and when their eyes met, she knew that he knew what she now understood. Eva waved with one hand and held her heart with the other. She would later write in her diary that the day was glorious and that she had never felt so grateful for anything in all her life.

But there was another who did not think the day glorious at all. Ignoring the others, Hans Bieber stood alone, cap in hand, his face set against an invisible wall of heat. He had built the winery with the help of his father so many memories ago. Its sturdy timbers had faithfully sheltered the secrets of his lifetime. And though some judge and visored clerk may have scrawled others' names on a paper deed—names that went on to defile its sanctity with greed and excess—Hans believed that the soul of the place had always belonged to him. After all, his hammer had fixed every board; his callused hands had cradled every stone. Here he had shared life with those he loved and here he had grieved for love, lost.

But now this. What happens to the soul of a place when it turns to ash?

And so Hans Bieber wept.

⌖

For a young man of twenty, Andreas Bauer was anchored with patience. Yet, through the weeks that followed the fire, his guilt fueled a simmering rage. Visions of little Daniel lying in the cold street kept him awake for nights. He wondered what kind of future the little boy might have had; what kind of joys and dreams he had been denied. Night after night Andreas stared at his bedroom ceiling through tear-blurred eyes wishing for all the world that he could rewind time.

He hated himself.

In addition, he was suffering the loss of Eva's affections. The young woman had refused to see him and had returned his letters, unopened. And as far as the other Volk's were concerned, Andreas was anathema. Rev. Volk had served him Communion, but with uncharacteristic coldness; Frau Volk once spat as he walked by their door.

Andreas was beset by other troubles as well. He had to come home each night to face Wolf who had managed to turn the whole business to his own gain. For starters, Wolf was enjoying 'whisper praise' for destroying the Swing Club. In one bold stroke he had avenged Daniel's death and rid Weinhausen of moral decadence. But Wolf was being credited with more. He, along with Richard Klempner and Adolf Schneider, had filed a formal accusation against the vineyard's managing director—Herr Blumenthal—for setting fire to the winery for the supposed purpose of insurance fraud. The three testified in court that they had been on an early morning hike when they saw Blumenthal running from the burning building.

Blumenthal and his co-investors were quickly found guilty of conspiracy to commit fraud. All of their holdings along the Mosel were confiscated by the State for resale to Aryan vintners and they were sent to the work camp at Dachau. (The decision had left Hans Bieber with mixed feelings: on the one hand he enjoyed a certain satisfaction in seeing his beloved vines taken away from those who had profited by his loss. But on the other he felt a twinge of discomfort for the dubious judicial process.)

In the wake of Wolf's victories, Andreas had become brooding and distant. On weekends he moped along the river bank, even as news of increasing employment and the boarding up of the poorhouse brought smiles to others. And when Weinhausen burst into celebration for the Saarland's overwhelming vote to rejoin Chancellor Hitler's Fatherland, Andreas took a nap.

""The struggle we are waging until victory or the bitter end is, in its deepest sense, a struggle between Christ and Marx."

Joseph Goebbels, Nazi Minister of Information and Propaganda

CHAPTER THIRTEEN

"HAPPY BIRTHDAY, WOLF." It was 20 April 1935—also Adolf Hitler's forty-sixth birthday. Eva and Lindie had followed Wolf to the race track of Mendig, a town about twenty-five kilometers from Weinhausen and situated near the popular Maria Laach, a peaceful lake in the region north of the Mosel known as the Eifel.

"Thanks." Wolf was off-loading his motorcycle from Oskar Offenbacher's truck. Oskar had become Wolf's sponsor. Like the lad, Offenbacher loved engines. He and the butcher's apprentice had helped make Wolf's newly acquired BMW R-32 motorcycle a contender for the Greater Rheinland racing circuit.

Eva watched Wolf roll the yellow cycle down the ramp. She liked how his leg muscles bulged. She thought the now nineteen-year old had grown stronger with every passing day. "Don't hurt yourself."

Grunting, Wolf eased the BMW into place. "Don't worry about that." The young man was oozing confidence. He jumped off the truck and stood close to Eva. "I'm glad you're here."

Eva was glad, too.

Wolf wiped his forehead with a rag. "I registered for National Service you know. But I hope I can go straight to the army instead of construction on the Autobahn. It'd make better sense for the chancellor to draft the older men for the roads instead of us."

"You could be a motorcycle courier."

"Nah. I'd rather be a Panzerschütze. "

"Oh."

"Hey, did you know that Klempner's a quarter Jew?"

"What?"

"Yeah, your father has to report genealogies to the State and Klempner's grandmother was a converted Jewess!"

"Wow. Klempner's not told any of us."

"He's too nervous. He thought he'd be put out of the Party but the region chief told him not to worry about it. The Wehrmacht can even enlist mixed breeds as long as they don't look Jewish." Wolf took a drink of water and laughed. "I caught him studying his nose in the mirror. Maybe it's good the Red broke it."

Eva laughed.

"Anyway, how have you been?"

"I'm the Party secretary now. I work out of the Weinstube."

"I heard. It beats waiting tables."

"My mother and I are fighting a lot. She's drinking again."

"Yeah. Klempner says he may have to put her out of the Party. How's your father holding up?"

"Not well. He's either at Daniel's grave or in meetings. Pfarrer Hahn took over the church, but my father still does clerical work and visitations."

"I hear he's in trouble for not reporting family backgrounds more thoroughly."

"People kept pressuring him," Eva said. "Nobody wants to know about Jews in their past. Oh, I hear your father's taking a KdF vacation later this month?"

Wolf nodded. "He told me that the government is actually buying cruise ships and chartering trains. Imagine, 'Strength through Joy' vacations...Hitler's a genius. You can go to Naples and Venice...even Madrid or Lisbon for next to nothing. Now *that's* how a worker's union should do it."

"And the Führer's talking about everybody being able to buy a cheap KdF car with coupons. I think he calls them Volkswagens."

"And did you know that Berlin is broadcasting the world's first television programs?" said Wolf.

Eva's mouth dropped.

"If your father still doubts God's blessing on National Socialism, just look around."

"Actually, my father is becoming something of a believer though he's not real happy that Pfarrer Hahn put the Führer's picture on the Lord's Table," Eva said. "And he's a little worried about some arrests of ministers."

"Remind your father that Hitler is a Christian. He's the one who does what Jesus would do. He feeds the poor and clothes the hungry. He's put men to work and restored their dignity. He's outlawed abortion and stands against the Reds. Only the radicals who use their church to promote treason have gotten into trouble. The Party doesn't preach; the Church shouldn't politicize."

Eva had heard enough speeches at the Weinstube. "Well, I guess you should get going?"

"Nah, we're a little early. By the way, does Lindie ever talk about her daughter?"

"No."

Wolf leaned close. "The baby was half African wasn't it?"

Eva fidgeted. She had never told a soul. "Why would you ask such a question?"

"Do you know that all the Rheinbastards are being sterilized?"

"But, they're not retarded."

"No, but they're racially unfit. The future of Germany should be Aryan, not African," Wolf said. "So, the baby is half Negro. I knew it!"

Eva didn't know what to say. She just shook her head. "I'm not saying anything of the sort." She hadn't wanted to talk about Lindie. She had something else to tell Wolf. She took a deep breath. "By the way, I never said, 'thank you.'"

"For what?"

"The fire."

Wolf grinned. "You're welcome. You know, I was down to my last match."

Lindie shouted to Eva over the roar of engines. "Wolf looks handsome."

Eva nodded. She thought Wolf did look handsome. He was wearing a black leather racing suit and a red helmet which boasted a swastika on either side. On his back was embroidered, 'Weinhausen und Vaterland.' She wondered if the words 'Wolf Kaiser' shouldn't have been added. The young man was notoriously full of himself—one of his traits that had kept her interest slightly at bay. Actually, Eva sometimes did fear his pride for she felt it drove him toward his excesses, but she was pretty sure she could help him calm down.

Wolf finished a practice lap and rumbled to the rail. He took off his helmet and pushed his close-cropped hair back into place. "A kiss for luck?"

The girl blushed. The two were the same age and both were blond and fair. Eva's only flaw, according to some, was that her eyes were brown. Nevertheless, people were saying that they were a natural match and the idea had gained appeal for her. Lately, she thought that a single act of grace could win her heart for good. Eva leaned forward and pecked the young man on the cheek.

Wolf smiled, then reached inside his suit and withdrew a leather necklace with a whistle suspended on the end. "Your mother gave it to Herr Bieber. If it's alright with you I'd like to wear it for the whole racing season."

Eva's eyes quickly swelled. She choked. Her hand moved toward the whistle. She remembered how brave Daniel had been through that meager Christmas.

"I'm...I'm sorry, Eva. I didn't mean to make you cry."

"No, no. Wear it." Eva wiped her eyes. "Wear it for Daniel and win."

⌖

To Eva's delight, Wolf Kaiser did win the Führer's birthday race in Mendig. And that would be just the beginning of a racing season sprinkled with victory upon victory. Wolf had become Weinhausen's favorite son.

The spring of 1935 was bringing others victories as well. Gunther Landes had finally won the hand of Lindie and the two had been wed on a soggy day in late April. After properly publishing their wedding bans the pair satisfied the state through a brief formality in Koblenz, and later that same week had bound themselves under heaven in the apse of Paul Volk's church. Then, after a dance and a hearty meal, the honeymooners took a train to Madrid. The normally not-so-clever Gunther had taken advantage of Hitler's new marriage loans in order to treat his bride to an otherwise unimaginable experience. Of course, somewhere in Spain the penny-pinching farm boy informed Lindie that she'd need to have four children as quickly as possible since the government would forgive one-quarter of the debt for every child born!

On the first of May another victory was announced. Midst much fanfare and ceremony the shapely nineteen-year old Eva Volk was elected Weinhausen's May Day Queen. Surrounded by a cheering crowd and alongside a colorfully decorated Maypole, Bürgermeister Beck wrapped her shoulders in a purple cape and set a ringlet of white flowers atop her head. She was then set side-saddle on a pretty Haflinger mare and led through the streets of Weinhausen by Wolf at the head of a singing procession of starch-shirted men and folk-dressed women. In the center of the winding column, Weinhausen's band played songs from the Hitler Youth songbook like *Dear Sister Dance with Me*, and *Zwischen Berg und Tiefem Tal*. The parade finally ended at the green banks of the Mosel where wild packs of boys in short pants and screaming, pig-tailed girls dispersed.

"Oh, Wolf, isn't this wonderful," said Eva as she dismounted. She drew a long breath through her nose. The air was heavy with the aroma of grilled sausage.

"I think it's you who's wonderful," Wolf said as he took her hand.

Eva blushed. "Thank you." She took her hand away, shyly, and then caught a fleeting glimpse of Andreas from the corner of her eye.

Wolf noticed him, too. "He's fine, Eva."

Eva didn't answer at first. "I don't see him very often." She had begun to soften toward Andreas; others had gently reminded her that the accident was truly an accident.

"Me either." He leaned close to Eva. "You know, I thought I'd cheer him up for his birthday with a plaque I made with my wood burner."

Eva was surprised. "Oh? That was so nice. What kind of plaque?"

"I copied a carving from the old city in Limburg. It says, 'Da hup di Welt wider an zu leben unde frolich sein. '"

Pleased, Eva smiled. "I do hope the world can be happy again."

"My brother's had enough troubles and he seemed a little depressed by turning twenty. Would you like me to get him?"

"What?" Eva was startled by the question.

"I could get him. He could eat with us. He seems pretty lonely...but maybe seeing him is still hard for you?"

Eva really wasn't sure what to say. "Well, maybe another..."

"Good. I'll try to find him."

"But..."

Wolf disappeared in the crowd and searched out Andreas who was sitting on the bank, far downstream. He was aimlessly tossing pebbles into the Mosel's sluggish waters. "Hey," shouted Wolf.

Andreas turned, saying nothing.

"You're being a jerk again."

Andreas was in no mood. "Shut up."

"You look stupid sitting here feeling sorry for yourself."

"What do you want, Wolf?" Andreas rose.

"I saw you following Eva."

"No I wasn't."

"Yes, you were. I saw you in the procession and so did she."

"Well, I wasn't following her."

"Yes. That is exactly what you were doing."

"Fine, if you want to be technical. The whole procession followed her. So what?"

Wolf leaned close. His mood darkened. "Leave her alone. She hasn't forgotten about Daniel. She wants you to stay away."

"Did she tell you to say that?"

"Yes."

"When?"

"Not ten minutes ago."

Andreas said nothing.

"Did you hear me?" prodded Wolf.

"Do you want to fight, Wolf, is that it? Because I really don't have much to lose anymore."

Wolf changed tack. "Just leave her alone." Another voice came from behind.

"Guten Tag, boys."

Wolf turned to see Hans Bieber.

"Have you had any sausage yet?" said Hans.

"No," they both answered.

"Andreas, you're missing a pretty good Fest. Offenbacher's brought baskets of bread, Silbermann has bananas and ice cream, Ulrich's busy with Wurst and even American hamburgers."

The young man nodded.

Hans peered from beneath his cap like a man who knew something. "So, Andreas, I hear your brother's made you a birthday gift with his wood burner."

Andreas was puzzled. "Huh?"

Bieber turned to Wolf. "Eva told me that you made him something?"

Red-faced, Wolf fumbled for words. "Well, actually, I'm not quite done with it. It was going to be a surprise."

Bieber feigned confusion. "But she said you made it for his birthday. That was last month."

"I…I had to make a little change before I actually gave it to him. But now you ruined the surprise."

"Ah. I'm so sorry." Bieber narrowed his eyes at Wolf. "I guess I misunderstood."

Agitated, Wolf returned to Eva with a small bouquet of blue wildflowers he had hastily plucked from the river's edge. "Almost as pretty as you," he said as he removed his brown cap.

Eva took the flowers into both hands, blushing.

"I'm sorry but I tried. He just wouldn't come. He can be stubborn, you know."

"That's fine, really. Maybe it's for the best right now."

"You've both been through so much," Wolf said. He laid his hand lightly on Eva's forearm. "I just wanted to help."

Eva smiled. The young man attracted her now more than ever. Perhaps it was because of his unexpected compassion. Or maybe it was how his uniform showed off his broad shoulders and narrow hips. Or maybe it was his blond hair shimmering under the May Day sun like ripened wheat in summer. At his touch she could feel passion rise within herself.

"I should clarify something," Wolf said. "I haven't really given Andreas his plaque yet."

"Oh?"

"No, I told you that I *made* him one for his birthday, not that I *gave* him one. I...I found a mistake so it's not quite ready."

"That's fine."

"Well, Herr Bieber was confused so I thought I should..."

"It's fine, Wolf, really. I think it's wonderful that you care about him so much."

Safely out of his corner, Wolf took Eva by the elbow and began to walk with her, quickly changing the subject to his motorcycle and the Hitler Youth. In time, however, he gradually moved his one-way conversation into a passionate speech about heroism, sacrifice, and 'Germanness.'

Eva smiled to herself. She decided that he was even more of a romantic than Andreas, though their differences were far more than those of degree. Wolf's romanticism was hard-edged and virile—even violent, where Andreas' was poetic and cultivated. Something about Wolf's boundlessness drew her, nonetheless.

At long last the young man cleared his throat. "Eva, I would like to ask you something."

She stopped and faced him.

"I, uh, well, I would like to court you, formally."

Eva's heart began to beat. She had been spending more and more time with Wolf, whether at the race track, at church, or at the market. He had even taken her hand during a walk by the river a few weeks prior. Courting would mean four o'clock Sunday coffees with her parents—and more. It was a precursor to marriage. Eva's mind recalled her diary. He really does make me feel safe and important. It's like I know who I am when I am with him; I feel happy with him, and somehow satisfied. But her mind suddenly flew to Andreas. She knew he would be crushed...but did that really matter any more? She laid her nose deeply into her little bouquet and drew on their fragrance. "Yes, Wolf. I would like that very much."

Diary entry: Niederberg Castle, 7 March 1936

Today the Führer is marching our army into the Rheinland. The radio says that the whole nation is celebrating but I doubt anyone else could be happier than those of us who live here. What a glorious day for the Mosel Valley! I am a little afraid that our enemies might attack us since the Führer is breaking the treaty. I'm glad he offered the world a peace plan but we are all holding our breath.

I'm now feeling guilty about Andreas. I stopped blaming him for Daniel but I never told him. I'm sure I really hurt him but Wolf says he's different now that he joined the Wehrmacht and that I shouldn't worry about him anymore. I wonder if he joined the army because of Wolf and me. I guess he'll be marching in the parade in Koblenz. I never really thought of him as a soldier.

I'm happy with Wolf but I get worried because he loses control sometimes. I thought he would hit me the day I said the government may be going too far with the Jews. He was so angry that he went to the market and threw Samuel Silbermann out of his door and screamed at him. We stopped talking for a few days until he said he was sorry.

I think Herr Silbermann and his wife should probably leave Weinhausen like most of the other Jews but he keeps saying that he's a German patriot and he says he votes for the Party to prove it.

I read about the laws that forbid Aryans from having sexual relations with Jews. Frau Krause says that it's the same way in Amer-

ica with Negroes. I'm waiting for Jenny to write me about that. She said that she and Bobby really liked Germany.

The SS says the Jews should be sent to their own homeland...maybe in Madagascar. Some of the Jews say they want to have their own country in Palestine. I think a special homeland for Jews is a pretty good idea. The Silbermann's would be better off.

Father hardly speaks anymore. I think it's good that he's not preaching yet. He's not ready. He's mad that the Führer banned all the youth groups except the Hitler Youth and he's been talking again to the BK. He's also mad that some Party man took the coils out of his RCA. I guess the state is worried about the lies our enemies are sending on radio waves. They might be right about that. Mostly, he's either at Daniel's grave or in his study filling out identification papers for the Gestapo.

I think mother still blames me for Daniel's death. But she says she likes Wolf. She's very angry that the Party cancelled her membership. Herr Klempner told her that she's not a good example of German womanhood. She wears too much makeup and drinks too much. Her smoking is another problem. I feel a little sorry for her because the Party was all she had.

I spend a lot of time here at the castle. I can be alone and think, although today others have come to watch the army. Something about the old stone walls and the mountains give me peace...like I'm connected to something else. And I love to watch the river from up high. The water looks quiet and calm, and I like the way it bends around the curves. This is my favorite place to write in this diary.

"The most important task in the new Germany is to educate the coming generation in Germandom based on Christian values...The objective is the creation of a strong, unified people in a Christian, National Socialist state."

Manifesto of the ecumenical Christian Parents League

CHAPTER FOURTEEN

"YOU LOOK PRETTY today, Eva," said Paul. The July 1936 afternoon was hot; the river busy with pleasure craft and swimmers.

"Thank you." The young woman paused to stare listlessly into the green water. She had little respect for the man but did pity him. Over the many months since Daniel's death she had watched him sink into an ever deepening melancholy.

"So, do you like being Richard Klempner's personal secretary?"

"Ja."

"Richard is lucky. Imagine, Hitler says you need *three* Jewish grandparents to be a true Jew. Three! If the radicals had their way, one would do it and Klempner would have been out of the Party." Paul Volk pulled the pipe from his mouth. He walked stiffly, like a man clenched around himself. His shoulders were tight and his voice was strained. "The chancellor's decision made a few folks in the congregation sleep a little easier. But I confess the man still confounds me. You know, Eva, the Hitler Youth are taught to hate Jews but then he turns around and goes easy. And this year he starts by being very patient with the complainers in the BK but then he turns around and has their newsletters censored and puts five hundred of them into protective custody."

"But he released them right away."

"Yes, but only after a few died under very mysterious circumstances." Paul shook his head. "I listen to every speech I can and I read the papers Rudi sends me. One day I think the Führer is a Christian man wanting to preserve Christian order in Germany. The next day he speaks of 'Fate' instead of Christ and removes prayer from the government schools."

Paul packed new tobacco into his pipe. He liked discussing politics; he had discovered that thinking was a ready substitute for feeling. "At least Hitler ordered his picture off the Lord's Tables. That really angered Hahn, by the way." He struck a match. "Of course when the chancellor did that I foolishly interpreted it as him stumbling across a bit of humility. I was wrong, of course. He just wanted order between the Church and the State. Yet now he expects personal oaths of loyalty to him, almost as if he's Divine."

"The people I know seem happy to trade some noisy extremes for the relief they are feeling. Some say that God is blessing the Führer," said Eva.

Paul nodded. "When I was a boy my minister told me to beware of fig leaves over idols." He drew on his pipe and released a cloud of sweet smelling smoke. "Enough said. So, have you heard anything from Andreas lately?"

Eva answered evasively. "He's stationed at the garrison in Wittlich." She didn't want to say more. Andreas had finally sent her a letter which she had read many times over.

"Good man, that Andreas. I hope you've forgiven him."

Eva changed course. "Herr Bieber says he won't take the Goldmann's bicycle shop."

Paul grumbled. "I don't blame him. The government shouldn't have taken it from Goldmann, Jew or not."

"The law allows it."

"Then the law is wrong."

Eva was surprised. For a German like her father, the law—and the order it represented—was always supreme. Besides, when had Paul Volk ever objected to anything? "When we said the law was wrong to steal Herr Bieber's vineyard you told us we needed to obey the law, no matter what."

The weary minister stopped walking. "I'm not suggesting we don't obey the law. Good heavens, girl. I would never say that. I wasn't saying that the State *couldn't* take Goldmann's. I just think they *shouldn't* have."

"So, you're saying that the law has a right to be wrong."

Paul Volk shook his head. "The law is the law...and nowadays I suppose Hitler is the law. As a Christian citizen I am expected to obey and allow God to deal with the State if it goes out-of-bounds. But I should add that in the past the State has never been very far off the mark."

Eva stopped walking. "So, if the State ordered Herr Bieber to take the shop would you tell him to obey?"

"Of course. Otherwise we'd have chaos."

The two continued their walk along the river. The bank was busy with revelers. The Mosel was lapped with wavelets running from the wakes of mahogany inboards. The songs of birds filled the summer air.

"So, tell me, Eva, are you happy?"

Eva hadn't thought about that very much. She didn't answer.

"Maybe I should ask what makes you happy."

Eva didn't want to open her heart. Not to him. Not to very many others. Not anymore. "Are *you* happy?"

"No." The man's answer was direct, but not sharp.

"Why not?"

Paul stopped walking. "Well, the government pays me to mind a church that considers me irrelevant. I do nothing more than push papers about my desk and keep the choir from bickering. I'm not even the assistant pastor, anymore, not really. I'm not sure who I am. The Superintendent wants me to go on retreat in Switzerland until he figures out how he can justify my salary to the Ministry.

"And the people love Hahn. He preaches with his SA uniform under his robes. Thank God the deacons put some limits on him. He wanted to take the headstones from the Jewish cemetery and use them as stepping stones to the church's garden privy! He was furious when they voted him down...And I'm very sad for your mother."

Eva watched a wave of emotion fill him but he seemed determined to not to lose control—not in front of his daughter. "But I will be fine, Eva."

Eva really did pity the man. "You don't look fine."

"I've not been feeling very well lately. Dr. Krebel says it's my nerves."

Eva said nothing as the two began a slow walk home. She watched her father put his hands behind his back and face the ground as he carried himself uphill on heavy legs. She thought he had become old overnight.

Paul and Eva walked on and eventually rounded the corner at Lutherweg in full view of the church grounds, alive with the color of its flower gardens. The women's auxiliary had done a marvelous job with this year's roses; the white blooms were particularly robust. "Daniel didn't like roses," Eva said. "He kept snagging his socks on their thorns."

The pair crossed the church grounds in silence and entered the adjacent graveyard. Like cemeteries all over Germany each grave was a miniature garden planted with the personal preferences of the tending family. The two walked to Daniel's grave. The mound had finally settled leaving the surface flat and firm, a reminder that time had really not stood still since the boy's death.

A low, stone border enclosed a lovely planting of yellow marigolds and multi-colored pansies well-tended by Hans Bieber. Daniel's monument was a marble cross inscribed:

Daniel Rudolf Volk
Child of God
Beloved son of Paul and Gerde Volk
11 November 1926—20 January 1935
Rest in Jesus

Father and daughter stood in silence for a long while. Eva felt closer in their common sorrow. "I picture him with the angels."

Paul stared thoughtfully at his son's grave until he finally answered. "Frau Klempner said those same words when she buried her son right over there." He pointed to another grave garden, one filled with ordered rows of red geraniums. "That day Richard Klempner told me he wouldn't believe in a God cruel enough to let his son die gasping for breath."

Eva waited.

"He asked me what kind of God would let that happen while a

few kilometers away some Frenchman hoarded the medicine that might have helped...He said it was easier for him to not believe in God at all."

"But then what hope would there be for his son?"

Paul nodded. "Precisely. No God, no resurrection—no Heaven...no hope. When I asked him that same question he spat on the ground. He called it my 'Divine Trap.' He accused me of leaving him with two choices: either worship a God he hated or abandon all hope for his son's soul." Paul's eyes began to redden; tears began to well. "At the time I judged him as a man of poor faith, but I was wrong to judge him at all. I am now that man."

⌖

"Wolf's here. I have to go now." Twenty-year old Eva was hurrying through the living room with her suitcase. She had agreed to be a kitchen helper at the Hitler Youth's two week summer outing scheduled to coincide with the 1936 Olympics being held in Berlin. Holding a brown suitcase, she was wearing a polka-dotted, powder blue summer dress that followed her shapely form to her shins. Her wavy hair was long and parted on the left side.

Gerde stopped playing the family's newly repaired piano and followed her daughter out the door. She scowled at Wolf. "I don't like this."

"Heil Hitler, Frau Volk," said Wolf. "Don't worry, I'll take good care of her. You can trust me."

"I don't care about that. She has work here to do."

"Mother, I've got to go." Eva's tone was firm. The two had been fighting all morning.

"You haven't cleaned the upstairs windows like I told you, and you said you'd weed the garden."

Eva turned to Wolf. "Take me away from here."

At twenty, Wolf was one of the supervising adults for the gathering of the regional Hitler Youth Bann—a unit of about 5,000 members. The wider organization was arranged like the Wehrmacht. Beginning with the smallest unit, the Kameradschaft of10 - 15 members, the Hitler Youth was a pyramid of larger and larger units until reaching the Obergebiet with 375,000 members, of which there were six. Though membership was not yet compulsory, boys—and girls—between ten and eighteen had flocked to the organization. For them, their Führer's words were a call to glory: 'The weak must be chiseled away. I want young men and women who can suffer pain. Flink wie ein Windhund, zäh wie Leder, und hart wie Krupp-Stahl.'

Indeed, the boys trained hard at outings like these so they could surely become 'fast as greyhounds, tough as leather, and as hard as Krupp steel.' Their days would be spent marching, running, and training in military maneuvers, mock grenade assaults and bayonet drill. For a select few, glider training would be offered as the precursor to a career in Germany's new Air Force, the Luftwaffe.

Girls would gather in a segregated location where they would train their bodies and their minds to be good mothers so that Germany's new Reich would be provided with generations of healthy warriors. Among other things, they'd have to be able to run 60 meters in 14 seconds, throw a ball 12 meters, complete a 2 hour march, learn to make beds properly, cook healthy foods and sew well.

"Every one of my boys took the oath back on my birthday." Wolf grinned, proudly, as he strutted alongside Eva toward the waiting busses.

"You mean on the Führer's birthday."

"Of course. Have you taken it yet?"

Eva shook her head. Some had taken Hitler's oath of personal loyalty by radio, some at the bewitching torchlight marches in Koblenz. She had not yet done so.

"Well, if you're working for Klempner you'd better. Your father had better also. He's paid from tax money so he really ought to affirm his allegiance."

The pair hurried along spotless sidewalks and past the brightly decorated houses of Weinhausen. Every window boasted a colorful flowerbox, and bright banners hung from the streets' canopies of leafy grapevines. Eva thought nothing seemed gray anymore; nothing was in disrepair. Road crews had filled pot holes and other workmen were fixing the docks by the river. Garden sheds were freshly painted and filled with rakes instead of the nation's poor.

Eva had marveled at the speed by which her village had been reborn. Men were busily employed in government projects or in the industries now booming in Koblenz. Area vintners were ecstatic; to relieve the effects of the French boycott Hitler had devised a brilliat scheme whereby towns throughout Germany would buy wine from a particular Rheinland village to which it had been paired. The results had been amazing.

"Things are good." Wolf was seeing what Eva was seeing. "People are smiling, children are playing. I like the flowers and I like all the flags. You know, the Jews in New York did us a great favor."

"Huh?"

"The Jews...in New York. They raided one of our ships and ripped down our Party flag. Ha! The Führer answered by declaring the National Socialist flag to be the official flag of the nation."

The two arrived at Flusstrasse and waited by the edge of the Mosel as two busses prepared to load. The girls had already left for their camp, leaving the forty-six boys standing in perfect order under the commands of their Scharführer, Otto Schneider. The Schneider lad was now eighteen and fit. Like his two younger brothers, he lived for the Hitler Youth. Otto barked a command and the forty-six snapped to attention, then saluted Wolf with a martial, "Heil Hitler!"

Wolf returned the salute and then supervised the group's loading into the busses that would deliver them to the outskirts of Mendig and the campground alongside the crater lake of Maria Laach. The diesel engines rumbled loudly and belched great puffs of black smoke from their exhausts. Then, with a few ground gears the busses lurched forward to begin the strain upward and out of the Mosel Valley.

Along the way Eva enjoyed the sites of the countryside. The young woman had not traveled much in her past. She used to joke that her world was horizontal because she always felt confined within a strip of train tracks running east and west. Now she stared through her window happily at planted fields, lush meadows and leafy hardwood forests patched with deep-green spruce.

She squeezed the window's clips and pushed it up. The air rushing past her face smelled of manure and pine. It made her think of those times as a child when she and Andreas would climb out of their quiet valley to run free through these very same forests and fields. She liked how he had picked her wildflowers in the springtime.

She wondered if Andreas was well.

After forty minutes the busses passed through Mendig and rumbled deeper into the Eifel. Here small ponds now lay like silver discs at the feet of green knolls and were blushed with rare water plants like candock and trefoil. Ducks and water hens floated lazily under the late July sun. The caravan slowed to let a tentative deer cross the road. In the quiet pause, Eva could hear a reed warbler. She smiled.

Finally, the group arrived at the beautiful Maria Laach, a shallow, circular lake ringed by low, lava mountains formed by volcanoes long since extinct. The mountains were tree-covered and green and cast their lovely reflection upon the lake's still waters. The busses made their way to headquarters which was a large tent staked by a pebbly shore. With a final shudder they finally stopped and their passengers disembarked.

Wolf led Eva into the tent where everyone saluted one another. "Heil Hitler." Instructions were clearly posted on a bulletin board where the chain of command was listed in large type. A superior presented a duty roster to Wolf. With all things in order, Eva was then pointed to the huge commissary grounds where she would report.

Eva spent the next week working hard in the kitchens while Wolf monitored swimming competitions in the lake. She found herself enjoying her time in the new surroundings despite the challenges of peeling potatoes without end and shredding cabbage until her knuckles bled.

The weather had remained fair and warm, though under the heavy canvas the air became oppressive. Eva didn't complain, however, for her routine was regularly broken by the camp loudspeakers which broadcast live programming from the Berlin Olympics. More than once she and the other women ran outside and listened to the announcer's excited voice cry out another Olympic victory for the Fatherland.

Eva and her co-workers had been surprised however to hear of American victories, especially those of the Negroes. The camp director had declared that America was an over-indulged, weak race of mixed breeds whose moral stamina and discipline had been eroded by Jewish materialism. And he also had reminded everyone that Negroes were actually subhuman; they were lazy and stupid like the Slavs. Nevertheless, the announcer's voice in Berlin was civil enough when announcing these Americans' victories and Eva was pleased that her companions offered respectful applause. To Eva, that sort of behavior seemed like the decent, German way to treat her nation's guests, subhuman or not.

In the evenings Eva would steal away from her women's discussion group and rendezvous with Wolf. Arm in arm the couple would walk the lakeside pathway while listening to the distant sounds of boys' choral groups or bands. Gentle willows and softwoods lined the shore, and water rail, coot, and swans bobbed calmly on the ripples that light breezes cast across the lake. There, with the air warm and sweet and the whole world set to right—with Wolf's words touching her heart and his strong arms around her—Eva felt as if she must finally be close to Eden's gate.

On one such evening, the air was pleasantly fresh and the young woman found herself leaning her head lightly on Wolf's strong shoulder as they strolled quietly along the lake's perimeter trail. They paused to look at the six-towered, Romanesque monastery of Maria Laach standing on the far side of a distant roadway. Founded nine hundred years before by the Benedictines, the peach-stoned cloister had been tucked neatly against a background of broad-shouldered mountains. "So beautiful." Eva leaned harder into Wolf's side. He put his arm around her and held her close.

The two stood silently for a time until Wolf noticed the first stars of the night rising in the east. He pointed to them. "The east, our future lies in the east."

"What?"

"Lebensraum—living space. We Germans are destined to expand eastward, just like the Americans were destined to expand west."

Eva sighed. "Politics?" She slapped his arm, playfully.

Wolf laughed. "No, no, sorry." He pulled Eva's body against his own and held her tightly as he looked into her wide, brown eyes. "Forget the east, mein Schatz. You are my destiny."

The young woman's breathing quickened. The arms around her felt so strong. Wolf squeezed her closer still. Now a little uncomfortable, Eva tried to move but as she did, he tightened all the more. Yielding, she let herself fall limp and he bent his face toward hers. Whispering her name, he kissed her lips.

Enveloped by the young man's passion, Eva now felt safe and adored—possessed by a man who really loved her.

The woman's heart soared.

The darkening sky above the round lake was now burnished by a dull yellow light cast softly from an encircling ring of small campfires. The water lay still and warm like a quiet pool, edged in hues of pale gold and brushed with a narrow glint of silver from the rising moon. A few horses snorted nearby and somewhere a dog was barking. Frogs croaked and insects chattered lazily. Wolf spotted the craggy silhouettes of a small apple orchard to one side and began to lead Eva toward it. He wrapped his right arm around her hip and held her tightly.

Eva submitted to his firm hold and laid her head against his breast. She could feel his heart racing as they walked. His breathing became shallow and rapid. Her stomach began to flutter.

"Can we sit for a time?" Wolf asked. "Look, the monastery lights are coming on and listen...yes, the bells. You love the bells."

Eva nodded. She did love church bells and she loved that Wolf knew her so completely. She followed him under the wide-spread branches of an old apple tree. A few grazing horses ambled away. From across the lake she heard a fife band playing a lullaby. A breeze cooled her perspired neck and she smoothed her summer skirt behind her legs to sit atop a dewy patch of grass. She removed the silk scarf from her head and shook her hair loose. She leaned back, allowing her weight to rest against her palms now pressing into the cool sod. She drew a deep breath of fresh air through her nostrils and closed her eyes.

Wolf sat close. He stroked Eva's hair and then laid his hand gently on her cheek. With his fingers he turned her face toward his and he kissed her again, deeply.

Eva felt all strength leaving her limbs as the young man's lips moved slowly over hers. They were firm and strong like his arms, and yet soft and moist. She felt so safe, so very safe. She felt wanted.

She was happy.

Eva quickly lost herself in Wolf's heated embrace and as she slid slowly backward, her body melted away.

But Wolf soon began to move differently. His weight felt suddenly heavy upon her. His breathing changed, his sounds changed. Eva's eyes opened; she was lost no longer. Anxious, the young woman began to protest, easily at first—in case she misunderstood—but then more strongly.

Wolf quickly relaxed. He rolled to his side and stroked her cheek gently, telling her over and over how he loved her; that nothing in the world mattered to him but her. "I would never disrespect you, dear Eva," he whispered in her ear. "Never. How could you think that?"

Eva softened. "I'm sorry, Wolf..."

"Shh." Wolf pulled her close to him again. "I would die for you, Eva Volk. I can make you happy...happier than you could ever imagine."

Eva trembled for joy. She nuzzled her nose against his throat and listened as he promised to protect her, to adore her—to love her as no other. The young woman felt warm and calm like the waters of the nearby lake.

Once more Wolf pressed more firmly against her, claiming her with whispers of devotion. He urged her to believe in him; to trust him.

Eva then felt his hands begin to climb over her. His body

moved atop hers, but she lay still, enchanted by his words, intoxicated by his touch. She felt him reach for his belt but, heady in the moment, she did not protest. His warm hand then moved under her dress and she willingly yielded in dreamy submission. In another moment, she felt a stabbing pain in her loins, and then another and another, but she did not cry out. Instead, she simply whimpered, but only slightly, contented in the taking, even exalted as the prize.

When it was over, Wolf fell slowly limp and Eva nestled close, lost in milieu of emotions. She lay in the young man's quickly fading embrace, unaware of his self-satisfaction until he stood and collected himself, leaving Eva alone in the grass and suddenly wondering.

"Get up."

"The Jews caused the crucifixion of God's Christ. They bear the curse and because they rejected His forgiveness they drag with them the blood-guilt of their fathers."

Rev. Martin Niemöller, future resistance pastor

CHAPTER FIFTEEN

1 November 1936
105th Infantry Regiment
Wittlich, Rheinland

Liebe Eva,

Thank you for your letter of 18 October. Seeing your name on the return post made me happier than I ever remember. I am relieved that you have received my past letters. I thought that someone was keeping them from you.

I cannot even put into words how much it means to me to hear that you have forgiven me. I was a fool and am without excuse. I will regret Daniel's death until the day I die. Thank you for your grace.

Your concern for me brings great comfort. I only wish you would have written more about yourself. Are you well? Though I fear to ask, are you and Wolf still courting? Are your parents well?

I am glad to learn that Herr Bieber is happy in his new apartment. I understand he works for the Roth Vineyards. Gunther tells me that Lindie is to have another baby in February. He wants a boy. I am very happy for them. By the way, I guess you heard that his father is making him take an apprenticeship with a machinist in Winningen.

You must also know that my father has taken ill in Heidelberg. I used my leave to visit him but he barely spoke. The doctor told me he has cancer of the liver and may not live past Christmas.

Since you asked, I am pleased to report that I am content in the

Wehrmacht, though I am still only a Schütze. We have the first draftees arriving now. They are born in 1914, the same year the World War started. Some think this is a bad omen but I think the Führer wants no war for Germany. I understand that a lot of the draftees are going into the Labor Front instead of the army, and some of them will be working on the Westwall along the French border. They'll be digging trenches, building bunkers and putting up many kilometers of barbed wire.

I'm a little embarrassed to say it but after all my training with machine guns and explosives, I've been transferred to a carrier pigeon platoon. No one needs to worry about me if the French attack!

To answer your other question: my comrades and I are proud to be in the Führer's army even though we don't like everything about the National Socialists. (We make jokes about Nazi supermen. We have a perfect Aryan specimen from Bremen in my barracks who's dumb as a stone!)

The Fatherland must be strong again and quickly. Only a strong leader can do that, even we don't agree with everything about him. We learned that the Reds in Spain have murdered thousands, including a third of the nuns and priests. I can't imagine leaving you and Weinhausen defenseless to that kind of brutality. So I took my oath of loyalty to the Führer with a clear conscience. We had to memorize it: "I swear by God this sacred oath that I shall render unconditional obedience to Adolf Hitler, the Führer of the German Reich, supreme commander of the armed forces, and that I shall at all times be prepared, as a brave soldier, to give my life for this oath."

I bet you never thought I'd think like this, but just because I like poetry doesn't mean I'm weak. I still hate Nazi art.

An SS recruiter tried to take me. (I am tall enough—you have to be over 1.75 meters.) But I'm glad I didn't go there. Many of the SS are better educated than I am or come from rich families. I doubted that I'd ever get a promotion even if the Nazis have broken down the old class barriers. I also think some of the SS men are more interested in National Socialist ideology than the rest of us. My comrades and I just want to protect the Fatherland.

Otherwise, the food is not terrible, our uniforms are good and we're getting better equipment every day. Please give my greetings to your father. I hope to see you again, soon.

Heil Hitler,
Andreas

Eva sat stone-faced on the side of her bed with Lindie's arm wrapped around her. "You didn't tell him?" asked Lindie.

Eva shook her head.

"But...but your wedding is in three weeks."

"I know, but I just couldn't..."

"Wolf's hitting you, isn't he?" Lindie pushed Eva's sleeves up to reveal the bruises.

"He says it's my fault that I'm pregnant. Maybe he's right..."

"That's ridiculous. And no real man would ever hit a woman. Gunther says if he ever sees him hit you, he'll tear him to pieces."

Eva touched a tender place on her cheek. "That's nice but Wolf would have the Party take your farm away."

"You shouldn't marry him."

"I have to. Besides, most of the time he really does treat me well. He bought me a nice dress for the wedding."

"You don't have to fool yourself, Eva. You could give the baby away and tell Wolf to stay out of your life."

Eva bristled. "Fool myself? You're wrong about Wolf. I know what you think but you're wrong about him. And, I'd never give my baby away."

Lindie winced. "You're going to live at the Kaiser house?"

Eva nodded.

"What's your mother saying?"

"She seems happy that I've been shamed...again." She blew her nose.

Someone knocked on the bedroom door. "Come in."

Wolf entered with a bouquet of hothouse flowers. He turned to Lindie. "Get out."

"So, you've been spilling your guts to her, showing her your arms, telling her how awful I am? Is that it?"

Eva's mouth went dry. She shook her head.

"Well, you should have." Wolf bent to one knee. "Eva, I...I've come to say that I'm so very sorry about everything. I get crazy sometimes. I've been awful to you but I really do love you, more than anything."

Eva stared at him, blank-faced.

"I love you, Eva, truly. Will you forgive me?"

She was confused.

"Eva? Will you?"

Eva looked into Wolf's icy eyes. They did not draw her like Andreas' used to, but there was power in them. She wanted to believe in him. "Yes." She answered cautiously.

Satisfied, Wolf kissed her on the cheek, lightly. "I got a raise today." He stood up.

Eva's mind was still whirling. Thrown off by the abrupt switch, she fumbled, "A raise?"

"Three hundred RM per month now. Enough to buy stamps toward one of the Führer's Volkswagens. Would that make you happy? We could have our own car."

"Uh..."

"Well, forget it. It doesn't matter. I'm meeting with an SS recruiter next week. You know, an SS officer gets whatever he wants for his wife and son. With my Party connections, I should be a shoe-in. Forget Volkswagens, you might have a Mercedes."

"What makes you think it's a son?"

Wolf laughed. "I'm the father."

"What makes you think you'd be an officer?"

Wolf turned away. "You really don't know me." His eyes fell on Andreas' letter. To Eva's alarm, he snatched if off the dresser and read it quickly, then tore it to pieces. "So, he hopes we're not courting. Well, won't he be surprised."

Eva trembled as Wolf stepped closer. His jaw pulsed. "This is exactly what I always thought...he still wants you. Do you want him?"

Eva made the mistake of hesitating.

With a roar, Wolf slammed his fist on to the dresser and grabbed Eva by the shoulders, shaking her violently. "You carry my son and you will be my wife. Why do you do these things to me! You belong to me, Eva Volk, don't forget it!"

On a gray Monday evening, 9 November 1936, Eva Volk stood with her father, her mother and a handful of witnesses in the church of Weinhausen waiting for the very late Wolf Kaiser to arrive. Eva managed a smile for Hans Bieber. The man was standing awkwardly in his well-worn suit and trying his best to offer an expression of comfort. Lindie and Gunther were there as well, as were Frau Diehl—the organist, Professor Kaiser—released from his hospital bed, and a few friends of both sides. Considering the situation, Rev. Volk and Gerde had agreed with Professor Kaiser that the ceremony should be discreet.

Nearly twenty-one, Eva was a beautiful bride. Her eyes were clear and set over high cheek bones; tall and fit, her figure was the envy of the village. She wore an ivory dress that fell to her shins, long white gloves and white pumps. Her hair was braided and rolled at each ear as per Wolf's instructions. Atop her head she wore a simple veiled hat.

She was stunning.

Holding a modest corsage of orchids bought for her by Lindie, Eva fixed her face toward the rear door and waited for her groom to arrive. The young bride had come to reconcile her decision to marry Wolf. Straining against stubborn doubts, she had resolved to love Wolf like a Christian wife ought. As to the night at Maria Laach, she concluded that he was a man with needs and she should have been more prudent; no one was to blame—or both were to blame.

Of course, Eva was well aware of others' concerns.

But who were they to cast stones?

No, Wolf was not perfect. Who was? She reminded them of his virtues: he protected her and would provide well, and when she walked by his side he made her feel unashamed—even important.

Besides, she had already given herself to him, freely.

So she had chosen to marry, and, yes, that meant making room for all of Wolf—for that's what marriage requires.

She would simply learn to manage his vices.

And her father had said something that helped. He suggested that even though Wolf could be trouble he wasn't *bound* to be trouble. She thought that made sense.

And she thought marriage should be a sensible thing.

The church door opened and Eva's thoughts were interrupted by the silhouette of a man moving from the shadowed rear foyer toward the light of the sanctuary. When he emerged, the young woman tensed. *Andreas*!

The young soldier walked slowly toward the fore of the church. He was dressed handsomely in his Wehrmacht field uniform—gray pants and a five button, gray tunic with a dark green collar and scalloped pockets. His tunic was wrapped with a black belt clasped by a brass buckle inscribed, *Gott mit uns.* Striding forward on his high-polished, black, hob-nailed boots he bravely approached the bride that he had always wanted.

Eva nearly melted in her place as she felt the whole of her spirit drawn once again into Andreas' soft eyes. In an instant, her inner whispers were shouting in her ears; her doubts came to new life. Her mind spun; she felt dizzy and disoriented.

Wasn't it Andreas who she had always really wanted? Wasn't love easy when he was near?

The truth was gut-wrenching.

Abandoning all her determined resolutions she now wanted to run to his arms; she wanted him to hold her, forever. *How could I have been so foolish*?

Andreas took her hand politely and kissed her on the cheek. His lips felt soft and warm. She wished he would have let them linger. "Hello, Eva," he said. "You are so beautiful today. I hope I am welcome."

Eva's heart raced; she wanted to cry out all the feelings she had so desperately denied: *Oh, Andreas, take me away*!

But was it too late?

She answered, "Yes, of course. I...I am sorry that I never told you..." The sound of her own voice returned to her to what was.

And it was too late.

Like a bitter blast of the north wind, Eva's cold reality numbed her heart. *I am marrying Wolf...Wolf. He will make me happy. It will all be fine. I can make it fine.*

I must.

"Eva? I understand. Wolf telephoned the barracks and we spoke. He invited me to be a witness. I only hope you are agreeable."

Agreeable? Eva thought. *Agreeable*? *What kind of word is that*? She stiffened a little and answered, "I'm happy you've come." *Wolf invited him to humiliate him*! *Can't he see that*? She glanced self-consciously at the others as Andreas turned away to shake their hands. *Oh, Andreas. How can you be so blind*?

The church door opened again and Wolf and Richard Klempner came striding forward with Adolf Schneider, his three boys, a contingent of SA men and a few of Wolf's co-workers from Koblenz. Eva took a deep, quaking breath, then greeted her groom with a forced smile. The pair turned to face the minister.

Rev. Volk cleared his throat and immediately thumbed through his well-worn Bible as he motioned for everyone to take their places. Eva slanted a quick look at Andreas who was making his way to his brother's side. She thought he moved like a man in pain.

As excruciating as was the moment for Andreas, however, few could have imagined the churning distress of Paul Volk. Dressed in his robes and holding his Bible securely in one hand, he looked over his spectacles at his dear Eva—the love of his life. Pictures of her running about his church as a gangly little girl in pig-tails came to mind. He swallowed against the lump filling his throat.

Paul faced Wolf. He had terrible doubts about the young man. Yet in the past years he had to admit a growing respect for him...until this. He had thought him to be honorable and morally upright, but Paul was fairly certain that he must have forced his daughter against her will. She had never said that, nor had Lindie when he had secretly pressed her. And both Wolf and Eva had asked forgiveness for their mutual sin. But he was also aware of rumors that Wolf had hit his beloved daughter. Suspicions and fear now filled the pit of his stomach. He hoped that the advice he had given his daughter would prove true.

Paul faltered. Inner whispers of self-contempt now condemned him. He wondered why his prior doubts had not prompted him to be more discerning about this young man. Perhaps he had felt that his dear Eva was safe with Wolf; perhaps he had thought the successful youth would provide for her well. Or, perhaps he had been afraid to stand against the young man.

Had he masked cowardice with tolerance?

Volk looked at his daughter and prayed that he was not failing her. He wondered whether she really wanted him to bless this union or if she secretly wished he would protest the marriage. Was his timidity endangering her? But he had only suspicions about Wolf Kaiser, and no proof.

And Eva had not asked to be rescued.

The troubled minister quickly reassured himself that his private doubts were not relevant anyway. He believed that he was powerless under the command of Scripture to sanction any other course; the deed that these two young people had committed had united them already. He had no option but to bind on earth what had been bound in heaven.

His hands were clean.

Paul Volk took a breath and began: "Whereas married persons are subject to many troubles and afflictions; to that end you, Wolf Kaiser and Eva Volk, who desire to have your marriage bond publicly confirmed, may be assured of the certain assistance of God in your afflictions, hear therefore from the Word of God, how honorable the marriage state is..."

Eva's mind spun wildly as her father offered his pastoral instructions regarding the nature and duties of marriage. She wondered what Andreas was thinking; she wondered what would be had she never gone to Maria Laach. Her world had changed and with terrible speed. Her attention returned when she heard her father say, "Wolf Kaiser..." She looked at her groom.

"...do you acknowledge here before God and His holy Church that you take to be your lawful wife, Eva Volk, promising never to forsake her; to love her faithfully, to maintain her as a faithful husband is bound according to the holy gospel?"

"Ja."

Paul turned moist eyes toward his daughter. "Eva Volk, do you acknowledge here before God and His holy Church that you take to be your lawful husband, Wolf Kaiser, promising to obey him, to serve and assist him, never to forsake him and to remain as a faithful wife is bound according to the holy gospel?"

Eva's heart pounded. She wondered what would happen if she turned and ran away; she wondered if her family would really be forever shamed—and what of the child she was carrying. Was this really her duty under God? Wouldn't He forgive her? *Oh God*!

It was too late.

"Yes," she answered weakly.

Paul nodded. "Then, may the Father of all mercies, who of his grace has called you to this holy state of marriage, bind you in true love and faithfulness, and grant you his blessing. Amen."

Eva stared at the Cross behind her father. She felt like a judge had just pronounced sentence. Instead of a bailiff's cuffs on her wrists, however, she felt Wolf's hand on her forearm. With the other he turned her face toward his. She forced a dutiful smile and received his kiss—a deep, possessive kiss that made her want to run all the more. *What have I done*? Her father's voice rescued her from the moment and she pulled away from Wolf, lightly. She looked deeply into her father's eyes as he bent to kiss her on the cheek. *You should you have saved me*. Eva closed her eyes.

She knew that he knew.

The next hours were a blur of music and food and a range of conversation in the hall of the Weinstube Krause. Wolf was bragging, of course; Andreas was grim, Lindie was sympathetic and Hans Bieber was grave. The band played loudly and people danced, but Eva was listening to whispers of regret.

Gifts were presented and the newlyweds received all the usual: vases, appliances, towels and the like. And they also received the two items both fast becoming the standard for the nation's weddings: a framed photograph of Adolf Hitler and a gift edition of *Mein Kampf.*

Finally the music ended and the food was gone, and the time had come for Eva to bid her guests farewell. She had hoped to say something kind to Andreas—just a simple word or two, but the young soldier had already left without a good-bye. Now she wanted nothing more than to hide within the cushioned confines of a winged chair or, better yet, to walk alone on Weinhausen's empty sidewalks. Instead, she felt Wolf's strong arm slide firmly around her waist and she was led away.

She would have to be brave.

"When I look back over the accomplishments of the last four years, you will understand that my first sentiment can only be that of expressing gratitude to our Almighty who has blessed us with success. May He grant us peace so that we might complete the work begun in Him."

Adolf Hitler

CHAPTER SIXTEEN

"THE MOVIE WAS good but I thought they were going to show *A Tale of Two Cities*." Eva wrapped her scarf around her neck as she and Wolf walked home from the Weinstube Krause. The Friday night movie ended up being Leni Riefenstahl's film, *Triumph of the Will* which had been preceded by a series of newsreels featuring the amazing achievements of the Labor Service like new bridges, dams, river locks, and the astonishing highway system know as the Autobahn.

"Klempner banned all American films from here on." Wolf waved to a few friends. "No one's permitted to show American or British films anywhere now. And he told Frau Krause to whitewash the wall. The picture gets hard to see sometimes."

"I know. I thought Hitler grew a big mole on his face but it was a mark on the wall!"

Wolf laughed. "Me too!"

Eva took Wolf's arm. She had decided she had no choice but to do all she could to be a proper wife; she was determined to nurture what good she could find. "So, tell me, Wolf, what makes you really happy?"

The young man thought for a minute. "Besides you?" He smiled.

"Yes, besides me."

"Two things: being right and winning."

Eva had hoped to discover some hidden well of virtue. "Oh."

"What about you?"

"Being in the center..." Eva caught herself. *What if he ever heard Andreas say the same thing*? "...Uh, being in the center of a circle of love."

Wolf laughed. "Ja, exactly what I thought. You women are all the same. Not me, I don't want to be in the middle of anything. I want to be out front...like the tip of a spear."

"Oh. Yes, of course. Anyway, the film was amazing."

Wolf nodded. "We need to get to Nuremburg someday. How about those hundreds of thousands of our people united and cheering the Führer...and the music and the flags...I'm going to tell Klempner to make the film mandatory. By the way, are you ready to join the Party next month?" He opened the front door of his father's house where he and Eva had set up housekeeping.

"I'd have to get in line. Membership is still closed," she answered as she took her coat to the closet.

"Get in line then." Wolf handed her his coat. He thought for a moment. "You know, you never asked me which makes me the happiest, being right or winning."

"Just forget all that."

"No, ask me."

"Really, just...

"Ask!"

"Fine. Which makes you the happiest?"

"If you loved me you'd already know."

"Eva?" Professor Kaiser called weakly from upstairs. He was suffering late stages of his cancer. "Eva, could you help me?"

Wolf grumbled. "He probably wants that light bulb changed in the hall. Tell him I'll get it in the morning."

The young bride climbed the stairs to the professor's chilly bedroom. Hans Bieber was sitting alongside the suffering man and reading from Hemmingway's *A Farewell to Arms*. "Ja, Herr Professor?" Eva tucked a blanket under her father-in-law's chin and cast a worried look at Hans.

"Are you ready for Christmas, child?" said the professor weakly.

"It will be a very nice Christmas."

"Your first one as a wife, that's good. You have lots of firsts coming. Next year that child you carry will be crawling all over the house." The professor sighed and Eva felt a lump form in her throat. She knew that he knew he would not see his grandchild. "The house smells good. You baked today?"

"Yes, of course. I baked Wolf his favorite, Linzertorte. And I made you two dozen Anisplätzchen and some hazelnut cookies, and I baked Herr Bieber a rum Stollen. I want this Christmas to be special for everyone."

"You are a good woman, Eva Kaiser."

"Indeed she is," added Hans. "By the way, I understand that Andreas has leave for Christmas. I think his favorite is Apfelstrudel with powdered sugar."

Eva hadn't been told of Andreas' leave. Her heart picked up a few extra beats at the idea of it. "I'll...I'll have to remember that."

"Wolf tells me you're hiding some egg liquor."

Eva playfully spanked the professor's arm. "Would you like some?"

"Only if you bring me a cookie, too."

Eva forced a light laugh and disappeared in the heavy-shadowed upstairs hallway toward the stairs. The Kaiser house was similar to the Volk's but it had only two bedrooms on the second floor. Downstairs were a small kitchen, a slightly larger dining room and a comfortable living room from which Eva heard Wolf dialing a broadcast on the government radio. *Andreas for Christmas. That will be nice.*

Lost in her thoughts, Eva missed the first step. With a sudden cry she stumbled forward, her hand grasping wildly for the handrail. Unable to catch herself, her knees buckled and she toppled down the hard, oak treads and landed at the bottom with a terrible thud.

Wolf dashed from the living room and Hans from the upstairs. In moments they were helping the stunned young woman to the sofa where she rubbed a fast swelling ankle. "How did you miss the step!" Wolf cried.

"Oh, Wolf," sobbed Eva. "It hurts." She squeezed her ankle. "I don't know how. It was dark."

"Well, if you knew it was dark why weren't you more careful?"

Hans hurried for cold compresses and returned to kneel in front of the whimpering young woman. "You'll be fine, my dear. Just lay these on the swelling and lie down." With Wolf looking over his shoulder, Hans examined Eva. Satisfied, he stood. "Well, a few bad bruises and a sprain. I don't think anything's broken. A little rest and in the morning we'll have Krebel have a look."

Eva nodded and offered a weak smile. "I guess you'll have to get your own Stollen." It was then that Eva felt her belly cramp.

⌖

Diary Entry: 30 January 1937

Krebel called it a miscarriage but I don't like giving it a name. When you give something a name it makes it seem like less than it is. I wonder what they did with my little boy. The nurses wouldn't tell me. They just kept saying that I am young and that I have lots of time for more babies.

I'm not being a very good wife. I cry a lot about my baby and I want to throw up when Wolf touches me. It's not because of the baby but because of the feeling I had at our wedding. I try hard to only find good in him but it's more than that. Before Maria Laach it was like I was his whole world but now that he has me, he's so different. In the past weeks he looks at me like he hates me and he is getting mean. Yesterday he slapped me on the face. I guess he was just frustrated by a lot of things but mostly I think he was angry that the SS rejected his application. They said he was too short and then I laughed a little. I shouldn't have done that. So maybe some of this is my fault. Anyway, he promised he'd take us on our wedding trip after his father dies. I told him we could use the money Opa left me.

He'll probably be drafted into the Wehrmacht next year but I think they could also put him into the Reich Labor Service. I can't picture him with a shovel. But maybe he'll go into the new Luftwaffe. Hitler says that National Service makes young men better. If he's right then I think it would be good for Wolf to go away for a while.

I'm glad Andreas stayed away at Christmas. I don't think I could have faced him. He wrote me a nice letter that I hid. He said he met a girl in Trier but she's a Catholic so he thinks he should stop seeing her. That was the first time I was glad someone was Catholic. I hope Andreas doesn't try to convert her. Am I wicked to think that?

The Superintendent gave the church back to Papa and he's happier.

Hitler ripped up the Versailles Treaty a couple of weeks ago and I wished I could have joined the celebration. I just couldn't bring myself to go. Everyone in the village finally feels really free.

Lindie told me the government is arresting Gypsies because they steal a lot. But I wonder why they arrest the Jehovah's Witnesses that Papa talks about. I never met one but I hope they learn their lessons. Papa says the camps are inspected by the Red Cross and even the foreign press, and they are clean and humane. Hitler says that the concentration camps are reeducating people through hard work. That sounds right to me.

Hitler is such a strong man. When I see his picture on the wall I can't help but feel good. It's a comfort to have someone who can make sense out of this world. Everyone is happy. Everything the Führer wants for us we get. Men are working, the roads are fixed, the poor are being cared for, and our enemies respect us.

I'm not sure I like the Nazis' ideas about Lebensraum, though. I don't think we should take land from other people even if they're only Slavs. But I do agree with Hitler that all German peoples should be allowed to join our Reich. Papa's cousins in the Sudetenland want to be free from the Czechs and come back to us like the Saarländers did. Everyone says the Austrians want to join with us, too. So do the Germans in the lands the Poles took.

I worry about Poland. Onkel Rudi says the Poles are passing more laws against the Germans who still live there and I have a feeling that the Führer won't allow that to go on much longer. With our new army he could probably beat Poland and make things right but no one wants another war. Herr Bieber says he's getting a little nervous about that even though Hitler says over and over that he only wants peace.

It was good to see Onkel Rudi at Christmas. His Jewish boss left for Switzerland and made Rudi the temporary president of the company. He came back from a business trip in New York and told us that the Jews there really hate the Nazis and are turning the Americans against us. At Sunday coffee he also said that the government schools are now supposed to make Christmas more of a winter celebration than a religious one. He said that some of the schools were told to replace their Nativity plays and caroling with Germanic festivals and folk songs. He said some schools were even changing the name of Christmas to Yuletide! He thinks these things are coming from the radicals in the Party. Maybe they just want us to be proud of our past.

I got a nice Christmas letter from Jenny and Bobby. They said the American papers complain a lot about Hitler and that their father made them burn the picture we took at the castle. Onkel Alfred wrote a nasty letter to Papa about it. Papa wrote back and told him that Americans should be careful judging others. Papa reminded him that the Americans murdered the Indians so they could take their land, and they had slaves for more than a hundred years. And where Onkel Alfred lives, Negroes aren't even allowed to use the same toilets as whites. We Germans never bought or sold Negroes to anyone, and we never killed a whole race of people to steal their land.

Heil Hitler

On a dreary Oculi Sunday at the end of February, Eva threw a colander full of potato peels to the family pig in the pen by her garden and hurried back to the kitchen to finish preparing the afternoon meal. Upstairs, Paul Volk, Doctor Krebel, Wolf, Hans and Andreas surrounded Professor Kaiser's bed. The February day was foggy and a layer of ice lay atop the slate roofs of Weinhausen.

Eva took a fork and stabbed a few of her boiling potatoes to see if they were soft, then finished setting the table with china once belonging to Wolf's mother. She stared at each piece as she placed them carefully atop the lace cloth covering the mahogany table. Memories had already begun to cling to them.

She heard her father finish a prayer for the professor upstairs. In the past weeks the suffering man had dwindled to less than half his prior weight. His skin had become yellow like a newspaper that had laid in the sun. She then heard footsteps treading down the stairway and in a few moments the five somber men moved to seats in the living room where they spoke in low tones. Eva checked her roasted pork and prodded her heated sauerkraut with a long fork. She hastily stirred the gravy.

Wolf came to the kitchen door. "I told you to be ready by two o'clock."

Eva wiped her hands nervously on her apron. "I'm almost done. How's your father?"

"Sleeping." Wolf opened the oven door and smelled the pork. "As sick as he is, he got mad at Andreas about the Party."

"Why?"

"Andreas said that some in the Party were crazy. I'll have to remember that."

"And what did your father say?"

"He cursed at him." Wolf pinched some sauerkraut out of the pot and tasted it. "Blah! Why did you add caraway? I hate caraway."

Eva stood stiffly and wiped her forehead with the back of her hand. She answered with a bite. "I thought you said you liked caraway. One day you like something, the next day you don't. How am I supposed to know what you really want?"

Wolf closed the kitchen door. "You'll not use that tone with me." He took a wooden spoon from the countertop and moved toward her with a menacing step.

Eva's eyes followed the spoon. She reached for it, slowly. "Please..."

Wolf slapped the spoon hard across Eva's forearm. The young woman muffled a cry and grabbed the stinging welt. "Yesterday I told you to water the pig and you forgot. Then I told you to get eggs from the nest and they froze. Now this." He swatted her arm again, this time harder.

Eva suppressed a cry.

"Just get our meal on the table."

"Ah, I never tire of our Mosel Riesling," said Dr. Krebel as he lifted the delicate white wine to his eye. "This is the only thing the least bit airy about us Germans." The diners laughed. Krebel turned to Wolf. "So, young man, you've a fine home here. Your father tells me you have a good job in Koblenz."

Wolf took his seat at the head of the table. "Thank you, Herr Doktor. I do my best, but sketching truck chassis isn't my dream."

"You'll be racing this spring? Weinhausen would love to see you the champion again."

"Unless I join up."

"That would make your father proud." The doctor lit a cigarette. "You know, the Wehrmacht has motorcycle combat units."

Wolf nodded. "I heard."

"The new army is interested in speed. The horse regiments will soon give way to tanks and armored vehicles. I can imagine a battalion of motorcycle infantry flanking an enemy with ease."

Wolf opened another bottle of Riesling and aimed a sarcastic sneer at his brother. "Would beat playing with pigeons."

Andreas said nothing. He turned, instead, to Rev. Volk. "So, the church school may close for lack of students?"

Paul grumbled. "I tell you, we ministers were shocked at the result of the referendum. Do you know that in nearly every province over 90% of the people voted in support of government schools over our church schools? I was astounded."

"I guess the BK pastors are really worried?"

"Well, you don't have to be a dissenting church to find this disconcerting. Just three years ago our schools were thriving. By the way, Klempner swears that I secretly carry the BK green card."

"Do you?" asked Wolf.

Volk sipped a drink. "I share many of their concerns but even some of their members are quitting now because their leaders are going too far. I've heard that of few of their radicals are suggesting that Hitler may actually be an enemy of Christ."

"Ridiculous," grumbled Krebel. "Don't they listen to his speeches? The Führer should keep them out of politics."

Paul reached for some more wine. "I'm glad that Hitler has shown some restraint. He's offered concessions and continues to stand by the Party Platform that expressly protects the Christian religion. He's never closed a church, you know. All he wants is unity in the Reich, especially in times like these. But BK extremists like Bonhoeffer and Niemöller are starting to torture him with their narrow doctrines."

Andreas had been listening carefully. "They need to remember that without the Führer we'd be under the Bolsheviks and then none of the churches would be open."

"Agreed," said Volk. "But some have been claiming that Christianity and National Socialism are polar opposites...even enemies."

"They ought to be shot," said Wolf.

"And what do you think, Herr Pfarrer?" asked Hans.

Paul shrugged. "I admit concerns, especially with the exaggeration of race issues, but the Apostle Paul told the Church of his time to even obey Nero. What am I supposed to do with that? The truth is that no government will conform perfectly to all things Christian."

"Not even in America," laughed Hans.

Eva stepped from the kitchen carrying a meat plate loaded with a steaming pork roast. "Meine Herren, enough of politics," she smiled. "Pork with horseradish and sauerkraut...Wolf, would you carve?"

Wolf took Eva's arm and kissed it. "Certainly, meine Liebe."

Eva stiffened and a fleeting glance at Andreas did not go unnoticed by anyone. She hurried back to the kitchen and returned with the rest of the meal including boiled potatoes, carrots, and gravy.

The diners stood as Eva took her chair.

The minister then proceeded with a prayer that covered the food, the plight of the professor and the state of the nation. He finished with a loud 'Amen,' to which Wolf and Dr. Krebel added a 'Heil Hitler.'

Eva surveyed her guests to be sure they approved. She wanted to let her eyes linger on Andreas' face and his kindly smile. She wanted to see him fill himself from her plate, to be fed and satisfied at her table.

"We must fight the destructive influences of Jews on religion, morality, literature and art, and political and social life."

Father Erhard Schlund, Franciscan publicist

CHAPTER SEVENTEEN

THE MEAL WAS finished soon enough and Eva cleared the dishes before presenting a plate of cheese. Wolf was busy boasting of a new promotion in the factory. Then he spoke of his likely rise to prominence in the Party and his future service in the military.

Eva listened to his voice which she found both disgusting and oddly inspiring. She was fast facing the reality that her husband was an indulged, favored son who had managed to manipulate an unbounded life of entitlement. In fact, for some reason nearly everyone gave Wolf all the room he wanted...even his father who let him have a bedroom of his own by sending Andreas to the attic.

Still, she could not escape his charm. Few could.

His power was irresistible at some deep level, as was the respect—even enthusiasm—she felt for the successes he had enjoyed. However, the conflict of these opposing feelings had fueled a simmering anger deep within the woman. She was angry at Wolf for his violence, but also at herself for needing his cruel passion. And she felt a rising anger toward her father for not doing something to protect her, even from herself. Exactly what, she didn't know. And Andreas...

"Did you burn yourself, Eva?" asked Hans.

"Huh?"

Bieber pointed to the red welt on Eva's forearm as she reached for a dish. "Did you burn yourself?"

"Oh, that, uh,...a mark of my stupidity."

The table fell quiet. Her father cleaned his glasses with a napkin but Wolf narrowed his eyes. "Exactly what does *that* mean?"

Eva felt color rushing to her face. Her private sarcasm had landed her in a dangerous place. She fumbled for words. "Well, uh, I just mean...I do stupid things around the house and sometimes I get hurt."

"Like what?" asked Hans.

"Oh, forget it." Eva laughed, self-consciously. "Who knows? I...I tripped in the pig pen once with a basket of eggs and I fell into the manure!"

Everyone chuckled, politely.

"You should have seen my face." She escaped by changing the subject. "Now, I've Apfelstrudel for desert...with powdered sugar." Eva noticed that her hands were shaking as she began to clear the rest of the table. She glanced tentatively at Wolf, now sitting calmly in his seat and enjoying his wife's discomfort.

"Well, the next time you break a dozen eggs I'll have to take a belt to you," he said with an insider's snicker.

The gravy boat slipped from Eva's hand and fell to the floor, shattering into a thousand shards. Wolf leapt from his seat with a roar and grabbed Eva's arm roughly. He squeezed it, hard. "Clumsy cow! That was my mother's."

"Shut up," shouted Andreas from across the table. He stood, eyes fixed on Wolf like two augers poised to drill metal. "Call her that again and I'll deck you."

Eva whimpered.

"And take your hand off her!"

"Boys!" cried Rev. Volk as he stood. "Boys, enough."

Wolf pushed Eva hard to the side. He slammed his fists on the tabletop; his neck pulsed and his face reddened with rage. "She's my wife; don't ever tell me what to do with my wife."

Andreas scowled and stormed away.

"Father?" said Andreas in a low voice. He pulled a chair to the side of Professor Kaiser's bed. The man did not answer. Andreas looked about the room, glad to be away from Wolf. On one wall hung the tin-type photographs of the professor's grandparents; on another hung pictures of Martin Luther and Adolf Hitler. The professor had insisted that Hitler was the consummation of the great Reformer's work. Andreas' eyes then ran over the window which was bordered by heavy, fringed drapes, and to a faded map titled, *The Holy Roman Empire of the Germans*. Another wall displayed the *Twenty-Third Psalm* in needle-point crafted by the late Frau Kaiser, Andreas' mother.

Andreas and the professor had never been close—the professor's unabashed preference for his biological son had been matter-of-fact and offered without apology ever since the day Andreas' mother died. But in spite of that, he had always thought the man to have treated him decently and even with paternal affection on some occasions. Andreas remembered the two of them studying the painting by Caspar David Friedrich and the professor teaching him how a radio works. As he looked into his step-father's bony, yellowed face, Andreas believed that the man certainly hadn't deserved to suffer like this.

But neither did Eva.

Dr. Krebel interrupted Andreas' thoughts. "Quite a scene down there...Your father is sleeping?"

Andreas nodded.

The doctor leaned over the man. "Hmm." Krebel felt for a pulse and quickly laid an ear on Professor Kaiser's chest. He snatched a small mirror from his vest pocket and held it under the man's nose. He listened to his chest again. "I'm sorry son, he's gone."

Andreas stood, quickly. "Gone?" A rush of unexpected emotion confused him. He swallowed against the lump in his throat. A flood of memories washed over him. And then another feeling emerged; the young man suddenly felt very much alone.

Eva Kaiser was quiet when she and Wolf disembarked the train from Koblenz. The May afternoon was warm and a stubborn river fog had made the air moist. Eva waved to a friend with a sigh and then lifted her suitcase. Her honeymoon had been a huge disappointment.

When Wolf had told her they would go to Rome she had been so excited. She had hoped to walk atop the black stone blocks of the Apian Way like St. Paul. She had looked forward to strolling amongst the flat, orange bricks of the ancient Roman forum. She had hoped to splash barefoot in the sun-warmed waters of the Trevi Fountain with a husband who loved her.

But there had been none of that.

Eva supposed that her husband's lingering grief had probably contributed to his distracted indifference. And she knew that her divided feelings had kept her from being the young bride he may have wanted.

But as a little girl she had dreamt of so much more.

So it was what it was, and the young woman now marched obediently behind her husband through the streets of Weinhausen. *I guess I should be more grateful*, she thought. *My parents barely had food when they married and I'm complaining about this*. But Eva really had wanted to bask in the sun outside the Pantheon and sip wine and nibble cheese at an outdoor café in the piazza Campo de'Fiori. Instead, she had spent much of the week following Wolf on his daily walks to Mussolini's balcony on the Palazzo Venezia where she stood under the hot sun pressed on all sides by jostling crowds of Black Shirts cheering for Italy's fascist dictator.

However, Eva was grateful that Wolf had at least been calm on the trip. He had treated her kindly and even bought a few gifts, though one was a brooch from Basel that she found unflattering. It was a silver hand-in-sword of the Germanic folk hero Hermann who defeated the Romans. But he had also bought her a smart silk scarf and an expensive cameo.

The tired couple walked slowly through Weinhausen's market. New shops had opened and the square was a palette of color from the flowers filling every window-box. Eva waved to jolly Oskar. "I hear he quit the SA."

Wolf nodded. "Schneider thinks he's getting uneasy with the

Party. He's been shooting his mouth off at the Weinstube...he says that Germany is whole again and enough is enough."

Eva waved to Ulrich Obermann, the butcher's apprentice. "He's a good man; too bad he's Catholic."

"He's leaving for training camp in June."

"Oskar told me he's angry about the trials of those priests in Koblenz."

"If you molest a boy you should be hung," grumbled Wolf.

"Ulrich thinks the charges were trumped up to keep the Roman Church in line." Eva paused to set down her suitcase and shake feeling back into her hand. "He told Gunther that before he leaves he has to take his radio to confession."

"What?"

Eva let herself laugh. "He said it lies too much!"

Wolf smiled. "I'll have to remember that. Come with me."

"Herr Silbermann, g'Tag and Heil Hitler." Wolf set his suitcases in front of the deli case.

Sam Silbermann nervously wiped his hands on his apron. He had stubbornly refused to leave Weinhausen despite threats and complaints by the Party. "G'Tag, Wolf...and Eva. I hope you had a good wedding trip?"

"Thank you, yes," Eva said.

Wolf looked carefully at the ageing grocer until the man lowered his eyes. Satisfied, he said, "So, you're the last Jew in Weinhausen."

Silbermann didn't answer.

"Where did the rest of the 'chosen few' go?"

Eva laid a hand on Wolf's forearm. "Wolf..."

"Well, the Goldmanns wanted to go to America but the Americans refuse to open their immigration policy. I think they went to Italy, and the Baums are in Geneva right now and hoping to emigrate to Palestine. The others have left for London."

Wolf nodded, approvingly. "I guess your Temple is shrinking. Too bad." He reached for a pair of tongs and lifted a pickle from its barrel. He put it in a brown wrapper. "You know, Herr Pfarrer Volk read me an article from some theologian who said we Germans have three choices about you Jews." He took a bite out of the pickle. "He said we can either put up with your conspiracies, or intermarry with you until your race disappears, or export you to a homeland of your own."

Eva wanted to leave. "Wolf..."

"The first is out of the question, of course. We've done that long enough." Wolf took another bite. "The second would make your Rabbis angry. They think you people are too good to marry us. 'Goyim dogs' I think they call us?" Wolf waited for Silbermann's response. The man remained silent. "So, it seems to me that the third would keep everyone happy, don't you think?"

Silbermann stiffened. "If it makes you feel better, the Zionists may be working with the Führer on some ideas like that."

"Imagine, Jews working with the Führer. See, maybe he's not as bad as you think." Wolf grinned. "Well, we all know what the Zionists want...they want to steal Palestine from the dumb beggars who live there. According to the papers your 'brethren' are already making life bad for them. Those poor fools won't know what hit them."

"How can I help you today, Wolf?"

The young man turned to his anxious wife. "Well, Eva, how about something sweet for Gunther's children...maybe some honeycomb or molasses?"

The grocer pointed to a small display and Eva hurried away. Wolf turned back to Samuel. "Now, there is something else."

The grocer waited.

Wolf leaned forward and whispered, "I want to surprise my bride with a box of your best chocolates."

16 October 1938
Feldpost
Karlsbad, Sudetenland

Liebe Eva,

I am writing to you from the beautiful mountain country of the Sudetenland. Nearly 3,000,000 Germans are cheering for us as their liberators from Czech oppression. You remember how the Austrians supported the Anschluss by a vote of 99.7%? It will be the same here. The same blood belongs in the same Reich and everyone knows it. Even the English and the French have agreed that these lands belong to us and the pact they signed makes this legal. Everything is in good order.

There are lots of soldiers here. I'm a little jealous of the SS men because the girls love their uniforms.

The Catholic girl from Trier has been banished from me by her father and her priest. It's probably for the best. I see now that I did not love her and the differences in our religions would have been intolerable.

I've been transferred out of my ridiculous carrier pigeon platoon and am in training as a machine gunner again. I will not bore you with the particulars. My enlistment has been extended and I've been promoted to Obergefreiter which is good because corporals get a little more pay.

Gunther and Lindie write sometimes. Lindie tells me she's pregnant with her fourth. That should cover Gunther's government debt completely! I guess she'll get some kind of motherhood award, too. She says Gunther has commanded her to produce a son this time. That made me laugh.

Gunther tells me that Wolf received his orders to report to Wittlich in July.

He also told me that you took the radio oath to the Führer along with a whole group. I guess we're all in the same boat now. But, I was a little surprised that you joined the Party. I guess you needed to do that so you could keep your job? Did you see the 'Eternal Jew' exhibit? A lot of the pictures were funny but the Nazis really don't have to go so far. (Dear Censor: my concern is simply about proportion).

I hear Pfarrer Hahn has a bee in his hat! Lindie wrote that he hasn't smiled ever since Hitler kicked all ministers out of the SA. My captain says Hitler is working hard to keep Church and State apart. I've heard that some ministers are arrested from time to time. I hope your father is safe. I can understand why some pastors are concerned, yet I think they've pushed the Führer to his limits. I hope he doesn't ever abandon his faith, even if he is a Catholic.

I also learned that the SS instructors have been officially reminded that Christ is a part of German history and that no one is permitted to denigrate His name. That gives me a better feeling. I hope the radicals get the message.

In your last letter you said you were worried about a war. If you could see how mighty the Wehrmacht is you'd know that none of our enemies would dare attack us. And the SS is very strong. Besides, the Führer has offered peace plans to nearly everyone. He's entered into an anti-Communist pact with Japan and Italy, so I think the Russians would think twice, even though they now have 40 divisions near their western borders. What's left of Czechoslovakia is mad as can be about the Sudetenland, but won't dare do anything about it now. I'd keep an eye on Poland, though. They still won't give us back Danzig, they still refuse a rail line to connect us to our own province of East Prussia and they are persecuting Germans who are under their heel. Hitler won't take this forever.

I hope that Herr Bieber is happy in his own apartment.

Heil Hitler,
Andreas

"Eva?"

The young woman jumped.

"What are you reading?"

"Oh, Wolf. I...I thought you were working on your motorcycle tonight." She slipped Andreas' letter into her drawer.

"We finished early. Let me see that."

"It's nothing. Just some office paperwork."

Wolf narrowed his eyes. "You never bring work home." He pushed her aside and snatched the letter from the drawer with a grease-blackened hand. He began to read.

Eva held her breath.

Wolf crumpled the letter into a ball and threw it into the kitchen stove. "Well, wasn't that cozy." He whirled about. "Paperwork? So you lied to me." He backhanded the young woman across the face.

With a cry, Eva stumbled to one side and then moved toward the dining room in case she needed to get out the back door.

Wolf took five long strides and shoved her to her hands and knees. With the sole of his shoe he then flattened her hard on the floor before jerking her to her feet by the back of her blouse. He spun her around and began slapping her face.

Covering her face with her arms Eva tried to pull away. "Please, oh please," she sobbed.

Wolf wouldn't listen. He slammed her against a wall and pulled the belt off his waist. He raised it over his head and swung hard. This time the shrieking woman dodged his blow. He swung again and she ducked, then sprang toward the kitchen. He caught her by the hair and threw her violently against a wall where he clutched her by the throat.

Eva's eyes widened as she gasped for air. She grabbed for the back edge of the china cabinet and pushed with all her might. The piece rocked and spilled dishes from its shelves, cascading chinaware to the floor.

Wolf released his hold in disbelief and Eva lunged toward the floor to snatch a long, sharp piece of a broken plate. She spun around and defiantly held the shard in a trembling hand. "Leave me alone."

Slack-jawed, Wolf stared at his mother's shattered china and then at his desperate wife now crouching like a cornered animal and ready to strike.

"Just put your belt away, Wolf."

Wolf slowly put his belt through the loops of his work pants. "Fine. There." He eased himself slowly forward. "This isn't like you, Eva. You must have had a bad day. Now, how about I help you clean this up?"

Eva backed away.

Wolf pulled a kerchief from his pocket and reached warily toward Eva's face. "Easy, now." He dabbed blood from her nose and lip. He then opened his arms wide, like a serpent exposing its underbelly. "I really am sorry." He waited. "But if you want to stab me, here I am."

Eva didn't move.

Wolf shrugged, then bent to pick up the broken dishes. "I never really knew my mother, you know."

Eva relaxed a little.

Wolf paused. "I only want what's best for us. I…I love you so much and I couldn't stand the thought of you and Andreas…"

Eva forced words from her mouth. "It's not like that."

"He always liked you."

She lowered her hand. "But I chose you."

Wolf stood. "No, I chose you…even though you bring the worst out in me." His voice was now hard as Krupp steel.

"Husbands are supposed to love their wives."

"I do love you."

"You don't hurt someone you love."

"Hurt? It's you who's been sneaking letters behind my back." Wolf sharpened his gaze and quickly grabbed her wrist. He yanked the shard from her grasp, cutting her palm. "If I ever see a letter like this again I will do more than slap you. Do you understand?"

Eva's eyes filled with pain but she lifted her chin. "Never hit me again."

"Don't give me orders, cow. I'll punch you right now!"

Eva stuck her face forward. "Then do it."

Wolf closed his hand into a fist and raised his arm. He cursed. "I forbid you to write to Andreas. And get his stuff out of my house or I'll burn it."

Eva didn't answer.

Wolf lowered his arm. "All I want is for us to be happy. We don't need this going on, especially with me reporting to the Wehrmacht next month. I can't be worrying about my wife and my brother in the same house when I'm serving the Fatherland somewhere. Can't you understand that?"

Eva faltered. Maybe he had a point. "Yes."

"I want you to promise you'll not write to him."

That was a painful demand. Eva was trapped in Wolf's world.

"Good." Wolf moved close to her and took both her hands in his. "Forgive me, Eva. I have a lot on my mind. I work hard and I hate giving up my racing just to go into the army. I might have been the Rheinland champion again, you know." He waited for a response.

Eva stood quietly. She could feel blood dripping from her hand. The mantle clock chimed.

"Yes, I promise not to hit you again. Not ever. And I don't have to tell you that my word is sacred."

Eva yielded.

She pressed his kerchief against the cut on her hand. "I'm sorry about the china. I'll buy some glue and I can try to fix what I can."

"Hopeless. It'd be better to get rid of it all and tell people we sold it."

"But...that'd be lying."

"Would you rather them know what happened? Should I tell them how you've been sneaking letters back and forth with Andreas?" Wolf shook his head. "I'm just trying to protect you."

Eva's mind was whirling. "But we weren't sneaking anything and..."

"Stop it, Eva," commanded Wolf. "Just stop it."

"But..."

Wolf grabbed her wrist again. "But what?" He squeezed, very, very hard.

"The Christian religion is not influenced by the racial characteristics of the Jews. Rather, it has had to make its way against this people."
Roman Catholic Bishop Hilfrich of Limburg, Germany

CHAPTER EIGHTEEN

Diary Entry: 1 December 1938

I've obeyed Wolf and not written to Andreas. Lindie told him that her mother reserved a room at the Weinstube for him and that Gunther moved his stuff over there. They hung Andreas' favorite picture on the wall across from the Führer's.

I haven't told Wolf that I'm pregnant again. Since he's training in Baden I thought I'd wait and be sure everything is good. I don't know how he'd react to another miscarriage.

Mother's been better. Now that I'm miserable she's happy. Since she stopped drinking again Herr Klempner let her rejoin the Party. She goes away a lot which makes Papa both happy and curious.

Last month a Jew in France murdered a German diplomat and all of Germany was furious. The radio was filled with angry speeches saying that it is typical for Jews to start trouble just as we are getting on our feet. Hans said that Jews are always lurking behind the scenes. The radio said that synagogues were burned and Jewish store windows were smashed all over the Reich. I think about a hundred Jews were killed. It's being called Kristallnacht because of all the broken glass.

The Information Minister says that the Jews will have to pay for all the damage. But some people are angry with the SA and the SS for causing so much disorder in our streets. Some say it's the Jews fault for giving the radicals so many reasons to behave badly. They're lucky the Führer let most of them out of jail.

The Silbermanns left Weinhausen yesterday. They're good Jews so I hope they'll be safe wherever they're going. Silbermann cried when he loaded his suitcase into Oskar's truck. His official name is now Samuel Israel Silbermann and his wife is Sarah Sarah Silbermann because all Jewish middle names have to be either 'Israel' or 'Sarah.' I think that's silly. They have to carry identification papers with them, too. He told Herr Offenbacher that the law forbids them to have a driver's license, attend the theater, or have any social connection with Aryans. Between that and Kristallnacht, he said he just couldn't stay. I feel very sorry for them both but they should have done more to keep the other Jews in line. Besides, if their grandparents would have converted they could have stayed.

I need to hide this diary at Lindie's farm from now on. I must keep writing in it or I will go mad, but if Wolf ever finds it I think he would kill me. I have to admit that sometimes I think he may be right about everything. Maybe I do bring out the worst in him. I've not been a very good wife. Sometimes I don't blame him at all. That's when I really hate myself.

I hope Christmas will be wonderful.

⌖

Christmas 1938 did prove to be pleasant enough for Eva Kaiser. On 18 December Wolf had been given a two week leave from his new garrison near Mainz. He had hurried home with three large cartons. Unable to wait for Christmas Eve, the young man had barely kissed his wife before he helped her pull the wrapping away. Inside was her Christmas gift—a complete setting for twelve of blue Delft china. Eva feigned excitement; Delft had never been her favorite. However, the sentiment behind the gift did not go unnoticed and she rewarded Wolf with a cautious embrace.

The next few evenings were spent with friends, typically singing around tables offering a bounty of Christmas cookies and cakes. Eva was relieved to be treated kindly by Wolf. She began to believe that his change of heart might be sincere and so she offered him warmth in keeping with the season.

And that made her feel better about herself.

Friday evening was spent with Gunther and Lindie at their farm on the edges of Horchheim, a hamlet about two kilometers from Weinhausen. They enjoyed a delightful supper of Sauermagen, turnips, pickled green beans and Weincreme dessert. But Eva could think of little else than the coming Christmas Eve.

At last the day arrived and eventually the mantle clock struck the hour. Finally, the very minute was upon her. Eva nervously cranked the phonograph and set the needle on to the vinyl of *Still, Still, Still.* She then led her curious husband to their candle-lit Christmas tree and at precisely 6:00, just as her father began to ring the church bells, she tinkled her own silver bell—the one given to her on that terrible Christmas those many years before. No happy children burst into the room—not yet, but with the light of candles shining in her eyes, Eva took her husband's hand. "Wolf, you're...you're to be a father."

Stunned, Wolf cried out for joy. He embraced Eva and lifted her off her feet with a happy laugh. He whirled her about their living room like a soldier at a military ball. The young man was overcome with happiness and when he later led his wife into the midnight church service, he strutted about the packed sanctuary in his uniform like a proud rooster, crowing his good news to all.

Beaming, Eva received the congratulations of many. Seeing Wolf so happy made her feel safe again, and hopeful. She took her place by his side in the pew and joined her voice with his as the congregation sang the songs of Christmas. To Eva it was like the church had filled with angels. She lifted her face to the Cross suspended over the Lord's Table and she felt loved by God again. Chills ran over her skin. She felt like she belonged.

And she felt whole.

The children's choir sang Luther's *Es ist ein Ros*:

A Spotless Rose is growing,
Sprung from a tender root...
Its fairest bud unfolds to light
Amid the cold, cold winter,

And in the dark midnight.

Eva closed her eyes. She imagined her own child dressed in a little robe and singing in her father's church. She smiled. She wished she had Oma's necklace to touch again.

She hoped it was blessing Jenny.

Eva took Wolf's hand as her Papa preached a short sermon, first reading from St. Luke and then proceeding to encourage his congregation. "The Christ child," he said as he finished, "is the Incarnation of Truth. His touch brings sight; His word brings hope. To take hold of His Cross is to be healed, to be reconciled, to be whole again." He looked at Eva. "May each new life remind us of His love and His forgiveness. For in Him, alone, my beloved, we find the power to begin anew. Amen."

The quiet congregation then passed candles along the pews, each wick being touched to the next. The lights were dimmed and the organ silenced. Then, in the warm glow of four hundred little flames, the people of Weinhausen softly sang, *Stille Nacht, Heilige Nacht*.

Eva closed her eyes. She let the music fill her soul with comfort and she felt warm. For those few precious moments the young woman put the world away and let her spirit float within the pleasant currents of the song. Eva sang, smiling. She opened her eyes and glanced at Wolf and then at her father. She saw Hans Bieber's face lifted toward heaven; she saw Oskar Offenbacher smiling alongside his plump wife. She was proud of him for keeping Lindie's secret. In the balcony sat Lindie, Gunther and their girls. She was happy for them; she was happy for them all.

But then she wondered about Andreas. Was he happy, was he celebrating Christmas alone or with friends—or perhaps with a pretty young woman in a church faraway? A lump filled her throat and she could sing no more.

⌖

On 31 December Eva sat close to Wolf by the radio where they listened to their Führer thank God for His blessings upon Germany's

Third Reich. "To be sure," he thundered, "it was the Lord God Who permitted this work to succeed but His instrument in the perfecting of that work was National Socialism!"

The next morning Eva packed several ham sandwiches, some cheese, and two rye rolls into Wolf's duffle bag. Wolf handed her a note. "Here, you can pick from these while I'm gone."

Eva scanned a short list of names. "First, you don't know that it's a boy."

"Yes I do. How could it not be? Let Gunther have the girls." He laughed.

Eva wrinkled her nose. "But, these names are awful. Why can't we name him Daniel, after my brother?"

"No. You want me to name my son after a Jew? No, no, the Führer wants the future to be filled with good Aryan names."

"But, honestly, 'Alarich,' 'Knut,'...'Faxon?'"

"Wonderful, aren't they?"

Eva shook her head. "Maybe 'Gunnar,' or 'Udo,' but...'

Wolf pecked Eva's cheek with a kiss. "You think about it. I should be home again at the end of July. The 29th is the Führer's anniversary as head of the Party and I'm told some of us may get extra leave."

Eva nodded. "That would be perfect since I'm due in mid-July."

"Be careful this time. No falling down any steps." He took her hands. "Right?"

"I know." Eva leaned against the wall and watched her husband move toward the closet. She thought he looked manly in his uniform. With his blond hair and icy blue eyes she thought he looked like the perfect Aryan soldier; he looked just like the posters plastered all over Weinhausen.

Standing by the closet in his high, black boots, Wolf put his long, gray outer coat over the shoulders of his Wehrmacht tunic, perched his cap on his head, kissed her, and headed for the door. He turned. "One more thing. Andreas is due home sometime around Fastnacht. He wrote to me and told me that he has no interest in you at all and that he hopes you don't come looking for him."

Eva felt suddenly sick. Wolf didn't look so handsome anymore. "You don't need to worry, Wolf. You never needed to worry."

"It's you who should be worried. I would kill you both, you know."

Eva felt a chill go through her. He had said the words so matter-of-fact. Her heart sank. She believed him. *Who are you, really*? She lifted her chin and turned away.

⌖

Alone on the cold, foggy winter's night of 30 January, 1939, Eva twisted the dial of her government issued People's Receiver in an easy search for the Führer's scheduled speech. For the past months she had begun to have an odd feeling about things generally, though she couldn't quite identify what it was. After all, life was surely not difficult anymore. To the contrary, life was good for everyone she knew. The nation's mood was euphoric, almost intoxicated—perhaps that was it? Discipline and order had been restored to every category of the day—perhaps too much so?

There was more, though. Her people's self-respect had certainly been reclaimed; the nation felt whole and Eva enjoyed the pride she now felt in being 'German.' Yet the young woman could not avoid a gnawing feeling that her people's pride was bloating into arrogance, an increasingly hostile self-righteousness that King Solomon had warned about.

As Eva walked toward her chair she recalled a co-worker's comment that Nazi literature didn't use so many exclamation points anymore. "Proof," he had triumphantly said, "that what was once revolutionary has become normal." Normal? What exactly is normal? Eva thought about the arrests she had heard of on the news and through gossip, and she recalled the scary swagger of some SS men in Koblenz. She thought about talk of Lebensraum; she worried what more land for Germans might really mean. It all left her feeling uneasy.

And what about the Jews, anyway?

It had become normal to not care about them, and hatred of them seemed less and less offensive every day. Eva had decided she wouldn't hate them; hatred wasn't the Christian way. But she also decided she didn't have to like them, or feel sorry for them, or ask questions on their behalf. It was up to the State to keep order, and if the State saw fit to pass laws that made their lives inconvenient—well, so be it. Besides, nothing really terrible was happening to them.

Nevertheless, something still felt off. Somehow the order the State sought was not exactly what Eva thought order should look like.

But what did she know about it? And who else was complaining?

Eva was well-aware of the radicals in the BK, but they seemed more interested in protecting the rights of the Church than defending the Jews. And the rest of the world was silent...even the Catholic pope. Furthermore, what could some Hausfrau in Weinhausen do about anything? Eva decided it was probably best to just leave the whole awkward business to the State.

That too, was the Christian way.

Finding the broadcast, Eva settled into her stuffed chair as members of the Reichstag offered thunderous applause for their Führer. With a cup of English tea, she snuggled within her flannel robe as Hitler's voice warmed the nation:

"Today, after six years, I am able to speak before the Reichstag of Greater Germany. We are better able than other generations to realize the full meaning of those pious words "What a change by the grace of God"...

Eva nodded. Hitler's tone hardened:

"The National Socialist State has not closed a church, hindered worship, nor has it ever exercised any influence upon the form of a religious service. It has not interfered with the profession of faith of any of the Confessions. In the National Socialist State anyone is free to seek his own religious belief...It is however true that if priests, instead of being servants of God, prefer to regard their mission as the abuse of our Reich, it's institutions or it's leaders, then the National Socialist

State will force them to realize that the destruction of the State will not be tolerated..."

Eva refilled her tea cup. Not unreasonable. She leaned forward as she heard the Führer assure her about other matters:

"The German nation has no feeling of hatred toward England, America or France; all it wants is peace and quiet...The nations will soon understand that National Socialist Germany wants no enmity with other nations; that all the assertions as to our intended attacks on other nations are lies...lies being used by unscrupulous profiteers to salvage their own finances...

...Never have German soldiers fought on American soil, unless it was in the cause of American Independence; yet American soldiers were brought to Europe to help strangle a great nation which was fighting for its freedom. Germany did not attack America, but America attacked Germany and as the American House of Representatives committee has concluded: 'from purely capitalist motives and without any other cause.'"

Nodding her head, Eva leaned back and listened as her Führer became suddenly sarcastic:

"...As for the Jewish question I have this to say: it is a shameful spectacle to see how the whole democratic world is oozing sympathy for the poor tormented Jewish people, but remains hard-hearted when it comes to helping them. They say: "We are not in a position to take in the Jews." Yet in these empires there are not 10 people to the square kilometer. While Germany, with her 135 inhabitants to the square kilometer, is supposed to have room for them... I see no reason why the members of this race should be imposed upon the German nation, while in the United States, which is so enthusiastic about these 'splendid people,' their settlement should suddenly be refused with every imaginable excuse."

Eva agreed. *I'll have to write Jenny and ask why America does-*

n't take them if they love them so much.

"Today I will again be a prophet: If the international Jewish financiers should succeed in plunging the nations into another world war, then the result will not be the Bolshevization of the earth and thus the victory of Jewry, but the destruction of the Jewish race in Europe...The nations are no longer willing to die on the battlefield so that this rootless international race may profiteer from a war or satisfy its Old Testament vengeance!"

The speech ended, Eva turned off the radio. She walked to the front window and looked into the fogged streets of Weinhausen. *I wonder what Papa thinks.*

"Where can the interests of Church and State be more convergent than in our struggle against degeneracy in the contemporary world, in our struggle against the Godless movement, against criminality, class hatred, and discord. These are not anti-Christian, but rather Christian principles."

Adolf Hitler

CHAPTER NINETEEN

PAUL VOLK ANSWERED the door with a smile. "Oh, Eva. Nice of you to stop by. I was listening to the Führer on the radio. Come in, sit, I'll get us some wine."

Eva sat on the sofa and waited until her father returned. She took a glass of white wine from his hand. "So, what did you think?"

"Well, he never fails to move me."

Eva nodded. "I know. It's a little strange. I started listening with some doubts but within minutes I was believing."

Her father was quiet. Eva could see the hesitation in his face. "You know, Eva," he began. "When I was a little boy your Opa came home very excited about some wonderful deal he had been offered. He was a start-up businessman in Dresden at the time and full of hope. He was so enthused that he mortgaged our house and even borrowed money from friends. But then he came home another night looking like a dead man. He had to tell us that he had been swindled out of everything.

"About a year later he took me fishing in the Elbe. I knew he was still ashamed of himself. But he told me something I never forgot. He said 'deception is best served with large portions of truth, but never the whole truth.'"

⌖

"You're ready for tonight?"

"I guess." Eva looked out her office window into the rain-swept streets of Koblenz. She laid a hand on her belly which was now swollen with six months of pregnancy.

"Is your father?" Klempner added.

Eva shrugged. She turned off the office radio which was still announcing Berlin's spectacular celebrations for Adolf Hitler's 50th birthday. "I don't know. He's getting a lot of pressure from his Superintendent and the deacons."

"I've had no choice but to involve the Gestapo." The man's voice had a quality of confession.

Eva turned about, suddenly alarmed. "The Gestapo? But why?"

"Your father is an employee of the State and refuses an oath of loyalty to the Führer."

"My father is a German patriot. He always has been. He's just concerned about mixing politics with his office as a minister, that's all."

"Well, he's splitting hairs. The Führer has made it perfectly clear that he, too, believes in separating the Church and the State. He won't allow Nazi uniforms in the churches anymore, except for funerals. And no more pictures of the Führer on altars, no more flags on the pulpits, no more swastikas on church newsletters...Hahn's still unhappy about all this, by the way." Klempner's voice gained strength. "I should tell you that a few of your father's parishioners have complained. They think he secretly belongs to the BK. They want me to search the house for a membership card."

"Not true. He has friends who are, but..."

Klempner lit a cigarette. "The Führer has had it with the Church disputes. All he ever wanted was unity. He kept the paganists in the Party at bay for a long time but I think he's giving up on the Church thanks to some Catholic priests and the stubborn radicals in the BK. I've heard that he is so frustrated by it all that he's secretly abandoned the Christian religion altogether."

Klempner drew a long, thoughtful smoke and exhaled it through his nose. He walked to Eva's window. "I hope that's not true." He stared into the darkness for a long moment. "You know, I'm not much for religion any more. I'm more like Dr. Goebbels—I read my

New Testament regularly like he does but I don't care about all the doctrinal nonsense. I think we ought to just help each other like Christ did and learn how to struggle like he did." Klempner inhaled another smoke. "But I really do fear the paganists in the Party. Rosenberg and his crazy ideas are showing up everywhere lately. I remember when the Führer laughed at him. He wouldn't even allow the Party to distribute the fool's book. Now the Hitler Youth meetings sound like ancient pagan gatherings. And the SS is becoming more and more unchristian. It used to be that a full quarter of the SS were registered as Catholics and the rest as Protestants, but now we have this new category called, 'Believer in God'. That's the group I'm worried about. To them, God could be Odin."

Eva was surprised at Klempner's candor. The man looked discouraged. He had never really gotten over his son's death and his wife was very sick. She also wondered if the rumors were true about his Jewish grandmother costing him promotions.

Klempner's mood darkened. He faced the young woman squarely. "But that's all beside the point. If your father refuses the oath, he will be arrested."

Eva paled. "Arrested?"

"Just make sure he cooperates otherwise he'll be in Buchenwald for reeducation."

Eva sat down.

"Are you alright?"

"No, I'm not," she snapped. The business day was ending and her co-workers were gathering their coats and umbrellas. "So what do I tell him?"

"Just do your best to get him to cooperate."

"And if he doesn't?"

"As long as I've known him he's been one to avoid trouble."

Eva didn't like Klempner's comment, even if she agreed.

"Enough of this gloom." Klempner retrieved a cream-colored envelope from his desk drawer. "For you."

Eva stared at it. A German eagle with a swastika was embossed on the back. She saw the return address and her fingers went light. "From the Führer?"

Klempner smiled.

14 April 1939
Office of the Reich Chancellor
Berlin

To the honorable Frau Eva Kaiser,

The German Reich thanks you for your valuable service to National Socialism as an employee of the Party's Rheinland District Office, Koblenz. On behalf of our Führer, our Party and our people, I wish you God's blessings as you raise sons and daughters in the cause of our beloved Fatherland.

Heil Hitler,
Dr. Hans Lammers, Director

Eva nearly swooned. "The Führer's office wrote a letter to me?"

Richard Klempner beamed, proud to have pleased his friend. "What he says is true, Eva. You've been a good worker and I am sorry to lose you."

"Thank you, Richard. I did my best."

The man nodded and handed Eva her rain coat and umbrella. "Yes, you did. But your duties are not quite over."

For Eva the train ride from Koblenz was a blur. She read her letter more than once and she was exhilarated at each reading. But the dread of the evening's meeting between Klempner and her father filled her with anxiety. In the background, passengers were chattering non-stop about the day's celebrations. In Berlin the nation's largest military parade ever had been held to celebrate Hitler's birthday and Eva wondered if Wolf and Andreas had been a part of it. She could picture Wolf riding his motorcycle in the battalion to which he had recently been assigned. He'd be telling everyone it was his birthday, too. She imagined Andreas snapping his legs forward in the 'goose step' he hated to practice. *I wish I could see him again.*

The rainy walk from Weinhausen's station to her father's house was hurried and quiet. When she and Klempner arrived she noticed an unfamiliar car parked across the street. Her heart began to beat. She knocked, and then opened the front door to find her father reading his paper in his favorite chair. The phonograph was playing Strauss' *The Voices of Spring.*

"Ah, Eva, Richard, yes, come in." He stood and kissed his daughter's cheek, then shook Klempner's hand. "Welcome, welcome. Let me take your coats. Gerde, they're here."

Eva and Richard took their seats in the living room and engaged the minister in a brief conversation about village business and such until Gerde invited all to the dining room where she presented a light supper of Eintopf, dark bread, and white Riesling wine.

However, given the stakes of the evening Eva had trouble eating. She listened politely as her father expressed his concerns over the Polish military mobilization and the British/French guarantees of Poland's defense.

"They're goading us, again," Paul complained. "You can't threaten Germany like this...not anymore, not without consequence."

The conversation abruptly moved to the new pope, the instability of Japan and the Far East, Franco's victory over the Communists of Spain, Mussolini's latest moves, and Russia's efforts to align with Britain against Germany. Gerde cleared the table and brought coffee and cake from the kitchen. Then, as plainly as a comment on the weather, she said, "Herr Klempner, should we invite the Gestapo agents inside for coffee? They must be cold."

Paul stared at his wife, blankly.

"Yes, that would be civil."

Eva's eyes widened. "You're serious?"

"Of course." Richard took a sip.

Paul paled. He had expected an evening of friendly debate

with Klempner over the oath but that was not what this would be. He tried to look indifferent by lighting his pipe. "Then you should have had them in for stew."

Gerde opened the front door and waved the two policemen into the house. In a few moments the men stepped into the living room and shook off their coats. It was then that Eva noticed the exchange of eyes between her mother and one of the men—a broad-chested, ruddy-faced man with a narrow nose and brown eyes half shaded by drooping lids. As the man removed a hat from his well-groomed gray hair, Gerde introduced him as Herr Manfred Schiller. "Heil Hitler," he said to Paul.

"Heil Hitler, Herr Schiller. Welcome." The two shook hands.

Schiller then introduced his younger counterpart, Fritz von Feldenburg.

"Heil Hitler, Herr von Feldenburg," said Paul. He had kept his attention on Schiller, however. "Do I know you, sir?"

"I was in the Navy during the war and was assigned to Berlin as an officer's aid." Schiller's tone was hard.

"I see." Paul's eye fell to the man's hand in search of a wedding ring. He found none. Paul then glanced at his wife who invited the men to the table where Eva had prepared settings for chocolate torte and coffee. The four took their places and began a quiet but firm conversation.

From her vantage in the kitchen Eva watched carefully as her father shook his head more than once. She became ever more nervous as the conversation grew louder. "Oh, please, Papa," she murmured.

Gerde laid a hand on Eva's shoulder. "If he doesn't take the oath, he'll have his next meal in Buchenwald...or Dachau, Sachsenhausen...only God knows where else. I've tried to tell him but he won't believe me."

Eva backed into the kitchen. "How do you know that Gestapo man?"

Gerde reached for some cherry schnapps. "I met him in Berlin before you were born."

Eva waited.

"Do you see him?"

A slight smile tugged at the edges of Gerde's mouth. "See him? Well, dear girl, yes, I've seen him at my NSF meetings in Bonn from time to time. He enjoys speaking to the League and I thought it was a good idea to have a friend in such a position."

Eva hesitated. "Is...is he more than a friend?"

Gerde's eyes narrowed. "What are you accusing me of?"

"Nothing, mother...I..." Sounds from the other room turned both their heads. Richard Klempner and the Gestapo agents were arguing over something.

"Eva, take in some cookies."

The young woman hurried into the dining room with a tray of fresh baked butter cookies. The look on her father's face frightened her. "Meine Herren...cookies?"

"No!" blurted Schiller. "Not until this matter is settled. Now, Herr Pfarrer, will you take the oath or not?"

White-faced, Paul Volk stared at the table linen. "Under God, I cannot pledge my loyalty as a minister of the Gospel to any other than Christ Jesus."

Exasperated, Richard Klempner threw up his hands. "You are splitting hairs! Almost every other minister and priest in the Reich has affirmed their loyalty. They aren't overreacting to all this, why are you?"

Schiller interrupted. "Volk, we're not asking more than your own New Testament demands."

Paul did not answer.

Fritz von Feldenburg tried to help. "Pfarrer Volk, you are aware that a year ago the Reich arrested exactly 5,737 abortionists? Who knows how many thousands of unborn Aryans we saved? Would not our Lord Christ be pleased?"

"Of course..."

"And," Von Feldenburg continued, "We arrested exactly 8271 sexual deviants...the kind that the Führer had executed within his own closest circle. Herr Pfarrer, the Führer unselfishly devotes himself and our movement to the sort of moral order I would have thought you'd support."

"Yes, yes. We in the Church appreciate that and his devotion to the poor, and to his being a bulwark against Bolshevism and materialism. Yes, yes, I know all of this. His Positive Christianity is virtuous. Yet, as I have said, my first loyalty is to Christ Jesus."

Schiller growled. "Jesus the Jew?"

Von Feldenburg corrected his comrade. "Jesus was no Jew. He was the enemy of the Jews..."

"Enough of this." Schiller faced Paul squarely. "I say again, nearly one hundred percent of the pastors outside the BK have taken the oath and more than half in the BK have taken it. In time, we expect at least 85% of the BK will finally understand that the Führer is no threat to their precious gospel. The others will leave us no choice but to believe they are subversives to the State." He looked briefly at Gerde, now craning her neck from the kitchen. "Apparently the huge majority don't see a conflict in their loyalties. What is it that sets you apart?"

Paul felt anxious. His palms began to sweat.

"By the way, one of your parishioners reported that you have books by Sigmund Freud."

Paul nodded, warily.

"He is a Jewish materialist. You do know that, don't you?" Schiller's nostrils flared.

"Yes, but..."

"Enough! What are we to think about you, Herr Pfarrer?"

"I...I'd have no concern about taking a personal oath, but you are asking for my office to subject itself to the Führer."

Klempner rolled his eyes. "You think too much. All we're asking is that you confirm your loyalty. But, since you say it, it occurs to me that your office is happy to take money from the State."

Paul squirmed. The man had a point. He did take his salary from the State like every other minister. Would it then be fair not to take the oath? He quickly supposed that he could stop taking any more money and refuse the oath, but where would that leave his family? His mind whirled.

Schiller had enough. "I have my orders. As we speak, the Reich is surrounded by enemies who are arming to attack us. Now, more than ever we must defend the Fatherland from those who would betray her within. Either you take the oath, Herr Pfarrer, or you will be taken tonight to Koblenz jail and then to Buchenwald in the morning. From there you can watch the beech trees bloom from your cell until your conscience is finally cleared."

Paul heard his wife and daughter gasp. His mouth went dry and his limbs tingled. He knew the man was not bluffing. He was well aware that one of his friends, Rev. Schneider from nearby Dickenshied, was sitting in a Buchenwald cell that very evening. He knew that the well-known Berlin minister, Martin Niemöller, had been arrested; he knew that some seven or eight hundred other pastors had been arrested as well as priests, and even though most had been released unharmed he was well aware that some had died in custody mysteriously. 'Ascension needles,' were the rumored cause.

And he also knew that the great majority of the eighteen thousand Protestant churches supported the regime. Less than a third had ever been represented in the dwindling BK and of them only a tiny handful had ever really challenged the ideology of the Nazi State. Even the Pope had given Catholic bishops permission to be loyal subjects of the Führer.

Maybe he had been over thinking this after all.

Paul looked up. "My primary reluctance has been that the oath is not to the State or even to the office of Chancellor but rather to a man who claims to be the State."

"I am losing patience, Volk," Schiller said. "Under our present conditions, it is necessary for the Führer to be the State and to be the people. Listen to me; Hitler must be the Fatherland!"

Paul swallowed. "You must understand that I'm no democrat. Like Luther, I have no problem with a strong leader...but he was also right to say that no man is absolute...no pope...and no chancellor."

Schiller turned red but Klempner quickly begged for calm and motioned for the Gestapo men to follow him into the living room where they huddled in low whispers. After two or three minutes of insistent bickering, Klempner emerged. "Herr Pfarrer, let's just be calm. You really are thinking too much. Have you actually heard the oath?"

"Yes."

"Are you sure?" Klempner laid a hand on his shoulder and repeated the words, slowly. "Now, are they really so threatening? Don't you think you're finding demons where none lie?"

Schiller began to pace. "You know, Herr Pfarrer, I've been listening to you and I can't help but wonder something. If you are not a loyal son of the Fatherland, why should we think your congregants are? After all, you do have an influence on them. I'd hate to see them cut off from their marriage loans or child grants. Perhaps we should investigate your deacons..."

Paul's mind raced. He looked into the kitchen and fumbled with his pipe. His eyes met Eva's now peeking fearfully around a corner. At last, he took a deep breath. "Perhaps I have been, uh, over zealous..."

"Then let's just be done with all this." Klempner moved quickly. Turning to Schiller he asked, "Have you the flag?"

With Paul Volk fidgeting in place, Schiller walked to the closet and retrieved a small national flag from within the deep pocket of his leather coat. It was displayed on a thin wooden shaft which Schiller held toward Paul.

Klempner beckoned Gerde and Eva to join them as the minister slowly stood. "Now, Herr Pfarrer, take the corner of the flag in your left hand and raise your right."

Paul hesitated again. He felt naked and ashamed, exposed as the coward he had always accused himself of being.

"Just do it."

The minister yielded and he slowly stretched his left hand forward and took the corner of the flag lightly in his grasp. At the touch, he felt nauseated; another wave of self-contempt washed over him. He raised his right hand, slowly.

Richard Klempner wanted the matter closed. "Now, Herr Pfarrer, repeat after me: 'Under God I pledge my faithful obedience to Adolf Hitler, the Führer of the German people and Reich, and I pledge myself to the sacrifice and service required on behalf of the German people such as befit a Protestant minister.'"

The words tasted like soured milk to Paul as he repeated them, and he pushed them out of his mouth hastily. When he had finished, he dropped his hand quickly from the flag and hung his head.

Schiller smiled. "Heil Hitler." He shook Paul's hand. "So, friend, as the Lutheran bishop at Wartburg said, 'One God, one obedience to the Faith—all hail our Führer.' Sieg Heil!"

"We set our entire power of life and spirit on this: to bring our Volk and Reich into a healthy, life protecting order, and to create for them a durable and honorable existence in the circle of the white ruling peoples to which God has entrusted the responsibility for the history of humanity."

Emanuel Hirsch, Protestant theologian

CHAPTER TWENTY

"I'VE BEEN FRETTING over this confounded vine for ten years," grumbled Paul Volk.

Eva nodded and wiped her brow. The June afternoon was sultry and the pregnant young woman was terribly uncomfortable. "Bieber says your problems are in both your leaves and your roots."

"I know." Paul pointed to angular, dead spots on some of his leaves. "*Phomopsis viticola*, he calls it. But here, see these tiny galls...from *phylloxera*, he says; tiny insects from America and France. Now he tells me he thinks we have *vitis vinifera, root phylloxera*, too. Now what do I do?"

Eva shrugged. "So just stop worrying about it. Maybe your vine will heal itself."

Paul grumbled and he turned toward his daughter. "They never do. Well, tell me about you."

"I don't feel very well."

"I should think not. Look at you."

Eva sat awkwardly atop a stool her mother brought from the garage.

"You look like you're going to burst," said Gerde as she came out the front door. She handed her daughter a lemonade.

"I feel like it. Last night I had sharp pains."

"You've a month to go," said Gerde. "What about this morning?"

Eva nodded. "At breakfast I had to sit down. I was so loud that

Frau Wicker knocked on the door." She took a long drink. "I was hoping to go to the village fest this afternoon."

"Well, don't worry about that," said Paul. "The summer solstice will return in exactly one year." He smiled. "Have you heard from Wolf?"

"I don't get too many letters. He says he's very busy in maneuvers. His battalion's being transferred to the Tenth Army. I think he's somewhere around Dresden." Eva held her belly and winced.

"Are you alright?" asked Gerde.

"I don't know. Something doesn't feel like it should."

"How would you know how it should feel? This is your first." Gerde took Eva by the hand and led her into the living room. "Lie down. I'm going to call Krebel."

Eva lay down on the soft sofa and sunk into stuffed cushions that smelled of pipe smoke and dust. She closed her eyes and listened to her mother's voice on the telephone. She wondered about her mother. The woman still sneaked an occasional cigarette in violation of Hitler's rules for Party women, but she had avoided alcohol almost entirely since Christmas. Furthermore, she had recently been elected as the chair of the local Nazi Women's League chapter. As such, she had been placed into a position that interceded for marriage loans and family subsidies. She was friendly with the Gestapo and the folk in Weinhausen grasped the value in that. In her new capacity she would also be in charge of the local Winter Relief fundraising as well as any number of parades, exhibitions, and celebrations. Gerde Volk had become important.

A sharp pain cut through Eva and she cried out.

⌖

Eva lay in her former bedroom, exhausted and covered in perspiration. She could hear her mother and father speaking with the doctor outside her door in low tones. A neighbor, Frau Nuber—a soft-spoken white-haired widow—gently dabbed her brow.

"Where's my baby?"

The woman's hand stopped by Eva's temple. "Dr. Krebel is examining him, now."

"Him?" Eva brightened. "It's a boy! Oh, won't Wolf be proud."

"Ah, my dear. All will be well."

Eva looked closely at Frau Nuber. The woman was a devout member of her father's church and known for near moral perfection. Eva knew she could not lie. "What's wrong?"

Frau Nuber began dabbing Eva's head again with the cool, damp rag. She thought for a long moment before answering. "You know, Eva, God's will is a mysterious thing."

Eva's eyes darted from the door to the old widow. "What's wrong?" She lifted herself on to her elbows. "Papa?" she cried. "Papa?" Gerde Volk came into the room and pulled a chair next to the bed. "Where's Papa?" Eva felt panicky.

"He's in the hallway with the doctor."

Eva summoned all her strength. "I want my baby." She listened for a moment, suddenly aware that the house was quiet. "Why isn't he crying? What's wrong, somebody, please, tell me what's wrong!"

"Get a hold of yourself, girl," answered Gerde coldly.

Dr. Krebel entered the room and took Eva's hand. "My dear, dear Eva. How are you feeling?"

"Tell me about my baby."

Dr. Krebel and Gerde exchanged anxious glances. He turned to Eva. "Well my dear, it is too early to know." His tone was painfully compassionate. "But I believe your son may suffer Apert syndrome. He is...well...he is not formed properly."

Eva was dumbstruck. She could not speak. Her eyes flew about the room until they rested on the *Good Shepherd* picture still hanging on her wall.

"It would be better for you to allow me to take the child to Koblenz at once. From there we will find a facility to care for him properly."

"No, no! Let me see him," exclaimed Eva.

"I think it would be better..."

"No. I demand to see him. He is my son and he must be hungry."

Paul entered the room. He had been crying. He took his daughter's hand. "I have prayed for your son and for you. I am so sorry, Eva, so sorry."

"Papa, please, they won't let me see my baby."

Paul turned to the doctor and to his wife. "It is her right."

Gerde could not bear the moment. She hurried downstairs as Paul called for Frau Nubel to bring the newborn to his mother.

Eva waited breathlessly as the old woman came through her door carrying a silent bundle. The child was laid upon Eva's breast and she gently—fearfully—laid back the folds of the blanket. She whimpered. The baby's face was severely retruded, yet his unfocused eyes were searching desperately for a mother. "Oh..." She began to cry.

"Eva, have you a name? Dr. Krebel must put a name on the record." Tears were running down Paul Volk's cheeks.

The baby began to move a little and then softly cooed. Eva ignored her father and instinctively led the child's face to her breast. The child began to nurse, slowly, and with great effort.

"Eva?"

The young woman closed her eyes and nodded. Paul and the doctor waited. "Is there nothing we can do for him?" Eva asked.

Dr. Krebel shook his head. "I am sorry. Some surgeons in Sweden have made a little progress but their help would be an unlikely prospect."

Eva stared forward. "Wolf chose 'Hermann.'"

Krebel held his pen above a note pad. "So, I should record him as 'Hermann Kaiser, born 21 June 1939, Weinhausen, Rheinland.'"

Eva nodded. She looked at the suckling child and slowly removed his hands from under the blanket. Her throat swelled. The child's fingers were fused into a small mass, like his feet.

Krebel put his pen away. He was uneasy, troubled. "Your son will need special care. His brain will eventually be squeezed by the malformation of his skull. We call it craniosynostosis. He will be subject to heart troubles, breathing difficulties, ear infections..."

"Enough, Doktor Krebel, please no more." Tears ran down Eva's face as she watched the helpless infant struggling to nurse. "He is my son. I'll find a way to care for him." Eva wanted to be brave.

Dr. Krebel gathered his instruments. "God bless you, Eva Kaiser. I will call on you tomorrow."

Eva thanked the doctor and assured him that he would be paid promptly. She tried to sound strong and determined. But then her heart began to race. "Oh...Papa, what will Wolf say?"

For Eva, nothing had seemed more difficult in all her life than the morning of Sunday, 2 July 1939. With Gunther and Lindie Landes on one side and Hans Bieber and Oskar Offenbacher on the other, she stood in the fore of the church with little Hermann in her arms. She had dressed the child in a beautiful baptismal gown and held him closely as her father prayed over him. She could only imagine what was being whispered behind her. She knew all necks were craned to see the monster-child they had all heard about.

She was glad that Wolf was not there.

The minister read from the Holy Scripture and asked Eva if she and her husband would raise their son in the doctrines of the Gospel. Eva answered with a bold, "We will." The congregation was then asked to commit itself to Hermann's Christian upbringing. The sanctuary returned a half-hearted assent.

But the congregation's whispers didn't matter to Eva. Her own mother had feigned illness; she was too ashamed to have the whole church see such a sight. As chairwoman of the NSF, the woman had even received letters from a few Party members who complained about the child being racially unfit.

She handed her son to her father who lifted his grandson into his embrace with swollen eyes. He carefully lowered the blanket from Hermann's face and removed the child's little hat. A murmur rippled through the congregation. Eva stiffened.

The minister tilted an old pewter pitcher to pour the waters of the Holy Spirit lightly atop the child's head saying, "I baptize thee, Hermann Volk Kaiser, in the name of the Father, the Son, and the Holy Spirit, Amen." The little Christian cried faintly and his grandfather quickly wiped the water from his face. Paul then bent forward and kissed the child on the cheek and handed him back to Eva with a prayer of blessing.

Strengthened by the knowledge of God's favor on her son and by the friendship of those standing with her, Eva turned and faced the congregation. With a determined smile she then walked her baby proudly down the aisle and out the door into the summer's day.

⌖

Three weeks later Eva stood stone-faced and well-braced at her door as she watched her husband march up-hill in his summer uniform. Released for leave two days before, Wolf had taken the train from Dresden which lay in the east of Germany near the former Czechoslovakian border. Eva thought he looked tired and out-of-sorts, even from a distance. She pinned on the silver brooch he had bought her in Basel in the hopes it might mean something to him.

The twenty-three year old soldier came through the front door and put down his duffle bag. Keeping his eyes off his wife and child, he removed a kerchief from his pocket and wiped the sweat off his face. He then removed his cap and ran his fingers through his sweat-soaked hair.

"Hello, Wolf."

He bent forward and gave Eva a dutiful kiss. "I need a beer."

Eva held the baby forward. "Don't you want to meet your son?"

Wolf had been warned about the child's condition; he was hesitant. But nothing had prepared him for what he saw. Little Hermann Kaiser had grown a little but his deformities now seemed all the more pronounced. Dr. Krebel's original diagnosis of Apert syndrome had been confirmed by a second opinion from a specialist in Köln. Wolf stepped backward, cursing. "Whatever that is, it isn't mine. Get my beer."

Eva pulled the child to her breast. "Yes, he is your son, Wolf. He is *our* son."

The man glared at his wife. "He looks like someone smashed his face with a rifle butt."

"What a horrible thing to say." Eva spun about angrily on her heels when Wolf grabbed her elbow. "We are not keeping him. He's a disgrace."

Eva's face reddened with rage. "Keep your hands off of me. It's you who's a disgrace."

Wolf held tightly to Eva's arm and cursed at her with a long string of profanities.

Eva's mouth went dry but she held her ground. "Act like a man and look at your son." She turned Hermann's face toward his father once more. "Look, Wolf, look at him. He needs you to love him and he needs you to get him help. Krebel says in Sweden..."

"Never." Wolf walked into the kitchen and poured a glass of beer from the pitcher. He drank it, then another. Wiping foam from his upper lip he turned on Eva. "How can I stay here with...with that? On my next leave home this...this thing had better be gone."

Eva quickly laid Hermann into the cradle that Hans Bieber had made for him. She tucked his blanket under his chin with trembling fingers and walked back to the kitchen. She lifted her chin. "I won't do it. I will not give up my baby."

Wolf turned his back to Eva for a moment and leaned on a counter. His shoulders tightened and his hands closed into fists. "Give that thing away, woman. I demand it."

"No."

Wolf whirled about with a face twisted in rage. "Tell me you will get rid of that thing or I will do it."

Eva started to shake so badly that she could barely move her lips. "No."

Saying nothing more, Wolf threw his beer glass into a wall, then slapped the young mother, hard. Eva fell backward, collapsing to the floor. Wolf bent over and slapped her again. "Did you hear me!"

Eva struggled to her feet and lunged at the man with a pitiful cry. Wolf seized her by her shoulders and heaved her into a wall, then grabbed her by the throat and squeezed. The woman gagged and her eyes began to bulge. She clawed at Wolf's face, desperately.

"This is not my son. I don't know who's been in our bed but this is not my son. Do you understand?"

Choking, Eva nodded.

Wolf tore the brooch off Eva's dress, then turned and grabbed the baby from the cradle. "A miscarriage and now this. You don't deserve me."

For weeks, Eva maintained a frantic search to find her child in the medical institutions of the region. Dr. Krebel insisted that he could not find the child, nor could any of his colleagues in Koblenz. Eva wasn't so sure. She made a list of every known institution between Weinhausen and Dresden, reasoning that Wolf would have taken a train back to his battalion and possibly dropped the child at a hospital along the way. She then spent a small fortune calling them from her father's phone. By mid-August, Eva had begun to fear the worst.

Nearly insane with worry, Eva had her mother contact Fritz Schiller, the Gestapo agent. Schiller went so far as to have Wolf detained for questioning in the field. The official report indicated that Wolf knew nothing about the alleged abduction. Considering his spotless military record and his recent promotion to Obergefreiter no charges were filed and the Gestapo began to look at Eva, instead.

Of course, the police and the military had greater concerns than those of a distraught mother in a wine village along the Mosel. The English government had recently instituted conscription and had formed alliances against Germany with Poland, France, Greece, and Romania—an act received by Hitler as provocation.

Eva paid little attention to any of it. She no longer cared about Poland. She didn't join in the outrage of Germans everywhere who thought the peace plan the Poles just rejected was fair. Her neighbors had told her that all the Führer wanted was protection for German ethnics within Poland, the return of the independent German city of Danzig which was still under the rule of the League of Nations, and corridor access to Germany's cut-off province of East Prussia. To many, war was becoming a frightening possibility.

But Eva didn't care

She was waging a war of her own. She had written unanswered

letters to Wolf, begging for him to tell her of Hermann; promising on her brother Daniel's memory to never tell a soul. "Even if you killed him," she had written, "I just need to know."

Paul Volk had written as well, as had Bieber and even Gunther Landes. But it was Gunther who received the only response, one informing him of the true parentage of Lindie's estranged mixed-breed daughter of rape.

"I'm so sorry, Lindie," sobbed Eva.

"How did he know? You must have told him."

"No, I swear to you, I did not. I think he just figured it out. Besides us, only Oskar Offenbacher knew and he swears on the Bible that he never said a word to anyone. I believe him."

"How could he have figured it out?"

Eva thought hard. "Maybe he knew someone at the hospital." Eva suddenly wondered something else. *Maybe that person knows of Hermann.* She changed the subject. "Does Gunther really think your body is forever soiled by the African?" asked Eva.

Lindie nodded. "He left for the shop without saying a word to me. I know his father does...he swears that one of our children will have kinky hair. And if not one of ours, then probably one in the next generation or the next. He says it takes ten generations to get rid of bad seed."

Eva put her arm around Lindie. "Gunther will forgive you."

"Forgive me? For what?"

"For not telling him."

Lindie's face flushed. "So, you think I should have told him? You never said that before."

"I..."

"Forget it. It's always been easier for you."

"What!" Eva was in no mood for this again. "Easier? You have no idea about my life, Lindie." Eva walked to a far wall. "You never have. You don't know what it's like to love two men and pick the wrong one. You never lost a brother; you don't have a drunken mother! Don't ever say that again." Eva headed for the door when the bells began to ring from Horchheim's nearby church. At the same time, Gunther's father began shouting from the pig yard.

"He says to put the radio on." Lindie hurried into the living room. In moments, Old Landes, Lindie and Eva were leaning toward the sounds of an urgent speech now being delivered by Hitler to the Reichstag in Berlin:

"...Danzig was separated from us; the Corridor was annexed by Poland. As in other German territories of the East, German minorities have been ill-treated in the most distressing manner. More than 1,000,000 people of German blood had to leave their homeland in the years 1919-20..."

"What's going on?" Lindie was confused.

"Last night the Poles attacked a German radio station," answered Old Landes.

"But I am wrongly judged if my love of peace and my patience are mistaken for weakness or even cowardice. Therefore, I informed the British Government last night that I can no longer find any willingness on the part of the Polish Government to conduct serious negotiations with us...These proposals for mediation have failed because they were answered with the sudden Polish general mobilization, followed by more Polish atrocities. These were again repeated last night. Recently in one night there were as many as twenty-one frontier incidents; last night there were fourteen, of which three were quite serious. I have, therefore, resolved to speak to Poland in the same language that Poland has used toward us in the past months."

"I don't understand." said Eva.

"I have declared that the frontier between France and Germany is a final one. I have repeatedly offered friendship and, if necessary, the closest co-operation to Britain...Germany has no interests in the West, and our western wall is for all time the frontier of the Reich on the west...and

as long as others do not violate their neutrality we will likewise take every care to respect it...

I will not war against women and children. I have ordered my air force to restrict itself to attacks on military objectives. If, however, the enemy thinks he can fight by other methods, he will receive an answer that will deprive him of hearing and sight."

"I think we're going to war!" exclaimed Lindie.

"For the first time Polish regular soldiers fired on our own territory. Since 5:45 a. m. we have been returning the fire, and from now on bombs will be met with bombs. Whoever fights with poison gas will be fought with poison gas. Whoever departs from the rules of humane warfare can only expect that we shall do the same. I will continue this struggle, no matter against whom, until the safety of the Reich and its rights are secured."

Eva trembled. "War! I cannot believe it. It seems like a..."

"A terrible dream," murmured Old Landes. He had fought in the Great War. "No good German wants this again."

"I am from now on just the first soldier of the German Reich...As a National Socialist and as German soldier I enter upon this struggle with a stout heart. My whole life has been only one long struggle for my people, for its restoration, and for Germany. There has been only one watchword for that struggle: faith in this people. One word I have never learned is surrender...I would, therefore, like to assure all the world that a November 1918 will never be repeated in German history..."

Old Landes stood and stared out the window. "Lloyd George predicted this would happen. You can't put two million Germans under the heel of the Poles and expect anything less."

"...It is quite unimportant whether we ourselves live, but it is essential that our people shall live, that Germany shall live. The sacri-

fice that is demanded of us is not greater than the sacrifice that many other generations have made. If we form a community closely bound together by vows, ready for anything, resolved to never surrender, then our will shall master every hardship...If our will is so strong that no hardship and suffering can subdue it, then our will and our German might shall prevail!"

Old Landes wiped his brow and slowly poured himself a morning beer. He looked sadly at the two girls now staring at him, waiting for him to say something. The old man took a drink and glanced at the old mantle clock, ticking as if nothing had really changed—as if nothing really ever changed. Old Landes knew better. "May God have mercy on us all."

The day was Friday, 1 September 1939

PART III
HE THAT HATH EARS, LET HIM HEAR
1940-1945

"My Christian feelings point me to my Lord and Savior as a fighter. They point me toward the man who, once lonely and surrounded by only a few followers, recognized these Jews and called for battle against them, and who, as the true God, was not only the greatest sufferer but also the greatest warrior."

Adolf Hitler

**"Our Hitler made every conceivable effort to prevent the clash of nations that he foresaw. And how often he has tried to end this war at the earliest possible moment...He did not want war, and did everything in his power to prevent it. Now that it has been forced upon him, he stands at the head of his people to wage it with every means."*

Joseph Goebbels, Nazi Minister of Information and Propaganda

CHAPTER TWENTY-ONE

26 AUGUST 1940.

Stunned, Wolf glanced at his twitching passenger who hung over the edge of the sidecar dead with a bullet through his forehead. Twenty meters away a black car lay on its side with its wheels whirling wildly in a cloud of summer dust.

Wolf swung his leg over the worn seat of his motorcycle and jerked a Luger from his hip. He pulled the goggles off his face. Not a half-hour before he and his companion had been sipping red wine and enjoying a plate of summer fruits and camembert cheese along the waters of the Eure just outside of Chartres. Now this.

With his cycle idling behind, Wolf walked toward the car and the body of a civilian lying awkwardly in the roadway. A few meters away lay a British-made Bren assault rifle. "Partisans." Wolf approached the car slowly, limping from wounds received almost a year before outside of Krasnystaw, Poland. He stopped and listened to some shuffling inside. A pair of hands then appeared grasping either side of a broken window as someone began to lift themselves out. Wolf raised his weapon.

"What?" Eva clutched her heart.

Andreas beamed. He thought he might float to the ceiling. He was on his last day of leave from his battalion in the Fourth Army now stationed in Poitiers, France. "Herr Bieber and I found him this morning."

Eva held a kerchief to her eyes. The woman had never believed that Wolf had murdered her child. She was convinced that he had acted out of fatigue and disappointment—that he could not possibly be *that* wicked.

For the last eleven months she had turned her world upside down looking for the child. In fact, while Wolf, Andreas, and 1.8 million other young German men had swept over Poland, Eva had traveled to every state and church institution from Frankfurt to Cologne. While others groaned when England and France declared war against Germany, Eva made phone calls. And when her neighbors held their collective breath for England and France to consider the Führer's peace initiatives, Eva had visited each institution a second time. Then, as Wolf and Andreas marched through the surrendered Netherlands, Belgium, and France, Eva had pressed on, widening the search eastward.

"How can I ever thank you! Where, where is he? Is he well? Did you see him?"

"Yes, Eva, we both saw him. He is well." The young man's eyes were wet. He wiped them, hastily, and turned to Bieber. "Go ahead. You tell her where."

"Hadamar—the Hessian state hospital in Hadamar."

Eva was stunned. "Hadamar? Near Limburg? But I was there...twice!"

"And what did you tell them?" asked Hans.

"I...I told them to check admissions for a Hermann Kaiser, born July 1939. I told them about his condition..."

"Of course. That's exactly what we all did."

Bieber slapped Andreas on the back. "*He* figured it out."

Andreas blushed. "I found Hermann under a different name. Just a lucky guess."

Eva was confused.

"It turns out that Wolf admitted him under the name, 'Paul Bauer'. And he even had a fresh diaper."

Eva suddenly wanted to take Andreas in her arms; she wished

she could chase old Bieber away and make love to him then and there. She bit her lip. "I need to tell my father at once."

Paul Volk had been nearly as desperate as Eva to find Hermann. He had enlisted the help of pastors and priests throughout the region and went so far as to humiliate himself by asking his wife's Gestapo friend to interrogate Wolf again. Unfortunately, Wolf was now a war hero. The soldier had managed to single-handedly save the lives of several senior officers (including two wealthy 'Vons' and an SS Death Heads colonel) from an ambush near Jedrzejow in the first week of the Polish campaign. According to Schiller, that placed Wolf "out of reach."

"Wonderful news!" said Paul. "But you'll have to convince the officials that you're his mother."

Eva furrowed her brow. "How will I do that?"

⌖

"Halt!" barked Wolf.

The crown of someone's head was rising from inside the overturned automobile. At the sound of Wolf's command, a woman's voice answered. "*Je n'y suis pour rien!*"

"In German!"

"*Non... ne parle pas Allemand.*"

"Out! Out of the car," Wolf motioned angrily with his arm.

The woman slowly pulled herself through the window. She was bleeding from both forearms and her face had been cut. She pointed into the car and begged something of Wolf in French.

Wolf walked slowly forward and motioned for the woman to climb down. He circled warily and peered through the windshield and spotted a small boy lying inside, still as death. Wolf glanced past the boy and into the empty seats. Cartridge casings lay scattered about near a lady's handbag. With the French woman trembling on the road, Wolf holstered his pistol and climbed into the car. He tossed the handbag out, then lifted the boy from the car and laid him by a nearby tree. The boy's mother started to cry.

"Shut up, woman." Wolf walked over to the dead partisan and

dug through the man's pockets. "Nothing." He looked into the man's face. "Looks like a Jew to me." Spitting, he returned to his motorcycle.

Under the tree, the woman was holding her son and stroking the boy's hair. She called to Wolf. Wolf ignored her for the moment, staring stone-faced at the body of his comrade instead. Wolf turned off the cycle's ignition, then pulled his companion from the sidecar and laid his body on the shoulder of the road. He had liked the young lieutenant. The man had just returned from his wedding in Stuttgart. He set the lieutenant's arms and legs straight, and covered his face with a blanket.

"I said, shut up." Wolf scowled at the woman, then noticed that the lad was beginning to wake. He retrieved an oval canteen from the cycle and handed it to the mother who poured water over her cupped hand into the boy's sputtering mouth. Wolf walked back to the dead civilian. "So, partisans."

The woman knew the word. A look of terror fell over her. "*Non, non*," she quickly answered. "No partisan." She pointed to the dead Frenchman. "*Non*....not mine."

Wolf smiled. "So, you know a little German after all." He imagined her to be thirty, maybe a little older. He thought her pretty. He noted that the boy was fair like the woman and not likely the son of the partisan. "So, if you're no partisan, than why were you driving him?"

"Eh?"

Wolf pointed to his comrade's body. "He didn't deserve this. Not from some coward in a speeding car." His lips curled. "We threw out your corrupt politicians, we bring you good order. We pay your shopkeepers for what we need. Lots of your countrymen are happy we're here. But not you and him, right?"

The woman turned away and gave her son more water.

"Don't turn your face from me!" He snatched the canteen from her hand.

The woman lunged for the water, shouting something about "Philippe" again. Wolf pulled the pistol from his hip.

The French woman stood, slowly. Perspired and still bleeding from the accident, she lifted her chin.

Wolf ground his teeth. He snatched her handbag off the

ground and dumped its contents. In the middle was a tangled golden chain that glittered under the August sun. He bent over and picked it up. "Now I understand." He twirled a Star of David in the air. "What a surprise. We are riding along minding our own business when three Jews in a car sneak up behind us and shoot."

The woman paled. "*Non, non,*" she insisted. "*Non* mine." She knelt by her son and held him, tightly. Her tone turned to pleading.

"So now you beg." Wolf squatted in front of the woman and gently hung the necklace over her head as he turned his face upward toward the drone of Luftwaffe bombers returning from a raid over England. "The Tommies have no business in this war...but I suppose you people are turning a profit from it." His face was relaxed; his voice was calm and reassuring. The woman, not understanding a word he had said, slowly stopped trembling. She offered a hopeful smile.

Wolf looked up and down the road. A car was parked in front of a distant cottage. He saw no one. He put his Luger into its holster and sat next to the woman. "I learned plenty about Jew partisans in Poland." The woman tensed at the words, 'Jew' and 'partisan' as he removed his helmet to look at a fresh dimple. "Hmm. Your friend almost got me." He laughed and winked at Phillipe.

The Luftwaffe squadron droned closer. Wolf watched their thin formation. "We lost quite a few today." He faced the woman and her son again, thinking. *Of course, the Major would object,* he thought. *He'd insist we give them a proper trial...all things in order.* His eyes began to move, unnaturally. "Major Koch is a Bavarian school teacher, you know, soft as one of their Dampfnudels."

Wolf patted Philippe on the head and then stood as he dug in the mess kit at his belt for a Belgian chocolate. He unwrapped it slowly. "I really should be in a Death Heads unit. They have the stomach for this sort of thing..." His voice faded a little and he stared blankly, lost in some otherness.

He abruptly popped the chocolate into his mouth. Then, with a face turned instantly hard as hammered steel, he snapped his pistol from his hip and fired it, twice.

The very next morning, Eva and her father took an early train from Weinhausen. They crossed the Rhein and changed platforms in Koblenz for the train to Limburg-an-der-Lahn. At the station they hailed a cab that took them the ten kilometers of freshly paved roads north to the quiet town of Hadamar. Finally, the pair stood at the entrance of the large, two-story hospital that overlooked the town from a small rise. The sign read, *Landesheilanstalt Hessen*.

"Are you ready, Eva?"

She nodded, anxiously squeezing a stuffed bear tightly in one hand. The two entered a tiled foyer and walked down a wide corridor toward the administrator's offices. The air smelled of soap and alcohol. Large ceiling fans turned lazily overhead.

Eva's heart was pounding.

A squat, irritable woman greeted the pair coldly and led them into a wood-paneled office where a narrow-faced administrator peered over wire spectacles. "Heil Hitler." He shuffled through some papers dispassionately. "Yes, here are the admission documents." The man scanned the contents of a thin folder. "So, young woman, you claim to be the mother."

Eva nodded.

"And can you prove it?"

Paul Volk leaned forward, calmly. "I am the child's grandfather and his pastor. I baptized the boy on 2 July 1939 in the Evangelical Church of Weinhausen. Here is the certificate."

The official read the certificate quickly. "This is for a Hermann Volk Kaiser. Our patient is Paul Bauer. I am confused." He set down his glasses and waited as Paul and Eva tried to explain.

"Preposterous."

A nurse knocked on the office door. She was carrying a baby boy in a summer blanket. "Mein Herr?"

The young mother bolted from her chair. "Oh, Hermann!" She insisted that the nurse yield the baby to her.

"No, Frau Kaiser," said the official.

"But… this is my son!" Eva shouted. "Papa?"

"You must be quiet! Sit." The official stared Eva into her seat. "Now, papers, please." Paul and Eva produced their national I.D.'s which consisted of their photos, thumb prints and racial backgrounds. Satisfied for the moment, he relented. "Let the woman hold the child."

Eva's heart raced. She stretched her arms to receive her baby and at the touch of his warm little body she shuddered for joy. Hermann had not changed other than having grown. His disfigurements were what they were and his eyes belied a dysfunctional brain. But the mother saw through it all to the soul cramped within the broken shell. Eva cooed softly into the boy's ear and nuzzled him, softly; she laid the stuffed bear in his arms.

With Eva's attentions fixed on Hermann, the administrator and Paul Volk began a laborious review of the facts as they were known. The official reasoned that a minister's word ought to be sufficient. He further reasoned that no woman in her right mind would claim this particular child as her own unless she really was the mother. Yet, it was also true that a soldier claiming to be Ernst Bauer had admitted the boy on the night of 29 July 1939.

Paul asked to see the admission form. "Did no one ask for his identification?"

The official shifted in his seat. "He arrived late in the evening and met with a junior administrator. Apparently he was very persuasive." The man poured some coffee. "I am sorry for any confusion but until this matter is cleared up I simply cannot release the child. You must understand my position."

Eva's ears cocked. She stood. "Hermann is my son and I'm not leaving without him."

"Eva," began Paul. "I'm afraid the law does not allow you take him. Not yet."

"Frau Kaiser, the law requires doctors and midwives to report damaged children at birth. Your doctor would have reported him under his correct name so we'll have to search the records."

Eva grit her teeth. "You can check what you want while he is at home where he belongs."

"You will not leave this building with the child. Now sit"

Paul laid an arm around Eva's sagging shoulders. "My dear Eva, perhaps you can visit the child?" He turned to the official. "You allow groups to visit the infirmed all the time."

"This may be different."

"How so?"

The man shifted again, this time more uneasily. "We...we have inspections from the government. I...I would not want to interfere."

"How would my daughter interfere? You would think the State would be glad to have another caregiver here. This one's free!"

"So I may come then?" Eva's red eyes were imploring.

The man removed his glasses. "You may visit weekly, on Sundays, from one o'clock to five. But if you cause us trouble I shall have to end it."

"But..."

"Be happy, Frau Kaiser. Be happy for this. If we can sort out the rest, who knows, maybe you can take him home sometime."

⌖

Wednesday, 4 September 1940 found a contented Eva helping Lindie at the Landes farm. Nothing concerned her now; her son had been found and she would be holding him in four days. Her father had assured her that in a matter of weeks the whole business would probably be settled and Hermann would come home.

"Listen," grumbled Old Landes from the living room. He was sitting in front of the radio drinking beer with his Polish POW farm hand. The Pole was a pleasant, broad-faced lad from Posen who the family called, 'Ski.' "The Führer's addressing the Winter Relief gathering in the Berlin Sports Arena." He adjusted the dial of his radio. "Sounds like a million screaming women in the background."

Eva and Lindie put down their towels and sat by the radio. Adolf Hitler was furiously lambasting the British for their 'terror bombings.' Eleven days before, German pilots—confused by fog according to the press—had dropped bombs into London's town center during a Saturday raid on military targets. The violation of Hitler's express orders had evoked a vengeful response from Winston Churchill, for on the Sunday that followed the English retaliated by bombing Berlin's city center and killing thousands of civilians.

"...As you know, they release their bombs recklessly, with no plan about residential neighborhoods, farmhouses, or villages. Wherever they see a light, they drop a bomb on it... I have tried to spare them, thinking they would stop this mad behavior. But Mr. Churchill has taken my humanity for weakness and has replied by murdering women and children.

You will understand that we must now give a reply, night for night and with more power.... If they will attack our cities on a large scale, we will erase theirs! We will put a stop to these night-pirates, as God is our witness."

The four looked at each other as thunderous shouts of 'Sieg heil' rocked the stadium. Old Landes stood and walked to the kitchen where he poured himself a glass of warm beer. "Only the beginning," he muttered.

Lindie heard the rumble of an engine outside and Gunther's voice calling to someone. A dark car parked just out of view. Lindie turned to Eva. "Do you think it could be..."

Eva held her breath. *Could it be a Party man delivering news of Wolf's death*? She hoped so.

And she hated herself for hoping.

The two hurried to the door that led to the barnyard. The engine stopped and they could see Gunther talking to someone. Eva's heart began to pound. She followed Lindie through a group of clucking hens and moved toward the ox stalls. Eva blew a wisp of hair off her forehead and removed her apron. Her hands were shaking.

Gunther turned and walked toward the women. The young man's face was sober and when he looked at Eva, his eyes dropped. "Wolf's here. He's in the privy."

Eva was dumbstruck. "Wolf?"

Gunther nodded. His round face was flushed. "He said Oskar told him you were here."

Eva took a deep breath. The door to the outhouse opened and Wolf stepped out. He was wearing civilian clothes and a brown cap. Eva's limbs felt weak. She tried to stand erect as she watched him approach.

"Ah, meine Liebling," said Wolf. He limped toward his wife.

Eva could barely speak. She hated him for so much; she remembered his rage, the sting of his hands across her face and the day he stormed out of the house with her Hermann under his arm...

"A kiss? A kiss for your soldier?" Wolf removed his cap and held Eva by the shoulders, lightly. He leaned his face close to hers. His breath was sweet with mint. Eva wanted to run; the thought of his touch made her feel sick. But she yielded.

"So, what do you think of my limp?" Wolf laughed at himself.

Eva quickly wiped her lips. "I hardly noticed."

"And you two, how are the Landes'? I hear there's six of you now!"

Lindie refused to answer. She had not forgiven Wolf for anything—his wicked treatment of Eva or his telling Gunther the truth about her rape.

Wolf looked at the Mother's Badge which had been presented to Lindie just three weeks prior on 12 August (Hitler's mother's birthday) for having born her fourth child for the Reich. It was an elongated, blue German cross with a bronze shield bearing the swastika. "Impressive. Keep it up, Gunther, and she'll get one in gold."

Three of the Landes' four daughters appeared from behind an outbuilding. Wolf turned toward them. "Beautiful. Perfect specimens." He knelt and beckoned the shy tikes to come close. The oldest was four; the middle three; the youngest a few months past two. All three were pig-tailed and blond. The baby was fast asleep inside. Wolf reached into his pockets and retrieved some Belgian chocolates. "If Mutti says I can, I will give you each a piece." He looked at Lindie.

The woman was scowling. She folded her arms. "I suppose."

"Good." Wolf handed each girl a chocolate and patted them on the head. He stood and waved to Old Landes, now ambling toward the swine shed in a wide circle with Ski in tow. The man grunted and looked away.

Wolf turned to Gunther. "Now. I need to apologize to you. You've been a good friend and my letter about Lindie's past was unnecessary...and untrue."

"It doesn't matter, Wolf," snapped Lindie. "I told him everything. You don't need to lie about it."

"Oh," he said. "Well, I am still sorry." Wolf held out his hand and the farm boy took it.

Eva watched with intense interest and not a little fear, evaluating each gesture and every intonation. *Who is this man*?

Wolf nodded. "Thank you, Gunther. You're a good friend…the best." He turned to Eva. "I stopped at the house before coming up here. It was nice to be there. After the hard times in Poland and the fighting in Holland, I thought I'd never see it again."

Eva said nothing.

"Of course, I don't mind France too much. Good wine, not so much fog and all that. Except for a handful of partisans I'd say most of the people are glad we came. Their government was no good and the people know about the Jews. They're hoping we give the Jews' businesses to them."

"That's nice, Wolf," answered Eva. She found it suddenly hard to breathe.

"I checked the Bible."

"What?"

"I checked the Bible. You still have the daffodils pressed inside. That made me happy."

Eva looked down. She had forgotten all about them. Now she wished she had opened the Bible herself so she could have thrown the flowers away.

"So what's with the limp?" Gunther blurted.

Wolf turned. "Polish shrapnel. It got me a little promotion and the Iron Cross Second Class. How about that? Of course, I'll be getting a First Class medal sooner or later and probably a Knight's Cross at my throat eventually."

Gunther was impressed. "I guess a Wound Badge, too?"

"In silver."

"And they let you stay in the army?"

Wolf laughed. "General von Faustenburg ordered me transferred from my combat battalion to Sixth Army General Staff. Now I deliver messages on a brand new BMW. Not bad."

Gunther was wide-eyed.

"So, what's new here?"

Gunther shrugged. "Lots of men are being drafted so the Rheinland's losing farm hands. My father picks up his prisoner in the morning to help, then takes him back to the POW camp at night. Ski's pretty nice. He can't speak German but he works hard. Papa lets him stay over for Sunday meals now." Gunther lowered his voice. "I'm officially classified as a machinist apprentice so I'll probably get drafted."

Wolf smiled. "They'll never take you. Your ears will stick out of your helmet." He abruptly turned to Eva. "So, we're going home now."

"You women and mothers, be real Christians; protect Christianity and your family, rear your children to love the Savior."

Lilli Otto, Nazi Women's League

CHAPTER TWENTY-TWO

EVA WISHED THE service would just end but her father seemed planted in his pulpit, preaching to a congregation that had steadily shrunk in proportion to the nation's material gains. A few years before the pews were packed as Hitler rekindled hope for a broken people. But once he had delivered, hope seemed no longer necessary.

Eva's gloved hands fidgeted and her toe began to tap. She did feel a little guilty for her impatience, though. The service had gone long because of special prayers offered on behalf of two grieving families whom Nazi Party officials had visited in the week prior with official notices from the Wehrmacht. She looked over at Herr and Frau Herbst. Both sat stone-faced. Their son had been killed the week before in an ambush outside of Warsaw. Eva felt a lump in her throat. She then glanced at Herr Dormeyer, the cobbler. His only son had died in the skies over London.

Eva felt Wolf shift in his seat. In her heart of hearts she had often wished that a telegram would cross her desk with the name, 'Stabsgefreiter Wolf Kaiser, Weinhausen' typed in large, black letters.

At last Frau Krause pushed the pedals on the pipe organ and the congregation stood to sing the final hymn, *Christ, unser Herr, zum Jordan kam*. The benediction then given, Eva hurried Wolf out of the sanctuary and waited for her parents for the train ride to Hadamar.

"You look handsome in your uniform, Wolf," said Gerde as passers-by admired the medals fastened to his tunic.

"Thank you," he answered. His fingers went immediately to the steel, black medal Iron Cross attached to his second button. Eva thought he toyed with his medal like a Catholic with a rosary. "And you look lovely today, Frau Volk."

Gerde smoothed her new Parisian dress. She had told her husband that the polka-dotted silk outfit was a gift from the Party Gauleiter in Hamburg. He knew better.

"Are we ready?" Eva wanted to fly to Hadamar, to run to her baby and hold him in her arms. She was certain that Hermann would be released; Wolf had agreed to cooperate out of 'seeing his duty more clearly.' But Eva had paid a high price for his help. When his hands came for her on that first night of his leave she had yielded for Hermann's sake. And she knew she would do it again, even if she spent the dark hours vomiting out-of-doors. That's when she had wished she could hang herself by a long cord tied fast to the crescent moon. Only thoughts of Hermann's homecoming had kept her from throwing herself in the Mosel.

But in the few days that followed she had been surprised at Wolf's unexpected kindness. He had been patient, generous, and even warm. Wolf had asked Richard Klempner to give Eva time off work so they might spend it riding along country roads on his motorcycle or walking the green banks of the Mosel. He had picked her flowers and bought her a new dress in Koblenz; he had been good to her; he gave her back the sword brooch. More importantly, Wolf had acknowledged his need to behave better and even his need to change. He had listened patiently to Eva's wary listing of his litany of offenses and answered by saying that he was without excuse; that he had learned much in war.

And so Eva soon found his touch to be less violating, less contemptible. She concluded that Wolf might not be the actual Devil enfolding her at night; he might just be a lesser demon or, more likely, just an unsettled angel. Her skin had stopped crawling when he held her and the knots in her belly had begun to loose.

She had found a way to believe in him, again.

But Eva still struggled with forgiveness. Wolf seemed sorry enough about Hermann, she thought. But even if she had the strength—if God gave her the grace—*would* she forgive him?

She had found her answer while walking through the ruins of her beloved Niederberg Castle just the day before. There he had taken her to the narrow door of the castle keep and whispered that she was the object of his every waking moment and his sole comfort in sleep. "You are the fair princess of my heart, dear Eva, and I am a fool," he said. Heavy tears had sagged beneath his eyes. It was then when she reached a hand toward his and touched it, lightly.

Later, walking quietly through the streets of Kobern, Eva listened carefully as Wolf explained how painful it had been for him to take Hermann from her, how devastated he had been to inflict such pain on one he loved. He said that he had imagined Eva's heart-wrenching wails over and over, even as the rockets screamed over his head in Poland. He said no wounded comrade's cries in Maastricht were more haunting than the sound of his dear Eva's broken heart. But he added that he truly believed what he had done had been necessary for the child's ultimate welfare. He begged her to understand.

She leaned close to him then, and heard him go on. "I had to use deception, Eva, because I knew how powerful your mother's love is. I honestly believed Hadamar to be the safest place for him."

Sitting along the Mosel on the past evening, she had listened again as Wolf went on to say that he had never intended to be cruel but that sometimes life required hard things to be done. He then asked, very cautiously, if maybe she should be thankful that she had a husband with the strength to do what others could not.

All of this had made some sense to Eva. With each explanation, apology, or gift, she found herself considering whether she had been unreasonable, after all. She began to think that her expectations of Wolf may have always been unrealistic, even unfair. She had been desperate for someone to protect her and to make her whole. Perhaps she had expected too much from him.

The more she had listened, the more she believed that she might have been the selfish one. She, like everyone else, had expected Wolf to win every race; she had expected him to excel in the Party, to work overtime and earn a promotion while paying close attention to her needs. And when the Fatherland called him to duty, she had not been sympathetic. No wonder he had acted badly.

Wolf smiled. "We'll take Herr Offenbacher's car instead of the train."

"What?"

Wolf laughed. "He offered it to me before church. He says it's the least he can do for us today."

Paul Volk arrived. "Now that is a good deed to be sure."

With a grin spread across his broad face, Oskar pulled around the corner and honked. He stepped out sporting a brand new suit. The nation's prosperity had found its way to nearly everyone in Weinhausen. Offenbacher had expanded his bakery business to a food service in Koblenz from which the government's Winter Relief program bought bread to feed what few poor were left. His company was also baking bread for the Wehrmacht and he was negotiating a contract with the combat arm of the SS, the Waffen-SS.

Offenbacher greeted everyone with a laugh, told a quick joke, and then presented Wolf the wheel of his shiny new Mercedes 170V Stationcar, complete with wood siding and room for plenty. "And don't mind the curves. She'll stick to the road like wet dough on a rolling pin."

The two hour ride to Hadamar proved to be uneventful. New highways made the ride smooth and a warm September sun had kept spirits high. Wolf eased the car over the gray bridge which arched over the Elbach—the town's quiet stream, and parked on the shoulder.

Gerde and Eva hastily spread a blanket along the bank of the lazy waterway so they could eat a quick meal of rye bread, Wurst, cheese, and pickled vegetables. Eva, of course, was restless. She had no time for eating. She wanted to get her baby. She gobbled down a slice of Leberwurst and urged Wolf to hurry. But the young man seemed suddenly glum. "Are you alright?"

"I'm just thinking about the end of leave. Tuesday's almost here."

"Well, unless the British invade it shouldn't be so bad. You're stationed along the coast, right?"

"Ja. Normandy, to be exact. Cool breezes, blue ocean and great wine. Most of the officers are bird-watching or fishing in the surf."

"You should be glad. Some aren't so lucky."

Wolf looked oddly at Eva. "Lucky? You think I'm lucky? Sorry, Eva. Give me six healthy sons and then I'll be lucky. You watch what I can do with that! We'll move to the new frontiers in the East. We'll build the new German Empire. But that won't be luck at all. It will be sacrifice, blood, and honor. Forget about luck, Eva. Luck is for the Irish and look at them!" He laughed, loudly.

Eva was now uncomfortable. Wolf had spent much of the car ride rambling on and on about notions that she thought were bordering on insanity. He had blustered about shining cities in the new *Germania*, temples to Nordic supremacy and a thousand years of Aryan order. He talked about becoming a provincial ruler in a conquered Russia while she bore him warriors to lead into battle.

Eva liked dreamers and Wolf had always been something of a dreamer, but not in the same way as Andreas was. Wolf's fantasies seemed heavy-built and plodding, immutable and overwhelming. Like the fanatics in the Party, he and his ambitions lacked subtlety and dialectic. Consequently, she had begun to understand that his dreams were not dreams at all and not even fantasies.

They were incredible delusions.

On the other hand, Andreas' dreams had always been inviting. She remembered him talking of misty forests filled with songbirds and happy woodsmen. His dreams were subtle and shaded with variations of purpose. They were aromatic, breezy, and imaginative. And if they were occasionally out of proportion, they never overstepped the bounds of normalcy.

She wondered how Andreas was doing.

She wondered if he had found the center of things.

"What's the matter with you?"

Startled, Eva answered quickly. "Nothing."

"No, tell me. You don't like our future?"

"Huh? Oh, no, it's not that. I...I just...well, you seem a little...different today."

Wolf's face tightened. "What kind of different?"

"I don't know, I..."

"Dear?" Paul Volk started gathering plates.

"Yes, Papa, of course." Eva looked at her feet. "I'm sorry, Wolf, I didn't mean anything."

The soldier relaxed his face into a smile. "You really should get more rest, Eva. Come on, let's go."

As Wolf parked the car at Hadamar Hospital, Eva noticed two busses with their windows blackened and several SS soldiers milling about. The sight was curious to her. Why blackened windows? Why SS? Why on Sunday? She had never forgotten a former co-worker's ideas about the 'elimination' of the mentally ill and incurables. A jolt of fear cut through her chest. She felt suddenly clammy and faint as she walked toward the entrance. *But Klempner said it wasn't true.*

The family entered the front door and walked the corridor to the administrator's office. Eva's heart was pounding. A new official had taken over, one named Dr. Horst Schroeder who was now sitting comfortably at the desk and talking to a man in a Gestapo uniform.

As the family entered, both men stood. "Heil Hitler." The Gestapo agent quickly stepped into a corner as Dr. Schroeder introduced himself. He called for a secretary to bring coffee and cake. "Yes, yes, I am happy to help a soldier, even on my day off." Dr. Schroeder smiled. "Now, you've come to straighten out some mess regarding the child presently recorded by the name of Paul Bauer."

Wolf answered. "Ja, Herr Doktor. I shall explain..." When he finished, he strode across the oak floor and handed Dr. Schroeder a formal statement.

Schroeder read the statement quickly, then looked at the young man, knowingly. Eva thought the moment odd, at the least. She felt anxious, panicky. Finally she stood. "Please, Herr Doktor. Can I see my son?"

The doctor handed Wolf's statement to the Gestapo man. "My dear Frau Kaiser," Dr. Schroeder said. "Since last August the

Interior Ministry has required mid-wives and doctors to complete proper forms for any defective child born since '36."

Eva didn't like his choice of words. "Yes."

Schroeder took off his spectacles and began cleaning them with a pocket kerchief. "We are not your enemies, Frau Kaiser." He pulled the wires behind his ears and poured coffee for everyone into fine china cups. "Quite the contrary." He rang a bell on the desk and a duty nurse entered. "Would you kindly bring Frau Kaiser the child. I believe his official card is still 'Paul Bauer.'"

Eva nearly fainted for joy. Her father wrapped an arm around her. "Oh, Papa," she whispered. "I was thinking the most ridiculous things."

"Now, as I was saying, Frau Kaiser," said the doctor. "We are not your enemies. Cake anyone?" The man proceeded to cut six perfectly equal slices from a white-iced layer cake. He handed each person a plate and a silver fork. "It is our honor to serve a brave soldier such as your husband and a faithful Party employee as yourself. And we are here to serve the Pfarrer and Frau Volk, who I understand has friends in high places and is quite active in the NSF."

Gerde proudly blurted, "Ja, Herr Doktor. And I serve the Führer in our Frauenwerk and several of our properly Nazified Protestant organizations like the Ladie's Aid." She folded her arms like she was expecting a shower of adulation. She received a polite smile.

"Indeed. What a wonderful family, what a *German* family." Dr. Schroeder leaned forward, smiling. "My dear, we all want the best for the child." The man paused and lit a cigarette. "Stabsgefreiter Kaiser, you've seen horrors on the battlefield, I'm sure. But you should see the suffering in this place." He looked into space as he puffed on his cigarette. He took a sip of coffee and pressed the edge of his fork into his cake. "The nurses tell me that your son enjoys a certain peace here. Good for him. He's one of the lucky ones." Schroeder turned his face to Rev. Volk. "I'm glad you came." He took another bite. "Could you please tell me why the Church allows men of science to continue to make gods of themselves?"

"I'm not sure I understand you, Herr Doktor."

"Well, I could show you the horrible, disfigured, tortured souls that live here. They endure endless days of suffering because we scientists have concocted the means to extend their lives...unnaturally. You should see their eyes, Herr Pfarrer. Haunted. Desperate to be freed from the broken shells that hold them. But we little gods stand in nature's way, don't we." He took another bite of cake. "Pitiful, don't you think?"

Eva was uneasy. *What's he trying to say*?

The doctor went on. "I've heard all the talk about 'lives not worth living.' But that's not it, no, not at all." Schroeder leaned forward. "These people are human beings with souls. I see these wretches as, well, shall we say...lives worth mercy."

"I've heard rumors of fanatics..." Volk paused as the Gestapo agent took a notepad from his pocket. "Never mind, I'm not making any accusations..."

"Exactly what kind of accusations are you not making?" The Gestapo agent was a hawk-faced man with a Swabian accent. He waited.

"Forget all that," Paul answered quickly. His forehead and upper lip began to bead perspiration. "But let me answer your question directly, Herr Doktor. I would say that I...um, I am thankful that we rely on God to be sovereign, even over the advances of science."

That's it? Eva was disappointed. She didn't think it was an answer at all but rather a diversion. Unfortunately, her father was woefully unprepared to discuss such matters. But who had ever asked about these things before? Eva laid a sympathetic hand on her father's forearm.

All heads turned as the nurse appeared with a bundle. At the sight, Eva stood and ran to take Hermann into her arms. "Oh, dear, dear Hermann." She pulled the cotton blanket from his face. "What's wrong with him?" Worried, she took her seat and showed her father, mother, and Wolf the reason for her concern. Hermann had lost weight in the last week and his skin was sallow.

The nurse answered coldly. "Frau Kaiser, I told you before not to expect too much. Be glad your husband brought him here in the first place or you would have lost him long ago."

"But, what's wrong?"

Dr. Schroeder finished a brief conversation with the Gestapo agent and leaned forward. "My dear, the sad truth is that your little Hermann is in failing health."

"No!" cried Eva. "Oh, please God, no." Tears dripped atop the child's cheeks. "He's lived more than a year. I was told that should mean he'll live longer."

"Sometimes. But his condition is severe."

"Well, I'm taking him home, today. Dr. Krebel will look after him with me." Eva was defiant. She held Hermann tightly.

Schroeder lifted his hand. "First, I am pleased to tell you that we have approved the corrections to our record. This child is officially Hermann Volk Kaiser."

Wolf listened dispassionately to the pronouncement. Had Andreas and that meddling Bieber not found the little monster, he would have been happy to forget all about him. "Thank you, Herr Doktor. This means a lot to us." He forced a smile and put his arm around Eva.

Eva took a deep breath and nodded. "Yes, I'm sorry. Yes, thank you for all your work."

Schroeder looked carefully at Wolf. "Now, Stabsgefreiter, I hope you realize that this statement you presented includes enough of a confession for us to bring charges."

Wolf nearly dropped his cake plate off his knee. He hadn't figured on that. The room fell silent.

The man tapped his fingers on his desk. "Obersturmführer Schnitzler here tells me that you were a commander in the HJ before the war and have a stellar combat record."

"Jawohl, Herr Doktor," Wolf said. He unconsciously lifted one hand to his medal.

"I told him that the hospital is willing to drop all charges but the decision is his."

All eyes fell on the agent who moved in front of the mahogany desk with a brown folder in his hand. He looked sternly at Wolf. "As you know, the law required your doctor to fill out proper forms at this child's birth. Our office contacted the ministry to see if either a

Paul Bauer or a Hermann Kaiser had been so recorded. Neither name appears."

"So?" Eva leaned forward.

"So, we investigated your Dr. Krebel and it would appear that he failed to file the proper documents."

Anxious for his friend, Paul attempted a defense. "I'm certain this was merely a clerical oversight. Krebel is busy with three villages right now; the Wehrmacht's taken the younger doctors from the whole valley. He has too much paperwork as it is. I doubt that he even knows about the law."

Schnitzler snorted. "He knew enough to file a report on a blind/deaf child born in Winningen two days after Hermann."

Paul could not answer.

The agent faced Wolf and Eva. "So, your doctor is guilty of obstructing a Reich regulation with clear intent, leaving me to wonder if you were in conspiracy with him."

"Conspiracy? Of course not. I'm confused." Eva turned to her father.

Schnitzler looked at Dr. Schroeder. "I am in a bad way, here. We have a family supposedly loyal to the Führer." He paused and turned to Paul. "That is correct, isn't it?"

Paul felt the strength draining from his limbs. He nodded.

"You are sure?"

"Of course. I took the oath." To Paul, the words sounded more like a confession than a defense.

Schnitzler pulled out another note pad. "According to a member of your church, you complained in a sermon about the 'deification of the Führer'—as you put it. Is that so?"

Paul was not completely surprised. Denounced by a member? Why not? Dissidents in his congregation had always taken pleasure in putting him in the hot seat for everything from forgetting a meeting to this; it had been easy to bully a weakling.

Eva answered, boldly. "Has the Führer ever said that he is God?"

Schnitzler didn't take the bait. "I'm waiting, Herr Pfarrer."

"I don't see how..."

"I need an answer, Herr Pfarrer, one that you'd swear to under oath."

"I would tell you the truth with or without swearing." Paul had found his legs. "Yes. And if I never said it, I should have and certainly would again if the Führer ever claimed such a thing." He was delighted with the taste of a little defiance.

Schnitzler nodded and made a note. "I see." His voice was even, unmoved. "So, maybe not such a perfect German family." The man looked at Hermann. "Indeed not." Schnitzler spoke in low tones to Dr. Schroeder and then turned to the others and simply said the word, "Cooperation."

Anxious, the family listened.

The agent continued. "Cooperation is what National Socialism is all about...community helping one another. Ja?"

The four nodded.

Schnitzler looked at each of them carefully. "Good." He stood in front of Wolf. "The State will not prosecute you for your attempted fraud. How would it look for us to arrest a decorated veteran."

Wolf released his air.

Schnitzler turned to Paul with a voice sharpened to a fine edge. "I am disappointed in you, however. This is not the time to undermine the confidence of the people whom the State pays you lead. Is that clear?"

Paul felt a chill. "Perfectly." His prior confidence had drained quickly away.

Schnitzler looked at Gerde. A little smile broke the otherwise granite face. "You, Frau Volk, are well-known as one to 'cooperate.' Please keep your husband educated." He folded his arms and leaned comfortably against the desk. "And I think your dress is lovely. More coffee?"

Gerde smiled but Eva sat still as death, holding Hermann tenderly as she awaited her turn. The agent looked at her and tapped the toe of his black leather shoe on the wooden floor. "I will say this plainly, Frau Kaiser. Dr. Schroeder informed me earlier that it is in the child's best interest to remain in this hospital."

Eva opened her mouth.

"Silence. Your child is a child of our community. What is good for your child is good for the State; what is good for the State is good for the child. Is that clear?"

The young mother did not answer.

"Listen to me, woman. We are at war. You must understand sacrifice. We cannot have a sick, helpless child sapping the strength of a young woman who should be bearing more children. We have professionals who know how to handle this."

Eva wanted to be strong but tears now slid down her cheeks. "If he's so sick, I should be caring for him. Oh please, Ostuf Schnitzler, I am his mother."

"You are first and foremost a mother of the race. You are a German woman whose body belongs to the Volk. The Fatherland cannot afford to be distracted by your whining over this…this error."

Shocked, Eva stood. "Error? You're calling my Hermann an error?"

Dr. Schroeder ordered her to sit. He waited as Eva slowly obeyed. "Our policy, Frau, is that a child in this condition is to remain with us unless we cannot care for him, in which case we will need to transfer him elsewhere. However, for now you may now visit him twice a week: Wednesdays and Sundays."

"Transfer him?" Eva looked to her husband. "Wolf? Are you going to help me?"

Wolf shook his head. "This is best."

"Papa?"

"Policy is policy," is all he could say.

Eva felt so very alone. She held Hermann tightly. Anger quickly overwhelmed her fear. She squinted at her mother. "Can't you sleep with someone?"

Gerde stood and slammed her cake dish on the desk. "You self-righteous, ungrateful little…" She slapped her daughter's face and stormed out of the office.

The room fell quiet, other than the halting sobs now heaving from Eva's chest. She held on desperately to her helpless baby wrapped firmly in his government blanket. Through blurred eyes she looked at him and thought she saw him smile. "Oh, Hermann, I'm so sorry."

"We joyfully recognize that the National Socialist Movement has accomplished marvelous deeds for the German Reich... The bishops promise their cooperation and add their benediction. They also will admonish the faithful to follow their example."

Roman Catholic Archbishop T. Karl Innitzer of Vienna

CHAPTER TWENTY-THREE

Telegram Post: 27 September 1940
To: Feldwebel Andreas Bauer
Sixth Division, Sixth Army, Wehrmacht
Glanville, France

Hermann has died...Best not come...Best not contact Eva...

Gunther Landes, Weinhausen, Rheinland

Standing outside the L'église Saint Jean in the tiny village of Le Mont, Normandy, Sergeant Andreas Bauer held the telegram in a limp hand and groaned.

"Feldwebel Bauer, get these people lined up."

"Ja, Herr Leutnant." Andreas folded the telegram neatly and put it inside the small New Testament that Rev. Volk had sent him. He half-heartedly ordered his men to get better control of a noisy congregation of French Catholics who had been driven from their sanctuary by a three-man squad of the German Order Police (the ORPO) under the command of a pock-marked corporal with alcohol on his breath.

The civilians finally shuffled into place and fell quiet. "Alles in Ordnung, Herr Leutnant. Four rows, fourteen in each," said Andreas. His mind was still on Eva.

"Good." Lieutenant von Schauer took a deep breath. He was about twenty-four and, by his accent, Andreas had assumed he was from Berlin or its environs. "It seems that the police want to make an example of these people."

Andreas looked at the group of trembling civilians. Most were elderly. A frail priest was on his knees. "They don't look like partisans, sir."

The lieutenant pursed his lips. "Good grief, Bauer, of course not. But the ORPO's complaining that they refused to sing the German Anthem before Mass. That nun walked out and then the others followed."

Andreas surveyed the faces staring blankly at him. He felt a twinge. The rumors about the ORPO in Poland had been troubling, at the least. But until now he hadn't experienced them for himself, probably because the French had been generally cooperative in both the German occupied zone and their own self-ruled region of Vichy.

He waited with one eye on the police and with one arm lying across the menacing MP40 (Schmeisser) sub-machine gun slung from his shoulder.

Von Schauer addressed the civilians in a stern voice. His French was impeccable. "Who is responsible for this problem?"

A young nun stepped forward. "*Moi.*"

Von Schauer answered. "I see, *Soeur.* You do not like our song?"

The young woman was spunky. "If I were a German I would think it wonderful."

"Was it necessary to walk out?"

"Of course. We never did such a thing as this before in church so I decided it must not really be Mass. I had other duties."

Von Schauer suppressed a smile. "I see. And why did the rest of you leave?"

An old man answered, "Because she did."

Von Schauer remained expressionless. "If she jumped into a lion's den you would not have followed."

Nervous, the old man rolled the beak of the cap in his hands. He looked to his nodding friends. "With pardon, but yes, we would."

"And why is that?"

The man faced his feet. "Because no lion could have eaten us all at once."

Von Schauer raised his brows. He was amused but dared not show it. He clasped his hands behind his back. "Of course, yes, I understand, but ..."

Bang, bang, pop, bang, zzzip.

Shots rang out from behind a garden shed, missing the Germans and grazing an elderly French man. With sudden screams the panicked congregation scattered in all directions. More shots were fired. Andreas whirled about, barking orders to his startled men. "Cover, get cover!"

Lt. Von Schauer emptied his pistol at a muzzle flash inside a shop window and then ordered Bauer to flank an alleyway. "There, Bauer! And on that roof. I count six."

Andreas led his flanking squad forward. One of his men collapsed with a leg wound, another gasped and fell to his side.

"Radio for support," barked Von Schauer. He was pinned behind a truck. "Bauer, the radio!"

Andreas dashed behind the cover of a row of parked cars toward the company's truck in which the platoon's communication gear was stowed. He barely kept ahead of the bullets pinging behind.

A partisan lunged from an alley and turned to shoot. Andreas squeezed a quick burst from his Schmeisser. Tat, tat, tat, tat...The man fell away. Emptying his 32 round clip at another fleeting figure, Andreas raced for the truck and reached for the handle. His hand grabbed hold and he was about to jerk open the door when everything vanished in a deafening, white blast.

⌖

Eva stared sadly out of her window into the grayness of a late October sky. A heavy mist was slowly rising from the river and an east wind was bringing rain. "I hate this war." She pressed a kerchief against her eyes. "And I hate being alone."

"You say that until Wolf comes home."

"Well, I upset him at the train station."

Lindie lifted a whining daughter from the floor. "Eva, listen to yourself. He slapped you after all his apologies and gifts and flowers...you cannot trust him! When are you going to believe that?"

"He wanted to kiss me good-bye. We just mourned our baby's death..."

"You mourned, Eva. Wolf didn't seem to care."

"Well, I could have at least kissed him good-bye. He said it might be our last one ever. And he was right. He could be killed in an air raid...or the Russians might attack...maybe he'll be transferred to the Balkans. I should have kissed him; I am his wife." She hardly believed a word she was saying. But what else could she say; what choices did she have?

Lindie shook her head. "What about Herr Bieber?" Hans had tried to restrain Wolf at the train and Wolf had knocked the old man onto the platform with a single punch to the face.

Eva bit her lip.

"Listen to me. Something has to change and you have to change it."

"But...I don't know what to do." Eva put her face in her hands. "Maybe I should move home, at least until the war is over. Maybe Wolf will calm down then."

"Oh Eva...no, he won't! God in heaven!" Lindie gave up. "Did you ever hear from your Uncle Rudi?"

"I got a letter from him a couple of days ago. He said the day my letter came he was leaving the country. He's very busy now." Rudi had become successful in the past few years. The Nazi government had confiscated the Rosenstein Tinte Company and gave it to Rudi under a new corporate name, Tinte Europa. Rudi now provided inks, paper and printing services to much of occupied Europe.

"And you told him everything?"

"Yes. I just hope Wolf never finds out."

"Rudi can protect you from Wolf if he wants. He's an important man now, right?"

"I guess so. Mother says he's doing some work with the Abwehr."

"I'd be afraid to work as a spy. What else did he say?"

"All he said was that he would see me and talk about it as soon as he can."

A knock sounded on Eva's front door. She answered to see Hans Bieber and Oskar Offenbacher looking grim. Eva's heart began to pound. Something was wrong. "Come in, please."

The pair entered and took seats in the living room. Bieber's nose was still discolored from the blow Wolf had landed on him three weeks prior.

"Coffee? Beer?"

"No, no my dear," said Hans as he removed his cap. "Eva, I received a telegram from the Wehrmacht about Andreas."

Eva's eyes flew from Hans to Oskar to Hans.

"No, no, he's not been killed."

Eva released her breath. "But?"

He handed Eva a small envelope. She read its contents quickly. "He's in a hospital?"

Bieber nodded. "I phoned his doctor. He said that an explosion caused severe swelling of his brain. And, he has shrapnel wounds."

Eva's mind was racing. She suddenly wished she could go to him and hold his head on her lap, to feed him, to change his wounds.

Oskar interrupted her thoughts. "The son of one of my employees is in Andreas' battalion. He wrote about how brave Andreas is."

Eva nodded. She knew Andreas had always been brave. She now realized how much she preferred his quiet courage to the bravado of her husband. "I should tell my father. He needs to have the elders pray for him."

"He already has, Eva," said Hans. "I stopped at his office on my way here. You should have seen how fast he ran to the phone."

⌖

Diary Entry: 18 January 1941

Today I am 25 years old but I feel so much older. I was worried that I was pregnant again but now I know that I'm not. I should be sad about that but I don't want Wolf to be the father of anybody, at least not until this war is over and he gets normal again.

He wrote at Christmas and asked if Herr Bieber was alright and he said I should tell Hans that he didn't mean to hurt him. Herr Bieber just shook his head when I told him.

I was glad Wolf didn't come home for Christmas. I hope he never comes home but I am ashamed to admit that. I try not to think of Wolf anymore.

Yesterday I realized how ironic it is that my 'racially unfit' little Hermann blessed me by filling me with love. Hermann was the one with the life worth living.

I finally asked Papa today if I could move home. He said that I shouldn't because I am a married woman and not a little girl. That hurt me.

My days are boring and I feel very lonely. The train to work is always the same. It's filled with people talking about the air war. Then at work all I do is type. Herr Klempner is doing more whispering and he has a lot of meetings behind his door. His nerves seem bad and I noticed that ever since Hermann died he avoids me.

Lindie is busy with her daughters and I help her when I can. She wears her Mother's Badge nearly everyday. I'm glad for her but it hurts me a little to see that pin. She's really getting worried about Gunther being drafted.

I like our new postman's wife, Kätchen Fink. Her husband lost a hand fighting in France. They are Catholics from Trier. She's my age and has one baby. She came for coffee a few times and she had me to her house twice. She really hates the Jews...

Eva had not finished with her entry when someone knocked on her door. She answered, only to be happily surprised.

"Happy Birthday!"

"Onkel Rudi! I didn't know you were coming." Eva was delighted.

"I'm sorry it's so late but my car had a flat in Limburg. I nearly froze to death changing it."

"Well, come in, come in! Let me take your coat and hat. You

missed our little party. Coffee, cake? Mother baked a wonderful Schwarzwälder Kirschtorte."

Rudi's eyes lit. "Of course!" He swatted the snow from his wool pants and stamped his feet.

Eva hung his coat and hat, then hurried into her kitchen and returned with cake and coffee on a silver tray as Rudi made himself comfortable in a stuffed chair. "I passed your father's and saw that it was dark."

Eva nodded. "Saturday night. Remember?"

Rudi laughed. "Oh, yes—weekly baths in the afternoon and to bed early enough to wake Sunday morning 'fresh for church.' Yes, yes, and I remember how Daniel liked to be last in the tub so he could play in the soap scum."

Eva took a sip of coffee. "Yes." She looked at her smiling uncle carefully and thought he had aged some. His Führer style moustache was all gray now and so was most of his hair. "So, what's the matter?" She could spot his phony salesman's smile a mile away.

Rudi swallowed and took a bite of cake. He wiped his mouth with a napkin. "First, I am truly sorry that I couldn't come to Hermann's funeral service. I trust you received my flowers."

"Yes, thank you. And I understand."

"I am so sad for you." He leaned back and crossed his leg. "Now, in your September letter you told me all about Hadamar and about Wolf. I wish I could have helped you then."

Eva nodded. "I understand, Onkel Rudi. I really do. Hermann was sick and he died quickly."

The man pulled a silver cigarette case from a pocket and opened it, offering a smoke to Eva. She declined. Rudi put one in his mouth and struck a match. "Have you seen Wolf lately or heard from him?"

"I got a letter around Christmas. He doesn't write much and I don't think he likes coming home anymore. I don't like to think about him at all."

Rudi exhaled a large cloud of smoke from his mouth and nostrils. "While I was gone I was able to have some people look into his military records."

Eva's breathing quickened.

"We have the Iron Cross, his Wound Badge, and several citations as to his personal bravery under fire and so forth. But I also uncovered some comments regarding the murder of a woman and a child just outside of Chartres."

Eva's jaw dropped. "Murder?"

"Ja. The investigation was closed by direct order of General von Faustenburg whose personal aid called the matter absurd."

"That's one of the officers Wolf saved. I think he's the one who presented the Iron Cross."

Rudi took another puff and pulled some papers from the inside pocket of his suit coat. "Your husband was reprimanded for cruelty to civilians on three occasions, two in Poland and one in France—Le Mont, to be exact. That's where Andreas was wounded. It seems that Wolf decided to inflict some revenge for his brother's injury."

"I doubt it was really for Andreas' sake."

"In any event, all the cases were closed."

Eva stared at her plate. "I know Wolf can be mean, especially when his nerves are stretched. But murder is another thing."

Rudi leaned forward. "I love you, Eva. I care about you and, frankly, I'm worried for you. You need to be aware that your husband may be more violent, cruel and dangerous than you already know."

Eva felt anxious. She looked at her uncle carefully. "You're afraid of him, too, aren't you?"

Rudi sat back and took another puff. "Yes, in a way I am. With two rich 'Vons' and a Death's Head officer in his debt he's nearly untouchable." He tapped ashes into his tray and took a sip of coffee. "But my real fear for you is that the more he gets away with, the more he'll do."

A chill ran through Eva. She had hoped that time and success would moderate Wolf. Imagining the reverse to be true was suddenly terrifying. And it would mean that she had been more than a fool.

She had been a blind fool.

Maybe even a willful fool.

Rudi snuffed his cigarette into the ash tray and opened an envelope which contained a smaller one. "As for the Hadamar business..." He handed the smaller envelope to Eva. "Your mother made some calls to her friends in the Gestapo who loaned this information to us. This is the statement Wolf gave to the official at the hospital. Do you remember him doing that?"

Eva nodded, then read the letter. Her eyes fell quickly from line to line. Then, there it was:

...and now to the final matter. My son deserves a life worth living. If Fate has denied this to him then he deserves the mercy of the State. The Führer envisions a Reich of racially fit men and women bearing healthy children for the future. I have pledged my life to the Führer and I pledge my son's to him as well. Do your duty.

Stabsgefreiter Wolf Kaiser 14 September 1940
Heil Hitler

Eva turned her face away. Her eyes swelled with grief, rage, confusion. She stood and paced; the world was spinning and she wanted to explode, to kill someone, to run and hide, to scream. "Do you know what this means!" she cried. "He had them murder my Hermann!" She rushed backward and forward, from wall to wall. "Klempner told us this was all a rumor, lies spread by the British."

Rudi stood. "No, Eva. We don't know that's what happened. It may be what Wolf wanted but..."

"You know the talk!"

"Yes, yes. Rumors. Don't get carried way. Listen to me. You must be careful. Wolf's cruelty is escalating. I don't know how far he'd go..."

"I don't care about myself! Don't you understand? Wolf killed my baby!"

"Calm down. You don't know that. But Wolf needs to be..."

"Dead! Wolf needs to be dead!"

Andreas' convalescence passed quickly and by February 1941

he had returned to his battalion still stationed in Granville, France. In April, however, his Sixth Infantry Division was transferred to the Wehrmacht's Ninth Army and sent to East Prussia. There, an invitation from Gerde Volk's second cousin—Helmut von Landeck—arrived, offering a home-cooked meal and some fresh country air.

Andreas coaxed a forty-eight hour leave from his battalion commander and took an early morning train into the former Poland. He arrived at Tarnowo where three-quarters of the German population had been murdered six months before by retreating Poles. As he stepped from the train he noticed black crepe and bunting still hanging about the station, along with German flags and tributes to the Führer. A tall man with white hair and a Franz-Joseph moustache waved. "Wilkommen, Feldwebel Bauer, und Heil Hitler."

Dressed in his field uniform, the young sergeant removed his cap and shook the man's hand. The man's grip was strong, like the lines of his jaw. "Thank you, sir."

Von Landeck directed Andreas to a waiting cab and the two ducked into a 1937 deep-fendered Citroën Traction Avant. They sped through the streets of Tarnowo until they entered a grey countryside yearning for the green of the coming spring. After a half-hour's ride of conversation ranging from life in Weinhausen to the air war over Germany, Helmut escorted his guest into the small living room of a hastily built cottage alongside the ruins of the original house. "It was in the Von Landeck family for generations," said Helmut as he gazed through a window at the rubble. "We resisted, but the Polish government finally took it from us three years ago...part of their "de-Germanization policy. Actually, if it wasn't for the violence of the PZZ we might have been able to hang on longer."

Andreas did not think Helmut's tone to be bitter; the man was far too disciplined for that.

"Beer?"

"Wonderful." Andreas took a seat on an old walnut chair.

"My wife and I fled to one of the border refugee camps." He poured two tall beers from a large pitcher. "Nearly 100,000 of us were crammed into those places and more were coming every day."

"So I've heard." Andreas took a drink and picked up a picture from the table. "Your wife?"

The man's eyes immediately reddened. "Ja. That's my dear Ida. I lost her on 30 November 1939...the very day the Russians attacked Finland." He swallowed some beer. "We should have destroyed those animals in 1917."

"I'm sorry."

Helmut's voice hardened. "My Ida was so happy to come home to our farm, even if it was just ashes. She was singing again and laughing, and she cried for joy when she got a letter from her brother. He had managed to survive the cattle-cars the Poles packed us into after the Reich invaded. He was taken east but the Wehrmacht blitz was so incredibly swift that he was rescued before they could kill him. Ida was certain that our son would come home, too. But the Poles marched him east on one of their death-treks. When the news came, my Ida lay down on our bed and died."

Andreas didn't know what to say.

The man looked out a small window. Droplets of rain began to slide along the glass. He took a long swallow of beer and gathered his composure. "But, here we are. My cook has a good dinner prepared and I have something of a surprise."

"Surprise?"

Helmut held up a ticket. "Yes, tonight we're going to the cinema. They are showing *The Blue Angel*. It's rather old in the Reich but new to us. I hope you haven't seen it?"

"No, sir." Andreas noticed that the man seemed less than enthused.

"And after dinner I have something to show you."

"The Church knows that her God-given responsibility today as yesterday points her into the fight against Bolshevism, against the horrible poison of destruction of all worthy order, all humanity. She belongs on the side of all who conduct this fight with earnestness."

Paul Althaus, Protestant theologian

CHAPTER TWENTY-FOUR

ANDREAS SEETHED ON the way to the cinema. As promised, after dinner Helmut had, indeed, shown him something. He had produced a letter from Eva's uncle, Rudi—a letter confirming Andreas' worst fears and more. Rudi had revealed specifics about Wolf's cruelty to Eva, his striking of Hans Bieber and the suspicions about his criminal behavior in the war. He also noted the letter from Wolf to the administrator at Hadamar.

In the letter Rudi explained his fear that if Wolf was not restrained, his madness would only escalate. *'I don't think it's an exaggeration to say that your brother has proven himself capable of horrible things. Therefore, I believe Eva is in peril as are other innocents in his path.'* Rudi went on to admit his own inability to motivate Wolf's elite protectors to act and finally suggested that Andreas consider a measure of 'brother's justice.'

"I know about your letter." Helmut's voice had a quality of confession. "This is why you were invited. I'm sorry if this feels like a deception but Eva is family to me."

Andreas didn't answer at first. "Rudi could have just sent it to me directly."

Ignoring his comment Helmut told a story. "I had a prize horse, once. He started biting as a colt. My wife thought it a sign of spirit. As a yearling he bit my groomsman hard on the arm. My wife said the man probably deserved it. One day he bit my wife. Then she wanted him shot on the spot. I didn't, of course. He hadn't bitten me. But I did hammer him across the nose with a rubber hose. He needed to know that he had reached his limit."

Andreas stared out the window. He remembered his concerns at the house years before and he remembered letters from Lindie that had said almost as much as Rudi's. He had taken them as likely exaggerations; he had reasoned that Lindie never liked Wolf. Now he wondered if he simply hadn't wanted to believe what she wrote; by not believing he didn't have to act. "So, I'm to lay a rubber hose into Wolf's face someday."

Helmut took a breath. The cab pulled up to the curb. "Whatever you think is best."

Andreas stared out the window into the rainy darkness.

"And one more thing, my friend." Helmut paused. "Rudi was also able to arrange a leave for your brother. He's standing over there."

A jolt of electric shocked through Andreas. He peered through the car window's wet glass at the brick sidewalk in front of the cinema. The lights from the marquis reflected a dull, blurry white glow in the puddles. Helmut pointed to a soldier in a leather coat pacing awkwardly in front of the theater now filled with German officers and their dates. "There. Rudi said he had a limp."

Andreas took a breath, then threw open the door and jumped over the curb, shouting.

Wolf whirled about. "Andreas?"

"This is for Eva." Andreas landed a crushing blow into the center of Wolf's face, knocking the stunned man to the slick bricks with a thud. Andreas then reached down and lifted his brother by the lapels. "For Bieber..."He smashed his face with another blow, and then another. He jerked Wolf to his feet. "And I should kill you for Hermann!" He knocked the dazed soldier into the rain-washed gutter with a wild round-house.

Wolf slowly stood. He staggered slightly, blood running freely over his lips. "Isn't this a nice way to see my brother again."

"Shut up. Hit her again and I'll kill you."

Wolf reached into his pocket and pulled out a kerchief. "My, my. No longer the soft poet, are you." He laid the kerchief against his nose and tilted his head back. After a brief pause he surprised Andreas by continuing in a gentle tone. "To tell you the truth, I suppose I have been a little hard on her—on everyone, actually. But I've also been good to her." He looked squarely at Andreas and spoke matter-of-factly. "She has a house and a good reputation, a solid job and connections. She has nice clothes and a full cupboard. You should ask her about it yourself...when you see her on leave." His voice was controlled, disarming...accusing.

"You're lying. And I...I don't see her."

"Ah, of course." Wolf answered, sarcastically. "So, tell me, did Eva tell you that I hurt her?"

"No."

"I see. Then you must be reading letters from Lindie."

Andreas squirmed a little. "No."

"Lindie never sends you letters? She never exaggerates? And she never lies, does she. She never lied about the African?" Wolf wiped the blood off his face again and narrowed his eyes. "You'd never turn against your own brother on the hearsay of some fat farm cow. You're too loyal for that. So, how about you tell me the truth? This is really about something else. You love my wife."

Andreas stiffened. He knew he did. "No."

Wolf smiled and dabbed his nose. "Well, who's lying now?"

Andreas licked his lips. He may have knocked Wolf over but somehow he had just lost the high ground. He never had a chance to respond. A deafening roar suddenly blew glass and bodies out the doors of the cinema. Andreas and Wolf were thrown into the street. Billows of smoke erupted from within the theater and bright flames thrust into the night's sky.

The morning following the partisan attack on the cinema, Andreas was nursing cuts and bruises in Helmut's cottage when his cab arrived.

"I checked with the hospital in town and your brother's no worse off than you."

Andreas lifted himself slowly off the sofa. "I'm so happy for him."

"Are you ready?"

Andreas followed Helmet out the door and tossed his duffle bag into the cab. He turned and shook the man's hand, weakly. "So what ever happened to that horse?"

"Oh, right. He bit me and I shot him, dead."

Eva received news of the brothers' confrontation via a telegram from Rudi but read it without satisfaction. Memories of Hermann stoked an unrequited lust for vengeance that she had turned to simmering rage against Wolf and his Nazis. She had already cursed at Klempner and quit her job; she had terrified her father with a public tantrum against a Party official; she had told war widows that their husbands had died for a criminal cause. Now she was counting the days to Wolf's next leave when he would come crashing through her door.

She'd be ready.

She lay in bed at night wishing for the most horrid things to happen to him; she wanted him tortured and hung by partisans, bayoneted over and over...or cut to pieces by a Jew.

And in the mornings she was not ashamed.

For the rest of that April, through May and into the June that followed, Eva was ordered to rest at home. Dr. Krebel had told Klempner and the Party that she was suffering a breakdown from delayed grief and was not responsible for her behavior. Happy for a rationale, Richard lobbied his superiors and the Gestapo on her behalf and the young woman was given a pass.

So she was excused from all the many projects busying the other women of Weinhausen. She didn't have to help the Women's Bureau organize gift packs for soldiers. Nor was she asked to fund raise for the Hitler Youth (whose members were now working on farms throughout Germany), or even donate to the spring raffle sponsored by the local Nazi Teachers League.

In the background, however, disturbing revelations about medical killings were circulating more openly. Just a few months prior a riotous crowd of citizens in Absberg (which included Party members) had protested the removal of mental patients to an SS bus for their certain sterilization and possible euthanizing. Remembering the busses at Hadamar, Eva had pressed the issue with her father numerous times, but he answered that she needed to be patient, that the Führer would certainly intervene if any of this had sneaked into State policy.

Besides, he had insisted that the rumors had never included Hadamar, demanding that she stop fixating on Wolf's letter. He argued that it was more likely that Hermann had simply died of natural causes. As to the other poor souls, Paul noted that some BK pastors were finding ways to quietly protect patients where 'aberrant' activity was feared. He thought they were wise to not make the matter a public outrage and thus endanger the patients all the more.

Nevertheless, Eva's imagination looped endless images of her Hermann being put to death by lethal injection in some cold, sterile room, all alone with no one there who loved him.

Eventually Eva realized that her anger was draining her, so she tried to conserve her strength by avoiding time alone with her thoughts. She sought the company of Lindie or her new friend, Kätchen Fink. But Kätchen was wrestling with her own rage and grief. Both of her parents had been killed in the recent bombings of Köln.

"I know." Kätchen pulled back her brown hair into a pony tail. Her thin face was flushed from spending the Saturday morning in the garden with Eva. "But at least I have my husband to go through these things with me."

Eva poured them both a blend of beer and lemonade. "I'm not alone. I have you, and Lindie, Hans, my father, and others. The village is my family."

"It's not the same as a husband."

"Lots of women don't have husbands at home."

"But at least they have husbands somewhere who love them."

The comment annoyed Eva. It reminded her of how unlovable she felt. She wiped perspiration from her brow and took a drink.

"Why did you ever marry Wolf, anyway?"

Eva chafed at the question. "I saw what I wanted to see in him."

"But..."

"Right. I know, Kätchen. I was stupid."

"I didn't say that."

"No? You think that, you and everyone else."

"I just feel sorry for you."

"Don't!" Eva stood and walked to the kitchen window.

Kätchen fumbled for words. "Do you think he learned his lesson?"

"I don't know and he's never come home since. My father says he probably got scared off, at least a little."

"Good." Kätchen thought for a moment. "And what about Andreas?"

"He sent me a letter asking if I was safe. I wrote him back and thanked him for helping me and I told him that I believed Wolf had learned his lesson. I lied."

"I thought Wolf made you both promise not to write."

Eva stared out the window.

"And...and how are your parents, by the way?"

Eva took a breath and turned. "My mother has a lover in Bonn." She took a drink. "Papa knows, but he's in a mess with the Superintendent for protesting the arrest of some pastors."

"Your father needs to be careful. He needs to stay loyal whether the government is perfect or not. His friends are wrong to cause trouble—not now."

Eva thought Kätchen's tone was suddenly grating. "Ja, I know," she snapped. "Don't worry about it. Papa's loyal and he's not stupid like me. He praised the Führer from his pulpit for banning some anti-Christian leaflet that Party chief Bormann was circulating."

"Good."

"I'm glad you approve. I hate Hitler."

Kätchen bristled. "You better be careful. This nervous breakdown excuse won't last much longer."

Eva turned her back.

"Last Sunday, Father Stefan prayed for the Führer and gave a homily on why the English should agree to peace. He can't understand why they declared war on us for invading Poland but not on Russia for doing the same thing sixteen days later. After church I reminded him that the Jews dominate both England and Russia. Did you know that Marx and Lenin were both Jews?"

Eva shrugged and reached for some dark bread and jam. "If it makes you feel better I'm told we've executed about 15,000 Jews in Poland, and Warsaw has a huge ghetto that's like a giant prison."

"Good. They deserve it."

"Like Hermann?"

"Nobody murdered Hermann! But the English are murdering lots of Hermanns! You don't seem to mind that they're killing innocent Germans...like my parents. The paper says that the RAF caused over 40,000 civilian casualties in Köln alone. That doesn't count how many they murdered in Berlin, Bremen and Hamburg, and they're just beginning...they've done this before."

A man's voice called from the doorway. "Eva?"

"Papa?" Eva walked to the door.

"Sorry to trouble you." Rev. Volk's face was taught. He looked deeply troubled. "I was wondering if you heard the news?"

"No, I was in the garden all morning."

"The Wehrmacht is massing on the Russian border."

Andreas had been promoted to Oberfeldwebel a week before on the eve of Operation Barbarossa—the invasion of Russia. The First Sergeant was now in command of an infantry platoon of forty men divided into four squads. His platoon was part of the 3rd battalion, Eighteenth Regiment, Sixth Division, Ninth Army and ultimately organized under the German Army Group Center commanded by General Fieldmarshal von Kluge.

Just before dusk the twenty-six year old returned from a briefing at battalion headquarters and stepped somberly into the barracks of his platoon. The men jumped to attention as the door closed behind him. Andreas stood quietly for a moment and then walked between their rows pausing to look into each face. *Just little boys,* he thought. Most were new recruits though a few had seen action in Poland or the Western Front. One group of eight had been transferred from tough duty in the Balkans. Looking into one fresh face, Andreas asked, "Are you ready, Dieter?"

"Jawohl, Oberfeldwebel! My life for Fatherland and Führer."

"How about the men around you?"

"Ja, Oberfeldwebel."

"Good." Andreas walked along the line, hoping that the rest of his men were fixed on being brave German soldiers and not fanatic Nazis. "Every one of you served in the Hitler Youth so I know what you are thinking. But let me be clear. Yes, we proudly fight for Fatherland and Führer. But when the world explodes under your feet you must fight for the man next to you."

The company chaplain entered the barracks. His face was grim and Andreas gave him permission to deliver a brief message and a prayer. When he finished, the man offered New Testaments to any who wanted them. Many took them but others grumbled that they were perfectly content to rely on the Führer. Andreas thanked the chaplain and allowed a brief conversation to follow during which fourteen of his forty declared their personal faith as believing Christians to the chaplain. Their zeal suggested to Andreas that they came from churches in the BK. The first to do so was a plucky young corporal named Horst Detweiler from a small village along the Rhein in the Pfalz. Detweiler put it squarely. "I tell you all that I didn't care much for my days in the Hitler Youth but I know my Lord wants me to drive out Bolshevism."

Twelve others took their turn and then the fourteenth man stepped forward. He courageously declared that his mother was Jewish but that he converted to his father's Christianity as a child. Andreas watched some of the men squirm. *This won't do,* he thought. "So, Soldat Jakob Keck, you are a Mischling."

"Ja, Oberfeldwebel."

Andreas turned to the others. "Let me remind you all that the Führer has invited good men with mixed heritage like Soldat Keck to be one with us. Do we have any problems with that?"

The men were silent. "Good, now hear me. In a few hours we

will be entering the jaws of a giant." He paused. "But we bring giants of our own. Sleep well."

Six hours later, at 4:15 AM on Sunday, 22 June 1941, the German army sprang from its haunches. She had, indeed, chosen to fight a giant, firmly resolved to answer the highest calling of the Reich: the eternal duty of the German Volk to be the sword of Christian Europe, the defender of the Occident.

To do so, Adolf Hitler and his General Staff decided to be more of a trident than a sword. The invasion was to be launched along three primary fronts led by Army Groups North, headed toward Leningrad; Center, targeting Moscow; and South, ordered through Kiev in Ukraine and into the region of Stalingrad. The German arsenal consisted of 3,200,000 men, 3,600 tanks, 600,000 trucks, 600,000 horses, and over 2,000 aircraft. Like his campaigns in Western Europe and Poland, Hitler would rely on speed and fury—the Blitzkrieg.

In the month that followed, Andreas and Army Group Center raced across western Russia and now encircled over a million Russian soldiers in a lethal pocket around the city of Smolensk. Casualties had been high on both sides. The Russians were determined to break out.

"Bauer, get your men down!" The lieutenant's voice sounded desperate. The screaming of incoming rockets sent Andreas' platoon scrambling for cover.

"Down, down!" cried Andreas. The ground shook as a violent, seemingly unending volley of Russian rockets poured into Andreas' position. His platoon was exposed in a partially wooded field. Ahead lay a small rise of birch from which came the insistent crack of small arms fire. Andreas and his radio operator pressed themselves deep into the soft dishes of earth made by their own artillery days before. "Fire on them!" He pointed his two-man machine gun team to a scattered group of muzzle flashes moving slowly through the woods just ahead. The team awkwardly set their MG-42 on the edge of their little crater. With explosions raining dirt and shrapnel all around them, the two managed to load the belt and begin blasting short bursts of 1200 rounds per minute into the trees.

Andreas barked at his radio man. "Where's the artillery!"

"We have no coordinates, sir."

"Their rockets have a range of five kilometers so figure it out."

Another volley from the Russian 'Stalin organs' came crashing atop Andreas' platoon. Bright flashes filled the sky and the thud of vacuumed air sucked life from lungs. The bodies of men were disintegrated or tossed into the air, limbless. Andreas' machine gunners were blown apart.

"Bauer!" Lieutenant von Schauer rolled into Andreas' hollow. "Get your men forward. Go, go, go!"

Andreas grit his teeth. "Forward!" he cried. "Now! Let's go, go. Detweiler, get moving! Go, go, go!" Andreas led his men directly at the Russian infantry which was advancing with steady fire from the birch grove. This would be a race for the cover of a stream bank lying about fifty meters ahead.

German mortars fired from behind. Plop, plop, plop. The swooshing sounds of their ordinance arced overhead.

Andreas' men charged forward.

One fell, dead, then another, then Horst Detweiler.

At about 25 meters Andreas barked at his second in command. "Kube, now!" The sergeant knelt to one knee and popped the cap from his wood-handled grenade and tossed one, then another, and another.

It was enough to give Andreas the advantage.

Nineteen survivors of the platoon pounced on to the bank and immediately returned fire at the Russian infantry now hesitating in the wood. German mortars continued to drop 50 mm rounds over a wide area of the woodland and beyond.

The rockets had been finally silenced.

For the next half hour Andreas' platoon traded small arms

fire with Ivan. To their right, remnants of the 2nd battalion were stubbornly defending the flank from a fresh wave of Russian infantry. Andreas grabbed his field glasses and peered into the broken birch and spruce ahead. "Not good," he muttered. "Too much cover. If the 2nd fails we'll be routed."

Two bullets sang past Andreas' dimpled helmet. He grabbed a carbine and fired its five rounds quickly. He reloaded and emptied it again.

His Germans held.

They had been trained well and the green troops were proving both bravery and skill. But Andreas needed more of both. He ordered them forward with a loud cry.

Surprised, Ivan began to falter and then slowly retreat in the face of the grey line's determined press. To the right, the even tap-tap-tap of a Russian Maxim machine gun was silenced and the patter of small arms sputtered.

In moments, it was over.

Andreas closed his eyes and reached for his canteen. "Casualties, Kube."

In a few minutes Sergeant Kube returned with the count and Andreas dutifully reported to battalion over the radio. "I'm less than quarter strength, sir."

After a pause, an order crackled from the speaker. "Hold position. Will advance soon."

"Ja." Andreas stood slowly and watched teams of medics load broken bodies on to stretchers. He moved amongst his men still lying about the battlefield. He stepped between shell holes to encourage the living and honor the dead. He removed his helmet and squatted by the body of a soldier. "Soldat Keck." Were he not so weary he'd have wept then and there for the boy, for the others, for himself, and for his dear Eva whom he thought of night and day.

Andreas laid a hand on Keck's shoulder. He closed his eyes, hoping to see the green Mosel in his mind's eye, but, instead, he could only recall the sights, smells, and sounds of his month along the highway to Moscow. He could almost feel the heat from the smoking hulks of Russian tanks, and smell the stench of diesel, cordite and dust. And then, of course, were the corpses rotting under the summer sun.

And he remembered more. He had seen, first hand, the evidence of Stalin's brutality against the tyrant's own Russian people. Mass graves had been unearthed, mutilated peasants had told stories of torture; churches had been turned to rubble or used as privies. The list was long. No wonder so many of the peasants had cheered them as liberators when they marched through their villages.

He shuddered.

But it was again time for Andreas to set his former self aside; he could no longer be the melancholy vintner from Weinhausen. He needed to be that other self—the soldier. He needed to do and not feel. His men needed him to be hard as Krupp steel.

And right now he needed to find Kube.

Andreas spotted Kube. He liked the boy; Kube was smart, brave, and decent. Less than a year ago he had been a machinist's apprentice in Hamburg. "Kube, make ready a skirmish line. Ten meters between. I need a team at the center. Send three scouts forward. At two red flares, we advance." Always counter-attack or advance. Always. That's how he had been trained and that's what he would do.

"Bauer?" Lieutenant von Schauer appeared. His face was smudged with soot and sweat.

Andreas looked up. "Ja, Herr Leutnant." He stood.

"Almost to Moscow. Then, who knows? Maybe this will all end. Army Groups North and South are pushing hard. The panzers are so far ahead we're having trouble keeping artillery behind them; the horses are exhausted." He looked at Keck's body. "One of your men?"

"Ja."

"Special to you?"

"They all are." Andreas looked sadly across the field. Every one of the fourteen was gone. He set his jaw.

Von Schauer didn't have time to answer. Two red flares burst overhead.

"The knowledge of God's grace must be awakened in our people. We expect our German women will view their work for the German Volk as a command from God as our Führer, Adolf Hitler, stresses how he views his office and his task as God's calling."

Gottfried Krunmacher, Nazi Women's League leader

CHAPTER TWENTY-FIVE

THURSDAY EVENING THE 21st of August found Eva picking clothing off the taut line strung in her side yard. Routines had become her escape: Every Monday after work she washed her windows; every Tuesday night was a church meeting; every Wednesday at 6:00 PM was either sewing circle or baking club; Thursday dawn was for washing, and every Friday—after others returned from their mandatory Party meeting—she sponsored a Weinstube meal for the growing number of war widows in Weinhausen. Saturdays were lawn mowing, housecleaning, her bath and a social event such as a village sing or dance. Sunday was reserved for church, time alongside the graves of Hermann, Daniel, and Opa, and four o'clock coffee with her parents.

But she no longer felt like she belonged.

She no longer believed.

So Eva needed to be doing rather than either thinking or feeling. Busy-ness had become a necessity. But in those moments when exhaustion demanded that she stop the doing, she could barely keep her feelings at bay; like sleepless demons they were always there, lurking just below her thoughts, ready to hang on her with heavy arms and pull her toward the dark chambers of hatred and depression.

Eva folded her final piece of clothing and set it in her wicker basket. The summer evening was warm; a thundercloud loomed large over the ridge behind the village. A voice turned her head. It was her father.

"Hello, Eva."

"You've news of Hans?"

"Yes. Your mother feels quite certain she can have him released."

"Do you know who denounced him?"

Paul picked up the empty basket and followed Eva into the kitchen where she set a bowl of berries and a pitcher of beer on the table. "It was Wolf."

"Wolf, again." Eva poured a glass of beer. "He's taking vengeance for Uncle Rudi's letter, isn't he? He knows that Hans told Rudi...things."

"It seems so."

The pair sat down.

"Andreas wrote to me twice, now," Eva said. "Both times he's asked if Wolf has done anything to anyone. I wrote back and said no—but now this." Eva took a breath. Her tone turned bitter. "Not long ago Wolf wrote to me that he heard about Hans and would do what he could to have him released." Eva squeezed her hands into fists. "He's evil."

Paul shifted in his seat. "You should be cautious about writing to Andreas. You are a married woman."

Eva stiffened.

Paul changed tack. "But right now I'm concerned about Hans."

"What are the charges?"

Paul took a long draught of beer and wiped the suds off his lip, slowly. "I think defeatism, but maybe treason. Wolf sent the Gestapo a letter that he claimed was given to him by a censor. It was supposedly written by Gunther and on its way to Lindie. The letter said that Hans once told Gunther that the war couldn't be won as long as Hitler was in charge."

"I never heard Hans say that. And why would..."

"No, Eva. *Wolf* wrote the letter. The whole thing is a deception."

Eva bit her lip. "Of course. With Gunther in North Africa, who'd bother checking!"

"We need to pray that your mother is successful. Hans was

transferred to the work camp at Buchenwald."

Eva's eyes filled with dread. Buchenwald. Murmured rumors of mistreatment had found their way to Weinhausen.

Paul reached for his glass and noticed a leaflet lying on Eva's table. "So this is what the English are dropping all over Germany." He pulled on his wire glasses and began to read. It was a copy of a sermon delivered just days before by a Roman Catholic Bishop, Count von Galen of Münster.

...There is little doubt that these numerous cases of death for the insane are not natural but deliberately caused and result from the belief that it is lawful to take away life which is unworthy of being lived...I am assured that at the Ministry of the Interior and at the Ministry of Health, no attempt is made to hide the fact that a great number of the insane have already been killed and that many more will follow...

"I can't talk about this." Eva walked to the radio and dialed in a classical music show. "I know what happened and I just can't talk about it."

Paul stood and laid a hand gently on his daughter's shoulder. "I'm so, so, sorry for you. But listen to me, Hermann's death is not your fault."

Eva pulled away and walked to a kitchen window. "I'm so glad I quit the Party. I hate them all." Eva waited for her father to say something.

Paul thought carefully. "But what if all the good people leave the Party? The radicals will have complete control and..."

"It's not just the radicals. Hitler is a criminal; they're all criminals."

Paul paled. "Shhhh." He hurried to the front door and closed it. "Please, Eva...Richard has tried to help you but..."

"And the Church is criminal, too. You did nothing even after you knew. Bishop von Galen and Bishop Hilfrich in Limburg are the only ones who did something. And they're Catholics! Where were your BK hypocrites?"

"They've tried to work through channels. The whole thing

turns out to be legal, you know. And some of their pastors think that this may be in the interest of some of the poor wretches, after all." His voice trailed away.

Eva looked at her father with contempt. "You're kidding, right? Since when did the Church allow any kind of killing other than the battlefield?"

"Well, criminal executions."

"And beside that?"

"You misunderstand me, Eva. I'm just saying that the State may be acting outside of norms but not out of cruelty."

"You really believe that?" Eva was disgusted. "Maybe some doctor will decide that you're insane." Eva wiped her face, angrily. "So, tell me, why didn't *you* do anything?"

Paul squirmed. "What was I to do?"

Eva grabbed the leaflet. "You do this!" she cried. "Hermann was your own grandson! You think you might be just a little angry."

"I am. But you can't blame euthanasia on the Nazis; the seeds of it are all over England and France, even America. Lay it at the feet of science, Eva, Darwinism to be precise. The Nazis just got to it first..."

"As I said: Hitler killed my baby and I hate him...and so should you."

Paul closed an open window and took a long, thoughtful drink. "That's another thing. We don't know if the Führer even knew about the program. He's busy with the war. He can't keep an eye on the fanatics every day. What if he knew nothing about it? And what if he stops it now that he knows?"

"Are you mad? If you knew about it, he surely did." She flung the leaflet at her father and stormed to the window.

"But what if you're wrong?"

Large rain drops were beginning to wash the streets outside. A rumble of thunder rolled through the valley just before a voice on the radio abruptly demanded their attention. An exited man from Berlin was announcing great victories of the German army in Russia. Eva turned up the volume in hopes of a report on either Andreas' Ninth Army or Wolf's Sixth.

"Unbelievable," mumbled Paul as the announcer boasted the good news. Russian resistance around Smolensk had been destroyed and all three German Army Groups were continuing their penetration of Russian territory. "This is why so many think God is on our side...despite this other business."

Then followed a different announcement; the broadcaster's voice became commanding. *"Beginning the week of 14 September all Jews living in Germany over the age of six must wear a yellow badge with the word, 'Jude,' displayed. This will help us identify the guests among us."*

Eva took a drink. "They're not 'racially fit' either. That makes them next."

"I wish the government would leave the Jews alone," Paul said.

"So why don't you do something for *them*?"

"It's just that...well, we're in a war of survival now. Believe me, when this is over we will set things right. I see some good signs already."

"Like?"

"The government's banned more anti-Christian literature and the occultists are now banished from public view. Your mother says the Party's really cracking down on homosexuals in the SS and the police. Things can get better."

"I don't care."

The room fell silent, leaving the radio to speak alone: "*In other news, the Führer has personally ordered the Interior Ministry and the Ministry of Health to immediately cease and desist the illegal euthanizing of incurables. In North Africa...*"

Eva's jaw dropped. "What?" Speechless, she moved slowly to her sofa and sat down. She was confused. She felt a quick flush of emotions: guilt, relief, joy....and anger for Hitler's late arrival.

I was wrong, she thought...the radio said it wasn't Hitler. It must have been the fanatics after all—just like her father had said. *Maybe the Führer will arrest the animals that killed my baby. Maybe he'll arrest Wolf!*

She felt a sudden sense of assurance. She was tempted to believe again, to belong again.

And she was desperate for both.

⌖

Through the rest of the summer of '41 First Sergeant Andreas Bauer led his men bravely across the plains of Russia toward Moscow, the golden prize. He had come to understand his enemy to be barbarous but brave, poorly equipped but stubborn. The summer campaign had been terrible in terms of bloodshed and misery. Lice, mosquitoes and parched thirst had competed with the horrid cries of the wounded in tormenting Andreas and his comrades. In battle, clouds of choking dust had scourged his nostrils. And when darkness let the world grow still and summer starlight turned the boundless Russian landscape silver, the air had filled with the nauseating, offensively sweet smell of rotting corpses.

The carnage of the expansive Russian plains had left Andreas longing for the flowers and gentle green landscape of his homeland—and for Eva. He had debated writing to her again. He had written three letters and she had answered each of them, assuring him that Wolf had not hurt her. Her letters had been short and guarded but reassuring, nonetheless. However, he couldn't escape his discomfort in the exchange. His prior vow to Wolf seemed irrelevant in light of all that had happened, but he had given his word and he believed that his word should mean something. Yet with life so tenuous, with Wolf so utterly undeserving, and with his heart so empty, he found the temptation to write irresistible.

But to think of Weinhausen was not safe for the lonely young man; it was to invite that other self back in—the self of poetry and circles. That self longed to wing away to vineyards and summer days by the Mosel, to Sunday coffees and village walks.

That self feared his soldier-self.

But that self could get him killed.

The first snows fell on the Eastern Front on the night of 12 September 1941 and Army Group Center's advance toward Moscow began to slow. Melting snow mixed with daytime rain had turned autumn roadways into quagmires. Andreas' platoon pushed trucks or pulled horses through shin deep mud for kilometer after kilometer. Supply lines had already been stretched by the army's rapid advance but the incomprehensible conditions now made transport nearly impossible. As a result, Andreas and his men did not receive their winter uniforms or coats. They shivered night and day, and sometimes huddled alongside Russian peasants at their wood stoves. But by 2 December the Germans had pushed the Red Army into the very suburbs of Moscow and Andreas stared at the tiny silhouette of the Kremlin some thirty kilometers to the south-east. "If we take out the heart, the beast will die," he said to Sergeant Kube. "Let's pray it happens."

Andreas just wanted to go home.

The Russians would not yield their heart willingly, however. They had already massed a stubborn defense and German casualties had reached 500,000 men. No one could calculate Russian losses but they were staggering. In the Smolensk pocket alone they had lost over a million soldiers. Despite the numbing figures, however, both sides remained determined in their cause. On 5 December the Russians launched a terrible counter-offensive in the bitter cold which threw the German army back a hundred kilometers to the west. A month later, Andreas and his men were shivering within the stark ruins of a nameless town in the Volga River valley just a few kilometers east of Staritsa.

"R...ready?" The young soldier shook uncontrollably. Seven of his comrades had been found frozen that very morning.

Barely able to stand, Andreas nodded. He and a dozen of the men under his command were huddled inside a small shop, thankful to have found shelter at all. Without a fire, the inside temperature was minus 20 degrees Fahrenheit. A rag was draped around Andreas' face, leaving small slits for his eyes and a breathing hole filled with ice crystals. He slowly unwound the tattered scarves he had wrapped around his hands. His fingers were white, the tips starting to blacken. He cupped his hands together as best he could, then looked away as his comrade urinated on them.

The warmth of the urine loosed his fingers just enough for him to squeeze his hands into fists and stretch them wide. He did this quickly, three times before yellow ice began to form on his skin. He fumbled for a match and struck it to light some kindling inside the shop's wood stove. "Keep g..g..g..gathering f..f..fuel..."

Andreas' new telephone operator called to him. A pioneer platoon had somehow strung a wire to headquarters some half kilometer away. "Bat..t..talion says expect an at..t..t..tack after dawn." The boy was a store clerk from Ulm named Rolf Weber.

Andreas grumbled. With a shortage of officers he was now in command of 165 men in a company reorganized from the survivors of two others. His and another company had retreated into the town that afternoon; the battalion's other two companies were stretched along an open plain. "Th...thrust or a f..full assault? Armor?"

Weber returned the answer. "F..f..full assault, sir, with T-34's. The lieutenant s..says to expect artillery s..s..support at 0900."

A young private in the group began to cry. He sat on the ground and sobbed for his parents. Andreas rewrapped his frozen hands and walked over to him. "Zimmer?"

The boy shook. "I'm s..s..sorry, sir."

Andreas laid a stiff hand on the boy's shoulder. Zimmer was the stout son of a brew master from Bavaria. He had been with Andreas' company since the capture of Klin where he had found his courage. Andreas' teeth were chattering, loudly. "W..we have n..no choices.. But we d..do have one another." He patted the boy on the back and checked his watch.

The dawn sun peaked over the distant horizon of the endless east casting a pink hue over the wind-carved, snowy plain. The sky was cloudless and soon to be arctic blue. Andreas moved his men into defensive positions along the east end of the shattered town. He shuffled about the ruins and through shin-deep snow to be sure his four platoon leaders were aware of the day's tactical options.

Waiting nervously and still shivering, the men tucked their trigger fingers inside their thin, summer-weight tunics. The first whines of German long range artillery sang overhead, arcing into the enemy about to advance from the cover of a forest about two kilometers east. Andreas and his communications shadow, Weber, leaned against the side of a plank-board shed. Andreas fumbled with his field glasses and watched plumes of smoke rising over the distant woodland. Russian artillery answered.

"Incoming!" cried Andreas. His men burrowed into basements and crawl spaces as a brief barrage of exploding shells tossed bricks and snow into the air. Andreas quickly climbed out with his binoculars and cursed.

From across the snowy waste the Soviet line was advancing. But to the half-hearted cheers of Andreas' company, a squadron of German Stukas suddenly roared from the west. The planes dove at the Russians, dropping bombs on the tanks and strafing the infantry. Another barrage of Russian artillery sent Andreas' men for cover.

The earth began to shake.

The advancing Soviets absorbed German artillery and air attack for nearly a half hour as they pressed closer and closer toward the grey line crouched in the rubble. The snow muffled the clanking and rattling of their tanks but when the Russian artillery stopped Andreas's company had no doubts that the enemy was upon them. A thud was heard, then another and another. "Down!"

Incoming tank shells exploded in the streets, heaving more mountains of brick and cobblestone into the air. The tanks groaned closer like dispassionate metal leviathans. "We need mortars," cried Andreas to Weber.

The giants cranked ahead. Alongside and behind them a thick line of white-clad Russian infantry shuffled through the snow-field tentatively, nervously poised to pour rifle fire into Andreas' position. Andreas held his breath. The night before pioneer squads were supposed to have set Teller mines with a web of trip-wires spun across the open field.

Whoom! One went off, then another and another.

Andreas raised his glasses. The Soviets had stalled as far as he could see to either side. Numbers of tanks were in flames and their infantry was hesitating. "Now!"

He and his men opened fire. Four Panzerfaust teams stood from their advance position screens and fired their bazooka-like weapons. Meter long flames of fire jumped out of each as their shells flew deftly into the stalled steel monsters. One T-34 exploded and then another.

At the same time, Andreas' machine gun crews began firing from their tripods. Rat-tat-tat, rat-tat-tat, rat-tat-tat. Belt after belt of ammunition raked the open field, decimating the Russian line.

Andreas strained through his field glasses to see Russian officers on horseback in the snow firing on their own men to push them through the mine field. He let his glasses fall to his chest and he set aside his sub-machine gun in favor of a scoped Mauser which he jerked his shoulder. He took careful aim...Bang—chamber round; bang—chamber round; bang—chamber round. One officer fell; one horse stumbled.

Four Russian tanks changed tactics and now creaked forward in a single line. The leader stopped. Its turret rotated slowly as its lowering cannon took aim at one of Andreas' scrambling machine gun crews. The Germans were blown into oblivion.

Andreas snatched his Schmeisser and ordered his men forward. He could feel Russian bullets whizzing past his body; he could see tracers zipping colored dashes all about him. German mortar fire dropped into the killing field but the advancing Russian line had moved to within 100 meters of the German infantry.

In moments the heavy work would be left to the anti-tank crews who were now receiving steady fire from the Russian infantry. "Cover them!" cried Andreas. A machine gun crew swung its barrel wildly to clear a swath of approaching Ivans.

Russian losses were heavy and their motionless corpses now stained the snow-field with red blotches of blood. But reinforcements were pouring in from the rear. Andreas quickly surveyed the field.

"Freedom is our dearest treasure. We will serve it steadfastly through the storms of war, following it like the good star that shines through the dark night to show the way to the coming dawn."

Joseph Goebbels, Nazi Minister of Information and Propaganda

CHAPTER TWENTY-SIX

"BACK, BACK!" ANDREAS ordered his advance teams to retreat under cover fire from positions in the town center. Off his hip, Andreas laid down a lethal stream of lead.

As the forward teams raced through their own lines, Andreas ordered a general retreat. Bullets ricocheted on all sides. Cannon fire exploded walls with deafening blasts, tossing cobblestones, bricks and frozen dirt high into the air.

Diving behind a pile of rubble, Andreas cried for Weber. The soldier appeared with a radio. He had been wounded in the arm and was bleeding badly. "Tell battalion we are being overrun!"

"I can't warm the radio, sir."

"Telephone?"

"I can't find the line."

Andreas stared at Weber's belt buckle: '*God with Us.*' I wonder. Russian tanks now appeared rocking over piles of rubble as they creaked down the town's three parallel east-west streets. Andreas had positioned at least one anti-tank crew on each street. From his own position on the center street he could hear them firing on either side. He glanced behind himself to see a crew dashing forward to take a better position.

Twenty yards ahead a tank was taking aim at the hurrying crew. Andreas whispered a prayer. "Go, go!"

The tank fired first and landed a direct hit on Andreas' men. He watched the two men fly apart, limbs torn from their torsos. A

German MG-42 then opened fire from atop a building, blasting a torrent of 7.92mm shells at the tank and the infantry surrounding it. Unaffected, the tank's turret groaned as it began to turn again. Andreas snatched a Mauser off a dead sniper and loaded it with the man's armor piercing bullets.

He flopped chest-down on the crest of a rubble hill.

Incoming small arms fire clicked off the bricks around him. He took aim at the driver's position and released his breath slowly as he squeezed his trigger, cutting three holes in a tight cluster through the steel.

But the tank's cannon fired and the MG-42 disappeared along with the top half of the building. Andreas slid behind the rubble and led his men on a mad dash deeper into the town. They spread themselves thinly across the ruins of a collapsed building. To either side he could hear Panzerfaust teams still firing on Russian tanks. "Hold here, men. If we're pushed much farther we'll be out the butt end of this town and in open country." He looked at his frightened soldiers.

The boy from Bavaria set his jaw. "Ready, sir."

Andreas slapped his helmet. "Good, Zimmer. Come with me. Weber, forget the radio. Stay with the others and shoot at anything in a white smock!" Andreas and Zimmer grabbed satchel charges and humped behind heaps of brick to an overturned automobile.

"Take my Schmeisser, Zimmer. When I give the order, empty your clip and then mine, then throw grenades at Ivan. I'll go for the tank."

The Soviet infantry advancing down Andreas' center street had the advantage of two tanks. The platoon on the north street was dealing with one surviving tank, but the south street platoon had cleared the tanks away and were defending against a heavy infantry assault. Their anti-tank crew had made a quick decision to support the center street and just as Andreas rolled from cover they fired their rocket from the German right into the rear tank.

Direct hit. The tanks magazine exploded killing dozens of Russian infantry crouched behind it.

"Gott sei dank!" muttered Andreas. "One to go."

The lead tank stopped and turned its cannon toward its left.

Inside, the crew was desperate to find the German team. The distraction proved an advantage for Andreas. He crawled forward, dragging his satchel charge. Then, barely hidden by snow and debris, he paused. He could hear urgent Russian voices and he could hear the gears of the turret.

Andreas signaled Zimmer.

Zimmer stood and fired savagely on the surprised Russian infantrymen. He emptied his magazine, then threw his rifle over and grabbed Andreas' sub-machine gun as he jumped to a new position.

Under Zimmer's cover Andreas grit his teeth and leapt to his feet. His legs felt heavy, the world seemed suddenly silent. He pulled the fuse of the satchel charge and leapt atop the tank's track to heave the satchel under the turret. With bullets now pinging all around him he rolled to the ground and covered his head.

The satchel exploded.

The tank's cannon lurched upward like a giant finger torn from its joint. Andreas felt a shower of debris fall all around him. He quickly lifted his head and looked for Zimmer. The soldier was throwing his last grenade. "Zimmer! Back!"

A large Russian rushed the youth but a shot from somewhere dropped Ivan dead. Andreas pulled his handgun and raced for Zimmer. The Bavarian grabbed his unloaded rifle and scrambled to the rear. He fumbled to reload as another Russian crowned the rubble. The Russian lurched backward from another unseen shot.

"Zimmer, back, back!" Andreas felt bullets nipping at his uniform. Something rang off his helmet.

Howling, Zimmer dove through a window with tracer rounds eating the frame around him. "Oh my God, oh my God!" he cried.

Andreas crashed through the door behind him and barked more orders into the street. "Everybody, back one block." Andreas knew his foe was better at defense than attack. He wanted to draw them into a trap.

The Germans in the center withdrew from one pile of debris to the next. Without tank support the anxious Soviets advanced, but slowly.

Andreas barked orders at a corporal and sent him ducking to

Sergeant Kube who was commanding the defenders on the south street. He then sent Zimmer with the same orders to the north, to a young corporal named Kurowski.

Obediently, Kube and his men set a machine gun at the fore of their right flank and began laying down a furious fire in advance of the platoon's hard press forward. That would drive their Russians toward the center. Similarly, Kurowski's men trained heavy machine gun fire on their far left and pressed forward with an aggressive grenade assault.

Sitting in the center of an inverted wedge, Andreas' group held and let the side pressure act like a vice against the Russians facing them in the middle. "You, Stenzel, I need a sniper on that roof. Go!"

Andreas held his breath and listened. His ear had been well trained by combat. "Yes!"

Ivan was slowly yielding to either side. "Grenades, men. On my command, rush forward and throw everything you have."

Each of his men jerked their wooden handled grenades from their belts and waited. Then, with Stenzel in place above, Andreas ordered the charge. His men ran forward yelling and heaving their grenades. The sudden attack caught the crouching Russians by surprise. Facing encirclement, Ivan began to retreat.

The German push was not easy, however. The Russians in the rear reserve had already dragged two Maxims forward on sleds and had set them up in the middle of the street. With no regard for their own back-stepping men their crews were ordered to open fire. Tak-tak-tak-tak...yellow tracers whizzed past Andreas.

Within a minute, the Germans were sent scrambling for cover, again.

Their vice had been jammed.

Hiding behind more debris, Andreas signaled his sniper and the man deftly took out one crew. The other Russian crew quickly raised their barrel and swept the rooftop with lead, nearly blowing it to pieces.

But Stenzel had anticipated that. He hurried to another side and began shooting. He dropped one of the Maxim crew but Andreas thought he had silenced the whole team. He ordered his men forward. "Now!"

Weber jumped first, only to catch a burst of rounds in the chest. The store clerk fell backward, eyes open.

Andreas cursed, loudly. He couldn't linger. He rolled to one side as another burst from the machine gun nearly took his head off.

In another few seconds Ivan's second Maxim was silenced but the Russian infantry had regrouped. "Kube," shouted Andreas through a hole in a building. "Keep pressing." He caught his breath. He knew he was outnumbered probably three or four to one.

He hoped Ivan didn't know that.

He slapped in his last magazine and picked off three Russians in one quick burst. "Forward!"

Suddenly two half-tracks filled with grey-clad German reinforcements rolled into view from behind. The vehicles had small mounted cannons that began pouring furious fire into the surprised Russian infantry. The half-tracks emptied with a stream of fresh troops; Lieutenant von Schauer jumped from one, screaming orders. Within a quarter hour the Russians were backed to the town's edge where they tried mounting a stubborn defense.

Von Schauer sought out Andreas. "Bauer! Ivan's got two whole divisions on the way. You need to pull back so the artillery can blast this place off the face of the earth."

Through the winter of 41-42, Eva continued to struggle with doubts about the Party, her Führer, and her duty. The passing months had brought her some reasons to believe and she yielded to Richard Klempner's pleas for her to return to work. But she had other reasons to wonder. She knew she could never be the enthusiast she once was, despite being assured by co-workers and neighbors that the medical killings really were an aberration—the radicals' abuse of Nazi fantasies that their Führer had properly redressed. Yet she had a feeling that something was still wrong. What if the killings were just hidden better than before? And what about the increasing number of memos crossing her desk that referred to the harsh treatment of Jews and dissidents?

The one thing she was sure of, however, was that suffering soldiers needed her help and she was not going to hold the men of Weinhausen suspect for the odd goings-on in Berlin. So Eva joined with every other woman in the village to knit socks and sew blankets. The army needed the whole nation to contribute to the success of its mission against Russia. No matter what gnawing suspicions any had about their Nazi government, everyone was united in the purpose of defeating the Red menace. Even Eva's father had reminded her and his congregation that this had become a war of survival: Either Christian Europe would be finally rid of the Bolshevik threat or Russian soldiers would be murdering and plundering their way to the Atlantic.

In the summer, Eva turned to her garden which she tended with the greatest of care. Rationing had stripped the meat hooks of Weinhausen's butcher shop, and other products were getting more difficult to find. She couldn't remember her last orange, and butter and cheese had become premium items. So Eva looked to her cabbages for winter sauerkraut and to cucumbers for pickling. And in August she spent hours picking berries with the Party hiking club; she'd make jam to send in soldiers' packs for Christmas.

Eva had not seen Wolf since October 1940 and she had spent the time pretending, even hoping, that he simply didn't exist anymore.

But he did exist

And Wolf had recently begun to write to her again. Eva found herself opening each envelope with a set jaw. She had not and would not forgive him. She may have been wrong about her Führer, but she had not been wrong about Wolf.

To her distress, however, Wolf's letters were not filled with the threats that she hoped would fuel her wrath. Instead the young man's letters were matter-of-fact. He had never commented on the confrontation with Andreas. In fact, he never once mentioned his half-brother's name. Instead, he wrote of camp life, of his bravery and of his great pleasure to kill in war. He wrote that the chaos of battle exited him like nothing else in all of life and that he found his brief leaves to be boring. He had ended his last letter by wishing her well and by expressing doubt that he'd be home for a very long time due to the distance of the Wehrmacht's advancing lines.

The first Saturday of September 1942 was humid and a river fog had hung heavily atop the Mosel until nearly lunch time. When the dew had dried Eva began rocking her hand-mower forward and back through long, green grass. She liked mowing the grass; she enjoyed the clicking whirl of the spinning blades. Something about the rolling reel and the rhythmic motion of her arms, pushing and pulling, calmed her. The sweet smell of fresh cut grass took her back to days of lemonade and summer song-fests in the market.

Frau Wicker rode by on her bicycle and waved. Frau Krause hurried by with a basket of provisions for her Weinstube. Martial music played from a radio near some opened window. Eva paused to wipe her brow.

"G'Tag, Eva," said a familiar voice.

"Oh, Herr Bieber, good to see you." Thanks to Gerde Volk's connections, Hans had been released from Buchenwald after serving six months wearing the red patch of a political prisoner.

Hans took off his cap and wiped his bare hand over his bald head. The village hadn't asked and he hadn't shared his story of life in the camp; he had been sworn to silence as a condition of his release. All he had ever said to Eva was that he hadn't been worked as hard as those wearing yellow, purple, or black patches. The camp had changed him, however. He tried, but the light had left his eyes. "I have something for you from Postman Fink." He handed Eva a small envelope stamped 'Feldpost' as he repeated an old rhyme:

Immer, wenn du denkst es geht nicht mehr,
Kommt von irgendwo ein Lichtlein her.

Eva smiled and wiped her hands on her apron. "Yes, a small light always shines." She took the envelope and invited Hans inside for a beer and some wurst. She hastily set his table and then found privacy in her living room.

2 August 1942

Field Post, Ninth Army
Mjesha, Russia

Dear Eva,

Forgive me but I cannot bear to keep my pen from touching this paper a day longer. Yesterday morning was still and quiet. I sat alone and stared at the endless Russian horizon and wished you were here to chase butterflies or pick wildflowers like we did as children. Later, when night had fallen, I spread my blanket on the ground and stared at the boundless Russian sky and wished you were here to help me count the stars.

I wanted to weep for all who I love but my heart barely feels anything anymore. Whenever I close my eyes, I pray for all of Weinhausen. I am very afraid for Lindie and her girls...Gunther is no soldier and I can hardly picture him fighting in the desert. I saw Heri Schneider in Warsaw. He's in the SS. He told me that Otto was killed in Norway. And Udo is in the Balkans. Bad luck for him.

As for me, sometimes I think that my mind and my body are separate. Sometimes I think I have two different spirits in one body. Maybe I'm going mad. But I am thankful for each breath.

I have seen things that make me ashamed. I don't mean the battles or even the executions of partisans, because these are necessary. But I've seen police pulling the beards out of old Jews' chins and I've seen them shoot Jews just because they were Jews. I've even heard of some units in the SS and the Wehrmacht doing the same. One soldier bragged about machine gunning 500 Jews. He said a Jewish cattle broker swindled his family out of everything so it was not wrong.

It's clear that we are losing good order. No good German should think like this. Someone needs to tell Hitler about these things soon. But sometimes I wonder if he already knows. Some say the Führer has changed.

I had a talk with a troubled chaplain. He used to be in the SA but he says that National Socialism has become National Arrogance. But he also says that we need to protect the Reich. This is confusing for me, because how do I separate what I fight for? Maybe it doesn't matter right now. We have no choice but to fight. The British are drop-

ping bombs on our civilians, and I will not even think about you falling into the hands of the Russians. So if I die under the swastika while protecting you, then I still die for a good thing.

I am glad to learn that Bieber is free. Give him my greetings. Also give my best to your father and tell him that I try to read the New Testament he gave me but it is hard to believe in anything here.

Please pray for me, Eva, and for my poor men. They are just little boys with helmets.

For those I love,
Andreas

⌖

Andreas distinguished himself through the rest of that summer and through the autumn during the savage contest around Rzhev, near Moscow. Then, in the first days of November '42 he heroically saved the life of his favorite Bavarian—Zimmer—and three others by leading a night raid behind enemy lines where they had been held captive.

Soon after the brilliant mission, Lieutenant von Schauer recommended Andreas for placement into officers' school; it was an opportunity that a poor village boy could never have had in the old Germany. Nevertheless, Andreas protested loudly at the thought of leaving his men. His complaints fell on deaf ears, however, and in less than two weeks his orders came. He soon found himself on a train bound for Dresden, Germany, via Warsaw.

In the meanwhile, for the last fifteen months Wolf had followed the advance of Army Group South through the mine-laden occupation of Kiev, the muddy springtime offensive around Kharkov, the bloody summer fighting in the area of Kljetzkaya, and finally into the snowy, skeletal remains of Stalingrad where he and his comrades were trying to hold their positions against a vicious Russian counter-offensive.

By this 19 November 1942, nearly 1,750,000 German soldiers had already been killed, wounded, or captured in the war and the

Wehrmacht recognized that Germany's resources were being terribly strained. Furthermore, both the military and political leadership feared that the Americans might soon declare war against Germany. To avoid a two-front catastrophe, Hitler knew that the Soviets had to be beaten and soon. His unyielding belief was that victory at Stalingrad would sever the spine of the Red Beast and lead to Stalin's surrender. Therefore, Hitler considered it to be *the* battle of the war; he had drawn the proverbial line in the sand.

Wolf understood the high-stakes of Stalingrad and he served bravely, negotiating his motorcycle through enemy artillery, partisan ambushes, and strafing aircraft. He delivered critical messages to stranded platoons and raced deep into the killing fields to rescue wounded comrades. On one occasion he drove his BMW cycle with a side-care over a mountain of debris to strategically position a Panzerfaust trooper who saved an entire company from a Russian tank. On another, he leapt from his cycle with a Luger and his knife to support an outnumbered squad engaged in a terrible hand-to-hand struggle.

But his heroism was overshadowed by his brutality, costing him more than one opportunity for promotion. He murdered wounded Russian soldiers with delight, often running over their contorted bodies with his motorcycle. And he showed no mercy toward the Russian civilians caught in the terrible cross-fire. The fact that their own government had prohibited their evacuation meant nothing to him, even when the peasants were simply cowering in the rubble.

Through it all, the young man felt invincible. He imagined himself as the epitome of an Aryan warrior—until something happened that did more to shake his courage than Russian snipers. While preparing to deliver a message from battalion headquarters he received a cryptic letter from Eva's uncle, Rudi, informing him that all three of his protectors had been killed: General von Faustenburg had been shot near Leningrad, the other 'Von' had died in a bombing raid over the Ruhr, and his reliable Death's Head Colonel had been assassinated by a bomb near Minsk. Rudi went on to write that Wolf's superiors would be reviewing his record carefully and without oversight, and that the Gestapo was planning to interrogate him on his next leave. "If you survive Russia, you'll have to face a reckoning in Weinhausen," was Rudi's final line.

Wolf re-read the letter before crumpling it in his fist and tossing into the wood stove at the Sovetskiy train station. *I'll fix that pompous fool and Andreas, too.* Waiting for the connecting train to Warsaw he spat. He had spent a very long time imagining how he'd take vengeance on his brother and Eva's uncle, and this news was not about to thwart him. *They will certainly pay. They'll all pay.*

Wolf had been ordered out of Stalingrad to deliver a locked satchel from the Sixth Army's chief of staff, General Schmidt. The order had proved fortuitous for Wolf; the Russians had launched a terrible artillery barrage against the Sixth Army's position in Stalingrad within an hour of his leaving. Now, even where he stood some 40 kilometers west of the city, Wolf could feel the earth tremble.

At 0800 the bombardment had not yet eased. Wolf grinned, wondering how Gunther Landes was faring. The hapless farm boy had recovered from wounds received from English bombers over El Alamein in the August just passed but then had been transferred out of Rommel's Afrika Corps to the Sixth Army. *Now, that's bad luck*! Wolf laughed.

An over-weight, middle-aged corporal checked Wolf's papers. He looked like a man who'd rather be buttering a pretzel than monitoring a military train depot. "Warsaw, Stabsgefreiter Kaiser?"

"Ja, Obergefreiter. Via Kiev."

"From Stalingrad, eh? You're lucky. Ivan's moving in from the north and east. I doubt the Romanians can hold the north. That'll mean trouble."

"You worry too much. The Fourth Panzers will hold the south. That'll help Von Paulus support the north."

The corporal nodded. "I hope so." He handed Wolf back his papers and lowered his voice. "The politicians are making a mess of this, you know. The peasants thought of us as liberators until..." He leaned close to Wolf like he had a secret begging to be told. "You should see the things I see."

"Like what?"

The man swung his eyes from side to side and lowered his voice to a nearly inaudible whisper. "I was in Ukraine last month and I saw box cars filled with Jews. They looked like frightened animals. I could see their eyes in the cracks of the cars. Some Nazi big shot told me they were being resettled to work camps in Poland. He said I shouldn't ask about it anymore."

"They *are* animals, Obergefreiter," grumbled Wolf. "Don't worry about it. They wanted a war and now they have one." A squadron of German fighters roared overhead. "But, I could tell your story to someone in Warsaw if you like."

"Oh, no, no, forget that. I'm just saying that some odd things are going on. None of my business, that's for sure. I just wonder a little."

"Don't." Wolf turned away and took a seat on a slatted, wooden bench alongside a few other soldiers waiting for their trains. He leaned his head against the wall and did some wondering of his own. He wondered how he'd muzzle Rudi and how he might put Andreas in his place. And he wondered about Eva. "Dumme Kuh," he grumbled. She doesn't know what she has in me.

Wolf closed his eyes and remembered how beautiful Eva looked when she was cheering for him on the edges of the race track all those years ago. He remembered the softness of her touch and the feel of her hair. He could smell the sweetness of her skin. *If she had blue eyes she'd be perfect.* He thought of the night near the shores of Maria Laach and he laughed to himself. *When I do get home, she'll remember who her husband is and she'll be glad about it—whether she wants to be or not.*

"And when now, after 10 years, I again survey this period, I can say that upon no people has Providence ever bestowed more successes than upon us. The miracles we have achieved in the last three years in the face of a whole world of enemies are unique in history."

Adolf Hitler

CHAPTER TWENTY-SEVEN

READING YOUR NEW TESTAMENT, Oberfeldwebel?"

"Ja, Hauptsturmführer. *The Gospel of John*." Andreas had been riding the train for hours along his 1,200 kilometer journey to Warsaw. At Minsk, a handsome, middle-aged captain in the Waffen SS named Heinrich Erhart had been squeezed into Andreas' compartment along with boxes of military mail. Andreas thought he had the bearing of a cultured man.

"I don't have much interest in that sort of thing. My father was disillusioned with God after the first World War." Erhart stared out the window into dimming light and lit a cigarette "I prefer reading Rilke." He closed his eyes and recited a few lines:

I'm circling around God, around the ancient tower,
and I've been circling a thousand years;
and I still don't know: am I a falcon, a storm
or a great song?

"I like that," said Andreas,

Erhart looked carefully at Andreas, studying him. "You have the most remarkable eyes, young man. I was something of a painter before all this chaos. I see things like that."

Andreas blushed.

"And you are a deep well of feeling."

"So I've been told."

Erhart released a cloud of smoke. "Yes, I see it in you."

Andreas looked at a wrist bandage peaking out from under the man's sleeve. "Wounded, Hauptsturmführer?"

"A little thing. I'm going home for a brief leave."

"And where is home?"

"Oldenburg..if Mr. Churchill and his RAF haven't destroyed it yet." His tone was suddenly bitter.

Andreas thought the captain seemed weary and reflective. He looked at his uniform. Every thread was in perfect order. His insignia patch was something of a swastika with curved arms. "Panzer Division?"

"Ja. Fifth SS-Panzer-Wiking. We've been in the Caucasus. Terrible losses there. But I'm proud of my men, more than words can say. We've lots of foreign volunteers, you know. We've Norwegians and Danes, Dutchmen and some Swiss. God bless them all. If only their governments would join us we could stop this Bolshevik monster dead in its tracks." His voice had become hard. "I will never understand why the West stands against us." He stared out the window.

By their second morning the two had developed a trusting bond born of common values and mutual peril. The train paused by a siding where they shared a bland breakfast of rye bread, liverwurst, and a cup of ersatz coffee brought by a porter along with a long apology to the SS officer. Erhart listened politely and then rolled his eyes as the porter disappeared. "The little fellow is terrified of me." He lit a morning cigarette and looked out the window for a moment. "My wife would laugh about that," he chuckled. He pulled a picture from his wallet. "Annerose. Isn't she beautiful?"

Andreas looked at the picture of a smiling woman standing by the sea. Her hair was light and wavy; her figure athletic. "Indeed."

"I took that picture when we were on holiday at the island of Borkum near the Dutch coast. We danced under moonlight on the promenade by the sea. Wonderful." Erhart's voice tightened a little. "She loves to waltz with me. Now I wish I had done more of it with her, and..." A gunshot cracked outside of train's window. The two jumped to their feet.

"There," Andreas pointed out the window. "A man's running."

Erhart grabbed hold of the window frame and jerked the window open. He drew his sidearm—a Walther P38. "Halt!" he cried. "Halt." The man turned and clumsily shot his rifle toward the sound of Erhart's voice. A bullet skidded into the turf ten yards from the tracks. Squatting at the window, Erhart aimed carefully and returned fire, emptying his eight round magazine rapidly. The man staggered backward and fell.

Erhart holstered his weapon and sat down. Outside, a group of soldiers dashed from the adjoining car toward the fallen man. Erhart sighed. "I am sorry to have disturbed our breakfast." The man stared into his coffee for a long moment. "That sounded cold, didn't it, even indifferent. You must understand that I find no joy in what we do. That poor fool belonged to someone who loved him."

"Ja, Hauptsturmführer, I understand." Andreas struggled with a disturbing memory. "I...I had to execute ten men along the banks of the Dnepr west of Smolensk. Two of my men refused—thank God the Führer forgives that—so I took their place. I remember the looks on the prisoners' faces as I aimed at them. I closed my eyes when I fired." Andreas quickly put bread into his mouth.

The two ate in silence for a while until Erhart finally spoke. "Bauer, these partisans do more than blow up trains and murder our men in their sleep. They do more than rape the wives of our officers or kill children. They change warfare, itself.

"I found two of my men mutilated in a forest behind our lines. They were naked and hanging upside down with their throats slit. Their genitals were stuffed into their mouths and a sign was hung above them that read, 'German Pigs.'" Erhart lit another cigarette. Andreas noticed that the man's hand was shaking.

"You see, Bauer, the greatest threat of the partisan terror is in making warfare total. So I hold my men—like you must—to the very letter of the *Haager Landkriegsordnung*. These orders keep warfare constrained by rules. Without some limits, war would become bottomless; civilization, itself, would be destroyed."

Erhart took a long draw on his cigarette and released. "In contrast, I have read a copy of the *Stalin Directive*. In it, he orders his Russian partisans to dress up in German uniforms and burn Russian villages and slaughter their own people. The deception has worked to spread hatred against us. You see, the Soviets have no fear of total warfare. I tell you, they are without conscience. If they'd do that to their own, imagine what they'd do to us."

He finished his coffee. "Of course, the Soviets are not the only masters of deceit." He looked carefully at Andreas and measured his words. "You know, Bauer, we Germans freely gave absolute power to our government to protect us against our enemies."

Andreas leaned forward. "Ja. So?"

"In the beginning our enemies were the Bolsheviks, the liberals and *some* Jews." Erhart leaned forward and began to whisper. "But notice how the State has gradually expanded the definition. We are being told that our enemies are now to include *every* Jew and Germans of conscience who disagree with government policy. And the way we are dealing with these so-called 'enemies' is becoming very troubling." Erhart sat back and squashed his cigarette.

Andreas stared out the window at the passing war-scarred countryside. After a few moments he whispered so softly that Erhart had to strain to hear. "But what of the Führer?'

Erhart eyed Andreas carefully. "Honestly, I don't know, but I'm quite sure that some in his circle are criminal in their intentions."

Andreas shook his head. "I would hope the Führer would restrain them."

Erhart smiled. "An Irishman named Edmund Burke once wrote: 'criminal means, once tolerated, are soon preferred.'" He leaned forward again. "Hitler has to know that prisoners in the Reich work camps are being mistreated...even murdered. If he's tolerating that, he may soon prefer the State to go further. Only God knows what may happen to the Jews in the Polish camps.

"Not that I care a whole lot about the Jews—I've always thought of them as the 'fat on top of the soup,' as they say—but I'm disgusted with the coarse behavior of the Party fanatics. It's all very disorderly and even bestial. I'm afraid that with the Jews far from sight the radicals could get away with more than I'd like to think about."

"But I thought the Jews were being sent east to work and for resettlement after the war," said Andreas.

"Yes, I think that's probably true and I find that to be acceptable. I also know that there's lots of talk about Jewish partisans behind the lines, so gathering up whole villages would make sense from a security standpoint. The Americans are corralling their Japanese citizens into camps for the same reason, and the British stuffed thousands of Dutchmen into camps during their war in South Africa just forty years ago. But mark my words, son, if we lose this war *our* methods will be the only ones examined and we will all be blamed for the misdeeds of a few."

Andreas felt his spirit sagging. "Just like how we blame all the Jews."

Erhart lit another cigarette. "Yes, Bauer, ironic, isn't it. We may become victims of our own way of thinking."

The pair rode in silence as their train raced westward under a bending column of white steam. It stopped for coal and water, and exchanged cargo and passengers until late on the third day when the train slowed as it finally entered Warsaw's large rail yard. The engineer eased the brakes and the train shuddered to a squealing halt on an outside track. Soon all that could be heard was the steady huffing of the steam engine and the voices of yardmen outside.

After a minute or two the train lurched forward fifty meters or so and hissed to another stop. A white cloud of steam passed by Andreas' window which faced the inside of the yard. Waiting, the weary sergeant watched jack-booted soldiers with leashed German Shepherds hurrying along the tracks. As they spoke, puffs of white vapor drifted from their mouths into the damp air of late November. The conductor knocked on the compartment door and told the pair that the train needed to be vacated; they'd have to walk the half-kilometer to the busy terminal.

Andreas followed Erhart through the car.The two climbed down three metal steps and stood in ankle deep snow made black from coal ash. They started to walk with others toward the terminal when Andreas noticed a windowless shed in an empty field about a hundred meters from the rails. A thin column of smoke fell heavy from its tin chimney and outside was parked a vehicle alongside a motorcycle with a sidecar. "Does that look odd to you, Herr Hauptmann?" asked Andreas.

Erhart stopped and looked carefully. "A brand new Volkswagen Kubelwagen with an MG-34 mounted in the back seat. And the cycle is armored."

"But I don't see anyone..."

Erhart furrowed his brows but before he could do anything he and Andreas heard a commotion on the opposite side of their train. They hurried to the gap between two cars to see a soldier beating a young boy. Two other soldiers were standing by, doing nothing. Erhart led Andreas hurriedly to the scene. "Halt, Gefreiter! What are you doing?"

"He's a Jew, Hauptsturmführer. He tried to escape under the cars."

"Where's his family?"

The soldiers laughed.

"I said, where is his family!"

The corporal pointed vaguely. "Somewhere in there, sir."

Erhart looked up and down the tracks, then into the wide, blue eyes of the terrified youngster. "German?"

"Ja, mein Herr." The lad's nose was bloody and his skin, pallid.

"Jew?"

The boy answered bravely. "Jawohl, mein Herr."

Erhart turned to Andreas. "In case you haven't heard, Himmler's now ordered all the Jews without special exemptions out of Germany." He turned and put his finger into the face of the corporal. "Find his parents. When I come back, you will take me to them and we will give them their child. Do you understand?"

"But..."

Erhart curled his lip and leaned forward.

"Ja, Hauptsturmführer. I understand."

Erhart turned to Andreas again. "Now, let's see about that shed."

"I hear three men." Andreas spoke softly as the two crept toward the shed's door.

"Four."

As the two moved closer they began to make out German words and the occasional whining sound of a woman. Andreas removed his sidearm from its holster and looked at the officer. Erhart held his forefinger to his lips and pulled his pistol from his hip. Outside, empty bottles of Russian vodka lay strewn in snowy footprints. Inside, four men were laughing loudly and two women could now be plainly heard, crying.

One of the men roared, "My turn," with a Hungarian accent.

Erhart took a breath. "Now!" He kicked open the door. "Halt!" he bellowed. The shed was dim and both Erhart and Andreas strained to see. "Hands up...outside!"

Andreas pointed his pistol at a blur of grey uniforms. He backed away slowly as the first two soldiers emerged. Andreas immediately directed them to one side where he had them throw their weapons to the ground and lie face down in the snow.

But Erhart was backing slowly away from two others who had not yielded. "You will be hung for this."

"We'll take our chances."

Andreas whirled about to see a grinning Hungarian and a leather-coated German soldier who was aiming a Schmeisser at Erhart's chest. The German was walking with a limp. Andreas' heart seized. *Wolf!*

One of the women suddenly dashed from the doorway, half-naked. Wolf's comrade, the Hungarian, snatched the fleeing woman by the hair and flung her to the ground.

Ignoring them, Andreas pointed his pistol at his brother. "Wolf!" Waves of emotion rolled through Andreas; his heart raced, his mouth went dry. "Wolf, drop your weapon." Andreas' hand felt weak.

Wolf's eyes arched. "Ha! If it isn't Andreas. Can you believe this? What are you doing in Warsaw?"

"Drop the gun, Wolf. You're drunk."

Wolf grinned at Erhart. "This is my big brother, Hauptsturmführer. What do you think of that?"

"Drop your weapon, Stabsgefreiter, now." Erhart was firm, mechanical.

In the meantime Wolf's accomplice had taken control of both women and now had his rifle pointed at Andreas. "What should we do, Kaiser?"

"Just shut up, Lazlo." With his gun still on Erhart, Wolf turned his face to Andreas again. "Time to set things to right, don't you think?" The safety of his Schmeisser was off, his finger tensed on the trigger. He looked back at Erhart. "He loves my wife, Hauptsturmführer. What do you think of that? By the way, you really ought to lower your pistol. You're making me nervous."

Erhart stood steady. "Drop the weapon or I will shoot you dead."

Wolf smiled. "Lazlo, leave the ladies where they are and put your gun on the nice SS man for a minute. If he flinches, shoot him." The Hungarian obediently moved to a position directly behind Erhart from which he held his rifle against the back of the officer's head. Wolf then called to the pair of soldiers still lying in the snow. "Get up you fools."

Andreas fired a round into the ground next to one of them and then fixed his aim on Wolf's chest. "You men stay where you are," he said. "Wolf, lower your weapon or I will kill you."

"I'm impressed." With Erhart held in place by the Hungarian, Wolf swaggered toward the women. "Of course, it's easy to shoot the snow." He grabbed one of the women by the arm and hiked her to her feet. She was a dark-haired Jewess marked by a yellow star on her torn dress. "So, Andreas, have you ever had Kosher?" The Hungarian laughed.

"Let her go, Wolf." Andreas' mind was spinning. He could pull the trigger; it would be easy now with Wolf's gun swinging casually from his shoulder.

Wolf shoved the dark-haired woman to the ground and hoisted the other one to her feet. She was another Jewess but this one was blond—a German Jew or maybe Dutch. Wolf pushed the barrel of his gun between her breasts and smiled. He turned his face to Andreas and snapped, "Lower your weapon or she will die."

Andreas' heart was still racing. His mind spun. He decided to make a move. With his pistol still aimed at Wolf, he took three long strides toward Lazlo, swung his pistol away from Wolf and set the barrel against the surprised Hungarian's temple. "Let her go, Wolf, or I'll kill him where he stands."

Wolf laughed. "What do I care about some stupid Hun? Go ahead, shoot him."

Andreas stalled.

Erhart then spoke in a voice as calm as a grandfather settling a boys' backyard quarrel. "Oberfeldwebel Bauer. You will follow my orders, precisely." He paused. "I order you to shoot the man behind me…shoot!"

Andreas was a well-trained German soldier. Without hesitation, he fired. The Hungarian's head exploded and his rifle fell away, harmlessly. Andreas immediately swung his pistol toward Wolf.

Stunned, Wolf jerked his sub-machine gun away from the woman and pointed it at Erhart and Andreas. His hands tightened around the grip. "Both of you, drop your guns. I will kill you."

Andreas answered. "Wolf, please…"

"Please? You are so polite." Wolf snatched the blonde's hair and yanked her against him.

Erhart spoke again, calmly. "Stabsgefreiter, if you do not lower your weapon we will kill you at my order. Your Jewess is no shield, you fool. What would we care about killing her?" He directed his voice to Andreas. "Bauer, listen to me. Again, you must do exactly as I order. Is that understood?"

Andreas felt suddenly weak in the legs. Shoot his own brother? Who can do such a thing? Yet wasn't he hoping Erhart would order it? And wasn't that a horrible thing to hope for? "J…ja."

Feeling suddenly anxious, Wolf noticed guards at the rail yard now hurrying toward them. His eyes flew to his motorcycle. *Now or never*. "I'm leaving." He pushed the Jewess aside but pointed his Schmeisser at Erhart.

"No, you are surrendering to us, now." Erhart took a step closer; his glaring eyes were aimed just over the top of his pointed pistol. "You threatened a German officer and I'm placing you under arrest."

"Back away!"

"Drop your weapon!" barked Erhart. The captain knew men. He could see the panic tightening Wolf's face; he saw the man's shoulders rise; he knew what desperate men could do. Barking his command again, Erhart stepped forward in three long, bold strides, pistol arm extended. And then he saw Wolf's lip twitch.

Erhart squeezed his trigger.

Click...empty. Erhart's jaw dropped—he had never reloaded.

Wolf reacted. His eyes pinched and he fired a burst from his Schmeisser throwing Erhart backward into the snow, dead.

Stunned, Andreas hesitated as Wolf swung his weapon about. Their eyes met for an instant—a mere fragment of time.

An eternity.

Then Wolf's eyes pinched.

But Andreas fired first, then a second time and then a third.

Wolf staggered backward with his gun firing wildly to one side. He stumbled over his own feet and collapsed into the snow where he arched his back, gurgling in his own blood.

Charged with surging emotions, Andreas flew to Wolf's side and fell to his knees. He reached under his brother's body and cradled Wolf, weeping. Andreas held his brother tightly as the man's lurching slowly gave way to short, desperate twitches. A moment later Wolf's throat rattled and he sagged heavy and still in Andreas' arms.

⌖

"Maybe, but Klempner's grandmother was a baptized Christian." Eva looked over her typewriter at an elderly co-worker.

"A Jew's a Jew. Baptism is good but it can't straighten noses." The woman snickered. "But Klempner's nose is straight enough...which is why he may be drafted even though he's not fully Aryan."

"How old is he?"

"Thirty-eight. The army's taking everyone now."

Eva nodded. "Klempner said if Stalingrad falls the war will be lost."

"Eva?"

The young woman nearly jumped off her seat. "Oh! Herr Klempner?" Klempner looked sullen. In his left hand he was holding a small envelope. Eva's eyes glanced about the room. The office had suddenly fallen quiet.

As always, Richard Klempner was dressed in his Party uniform. But this morning every crease was particularly straight, extra starch stiffened his collar and his tie had been pressed. The leather holster at his side had been polished. He stood at attention and raised his arm. "Heil Hitler!"

Eva stood and returned the salute, weakly. Her heart was pounding.

Klempner took a deep breath. "Frau Eva Kaiser, friend and comrade, I regret to inform you that Stabsgefreiter Wolf Kaiser has fallen for Fatherland and Führer." He handed Eva the envelope. "Heil Hitler." He saluted and turned away.

Eva stared into the air, blankly, clutching the envelope in her hands. Her throat tightened and she felt her belly swirl with sadness, relief, joy, regret—shame.

She wanted to dance and wave her hands; she wanted to fall down and weep;

She wanted to clap; she wanted to vomit;

She wanted to sing and laugh; she wanted to run and hide.

She wanted to jump out of her window.

But she fell into her chair.

She felt as if some snake of guilt was slowly constricting the life from her. She had trouble breathing; time fell away; the room moved oddly around her and its silence roared hollow in her ears.

A tear rolled down her cheek.

The light touch of someone's hand abruptly returned her to an explosion of sound and color.

"Poor dear...poor Eva...brave girl...such times..." Helga and others surrounded the young woman. They stroked her with caring hands and lifted her to her feet. She was walked slowly to the coat room.

Eva nodded to this one and that, accepted a kerchief from someone and wiped her eyes. She put on her coat and hat, and took her umbrella in hand.

Then it came back to her.

The blessed numbness returned to settle her heart and quiet her mind. She paused and faced her co-workers with a brave smile. Their faces looked genuinely sad for her. *If they only knew.*

"Eichmann assured me that the entire Jewish question for Germany was only a transportation question."

Unnamed representative of the German Church Chancellery

CHAPTER TWENTY-EIGHT

ON THE SECOND Sunday of Advent, 6 December 1942, Andreas Bauer stood in front of Eva's door, trembling. He had been granted a seventy-two hour leave to settle matters regarding his brother's death but he hadn't had the courage to attend church that morning, nor had he visited with anyone other than Hans Bieber to whom he had bared his soul. As the shadows grew long in the fresh snow of the sidewalk by the place he once called home, Andreas closed his eyes and said a prayer.

A brief military investigation had cleared Andreas of any wrongdoing but that hadn't prevented his own conscience from accusing him. Hans Bieber had been a wise counselor and assured him that circumstances had driven the shooting, not desire. And even if desire had unconsciously nudged him, Andreas should know that no motive was ever purely good or purely evil. Hans urged the young man to consider the patterns of his life rather than the chaos of a single moment; he insisted that the soldier not judge himself too harshly. The old man's words had helped the soldier find just enough courage to bring him to Eva's door. But what would Eva say when she learned the whole truth?

Andreas adjusted his army overcoat and cap, instinctively checked his boots for shine and knocked. He heard steps coming toward the door. He shifted nervously in place.

Eva answered. "Oh!" She was startled. She had certainly not expected Andreas.

Andreas removed his cap. "May I come in?"

"Of course." Eva welcomed him with an outstretched hand. At his touch, Eva felt a surge of life. The numbness that had plagued her since the day in the office abruptly vanished and feeling burst through her filling every empty chamber of her heart. With feet light as an angel's she led Andreas into the living room and offered him a seat. "Uh...let me get you something from the kitchen..."

"I'm really not hungry, Eva, I..."

"Nonsense. I'll only be a minute." Eva's skin was tingling. A smile spread wide across her face.

Andreas sat stiffly. He listened to Eva rustle through the cabinets. He heard her drop some silverware and bump into a chair. He tried to calm himself by looking about the room. He let his eyes linger on the many familiar things that had once been his father's. But he saw Wolf in every corner. A chill of dread came over him. He squeezed his cap.

Frightened, he summoned the soldier within.

He closed his eyes and took a deep breath, and then another. He heard Eva's footsteps and then tried to chase the soldier away.

Eva entered with a tray of china plates and a small butter cake. "The coffee will be ready soon. Ersatz, of course." She set the coffee table nervously. "I want to show you something. Wait there."

"But..."

Eva scurried away. Her heart was now pounding; her emotions were swirling. She returned from a back room with a blanket over a square object. She removed the blanket. It was Andreas' print, *The Man above a Sea of Clouds*. "I didn't want anything to happen to it."

Andreas stood and took the picture in his two hands. His throat swelled, the dam behind his eyes nearly burst. He was moved by a thousand memories but knowing that Eva had thought enough to protect it moved him most of all. "Oh, Eva, I..."

"So, what do you think? Is the man watching a sunrise or sunset?"

Andreas knew his answer. His faith in faith was failing. He had seen the slaughter on the steppes of Russia. His trust in the Führer had eroded...and Stalingrad was about to fall. The sun was fast setting on the new Reich. He forced a smile and put the painting down. "Eva..."

"Just another moment." The woman hurried into the kitchen and poured the coffee into a silver pitcher. She felt flushed, confused. She was still wearing mourning clothes but hardly felt like a widow, especially now.

She was happy that Wolf was dead.

But the thought of it crashed in on her. She felt short of breath. It was as if the snake was coiling around her again, whispering words of shame.

And then she remembered Hermann.

She closed her eyes and breathed deeply, then wiped her hands on a dish towel and fluffed her hair. Ready, she returned to the living room and filled Andreas' cup.

Andreas waited patiently and when both cups were poured he reached for Eva's hand. "Eva, please sit next to me."

She obeyed.

She noticed that Andreas was pale, even gaunt. His beautiful eyes were faded as if the deep pools of feeling behind them had been drained. Eva felt sad for him. She could only imagine what he had been through. He suddenly looked frail and vulnerable to her; she wanted to hold him.

Andreas licked his lips; he took a deep breath. "Eva, I am so sorry about Wolf."

Eva nodded. "Thank you." She knew there was more. His voice was hesitant, incomplete.

"I heard your father's service for him was very moving. I'm sorry I wasn't there."

She nodded, waiting.

Andreas stared at the floor. "Eva, you need to know something."

She watched his cheek twitch; she had never seen that before. His chin quivered. "What is it, Andreas?"

"I...I have something to tell you that you must know."

Eva suddenly wasn't sure she wanted him to go on. She bit her lower lip and shifted in her seat.

"Eva, I...I am the one who...who killed Wolf." The words felt like bricks falling from his lips. The tick-tock of the mantle clock sounded suddenly loud, like hammers on an anvil. *Oh God...*

The words pierced Eva's ears like painful stabs from a workman's awl. She felt her belly twist; her throat tightened. She heard hissing in her ears and her world went cold.

The woeful young man waited and waited. Would she never answer? He was desperate for a gentle word or a knowing touch, but a jumble of emotion had left Eva sitting still as stone. Andreas could bear the silence no longer. A flood of explanations poured from his mouth. He was desperate to be understood. He fumbled through his story, terrified of either incriminating Wolf too aggressively, or defending himself too vigorously.

He only wanted to be truthful.

Eva stood, confused and overwhelmed by the news. "This...this is too much," she choked. "You...you should leave."

"But..."

"Please, I need to be alone." She walked to a far wall and stared at nothing.

Andreas stood. His fingers raced around the hem of his hat.

Eva could feel his eyes. "Please don't look at me like that. What am I supposed to say? How am I supposed to feel?" She wrung her hands and whirled about. "I hated Wolf, but...I..." She began to pace. "I just can't think right now."

"But...but I had to do it. He would have killed me and then the women..."

Her voice now trembled. "Can't you see! All of this is my fault! All of it! Wolf is my fault...I killed Hermann...and now I've killed us." Tears streamed down her cheeks. She flung herself into a chair and bent over her own lap, sobbing.

CHAPTER TWENTY-EIGHT

25 December 1942
Sixth Army
Feldpost, Stalingrad

My Dearest Lindie,

Feldwebel Bittmann tells me that this letter may never find you because he thinks the last planes have flown away. I hope he's wrong. The Führer will save us.

Last night was Christmas Eve and all I thought about was you ringing the silver bell for our little girls. I hope you had cake and a nice tree with candles. Here we pretended that our black bread was Weihnachtsstollen. We shared some with a Russian woman and her sick children who a priest found in a collapsed cellar. Then we melted snow to drink and we pretended it was egg brandy. At midnight we had permission to shoot rockets into the air. You should have seen that. The whole German army shot rockets. It looked like the angels might be coming to save us. We took off our helmets and sang 'Stille Nacht.' Some of the men cried.

This morning the priest gave about twenty of us Communion and read the Christmas Gospel. It didn't bother me that he was Catholic. He reminded us that God takes pity on people and then he prayed for us, each by name. When he put his hand on my head I felt peace.

Afterward, I prayed to God and put my soul in His hands. When you get this letter I may already be with Him. Whatever happens, Lindie, I believe that God will protect you and Germany from the Russians. He must.

I hear artillery coming close now. Please put my Lieblings on your knee and tell them that their Papa loves them. Tell Clari and Frieda to keep singing. Tell them that I hear them in my dreams. Tell Trudi and Irina to keep baking cookies because I can smell them all the way in Russia.

Lindie, I never had much money to give you but you have made my life rich. I love you with all my heart. Pray for me and my comrades in this terrible place.

Your loving husband,
Gunther

On Monday evening, 1 February 1943 a bitter wind blew through the Landes farm. The house was dreary and cold. Gunther's letter had arrived a few days before—nearly a month after he had written it. But a full week before the letter had arrived Lindie had been visited by Richard Klempner with the dreaded notice informing her that Gunther had been reported missing in action on 7 January and presumed dead somewhere in the stark ruins of Stalingrad. At her office, Eva had learned that thousands of German soldiers had perished that day in a vicious bayonet battle. The report also said that bodies of German soldiers could no longer be recovered.

Lindie held Eva tightly. "Remember, the notice said Gunther was *missing*. I don't believe he's dead. He will come home. I can feel it. How long would it take him to get here from Stalingrad?"

Eva stroked her friend's hair. She was worried about her. "I don't know, Lindie."

"I'll go the station and wait. I'll go everyday. And Hitler can burn in hell forever, that wicked little fool," Lindie sobbed. "How could he be so stubborn?"

"Why did you say that about the Führer, Mama?" Six-year old Irina had been listening.

Eva answered, anxiously. "Mama was just telling me what someone else said. Now go into your room and read with your sisters."

Eva waited until Irina closed the door behind her. "You need to be more careful."

Lindie wiped her eyes and nodded. "I know. But Hitler put my Gunther in a hopeless place. I hear the whole Sixth Army is gone—except for a lucky handful." She lowered a voice to a whisper. "I hate him."

Eva turned off Lindie's radio. Every station was playing funeral dirges in honor of Germany's heroes who had been lost in yesterday's official defeat at Stalingrad. Of the nearly 300,000 German soldiers who had been trapped there only 34,000 had been evacuated to safety. The others had been either killed or captured and, if captured, were doubtlessly being marched to Siberia.

Eva walked to a window and stared into the blackness. She pulled her sweater over her shoulders. "I heard rumors at the office that the whole Eastern Front is beginning to crumble." She squeezed her fists. "The Russians are pushing back, hard. They have to be held."

Lindie blew her nose. "I'm glad your father cancelled Gunther's funeral service."

"He understands, Lindie. He hopes for Gunther like we all do. Besides, he's done too many of them. Tomorrow he has Heri Schneider's."

Lindie wiped her eyes. "I hear Adolf is going mad."

A car pulled up outside. Eva and Lindie cupped their faces against the glass to see a dark figure making its way to the front door. "G'Tag, Lindie." The visitor was Paul Volk. His eyes were red from crying. He, too, held a letter in his hand.

"Please, Herr Pfarrer, come in," said Lindie. "Old Landes should be home soon. He's taking Ski back to the camp." She heard a truck parking in the barn. "Oh, maybe that's him now. I'll fix some coffee."

Paul stepped inside, removed his hat and coat, and shook snow from his pants. "Ja, thank you, but I didn't come for him." His chin trembled. "I shouldn't have come here, Eva, but I needed to see you, tonight."

"What is it?" Eva was suddenly anxious.

Paul looked self-consciously at Lindie, then handed Eva his letter. He took a seat and faced the floor. "I just opened it."

Eva sat and read the letter quickly. "How could she!"

Tears dropped from Paul's eyes to the wooden planks. "I've not been the best husband; you know that. And ever since Daniel's death I think she's been so empty."

"But this? Divorcing you to marry that Gestapo man?" Eva put her hand on her father's arm. "I'm so, so sorry, I..."

"She has never forgiven me for any of my weaknesses..." An explosion suddenly rocked the house. Glass sprayed across the kitchen and Lindie collapsed against a wall; Eva and her father fell to the floor. Outside, flames leapt into the black sky from the adjacent farmyard. "A plane...I think a plane crashed!" cried Paul. He and Eva scrambled to throw the door open. The barn was in flames.

"There!" Eva cried. "There, look there!" To one side of the barn she spotted the burning wreckage of an RAF Beaufighter.

"The pilot..." Paul danced around burning debris and ran toward the cockpit just ahead of Eva. Inside, a pilot was slumped over next to a dead crewman. Paul struggled to wrestle him free from his seat. From another side Eva heard Lindie shrieking. "Help! Help me!"

Lindie was at the door of the burning barn shielding her face with her forearm. She was inching her way against a wall of heat. Inside, Old Landes' truck was engulfed in the center of what had become a roaring furnace. A black outline of a burning corpse stared back from within the inferno. Eva abandoned her father and raced toward her friend. "No, Lindie, no!" Eva wrapped her arms around Lindie's back and tried to haul her back.

"Let me go, let me go...it's Papa!" The smoke was choking, the air scorching. The skin on Eva's face felt like it was blistering. Lindie was fixated on the sight of her father-in-law's charred form stiff and motionless within the flames. "Come away!" cried Eva. "Your daughters are seeing this!"

With a heave, Eva turned Lindie and chased the girls into the kitchen where her father had just dragged the pilot. The Englishman was sprawled on the floor, still conscious and staring at the ceiling. He was bleeding but not badly burned.

"We need water," cried Paul. "And bandages."

Eva pumped water into a cup, then lifted the pilot's head and held the cup to his lips. She thought he looked young. He looked at her for a moment, gratefully. But when he did, Eva abruptly recoiled. She scowled and poured water into his mouth. "Why couldn't you English stay out of this war!"

Within a quarter hour a military vehicle roared into the farmyard along with a fire truck. Four German soldiers dismounted and hurried into the house. A medic was among them and he quickly checked the pilot. Eva backed away and watched the medic examine the Englishman's wounds. She thought the medic looked a little like Andreas. Something about the way he moved, the way he wiped his hand over his hair—maybe it was the breadth of his shoulders or the quiet strength of his face.

The medic gave the soldiers some instructions, pressed bandages into the pilots bleeding wounds and then turned to Eva. "Let me see your face, Frau."

Eva yielded to his hands. It felt good to feel the touch of a man. She kept her eyes on his as he lightly rubbed salve on her burns.

"You'll be fine. No scarring. I'll leave you with some salve."

"Are...are you stationed in Koblenz?"

"Only for another day."

"Oh. And then..."

"We're being sent to the front."

"Russia?"

The man nodded, grimly.

⌖

"All she talks about is her Opa and the Englishman who killed him," whispered Lindie. She motioned her head toward the now seven-year old Irina who was cutting potatoes at the sink. "I'm worried about her. She's so angry."

Eva watched the little girl snap her knife against the cutting board. "That's good work, Irina." Eva walked to Lindie's window. Outside, dairy cows were being herded toward their milking stalls by a few Hitler Youth boys. The Party had seen to it that the farm was rebuilt and furnished with new equipment. After all, every farm in Germany was needed. Oskar Offenbacher had financed a great deal of the project. Lindie now had a dozen milk cows, twenty pigs, and ten dozen laying hens all tended by the Hitler Youth and a farm manager assigned by the Party. A healthy crop of wheat was wending silk-like under the July sky in far field. To one side, Ski and another Polish POW were weeding a large kitchen garden lush with vegetables.

Eva helped herself to some beer and watched Lindie fuss with her daughters. She wondered if she'd ever have a family of her own. A lump filled her throat as she thought of Hermann.

She thought often of Hermann.

Eva closed her eyes. But when she did, she risked images of the cold tile of Hadamar. And closed eyes also invited the dark weight of loneliness...unless she thought of Andreas. She suddenly pictured him laughing in a vineyard.

She smiled.

Six weeks ago Hans Bieber had scolded her for the way she had acted toward Andreas when he confessed the killing. "The man loves you, girl. But that's not why he shot Wolf. Have you no heart, no courage against the lies of others? Your Opa would be ashamed."

That was when her demons had finally emerged. She flew into a rage, screaming a litany of contemptuous accusations at the wider world until she collapsed and sobbed about how it was that she had been made the fool; and how it was that she blamed herself for Wolf and all that happened in the wake of his wickedness. Then, when all the words were spent, she leaned on Hans' shoulder.

But to her surprise the old man had remained unmoved. "You were not *made* a fool. You were a fool. And now you bear a fool's burden."

The old man's words had stung: '*You were a fool.*' She had hoped he would have agreed that she had surely *been* fooled.

But that's not what he said.

He said that she *had been* a fool.

The truth was plain and cruel and bitter. And he had given her no way out. He went on to hold her face fast to the truth until her dodging eyes could dodge the truth no more: Whatever the reasons, she had foolishly made room for evil and it had gladly filled the space.

That's when Eva had collapsed and sobbed true tears.

And that's when Hans Bieber took her in his arms and hugged her. Then he said, "Now listen carefully dear Eva. We are all fools. I was a fool not to warn you about Wolf...and so were others. So if you'll forgive me, we'll cork our foolishness together in a bottle and sink it in the Rhein."

His was a gift of grace.

The next day Eva had written a painful confession to Andreas, baring all her heart and without defense. Rending her soul with a pen proved to be a healing act. It had been a courageous thing to do.

But Eva had always been brave.

Eva opened her eyes and turned up the radio. The announcer was offering more information about the terrible fire bombing of Hamburg which had ended two days prior. More than 50,000 civilians had been burnt to death and the announcer predicted the count would go higher. Eva shuddered. The announcer then denounced the Allies' arrogant demand for an unconditional surrender as a pretense for their plans to utterly destroy a defeated Germany. "*It is time for all Germans to lock arms in our common defense.*"

Eva turned to see Lindie slapping Irina hard across the bottom. The little girl screamed and then shouted another 'no' just as a long, black car rolled slowly into the farmyard. Two men got out.

Gestapo.

"Lindie?" Eva said.

The pair approached the door and Lindie let them in, anxiously.

"Heil Hitler, Frauen, Kinder."

The women and the children returned the salute. Eva held her breath.

"We were told in the village that Frau Eva Kaiser may be here?"

Eva summoned strength. "Ja. I am she."

The agents stepped forward with an envelope. A distinguished looking man with silver hair and a monocle took command. "Tell us what you know of Fräulein Anna Keller?"

Eva had nearly forgotten her old friend, the Swing kid. Anna had moved away soon after Daniel's death. "I haven't seen her in years."

"Hmm. Well, what about her letters?"

"What letters?"

"We found your name on her mailing list in München and your postman gave this to us a few days ago." He held up the opened envelope containing an enclosure.

"I don't understand."

The man looked at his companion. "Are you loyal to the Führer, Frau Kaiser?"

Eva's heart began to race. "Loyal? Of course, I..."

Irina climbed out from behind her mother's apron. "Mutti called the Führer a little fool." Irina folded her arms, proudly. "Ask her."

The Gestapo agents turned to Lindie.

"I...I...I..."

The agent motioned for a third man to come from the car. He was an armed escort. "We'll need to take you both to Koblenz for questioning."

"No," snapped Lindie. "I need to go to the train station. My husband is due home from the Russian front any day. And what about my girls?"

Eva took Lindie's hand. "We've done nothing wrong."

"We'll deliver the children to a woman at Party headquarters."

"What? You can't..."

"Silence! We can and we will." The agent reached into the envelope and withdrew a smudged leaflet printed on poor quality paper. "Your friend has been arrested for belonging to a seditious group known as The White Rose. However, before her arrest she was kind enough to send this to you." He smiled, sarcastically. "We have to assume you are sympathetic. Why else would she do that?"

"Sympathetic? To what?"

The agent handed the leaflet to Eva. "You'll see that they consider our Führer to be 'evil.' But you already know exactly what they think." The man looked squarely at Lindie. "Perhaps they would call him a little fool, too."

"The orders to the British air force should be: Wipe the Germans out! Kill them all! We should use all of our scientific knowledge to invent new and more terrible explosives. But I will go even further. I will say it openly: If I could, I would wipe Germany off the map. The Germans are an evil race."

Rev. C. W. Whipp, English vicar of St. Augustine's

CHAPTER TWENTY-NINE

ANDREAS COMPLETED AN abbreviated officer training program and was graduated from school in Dresden in May 1943. Abbreviated or not, his instruction had been thorough. In addition to rigorous physical training he had spent hours in the classroom studying strategy and logistics, including a particular emphasis on Fieldmarshal Rommel's military text book, *Infantry Attacks*. His training had been made even more difficult by his recent disgust with Hitler—a feeling shared quietly by others. As he saw it, the Führer's arrogance had unnecessarily cost the lives of tens of thousands at Stalingrad, including the life of his dear friend Gunther.

Nevertheless, the time had gone quickly for Andreas especially because his heart had been lightened by letters from Eva. She had written her gut-wrenching first letter a month or so after he had left on that cold December evening. A second letter came within days of the first and in this one she added her absolute belief in his account of the story. Andreas had responded graciously to both, genuinely appreciating her honest self-appraisal and apologizing for his unfair expectations in light of the shocking news he had brought. Such mutual repentance had set the stage for an immediate reconciliation. So when Andreas was given the insignia of lieutenant, he returned to active duty as a contented man.

His battalion had been temporarily assigned to the Fourth Army and was then moved in reserve to the Second Panzers where it fought bitterly around Smolensk, this time in retreat. By the middle of July Andreas and his men were back with the Ninth Army and falling back to the Gomel-Orscha line. The battles had been unspeakably horrid and losses had been heavy on both sides. The hordes of Russians rushing at his men day and night were fearsome and lethal. Day after day, night after night, they pressed. Yet Andreas was now more concerned about the plight of his dear Eva than the miseries he was suffering. He had not heard from her in some time.

Then he received a letter from Paul Volk who told him that Eva and Lindie had been arrested and were being held for trial in Koblenz. For a week Andreas could barely breathe but in a letter dated 8 September—the very day Germany's ally, Italy, surrendered—Eva wrote to assure Andreas that her mother, the soon-to-be Gerde Volk Schiller, had successfully intervened in the trial. Eva's penalty was that she be dishonorably dismissed from the Party, to be stripped of membership in any Nazi affiliated clubs, and to have her house and person subjected to random searches. As for Lindie, a stiff reprimand and a small fine were imposed along with a severe warning.

Frustrated for the injustice but relieved that Eva had suffered no worse, Andreas fought on. In late September his friend and much beloved comrade, Lt. Von Schauer, was killed by a sniper while standing in a potato field at Andreas's side. Andreas was immediately given Von Schauer's command.

For days afterward, Andreas and his men engaged the Russians in a defensive battle along the Dnepr River. On one particularly savage morning, Andreas single-handedly destroyed two Russian tanks in the fierce fighting around Sshosh—including one of the giants, a KV II. His uncommon courage under extraordinary circumstances earned him the Iron Cross First Class.

⌖

"Yes, Herr Pfarrer. I do love Christmas but I find it very hard to be apart from my men. I've news that they've been pushed out of Kursk and are fighting in the Pripet Marshes northwest of Kiev. I should be with them." Nervous, Andreas sat in Paul Volk's study like he had more than a decade before.

The minister leaned back in his chair. He set aside a letter he had been reading from his brother, Alfred, and reached for his pipe. "I wish all of you boys could be home for Christmas and never have to leave again." He packed tobacco into the bowl. "I can hardly bear another day of casualties. I fear this war is another disaster for Germany. Stalingrad was the beginning of the end for us."

"You wouldn't want to say that too loudly."

"I know, son, and I'm no defeatist. I understand why you must fight, perhaps harder than ever. Mr. Churchill has mounted a war of annihilation, like the Russians. It seems that our enemies are envisioning a future with the German people utterly destroyed and our country divided into tiny farm districts. Oskar told me that some Jew in America wants our men to be castrated so that the German race will disappear."

"Well, that sounds like propaganda. But it's so hard to know what's true. I can't forget the images of the Jews I saw packed in trains in Warsaw. We were told..." Andreas was about to say more when he thought he heard some rustling in the kitchen downstairs. His heart skipped.

"This whole relocation thing has a bad smell about it." Paul lit his pipe. "I know we're using Jews as workers in Polish camps, but last Christmas the pope made some veiled reference to the murder of a 'people.' I have to assume he was referring to the Jews but he's never said more. Maybe he had bad information? I tell you, I fear the radicals. I know what they're capable of and I no longer know where Hitler stands. But you're right, Andreas, with all sides spreading propaganda it's hard to know the truth.

"Anyway, right now I'm mostly concerned about an invasion from the west. Sooner or later the Americans will join the Tommies and attack us. We'll be squashed in a vice. Hitler should never have declared war on the Americans. Never. I know the Amis are busy with Japan, but they'll be coming. I found out that my nephew, Bobby—you met him—is teaching basic German language skills to infantry officers."

"Well, the Americans were supplying our enemies," said Andreas. "I guess our treaty with Japan..."

The minister nodded. "Still, we should have left them alone. I tell you, world politics is nearly as strange as village life. The West should be our ally, not our enemy. Together we could have smashed the Bolsheviks." Paul drew on his pipe. "On another subject, Bieber and Offenbacher have put a stop to any gossip about you and the Wolf matter."

"I only care about your daughter, Herr Pfarrer, and nothing else." Andreas took a breath and squeezed the cap in his hand. "I love her more than my life...but I worry about her."

Paul nodded. "Me, too. Eva seems better but she still wrestles with self-condemnation for allowing herself to come under Wolf's spell." He sucked on his pipe, thoughtfully. "Ever since that terrible business in the market she has struggled with fear and shame. Wolf seemed to be the way out of it for her. He made her feel good about herself and safe. To be honest, she was in no condition to see who Wolf really was...she never *could* have wanted to see. She was too broken. She needed the eyes of others...and I failed her most of all." Paul wiped an eye and pointed his pipe at his print of the *Peaceable Kingdom* hanging on the wall. "You see, Andreas, peace is ultimately about forgiveness." A knock sounded lightly on the office door. Paul collected himself. "Come in."

The door opened, slowly. It was Eva. Her cheeks pinked and she smiled happily. She self-consciously fluffed her hair. "Andreas..."

The sparkle in her wide eyes made Andreas' heart leap. Paul climbed out from behind his desk. "Well, I've got some cookies waiting for me in the kitchen."

Eva's belly fluttered, her legs felt weak. She fixed her gaze on Andreas. She thought she had never seen a more handsome man in all her life. His Iron Cross First Class was pinned to the left breast pocket of his officer's uniform. She melted into his eyes.

"Oh, Eva," said Andreas. Heavy tears began to sag. His chin quivered. "I've missed you so much."

The young woman was powerless. She could not resist him

another moment. She rushed into his embrace and held him with all her might. "Andreas, I'm so sorry for everything."

Andreas could not speak. He could only hold her tightly against him as if binding her soul. Here, in his embrace, was all that he had ever loved. She was the object of his longing, the purpose of his life. She was the circle he longed to fill with all that he was.

Andreas took her by the shoulders, lightly, holding them in his strong hands as if they were the tender petals of a fragile flower. "Nothing matters to me other than you. Eva, I...I love you more than words can say."

Eva trembled. The condemning whispers were gone; his love had crushed the serpent's head. She wanted to fly like a happy little bird and sing from the rooftops. "Oh, Andreas." She leaned into his chest as he enfolded her once more. Then, as he moved his face slowly toward hers, she closed her eyes and touched her lips softly to his.

⌖

The next morning Andreas hurried from his room at the Weinstube and knocked on Rev. Volk's door. The minister answered and led him into the kitchen where Eva was already hard at work. Andreas presented her with a gentle kiss and a wreath of greens for her dining room wall.

With a giggle, Eva handed him an apron and the couple went to work preparing a wonderful Christmas Eve meal. Despite growing shortages, the Volk table would be soon be graced with two bottles of delicate Mosel wine, roast goose with stuffing, saffron buns, fruit cake, roasted potatoes and Preiselbeeren.

Paul returned from the six o'clock ringing of the bells and as he entered the door Eva rang her very own silver bell to summon Andreas, Hans Bieber, and her father to the living room where she had decorated a plump Christmas tree. Gathered around the tree, the foursome sang their favorite Christmas carols and opened a few gifts including Eva's gift to Andreas—a silver pocket watch with a grapevine etched around the edges. Andreas presented Eva with hers—a lovely dress from Berlin.

Afterward, Eva served her guests Andreas' favorite, Apfelstrudel (but without the powdered sugar), as well as a modest Weihnachtsstollen and a small plate of marzipan candy. Then, with the formalities of Christmas Eve behind them, the couple excused themselves to take a starlit walk to neighboring Kobern and its Niederberg Castle.

⌖

"This way, Andreas." Eva retied her red scarf and fastened the top button of her green woolen overcoat. She pulled a flashlight from her pocket and pointed it into a small stand of leafless hardwoods at the base of the castle's knoll. Snow had fallen earlier but only enough to powder the countryside. Above, the broken clouds were running invisibly across the sky leaving rich, black patches of starlight in their wake. Dressed in a dark overcoat and a heavy wool cap, Andreas took Eva's hand and followed her up the winding trail.

"And you're absolutely sure your father won't be angry that we're not at the midnight service?"

"Of course not."

The two climbed upward until they finally emerged into the dark shadows of Eva's favorite escape. The air was brisk; the castle smelled of snow-wet stone. Its ancient walls loomed large like silhouetted sentries standing watch over the Mosel. The pair climbed onto the sill of a broken window and stared at the scene before them. "It's so beautiful, Andreas."

Beyond their window the Mosel River curved gently between mounded hills that were shadowed soft and gray in the moonlight. The river shimmered silver. Below, the fairy-tale village of Kobern lay still, quietly lit by the warm candle-glow of Christmas. A train whistled in the distance and Eva snuggled all the closer to Andreas.

The young woman closed her eyes for a moment. "I can imagine Christmas elves scampering along the battlements and the Castle Queen singing. I think she keeps her treasure in the well."

"And I see happy gnomes dancing around a circle of candles burning brightly over the snow." Andreas laughed.

Eva tittered. "And what about the water sprites?"

"Ah, the water sprites. Who could forget them! Look, out there. Can't you see them? They are floating in the air just above the river singing for Count Andreas von Weinhausen to saddle the good River Dragon and rescue fair Eva from the wicked dwarves!" The soldier laughed and recited a poem he had written:

You evil dwarves beware this night,
I ride on dragon's saddle light
To fly o'er keeps and castle walls
To free my love; to be her all.
No dungeons and no werewolf's lair
Shall keep me from my Eva, fair.

Eva clapped. "Oh, Andreas! That was wonderful." She stared at his face, shadowed heavily by the deep-set window. "Don't ever lose your magic."

For the next moments the couple lost themselves in one another. No more the widow, no more the soldier, the two pushed the world away. The midnight church bells of Christmas Eve began to peal through the valley. From villages up and down the Mosel their soothing resonance filled the winter air with the peace of things certain.

Soon the songs of a choir drifted faintly upward from the rooftop of the Catholic church below. Together, Eva and Andreas sang with them *Stille Nacht, Heilige Nacht*. And when the song ended the world was still again, more still than either Eva or Andreas had ever known. The couple stared into the dark, tranquil landscape, wishing that the spirit of the moment might last forever.

Then from behind an unseen bend the rhythmic chugs and hissing steam of an approaching train broke the silence gracefully and with music of its own. The panting of the iron horse grew closer and the heaving engine soon led its obedient cars past the village. From the castle heights, Andreas and Eva thought the train looked like a toy in a young boy's room; a little thing rattling happily on its way.

As the steam puffed into the dark beyond, Andreas turned and kissed his Eva. "You are my sunrise at every day's dawn," he said. "You are the starlight over my head. In the heat of battle your breath cools me and when I am cold I feel the warmth of your heart."

Eva nestled in his embrace and the two held each other until Andreas led her from the window to the timeless castle well where he took both her gloved hands in his and kissed her once again.

"I love this place. I love you," said Eva, softly.

Andreas' legs felt weak. "Then...then let this place love you, Eva." He looked up. "Let the stars light your hair, let the night sky be a blanket." He looked about the castle. "This is a good place, Eva, one filled with hope. Feel it, feel how these walls protect you and how they let the beauty of the valley fill your heart with peace." His heart was racing. He brought his face close to hers. "Let me love you, Eva, let me love you with all my soul." He could barely hear his own words as he slowly lowered himself to one knee. He swallowed hard against the lump filling his throat. "I love you Eva, more than life." His eyes filled. "Would you marry me?"

Eva felt suddenly lifted to places she had never been; she felt as if she had been given a taste of heaven's joy, a gift long buried in her dreams. "Oh, dear Andreas, yes, yes, I will marry you."

Ecstatic, Andreas stood and swept his bride-to-be into his arms where he held her tightly. His spirit soared, his heart had flown to paradise; he felt as though he was swimming through starlight with the angels.

⌖

Christmas Day had fallen on Saturday that year of '43 leaving Sunday a seemingly unending day for the happy couple. In a whirlwind of emotion, they had decided to marry right away; the war had made every tomorrow too much of an uncertainty. Since theirs was a War Wedding it was exempted from custom and their marriage was quickly approved *sine praevia proclamatione*. So, at four-thirty on Monday, 27 December 1943, Andreas stood with Eva in the in front of Bürgermeister Beck for a brief civil ceremony.

Eva had chosen to wear the dress that Andreas had bought her for Christmas. Of course, wartime shortages had prompted the government to put some controls on style and fabrics. To save material, hem lines were raised to just below the knee and all pleats forbidden. With cotton, wool, and silk needed for other things, the dress had been made of dark green rayon. The double-breasted, button-front dress was pretty, nonetheless, with full shoulders, a tight waist, and long sleeves. Eva also wore ivory colored gloves and a rather daring brown felt hat with a few feathers set smartly atop her long, page-boy styled hair. Andreas thought she was utterly stunning.

The groom was dressed in his grey uniform. His Iron Cross First Class was pinned to the pocket of his freshly pressed tunic; his Wound Badge in Silver shined neatly on his chest. His shin-high boots were polished to a high sheen and the crease of his pants rose straight as an arrow.

After the official paperwork was settled at the mayor's office, the happy couple walked quickly to the church where Paul would perform the religious rite.

"He invited *everyone*?" Andreas whispered as the two made their way uphill.

Eva nodded, suddenly a little anxious. "Ja. He mentioned it at Sunday service yesterday. I suppose all the old gossips will want to see *this*."

Andreas laughed. "Good. I want the whole world to see!"

"My father called my mother yesterday."

"Oh?"

"I'm not sure if I want her to come or not. I don't think he could bear to see her and he's very touchy about what his congregation thinks."

"It was very kind of him to call her, then."

A voice from behind turned the new couple's heads. "Oh, Eva." Lindie Landes and her four girls were hurrying toward the church. They had spent the day at the train station waiting for Gunther. Panting, she said, "I'm so happy for you both! I can't wait to see this." She was wearing a nice silk dress that she had bartered from a city woman for two large hams. Around her neck she proudly wore her Mother's

Badge. She took Eva's hands in hers. "Imagine, Eva *Bauer*...Frau Andreas Bauer! I love it." She gave Eva a big hug and kissed her on the cheeks. Her daughters stood behind her like a line of ducklings. Each stepped forward and wished the bride and groom happiness.

"Well, we had better keep moving." Andreas' heart ached for Lindie and her girls. "Let's have a dance afterward."

Eva and Andreas entered a side door and took their place in a small room behind the pulpit. Even Eva's Catholic friend, Kätchen Fink, had helped decorate the church with Christmas greenery and the candles now casting a soft light over the fast-filling wooden pews. Frau Diehl was playing carols at the organ in the balcony.

"Are you two ready?" Oskar Offenbacher poked his nose into the room. Flushed with excitement, he chortled and hurried away.

Eva cracked the door and sneaked a peak into the sanctuary. "Everybody did come!"

Andreas took a deep breath. "I don't know if they're happy for us or just nosey."

"Yes you do," laughed Eva.

"Nosey."

"Ja, of course, and I don't even care. I have you, Andreas, and that's all that matters to me now."

Andreas took hold of Eva and pulled her close. He kissed her deeply until Paul Volk tapped him on the shoulder. "Huh?"

Paul laughed. "Ready for a wedding, young man?"

Eva walked behind her father and at Andreas' elbow as the three made their way to the fore of the church. She could feel her heart beating. She looked into the audience, expecting the whispers and the stares. She held her breath.

But instead of hissing whispers the congregation abruptly stood to its feet and applauded. Eva was startled. She looked at her neighbors, speechlessly. Tears formed quickly and sagged beneath her eyes. In the audience was Hans Bieber of course, standing next to Widow

Nuber and clapping wildly. And there were Frau Wicker, Rev. Hahn and his wife, and Oskar Offenbacher with his wife. In the center aisle sat Ulrich Obermann in his wheelchair, crowing happily; a grenade had paralyzed him from the neck down. Dr. Krebel and his wife stood in the middle of a row of young widows. Frau Krause stood alongside Lindie and the girls, and to the far side was poor Adolf Schneider standing by his only remaining son, Udo.

Finally, Volk smiled and thanked the congregation for their kindness. Gathering his composure he began the liturgy. "Whereas married persons are subject to many troubles and afflictions; to that end you, Andreas Bauer and Eva Volk Kaiser, who desire to have your marriage bond publicly confirmed..."

Eva barely heard her father's words as he went on. She could only hear the song of her soul; she could only feel the strength in the arm she held fast. Love had led her to a new beginning; love had softened her heart—to others and to herself. Now, in this place, at this time, forgiven by God, forgiven by self, and loved by this man, she felt safe and whole, at last.

"Andreas Bauer, do you acknowledge here before God and His holy Church that you take to Eva Volk Kaiser to be your lawful wife, promising never to forsake her, to love her faithfully, to maintain her as a faithful husband is bound according to the holy gospel?"

"Oh, yes, I surely do." Andreas voice was strong, contented. He kept his gaze on Eva as her father then presented her with her vows. And when she said, "I do," he felt suddenly weak. *My wife*, he thought. *She is my wife*. He slipped a gold ring on her finger.

Paul paused only to notice Gerde now seated in the rear. He took a breath and continued the service, finally leading his congregation in a prayer for Eva and Andreas as well as the sons, husbands, and brothers serving the Fatherland in battlefields far away. "And may God's mighty Hand shield them each and every one from the wrath of our enemies. Lord, in your mercy, grant us peace."

Then, without being prompted, Udo Schneider stood and began to sing the Martin Luther hymn, *Nun komm der Heiden Hei-*

land. The congregation joined him, ending on the fifth verse:

Thou, the Father's only Son,
Hast o'er sin the victory won.
Boundless shall Thy kingdom be;
When shall we its glories see?

"God the Almighty has made our nation. By defending its existence we are defending His work. The fact that our defense is fraught with incalculable misery makes us even more loyal to this nation."

Adolf Hitler

CHAPTER THIRTY

ANDREAS BADE EVA a heart-wrenching farewell on the Wednesday to follow. He could barely lift his legs to the steps of his waiting train and when it pulled away from the station he hung far out the window, his eyes fixed on Eva until she slowly disappeared.

Then, without asking, the soldier-self displaced the other-self and he dutifully arrived in Berlin to accept his orders. He was to report to the 275th division now being organized as part of the First Army in Western France. The news was bittersweet. He, like every German soldier, considered Russia to be an endless horizon of death and misery. Yet he felt so bonded to the men under his command that he could not stand the idea of leaving them abandoned to such a place. Who would lead his men into battle now? He was angry. Nevertheless, his orders were what they were and he knew that Eva would be greatly relieved. He immediately wrote her a letter informing her of the change.

Andreas would need to wait at least two weeks for his train to Bretagne, and that was likely to change depending on the condition of the rails. So, when not performing mundane duties at battalion headquarters, Andreas walked the streets of Berlin by day, usually studying the faces of the people waiting in long lines to trade a few yellow ration coupons for a handful of groceries. By night he huddled helplessly with his comrades below ground waiting for the RAF to do their horrid business, all the while wondering who in the day's food lines had been killed.

The RAF had begun routine nighttime raids on Berlin in November and heaps of rubble now lay strewn about the streets where neighborhoods once stood. The majestic buildings of Alexanderplatz had been badly damaged, the renowned Kaiserhof Hotel was destroyed and the Reich Chancellery nearly ruined. Fire had swept through large sections of the city killing tens of thousands. To Andreas' eye, nearly a third of the capital city had been devastated.

From time to time he would stop walking so that he could help his countrymen pull over piles of bricks. But he wondered about them. *Why rebuild now*? *This is just the beginning*. Andreas hated to think like that but what sane man could deny the facts? The English were pounding German cities by night and their relatively new enemy, the Americans, by day. To be sure, German anti-aircraft had exacted a high price for the attacks but the enemy seemed to have an infinite supply of replacement planes and pilots.

On one particular morning Andreas helped a woman carry two of her children to their graves. They had been burned to death in their beds. Later that same day he helped a Red Cross nurse bandage the wounds of an old woman who fell over dead before they finished. Staring at her lifeless eyes he had imagined her as someone's Oma baking cookies on a winter's day or canning preserves in summer. With countless such pictures in his mind's eye, he wasn't sure whether to curse Churchill for his hateful brutality or Hitler for having pushed the world too far.

Talking with others, he found himself oddly grateful to the Americans for having the decency to focus their raids on strategic targets instead of old women and children. But he knew the ties between Churchill and Roosevelt, and he feared the Americans might be easily swayed into the war of annihilation that Churchill seemed to enjoy. Andreas spat. Walking with a young sergeant, he made his way slowly to his barracks—a cramped cellar deep in the earth.

"Oberleutnant, I think we'd be beaten already if the Tommies dropped as many bombs on our factories as they do our neighborhoods!" said the sergeant.

"Churchill is an evil man."

"And the captain says that their 'unconditional surrender' would mean the absolute end to everything."

"They want us to come to the table on our knees, completely dependant on their mercy," answered Andreas.

The sergeant said nothing for a long moment. "Mercy? We've both been to Russia. We shouldn't expect any mercy from Stalin and his savages. And look around at what the British do to the helpless."

"It would go worse for us than Versailles." Andreas cursed under his breath. "So, this is why we fight. Maybe if we make them pay a high enough price they'll have to offer terms."

"I hear the Führer is working on Wunderwaffen." The boy's voice had a quality of desperate hope.

"Wonder weapons? I hope you're right about that. We need something." Andreas had his doubts. He pushed his cold hands deep into the pockets of his overcoat. The January evening was bitter and raw. The city's lights were dull, most barely visible behind black-out curtains.

Suddenly the sirens began to wail and the pair began to run as the sky lit up over Berlin. Searchlights probed the darkness and soon flak began to burst over the city. "Hurry, Feldwebel!"

Andreas had not expected a raid this early and despite his years of combat he felt anxiety rising rapidly in his chest. He didn't like being trapped within the confines of buildings and rubble, and he particularly resisted the idea of burrowing underground like some frightened animal.

Unseen bombs began to whine from far above.

The earth began to shake.

Running wildly, Andreas and the sergeant leapt over debris and covered their ears. Whoom! A shock wave of air threw them both to the ground.

Whoom!

Another bomb blew the top of a nearby building to pieces. A thick shower of bricks cascaded over them, killing the young sergeant.

Clouds of dust rolled around the gasping Andreas as he desperately pried himself from the rubble. Fires began to erupt on all sides of him.

Whoom!

The man was thrown backward, the air sucked from his lungs. A piercing pain ran through his left arm and shoulder. He pulled himself upright, struggling to breathe.

A tower of burning debris collapsed just yards away. Andreas wheezed. Around him people were running like frightened mice, some on fire, all in panic. It was a scene from his worst nightmares.

Whoom!

Everything was suddenly like a slow-motion movie; sounds were hollow and distant. Andreas' vision blurred; he began to wobble. His head went light and his vision dimmed.

He collapsed atop a heap of gray ash.

3 February 1944
Weinhausen, Rheinland
Germany

My Dear Husband,

The letter came today from your battalion. They say you were injured in a bombing raid over Berlin on the night of 20 January and are in a hospital. I am so relieved to learn that you are alive but they did not tell me what your injuries are. I am praying for you.

My father told me that the RAF dropped over 2,000 one ton bombs that night. God must have spared you because the English surely wouldn't. Herr Offenbacher offered to pay my way to visit you but the Gestapo forbids my traveling because of the Anna Keller matter. So please forgive me but know that my heart is with you every moment. I'll write to Uncle Rudi and see if he can come see you soon. I just know that you'll be fine. I hope the nurses don't flirt with you. After all, you are a true German hero and holder of an Iron Cross First Class!

Mother wrote to tell me that Anna Keller was executed for treason in München. Even as I write the words I can hardly believe it. I don't understand why she would have undermined our people now, when the Russians are pressing from the east and Tommy and the Amis are bombing us night and day. That puts you and your men at risk and cannot be tolerated. But it still saddens me.

I'm now working in a factory in Koblenz. We make some kind of metal parts for Tiger tanks. It seems strange to work next to the women in a place like that. But we do what we must do.

On the weekends I sew with Kätchen. We make socks for the army and some blankets. If you ever get socks with bad stitches you'll know they're from me! On Wednesday nights I go with Richard Klempner for our weekly spoon collections. We ask for a spoonful of flour, farina, rice or anything like that from every house. We put each spoonful in a bag and then send the bags to the Party for shipping to the front. The people want to help but they have so little themselves.

Herr Offenbacher is sending all of his bread to the army or giving it to the new orphanage so I'm baking my own when I can find flour. The government says we should bake bread very densely so that we'll use less butter or jam. I think it's a good idea, but who has butter or jam anymore?

We all know that the Führer's stockpiles are almost gone now but don't worry about me. I think I am strong and knowing you love me makes me stronger. In the ration lines, women with children are allowed to go first. Maybe someday I can go first? I hope so.

Lindie still goes to the train station every evening. She always dresses in her nicest clothes and wears her Mother's Badge. She sits at the station with the girls eating cheese until the 17:45 train leaves. I usually arrive in Weinhausen on the 17:09 and sit with her. I can't tell you how sad it is. She really does think Gunther is coming. She made him a tin of molasses cookies last week. Sometimes she makes me almost believe it too. The women of the village think she's completely crazy now. Behind her back they're calling her the 'Mad Widow.' They say she never was quite right since 'that' night. I got in an argument with Frau Hoffman over it.

Papa says I should tell you that he prays for you every day and the deacons join him on Wednesday night prayers for you and all our soldiers. I worry about him. I found him crying in his study one Sunday afternoon and then I found out from Klempner that some Party men made him change his sermon that day. He never said so but I think Papa really hates himself for being weak.

I love you, Andreas. Please get better soon and come home to me, safe. I will write you every day.

Yours always,
Eva

⌖

"Ready to climb the terraces?" Hans Bieber nudged Andreas. Much to Eva's joy, the young man had been sent home in mid-March on a ninety day medical leave to free up hospital beds. The bomb blast had broken his upper left arm which would have healed quickly had it not been for a stubborn bone infection that Dr. Krebel was now treating. His left arm was in a sling but the plaster cast was gone. From time to time he had fevers and the skin around his break was tender and slightly discolored.

"I am," Andreas said with a wry smile. Lying on the sofa, he strained to sit up. "But not just yet. You've begun your garden?"

Hans raised his brows. "Well, it's April—I should think so."

"I hope your cabbages are in a straight line."

"Always."

"So, tell me about the vineyards"

"I'm afraid the vines look frail and tired like you. Herr Roth's worried."

Eva entered the living room with her father and a tray of thin ham sandwiches. "Sorry about the bread. I can only find oat meal to bake with."

Bieber grunted. "My horses loved oats."

"You're lucky to have what you have, Hans," said Paul. The minister looked pale and strained. "I stood in line for three hours last week and came away with a tin of wurst and one sausage." He took a seat. "I visited Adolf Schneider this morning. The poor man could only stare out the window. I wanted to read him some Scripture and pray for him, but he ordered me out."

"Udo was his last son," muttered Hans. "The boy deserved better than to be killed in Italy. Cowardly Macaronis—the traitors left us with a mess."

Eva sat by her father. "Remember how the Schneider boys used to get you with snowballs every Christmas Eve?"

Paul stared glumly into space. "I'd give anything to go back to those days. Anything. I would do so many things differently. So many things..."

The room fell quiet.

The minister took a deep breath. "I'm worried about Adolf." He turned to Andreas. "And how are you feeling, son?"

"Better every day."

"Good, but I hope this awful war is over before you're called back."

"Ja, I understand. But until then I have my duty." He dodged Eva's eyes. "I'm told that I have a new command waiting for me." He watched Eva hastily pour everyone a cup of ersatz coffee and walk away. "She doesn't like me talking about it." The young man looked into the kitchen where Eva was now holding a kerchief to her face. "I love her more than my life, but my men will need me."

"Your wife needs you, too." Paul's tone had an uncharacteristic bite. "The war is lost. The Führer should sue for peace before our enemies crush us completely."

"You need to be careful, Herr Pfarrer," said Bieber. He lowered his voice, instinctively. "The Gestapo has no trouble arresting defeatists."

"Then let them come for me. I'm sick of everything—death, destruction, misery...all because of the fanatics. And what have I done about any of it?"

"Are you sure it's only because of the fanatics?" asked Hans.

The room fell quiet. Paul shifted in his seat; Andreas stared at the floor, thinking.

"But nothing can be done about it now," said Hans. "Nobody

cares about anything other than surviving this war. Perhaps afterward..."

"I hear talk of our cruelties, especially against the Jews. I'm supposed to be a minister of the Gospel. I should be doing *something*."

"Maybe exaggerations or British propaganda," said Andreas. "But even if the worst is true you can do nothing about it now. Your congregation needs you. Nobody has the luxury of worrying about the Jews or anybody else in these times, not with the Russians coming." The soldier looked grim. "You don't know them; they're animals. That's why the war is now about extermination." His voice fell. "But it is true that we've learned to be like them."

"I tell you, we have one duty now," said Hans. "We must help one another survive. With an invasion from the West certain, we're about to be apples in a cider press. All we should care about is our boys at the front and the neighbor next door."

Paul took a deep breath. "Our neighbors? Who are our neighbors, Hans?"

The old man fell silent.

Andreas leaned forward. "We must pray that Fieldmarshal Rommel's Westwall can hold long enough for our enemies to grow weary. Maybe then they'll negotiate a peace. Rommel's a genius. If anyone can build a wall to hold, he can. He has the Hitler Youth digging pits and building bunkers, and his pioneer companies have strung mines along the entire coast."

Bieber reached for his coffee. "And let's not forget about the Wunderwaffen. Who knows what our scientists are doing with their rockets."

Paul looked at Andreas. "Where do you think the invasion will be?"

"Hard to know. We have 1300 kilometers to defend and I guess they could come anywhere, but probably Calais."

"And when?"

"The generals seem to think not until late June. Seems logical, since that's the end of the thaw in Poland. With the Russians able to advance from the east, we'd have to leave our western defenses thin." He lowered his voice. "I'm a little worried about it. The Führer sends the best men against Ivan and leaves boys, old men and the walking wounded to fight Tommy and the Amis." Andreas looked into the kitchen again. "Maybe we should talk about other things." He walked over to the gramophone. He put a record on the felt turntable and cranked the handle. "We still have music. This is Mozart's Piano concerto number 27, in B flat Major. It was a favorite of an officer I met on a train to Warsaw. I hope it lightens the mood around here a little."

A knock on the garden door took Eva across the kitchen. She answered to find Widow Schmidt, crying. "Is the Pfarrer here?"

"Yes, please, come in." Eva led her into the living room. "Papa? Frau Schmidt is here for you." Eva watched what little color her father's face had drain away as he bent over to listen to the woman now whispering in his ear. Widow Schmidt then handed him a note. Eva noticed how his hand trembled as he set the note on the coffee table. He pulled his wire spectacles over his ears. "Nerves," he had always said. "Just nerves." Eva certainly understood that. Her father was lonely and had been terribly embarrassed by Gerde's remarriage. Added to that was the suffering he now regularly shared with bereaved congregants. "Papa?"

Paul read the note slowly. When finished, he stared at the empty table top for a long moment. Finally he stood and bade Widow Schmidt good-bye. He reached under his glasses and wiped his eyes with a kerchief. He took a breath. "Adolf Schneider was just found floating in the river." He slowly read Adolf's short note to the room's stunned faces. '*I cannot stay another moment on this earth.*' Paul hesitated. '*I go to God to put my fist into his face.*'

⌖

"So you can do this for me?" Eva was sitting in Dr. Krebel's office on a warm day in early June pleading with him from across his desk. Her voice was imploring, desperate.

Dr. Krebel wiped his face with a kerchief, thoughtfully. Despite his many years of healing flesh, bone and even spirit, he still doubted his own wisdom. "My dear Eva, I don't know. I told you that I could, but I'm not sure that I *should*."

Eva was frustrated. "He loves the land more than the war. He and Bieber have been climbing all over the Roth vines since the first buds. And you said the war is lost. Why would you make him go back?" Her voice was strained. She leaned over his desk, pressing her hands hard on the oak. "All you have to do is say his arm's not healed enough. A little letter from you and Andreas can stay home."

Krebel leaned back. "Eva, first, the Gestapo hasn't stopped watching every move I make since that business about Hermann. And they haven't forgotten you, either."

"So you're afraid."

"Let me remind you that you have no business demanding that I lie to save your husband."

Surprised, Eva returned to her chair. "I'm sorry. Yes, you're right about that. But will you help me?"

Krebel stared at his notepad. "Honestly, Eva, I don't know." His mind was weary. He knew that a simple letter could keep Andreas home and probably save his life. But then what other young man would die in Andreas' place; how many others would perish because Andreas was not there to lead them? He looked into Eva's face and his heart broke. "If Andreas ever found out that you and I conspired in this he would hate us both. We would have stolen his manhood."

"But we would have saved his life."

Dr. Krebel nodded. He reached a hand forward and rested it lightly on top of Eva's. "I was in the first World War. I know how men cling to their honor when everything else is gone. I saw men cast themselves into certain death rather than be stripped of that." Krebel withdrew his hand. "Before I make a decision, I want you to consider what this would mean to him and to your marriage. He would resent you, Eva, maybe even hate you for this." He looked carefully into the young woman's face. "If I do this you will live the rest of your days hiding a secret. And secrets change people, my dear, I promise."

Eva started to cry. "But, but…it's only a letter." She walked to a window and stared into the streets of Weinhausen. The village had become grim again, like it had been in her youth. People now walked the cobblestones on weighted legs, faces hanging forward. Children were not laughing; music was not playing. All that was left of Hitler's Miracle were the flowers of the window boxes that now seemed out of place in the gloom. She turned and looked firmly at Dr. Krebel. "I want you to do it."

Krebel hesitated, then reached for a pen. "I will mail it tomorrow."

Eva walked home slowly. She paused in an alleyway by the market square where she looked up to see the heart that Gunther Landes had carved into the ancient cross-beam so long ago. '*GL liebt LK*' it said.

She wept.

When she arrived home she found Andreas and Hans Bieber fussing in the garden. They were laughing. She watched them for a long moment before announcing herself. "I'll have some supper in about fifteen minutes."

Eva hurried into her kitchen and wrapped an apron around her waist. Klempner had once told her that an apron was a German woman's uniform. Perhaps that's why it felt so heavy today. She opened her cupboard and stared blankly at her nearly empty shelves. The sparse cupboard said as much as anything about how things had changed since the pre-war days when her Führer had made life good for them all. She reached for a tin and an opener, then emptied a cylinder of Wurst on to a plate and cut some smoked cheese into small wedges. She spooned the last pickled beets from a tall jar. She put a few slices of densely baked oat bread on a plate, and scraped the bottom of her last jar of cherry preserves.

The springtime supper passed quickly. Eva did her best to smile and Andreas was attentive. Afterwards, she sat quietly and listened to her husband react to Bieber's wild chatter about grapes, new ideas in distillery, the Roth Vineyard's errors in pruning and so forth. Eva loved the old man but she was glad when he reached for his cap and finally said good-bye. She wanted to spend the rest of that June evening walking along the Mosel with her Andreas.

"We must continue to do our duty conscientiously in obedience to the Divine Will and out of love for our people and country. Our soldiers will continue to fight and die for their Fatherland but not for those men who, by their hateful deeds against our beloved Religion, break our hearts and bring down shame on the German name before God and man."

Roman Catholic Bishop Graf von Galen

CHAPTER THIRTY-ONE

"I LOVE YOU, Eva."

Eva held Andreas' arm tightly.

The pair paused by a swirling eddy and Andreas bade her to sit there with him. The Mosel was full and vital, running harder toward the Rhein than usual. A family of ducks was struggling against the current. "I am so happy, really happy," Andreas said. "I told Bieber that when this war is over I'd like to buy a small vineyard and build a new winery. What would you think of that?"

"I'd like that, very much," answered Eva, softly.

"See there?" Andreas turned to his left and pointed to the mountain curving toward neighboring Winningen. "Bieber tells me that a very good vineyard sits on terraces just out of sight. The owner and his son were both killed in Russia this winter. The widow wants to sell soon but Bieber begged her to hold it for me. He offered to help work the vines for free if she would."

Eva took Andreas' hand. She didn't care about vines or grapes or wine; she only cared about him. Seeing the light return to his eyes was all that she wanted. "I think that would be wonderful, just wonderful. Could we still live in Weinhausen or would we move to Winningen?"

"Oh, we'd stay here. And Offenbacher says he has a good delivery truck he'd sell me, cheap."

Eva nodded. *Oh, Andreas, we could live long lives and make wine for our grandchildren! Would you rather that or honor?*

Later that night, Eva lay in her bed staring at the ceiling with Andreas' arm lying heavily across her. *How would he ever know? Krebel would never tell him. I would never tell him.* She awakened to fix breakfast about 6:30.

It was 6 June 1944.

The two ate quietly, each having a boiled egg and a thin, half-slice of ham. Eva watched every movement her husband made—the way he cut the top off his egg, the way he chewed and swallowed, and the way he smiled at her.

Eva left the table and finished dressing, lost in a belly-churning swirl of conflicting emotions. She brushed her hair hard, almost violently, then hurried downstairs.

She hated her secret.

The chimes on the mantel clock rang 7:00. From the kitchen she heard Andreas fussing with the radio. She looked into the living room and listened as he suddenly turned the volume up.

"The invasion...in Normandy of all places!" Andreas cried.

Eva dropped a dish to the floor and clutched her heart. She ran to his side.

"It started with parachute commandos overnight...shh...but now they're landing on the beaches. If we let them get a foot hold we'll never get them out!" Andreas turned to Eva. "I don't think we're ready. Rommel is in Ulm with his family."

Eva felt weak.

Andreas took her hand. "But we will hold them, Eva. I know it."

Eva wiped her eyes and nodded. She then took Andreas' face in her hands and looked at him, lovingly. She could see the battle-flush in his cheeks. He was the soldier again and his Fatherland needed him more than she did.

Biting her lip she waited for the inevitable. According to his orders Andreas still had more time, but Eva knew his heart. She knew that he had a mistress.

Her name was Duty.

"Eva..."

"Your men need you now." Eva's voice was weak, but gracious.

She would not steal his honor after all; she would tell Krebel to tear the letter up.

Tears filled Andreas' eyes. He pulled Eva close. "If I could do any other thing..."

Eva held him tightly. "I know. I understand." Her mind filled with images of black crepe and death notices, of weeping widows and funerals without bodies. "Just tell me..."

Andreas stroked her hair, softly. "Ja, I will come back to you, Eva. You are my life." He held her by the shoulders and offered a weak smile. "Promise me that you'll be safe." His face abruptly hardened. "I don't know what will happen but the Americans and the British will want to drive us over the Rhein and Ivan wants to open our veins from the east." He tightened his hold on her. "Listen to me. You must stay out of Koblenz from now on. Promise me."

Eva nodded.

Andreas stood and paced. "They'll bomb it to pieces and they'll be attacking the trains, too. Stay off the train and away from the tracks. Maybe you should stay with Lindie. She's far from the rails...But she's more isolated and that could be bad, too..."

"I understand."

"Good. Very good." Andreas lowered his voice. "Now listen to me carefully. Your father has an illegal radio..."

"Papa?"

"Yes, believe it or not. He says the BBC is probably lying as much as Goebbels, but he figures the truth might be somewhere in the middle."

"It's dangerous..."

"Anyway, he should be able to warn you if the Brits or the Amis are getting close."

The idea of enemy soldiers marching through Weinhausen had seemed a far-fetched fantasy. Its sudden possibility made Eva anxious. Her breath quickened.

Andreas hurried to their bedroom and returned with his sidearm. "I'm going to leave this with you. I have four clips of eight rounds each. The Party trained you, right?"

Eva nodded. Her hands were beginning to tremble.

"Good. There's been talk about arming women for civil defense but that may only mean Party women. So, if the Gestapo finds it, tell them I rushed away and forgot it. You understand?"

Eva nodded.

Andreas looked at the clock on the mantle and at his beloved print. "The sun is probably setting, Eva. But that means a new day will come. Believe that." His eyes scanned the rest of the room until they fell on the picture of Adolf Hitler hanging on the wall. He stared at his Führer. "I want you to remember that I'm not fighting for him anymore...not since he betrayed our comrades at Stalingrad. Honor requires that I obey my oath, but my men and I bleed for one another and for the Fatherland...not for him. Not now. Leave the picture on the wall to keep the Gestapo happy but if the Amis come, burn it."

"Yes, yes, I understand it all." She reached for him. "Do your duty, as you must. But come home to me, Andreas, please come home."

By the end of 6 June the Allied armies had landed 155,000 men on the blood-soaked beaches of Normandy. By 9 June First-lieutenant Andreas Bauer had arrived at his battalion headquarters to take command of a badly depleted company of men serving in General Dollmann's Seventh Army. His arm was sore but serviceable, and he had been quickly apprised of his company's objectives as they defended their position between the Americans and the British along the river Drôme. However, by the middle of the month he and his men were slowly pushed out of their perilous corridor and found themselves dug in at the base of the Cotentin Peninsula, even as the Allies secured an ever-widening beachhead on which they had now landed nearly 1,000,000 men.

On 17 July Andreas was devastated to learn that his over-commander, Fieldmarshal Rommel, had been badly wounded and was being sent home to recover. On 20 July Andreas was stunned again when he learned that Adolf Hitler had survived an assassination attempt in the forests of East Prussia. Hitler considered his survival a demonstration of Divine approval and, to Andreas' chagrin, on 24 July the man ordered the Wehrmacht to replace its customary military salute with the Nazi salute along with the words, "Heil Hitler."

August found Andreas engaged in seemingly endless fighting along a slowly collapsing front. Reinforcements came and went from his company like passing breezes, dissolving into death like faceless shadows and remembered only by broken hearts far away. He wondered when he would have his turn to die. Would it be in the morning or at night, by artillery shell, or bayonet—would he see the man who kills him?

On 20 August Andreas and his exhausted men were among the last units to flee across the Dives River in a desperate night time maneuver that avoided their complete encirclement by the Americans near St. Lambert. Five days later he learned that Paris had fallen but that General Dietrich von Choltitz had disobeyed Hitler's orders and had not mined the city's museums. The General's defiance brought a smile to Andreas.

By mid-September the defense of the west had already cost the Wehrmacht 700,000 men. But in Russia, German losses were in the millions. There, Stalin was driving his armies on a relentless press from the east, slowly collapsing the entire German front with no regard to his own casualties. Andreas read letters from Sergeant Kube and Private Zimmer, each speaking of unimaginable losses and unspeakable barbarism. Kube had written that the ground they had once fought for was being taken back by a 'red tide of blood;' that mankind had never fought such a war as this. 'A war between savages,' he wrote.

"Bauer!"

Andreas turned. His whole body was trembling from adrenalin. A savage artillery barrage had just ended. "J..Ja, Herr Hauptmann."

"We're going to need fire on that field. They're coming!"

Andreas and his battalion were desperately defending their section of the Westwall. The wall was a 630 kilometer network of concrete defenses tightly linked by pillboxes, barbed wire, iron beams, and trench systems designed to defend the western border of pre-war Germany. The week before it had been breached for the first time. Andreas barked at a platoon sergeant. "Rausch, Feldwebel Rausch! I need a machine gun crew on that field, now!"

Four American fighters suddenly dropped from the clouds. Andreas dove for cover. Dirt flew along the line and men fell screaming to each side as the planes' gunners chopped the earth to pieces around them. "Get fire on that plane! I need a 15, now!" shouted Andreas. He heard the sound of cannon and whirled about to see four Sherman tanks rolling toward his line.

Cement and debris immediately blew into the air all around him. In another moment the planes were back.

"Come on, come on! Get me that gun!" From either side the heavy machine guns of the German pill boxes lay a rhythmic tak-tak-tak across the field. An anti-aircraft crew quickly trained its MG-15 on the incoming fighters.

Rat-tat-tat-tat-tat.

Tracers from the 15 streaked through the air just ahead of the first fighter. One plane suddenly banked right with smoke pouring from a wing. "Keep firing!" Andreas spun on his heels to see American infantry now crossing the open field toward him.

He hit the ground again as more strafing ripped through his line. He cursed, then jumped into a position behind a steel-reinforced fascine that stretched between two pill boxes. From there he looked through his field glasses at the American advance. "Three companies, with Shermans." He called for his communications man. "Metz, tell battalion we need another anti-tank squad." He turned to another. "Schuler, are the mines ready?"

"Ready, Herr Leutnant," answered Private Schuler.

Andreas thought the boy to be no more than sixteen. "On my command." Andreas watched four Sherman tanks roll closer. Clusters of young Americans humped forward on either side of the steel giants. Andreas studied them through his glasses. He thought they seemed anxious.

And why not?

He quickly surveyed his own men. He had just lost a dozen or so to the strafing and tank fire. The others were exhausted. And they were anxious, too.

More incoming rounds from the Sherman exploded, loudly, blasting huge pieces of concrete off the pillbox to Andreas' right. Another round took part of the roof off. He and Schuler fell under a cloud of white dust, covering themselves from falling debris.

The sounds of machine guns and cannon fire filled the men's ears but in the midst of the roar Andreas heard a plane sputtering from above and arc into a distant crash. He turned to Schuler. "Now!" Schuler set the charges on two long rows of Teller mines. The terrible sequence of explosions hurled bodies and great clods of earth high into the air. At the same moment Andreas ordered a just-arrived two-man anti-tank crew over the wall to a forward position in a shallow crater.

Andreas held his breath as the crew dashed through a hail of American small arms fire. Above, he heard the remaining two Mustang fighter planes burst from behind the clouds and streak toward the tank crew like angry wasps. The whole grey line opened fire on the planes. One exploded, the other came closer and closer. A long burst of gunfire danced across the field and found its mark. His Panzerfaust crew was gone.

Andreas ordered Schuler and another—a middle aged miller over the wall. "Take out those tanks!"

Small arms fire now ricocheted off the German defenses from the pressing American infantry. Andreas held his breath as his second team raced for the Panzerfaust.

The Mustang swung from the west.

The Germans shot everything they had at it but in a moment Schuler and the miller were chopped to pieces. Cursing, Andreas snapped his field glasses to his eyes and checked the field. Behind the first wave of Americans was another. He looked quickly from side to side. His pillboxes and his infantry were exacting a heavy toll on the Americans but the Shermans were still rolling.

Another explosion sent a screaming swarm of glowing shrapnel past Andreas. "Metz," he shouted. "Tell battalion we need artillery support, close. We haven't stopped the tanks." He turned to his sergeant. "Rausch. Send another team."

Rausch didn't hesitate. He tapped a young soldier on the helmet and leapt over the wall with him.

Andreas grit his teeth. Rausch was too valuable for heroics.

By now every bit of firepower the Germans could muster was being thrown at the Americans. Andreas could see that their reserves were advancing quickly and supported by more tanks. He looked overhead, nervously. The sky was clear. "God, send us some Stukas." He turned to watch Rausch and his comrade diving toward the Panzerfaust. He held his breath. More Shermans belched and a pillbox disintegrated in a terrible explosion. "Come on, Rausch."

From a dish in the earth a meter long flame suddenly flashed across the ground. In an instant one of the Shermans exploded. Andreas and his men cheered. In another instant a second missle was launched and a second tank was engulfed in flames.

Another cheer.

The American infantrymen now rushed forward. Andreas knew why. They would have to claim in speed what they were losing in armor. "Here they come!" He ordered the final detonation of mines. Two more rows of devastating explosives blasted huge gaps in the American lines.

Andreas snapped a fresh clip into his Schmeisser and threw himself on to the fascine. It was then that he saw Rausch and his comrade launch a third shell. They missed and were now in danger of being overwhelmed by enemy infantry. Rausch was spun to one side, wounded; his comrade tried reloading. Andreas grabbed three men and jumped over the wall, racing toward Rausch with heavy cover fire. Bullets zipped through the air alongside Andreas' head, nipping his helmet and snagging his clothing. Two of his three men fell away.

Ahead, Rausch was hunched in his hole alongside a now dead comrade. Badly bleeding, he was desperately trying to fire his Panzerfaust. With an American tank a mere five meters in front of him, Rausch lurched upward.

"No, no!"

Rausch fired, point blank.

The Sherman exploded, killing Rausch and a close squad of American infantrymen.

Andreas cried out and then heard his remaining comrade gasp and fall away. The American infantry was now closing to within forty meters. All around him bullets snapped and whined. His men were firing furiously from behind.

A thick shroud of smoke swirled toward him.

Andreas took a breath and turned to make a zig-zag dash back toward the wall. Ping-zip-hizz...the sounds of hot metal popped and cracked to all sides. He tripped headlong into a shallow gulley and twisted into a prone position where he quickly supported his Schmeisser on his elbows. Straining to see through the smoke, he emptied his final magazine at a hazy group of Amis.

With eyes burning, Andreas then spotted a lone green figure suddenly emerging from the smoke and charging toward him. He rolled to his side and pinched his eyelids to clear his sight as he desperately fumbled for his sidearm. The American's fresh-face abruptly appeared.

Andreas snapped his pistol forward.

The American snugged his carbine to his shoulder.

Andreas fired and missed, then rolled to one side as the American's shot nipped the dirt at his side.

He rolled again as the American's second shot rang off a rock; The German fired back, missing.

A third shot sang by Andreas' ear; he aimed again.

The American's rifle jammed; the astonished soldier's eyes met Andreas' for just an instant.

Whoom!

The earth shook. From somewhere in the rear the German artillery had found its mark. Huge heaps of earth suddenly leapt from the earth, heaving spinning rocks, dirt and screaming men in all directions. The sky flashed with light. Andreas and his American foe were thrown to the ground by unseen compressions thumping through the air like mighty, invisible hammers.

German Stukas screamed out of the sky above.

Andreas covered his head with his arms and prayed as fast as his lips could move. Whoom! Whoom! Whoom! Dirt and rocks rained down on him. He pressed his body against the earth. Whoom! Tat tat tat tat...strafing fire bit furiously at the ground nearby. The soldier pressed his body harder. Whoom!

And then it ended.

The world fell still for just a moment.

Coughing, Andreas slowly lifted his head and peered through the rising smoke and dust. His ears rang. He thought his head would explode. But, wary and with his pistol now pointed forward in a trembling hand, he eased himself to a crouching position and strained to see any sign of his young American foe.

Nothing moved.

The field had been cleared.

Relieved, Andreas stood slowly. He could barely hear his men cheering from behind. But when he turned and saw them waving him home, he ran as fast as his legs could carry him.

⌖

Diary Entry: 27 December 1944

This is my first wedding anniversary and I spent the day crying. Andreas wrote me a beautiful poem but the paper he wrote it on smelled like gunpowder. I love him so much but so many men are dying that I really doubt that I will ever see him again. Every day the newspaper is filled with obituaries. I had a dream about him last night. I saw him picking grapes and smiling. He says his men are hoping the V-2 rockets will turn the war around. I hope so, too.

Dr. Krebel says that my pregnancy is going well. I'm happy and sad about it. What if my baby has no father? What if the Americans kill me after it's born? Dr. Krebel scolded me for thinking like that. He says that babies are God's gift of hope. He says that's why Jesus was given to the world as a baby. And he reminded me that the Amis are not like the Russians.

I still haven't told Andreas and I don't know if I should. I thought he might come home for Christmas but that was stupid of me. Nobody is coming home this Christmas. Dr. Krebel says he doesn't know if I should tell him or not. He says it could make him fight harder or worry more. Papa says he wouldn't tell him because he thinks Andreas might change whatever he's done to stay alive so far. But what if he dies not knowing?

Everybody is hungry now. I'm a little worried that I'm not eating enough for my baby. The village has less food every day. Even the farmers are having a bad time.

I hear more talk about the SS murdering Jews in Poland. Papa thinks the fanatics are capable of it but he says that enemy propaganda always exaggerates things. He tells me he hears some things on the BBC that are ridiculous. Kätchen said she hopes it is true because the Jews started this war. She really hates them. I ask Klempner about it and he said we're relocating Jews. But he said they are taken to labor camps where they sew uniforms or assemble things for the war effort. He asked me if I thought it made sense to kill workers that we need so badly. I told Kätchen and she was disappointed.

The women at the church sewing club are talking about the Morgenthau Plan. They said it proves that the Americans are in league with world Jewry to destroy Germany once and for all. I am mostly worried about the part of the plan where every German would only be allowed to eat 1,000 calories a day. Would that mean children, too? We could starve to death. Frau Wicker says they want to take away all our industry and break us up into little farming districts. I think it's awful that the American president would even consider a plan like this. We must stop them, somehow.

Mother visited last week. She wants me to go to Dresden with her and her husband to wait for the war to be won. She says there's some kind of secret agreement between the governments. The Führer agreed not to bomb Oxford and Churchill agreed not to bomb Dresden. I told Mother that I couldn't leave Papa and that I wouldn't trust Churchill about anything. She said she was going anyway. Then I told her that the BBC was giving a very different picture of the war.

Papa and Herr Offenbacher were marching around the market today with the Weinhausen Volkssturm. I thought they looked ridiculous in their baggy uniforms and seeing Papa with a gun is too much.

He seems to like it though. I think it makes him feel strong. Hans Bieber is angry as a summer hornet because Richard Klempner won't let him join. Hans says that he's only seventy-seven and can still shoot straight! I don't think old men and school boys should ever have to fight against real soldiers. But if the Amis come, they may have to.

Poor Lindie still goes to the train station and waits for Gunther every evening.

I think the whole world has gone mad.

Yesterday I opened my Bible and found those daffodils that Wolf gave me long ago. I felt sick and threw them away.

"God, I hate the Germans."

American General Dwight D. Eisenhower

CHAPTER THIRTY-TWO

PAUL VOLK LOOKED up. Overhead a squadron of American B-17 bombers could be heard droning eastward above a heavy blanket of January clouds. "They're going to hit Koblenz again. God help those poor people." Paul pulled his collar over his neck. A cold wind started to blow and more snow was falling.

"I was with Lindie after church yesterday," said Eva. "She's supposed to get seven children from the city. Herr Klempner told me the Party was going to evacuate more as quickly as possible."

"I pity the city people. Lots are homeless. Some are beginning to starve and the rich are still coming out here begging farmers for food with their jewelry and clothing. I saw some ridiculous hats at church this week."

Eva shook her head. "But even the farmers are running out of food. Lindie's cupboards are bare."

Paul nodded. "Offenbacher's bakeries are all destroyed now."

Father and daughter made their way slowly from the sparse market square. They each carried a few items in their baskets. Eva had managed to find a tin of smoked pork, some pork bones for soup and a small bag of rye flour. She felt lucky because her yellow flour coupon would have expired the next day. "Have you heard from Andreas lately?"

"Yes. The military post is miraculous. He gets all my letters and I get all of his. Of course they're always censored." Eva stopped to tighten the scarf wrapped over her head. "He wrote that the battle in the Ardennes was horrible. That's all he said."

"I think thc West is surprised how much fight we still have in us." Paul looked from side to side and lowered his voice. "But we all know we cannot win."

Eva stiffened. "You need to stop talking like that. The army's working on new weapons and..."

"My dear," Paul stopped walking. "My prayer is that our brave soldiers can buy us a better peace."

" 'Buy us' Papa? What an awful thing to say. You do know what they're spending, don't you? " Eva's face hardened and she stared straight ahead.

Paul gripped his coat tightly to his throat. A wintry blast nearly blew his hat off. "I'm sorry, Eva, I didn't mean for it to sound like that."

As the two approached the Volk house they spotted a dark, four-door car parked in front. "Gestapo," murmured Paul.

Eva chilled. "Papa?"

"I think you should go your own way. Leave this to me."

"But..."

"Please, just keep walking."

Eva nodded. Her heart pounded and her legs felt like liquid. She paused at the stoop of her father's house and kissed him on the cheek. "Papa?"

Two car doors opened.

With a nudge from her father Eva kept walking.

Two Gestapo agents in black leather coats emerged from their car, each tilting their hats into the snow-stinging wind. Another was left sitting behind the wheel. "Pfarrer Paul Volk?" barked one as he approached the minister with long, menacing strides.

"Ja."

"Heil Hitler." Both agents snapped a quick salute.

Paul did not.

One agent was a large man with pursed lips and a long nose. "I am Obersturmführer Bruno Altmann. This is Obercharführer

Hirsch." The second agent grunted. He was a portly man with a pudding face and wide-set eyes. Both were cold and surly. "We've come to search your house."

Paul felt his chest tighten. A sharp wind cut through the gaps of his clothing. He pulled his collar to his throat with one hand and held his hat in place with the other. He cast a forlorn look toward Eva now watching from a shadowy corner in the church yard, then took a deep breath. "Well, come in, then."

The agents followed Paul into his living room where he turned on the only lamp with a working bulb. A dull yellow light struggled to find the corners of the damp room. "Would you like some schnapps?" He removed his hat and gloves.

Hirsch was in no mood for pleasantries. "You've been denounced for defeatism, sedition and contraband."

Paul rubbed his hands to warm them. "Ah, denounced. The word has a quite ring to it."

Altmann jerked a glove off his right hand and slapped the minister across the face. "Fool."

The slap stung Paul's cold cheek. Wincing, he closed his eyes. For months he had spent long hours in a dark, empty house reflecting on the man he had never been. Fool? Yes…but no more the coward. The minister opened his eyes and took a deep breath.

He exhaled a lifetime of timidity.

"You, Hirsch, should write this down. First, we cannot win this war. Second, Hitler has been our ruin, and third, I have a radio upstairs which broadcasts the most interesting programs from the BBC." Paul turned to Altmann. "Now, if you wish to strike my other cheek, have at it."

Paul was man-handled through his doorway and dragged into the street. He turned his head to see Eva rushing toward him in the snow. "Stop!" she cried. "What are you doing?"

The agents hurried the minister toward the car as Eva approached. Altmann turned. "So, you must be Frau Bauer, the suspect's daughter."

"I am." Eva looked at the radio cradled in Altmann's arm and then raised her face to meet her Papa's. She was stunned to see how calm he looked, how unexpectedly heroic. Sudden respect displaced her terror. She wished she could cheer for him, loudly, so that all of Weinhausen could know how brave their Pfarrer Volk really was. She quickly fixed her admiring eyes on his and she knew that he understood exactly how she felt.

"I love you, Eva..." A punch in the belly from Hirsch silenced the man.

Eva lurched forward, "I love you, too, Papa, and I'm so proud..."

Altmann pulled Eva to one side, then jerked open the front passenger door and threw the radio onto the seat. He motioned for Hirsch to put Paul in the back. His hand squeezed Eva's arm tightly. "So, Frau Bauer, you do realize that we are still watching you?"

Eva flinched, but just a little. "I don't care." She grimaced as she watched her father being muscled into the car.

"No? Well, I would hope you aren't planning to interfere. That would surprise me. A pregnant wife of a brave German officer should be...shall we say...cooperative, especially if her husband might be transferred to the Eastern Front."

Eva swallowed. "Obersturmführer Altmann, you must contact Manfred Schiller. He's an agent in your Dresden office. He...he can set this straight for you."

The corners of Altmann's mouth twitched. "Ah, well, you see, Herr Schiller is the one who ordered your father's house to be searched."

Eva's belly rolled and her head went light. "S..so who...who does he think put the radio in my father's house?"

Altmann laughed, loudly and released his grip. "Have a good day, Frau Bauer."

"But where are you taking him?"

Altmann climbed in the back seat, sandwiching Paul Volk between himself and Hirsch. He slammed the door.

"Papa?" cried Eva. "Papa, I love you!" She followed after the car as it pulled quickly away. She could see her father twisting his neck to face the rear window. Desperate, Eva ran after the car, awkwardly.

"Papa! Papa!" The car sped away over the snow-dusted street and she could go no farther. Eva fell to her knees and wailed.

By 1 March 1945 Andreas had become a staggering shell of a man. He had survived over five years of war under the most horrendous of conditions. He had fought with and against good men, evil men, brave men and cowards. He had wrestled with God's natural elements and with God Himself; he had done battle with things outward and inward. Now with the Americans over the Westwall and into Germany, he had little time to reflect, little time to consider; he had barely time to survive.

By 6 March General Patton's U.S. Third Army had driven Andreas and the German Seventh Army across the Prüm River and backward toward Kolberg which lay a mere fifty-five kilometers from Weinhausen. German casualties had been terrible and German morale had long since faded along with any hope of salvation.

Worse, Andreas could not escape the gnawing sense of moral dread that had secretly weighed on him for some time. Something about his government seemed wrong. He had always been offended by the ugly rhetoric of the fanatics, he was well-aware of the execution of dissidents and he had seen cattle-cars of Jews pointed eastward. But for years he had countered by reasoning that each could be explained: for the first, hyperbole; for the second, public safety; for the third, resettlement. Nevertheless, a disturbing impression of the whole was beginning to emerge that loomed larger than these parts. And he was hearing talk of other things.

Things he dared not even imagine.

In response, Andreas began to slip into a depressive resignation to the purposes of Fate. Confused, he found himself standing on the only ground that seemed plain and simple to understand: his love for Eva, for his men, and the obligation of his oath.

"You, come here."

Andreas turned to see a badly wounded officer lying in a heavily shadowed corner of a field dressing station. He removed his cap. "Heil Hitler, Herr Major."

"I need a priest," the man wheezed. His uniform was covered in dark blood from a bleeding stomach wound and his mouth was covered in pinkish foam oozing from a badly punctured lung.

Andreas looked around the tent, straining to find a chaplain in the midst of the frantic medical staff. "I'm sorry, Herr Major, but I don't see any..."

The man seized his arm, weakly. "What's your name?"

Andreas had hoped to check on the wounded from his own company, but he removed his cap and set a stool by the man's cot. "I am Oberleutnant Bauer." He reached for a rag and dabbed the man's mouth.

The officer nodded. "Major Lehrbach, Fifth Panzers." He calmed for a moment and stared quietly at the canvas overhead. Outside, the earth shook from American artillery that was steadily blasting the Wehrmacht line. Inside, medics and aids were frantically loading wounded men into waiting trucks. "I am a dead man within the hour." Lehrbach sucked hard for breath again. "But I cannot die without confessing to someone."

"There must be a priest..."

"No time, now," he wheezed. "Listen to me Bauer..."

"Well...I..."

Lehrbach strained to pull himself up on one elbow. "Listen to me," he hissed. The man's eyes found Andreas'. "We are murdering Jews in the east...tens of thousands..."

Andreas looked around, anxiously. No one else had heard the man.

"You don't believe me." He fell back into his cot.

"I...I know we've shot some..."

Lehrbach cursed. "No, it's bigger than that." He paused to breath. "We're exterminating them like vermin." He paused to breathe. "The camps in Poland are not just work camps. Himmler wants the Jews...annihilated. Those too weak to work are killed and when the war's over, he'll exterminate them all."

Andreas sat back. "With respect, Herr Major, the SS talked about a future homeland for the Jews. Surely..."

"Listen! I was at Treblinka. A Death Head's colonel told me... that he was duty bound to an 'unpleasant necessity.'" Lehrbach sputtered a long stream of blood out of his mouth and over his chin. "That's what he called it. He said he...needed to be strong. He told me things..." The man paused. "I closed my eyes and said I didn't want to know anymore." Lehrbach's whole body convulsed. "God have mercy; I closed my eyes and turned away."

Andreas looked at the morphine bag dripping into the major's arm.

"They try to keep it a secret. They fear the people. The Party's always feared the people..." His chest lifted and fell. "I kept their secret; telling would lead to our defeat." The man paused. "But we are already beaten. And the Russians are overrunning the camps. The truth will come out."

"Well, the Russians would lie..."

The major opened one hand and revealed a blood-stained picture of his wife and two teenage daughters. "My family, Bauer. Look at them."

Andreas stared at a picture of three faces smiling along a lakeshore. "They are beautiful, Herr Major."

"I swear on their lives..." Lehrbach's voice faded and he sank in his cot.

Andreas ran his fingers through his hair. His mind whirled. *Of course there's been atrocities, but this?* "I don't like the Jews, Herr Major...most of us don't. But I never hated them." He grew anxious. "And how could anyone hate them *that* much?" His tone was insistent, suddenly defensive.

Lehrbach didn't answer.

Andreas licked his lips. He knew that some of his men certainly hated the Jews. After years in the Hitler Youth why wouldn't they? *But they were still civilized,* he thought. And he supposed that some hated the Jews *that* much. *But aren't they the fringe?*

If it's true, when did things change?

Does it even matter now, with the Russians coming?

And what about the Führer?

A flood of images burst from his memory—images of beatings in the streets, and caricatures of Jews on posters, of movies degrading them and rabid speech making. Each in its time had seemed so separate from the other. But this? Could extermination be the *policy* of his government? "But if...if this is so, Herr Major, then no one will forgive us...not any of us. Not ever. Not even God."

7 March found Andreas as a tortured soul. Major Lehrbach's deathbed revelation weighed heavily on the man, so heavily that he could barely march. Through that terrible day he struggled with the monumental question of whether his own government might be genocidal; it was a question he thought no decent German soldier should ever have to ask.

On one hand he thought the whole idea to be an insane exaggeration, one too unbelievable to dignify with consideration despite Lehrbach's persuasive testimony. But on the other were the nagging rumors that had persisted for years. These always had a vague smell about them, but the smell was of things that had been easy to turn from—of things that were better forgotten.

He remembered the common table-talk at the beginning: 'The soup is never served as hot as it's cooked.' Now Andreas wasn't so sure.

He wondered if he had been a fool.

By nightfall, an exhausted Andreas could do nothing but stare the dead man's stare. He did not answer the questions of his men; he did not call in his casualty report to battalion. At 3:00 AM he threw off his blanket and vomited, even as artillery blasts thumped all around. He asked himself if his oath bound him to a betrayal. But what if there's a different explanation? The cold night's sky was alive with flames and flashes. Aircraft rumbled overhead. He collapsed to his knees and squeezed his temples with his fists. "Oh God, oh God."

At dawn on 8 March Andreas' and his men were ordered to retreat again. Farther north the Americans had crossed the mighty

Rhein—the jugular vein of Germany. The news was a terrible blow. Andreas' Seventh Army had wheeled south, however, and would be attempting to hold a defensive line parallel to the north bank of the Mosel.

Passing near the monastery at Maria Laach, Andreas knew that he was only twenty-five kilometers from his own dear Weinhausen. He looked across the grey, leafless countryside with longing eyes. His heart was heavy. He didn't want to be the soldier-self anymore. He wanted to throw away his weapons and abandon the war; he wanted to fly through the hilly forests and be with his wife.

He wondered about her; he always wondered about her.

And he worried, too. What was she doing that very moment? Was she sewing or standing in line for food? Had she kept away from Koblenz?

And he worried about her father, as well. To trick the censors Eva had written that Paul was 'serving' south of Stuttgart at Schömberg—where he was no doubt mining shale to be pounded into fuel. And he wondered if Eva's mother was one of the 200,000 old men, women and children reported as burned alive by the fire bombing of Dresden just weeks before. He pictured her blackened remains being bulldozed into a mass grave already filled with the charred remains of grandmothers and little girls.

Andreas looked woefully at his marching men. *Boys and old men, he thought. My God, what is this madness?* Each weary soldier was waiting his turn to die for a cause that all but a few believed was long lost.

But their heads were still up. He needed to lift his own.

They had all remained stubbornly proud in the face of inevitable defeat. Andreas marveled at that. He was proud of his comrades—and he loved them...despite the government that may have betrayed them all.

But he was not proud of himself.

He thought about what he should have seen.

Two American Mustangs suddenly dove from the grey clouds. Soldiers tumbled to both sides of the road. A hospital truck exploded. But Andreas just stood in the roadway and stared like a man watching a film flickering on a white screen. A boy sergeant, Willi Klemmer—a store clerk from Hamburg—pulled him to the ground by the sleeve. "Are you mad, Herr Leutnant?"

Andreas stared into the earnest face of his sergeant. The boy's voice sounded far away—a groaning, hollow blur of words.

Another grabbed his shoulder and shook him. "Herr Leutnant!"

Then the world burst in. Andreas' eyes focused; his ears piqued. He looked around, awakened. "God, that was bad...thanks." The all-clear given, Andreas ordered his company forward.

But Andreas' attention was still drawn away. *Maybe Lehrbach was confused. Maybe he was crazy with morphine.* Andreas thought it a relief to think so. *But even if he was crazy, he was right about one thing: the war is lost and my men are dying for nothing.* Andreas sucked a long drink of water from his canteen.

In the late afternoon Private Metz raced to Andreas with the company radio. "From battalion, Herr Leutnant."

Andreas answered. "Ja, Bauer here." He listened to his orders and as he did, his face tightened. American infantry was making a rapid flanking advance against a wooded hill just south of the column. If the Americans took the hill they could cut off the retreat and begin an encirclement of the whole column. Andreas double-timed his men forward.

Plunging headlong through heavy thicket, Andreas' company beat the Americans to the west side of the hill and quickly dug a shallow trench along a line about three-quarters of the way to the top. There they waited, anxiously.

Andreas ranged along his defenses, being sure that he had spread his machine gun crews correctly. He placed flame throwers at each end. "Our orders are to defend at all costs," he shouted. "The column needs to pass behind us on the other side of this hill and we need to shield them. Once passed, they will wheel back and flank the Amis from the east. Do we understand?"

"Jawohl, Herr Oberleutnant," came the weary response.

Night was settling quickly. Andreas hoped that the stalled Americans would not make a night fight out of it. He hated night fights. Flares, muzzle-flashes, and blinding artillery were haunting to him. He checked the springs of his eight Schmeisser magazines and loaded them slowly. He counted four grenades, wiped down his Walther P-38 side-arm and ran a finger over the edge of his knife. He had only ever used the knife once and he hoped to never see the silver steel again.

Where are they? In the quiet he began to think again. With the war truly lost, he wondered how he could kill another American or British soldier in good conscience. Yet he wondered how he could not. How could he not protect his homeland or defend his comrades: simple farm boys, milkmen, school teachers and clerks? He wished he could just make this all end. *Surely the men know the war is lost. Would they surrender? Better to the Americans than the Russians. Would it help if I tell them about Lehrbach? But was he telling the truth?* Andreas' heart started to pump, wildly. *I could order them to surrender. The shame would not be theirs. But the oath*. Andreas looked over his men. *Which is better...keeping my word to Hitler or saving them?* He wiped his face with a shaking hand. *Surrendering my company would expose the column to certain death.*

But somewhere this must stop.

But when? How?

The column only needs a delay to escape...

Andreas' mind spun until he heard a crack in the forest. One of his men sent up a flare, exposing a crouching American skirmish line advancing slowly uphill.

The Germans opened fire.

The Americans returned a few rounds of their own. As the flare sputtered, the Americans fell back leaving two dead. A young German near Andreas caught a final shot in his face. Andreas stumbled to the dead soldier's side and stared at what was left of his head.

For Andreas, it was enough.

He grabbed Sergeant Klemmer's arm and dragged him aside to whisper in his ear. Klemmer began to protest loudly. Andreas put his hand over his mouth. "A German soldier follows orders, Feldwebel."

Klemmer nodded. Andreas removed his hand. "You are as good a soldier as the Reich has left. You will obey me."

Nodding, Klemmer stared at his boots.

"Now leave your rifle and follow me." Andreas pulled the Schmeisser off his shoulder and laid it on the ground with his sidearm. His mind was racing. He looked deeply into the dark wood, took a breath, and without another word he began his trek downslope toward the American line.

Andreas' tentative creep was a far cry from the boasting goosestep of times past. Now every leaden step bore the weight of rising doubts; every stick cracking underfoot heightened anxiety. Indeed, the three hundred meters that followed were the longest, hardest, and most agonizing meters the man had ever marched. He stumbled and slipped; he struggled to find his footing. And why not? This was no ordinary jaunt through a dark wood. This was the painful journey of a man stepping out of himself to find himself.

This was a pilgrimage.

"Not to shoot, vee surrender." A terrified Klemmer blurted his poor English at a surprised patrol now surrounding the pair. The dumfounded Amis ordered the Germans to clasp their hands behind their heads and then hurried them to the rear where a disheveled captain pointed a flashlight into their faces.

Andreas saluted. "Oberleutnant Bauer." He pointed to Klemmer. "Feldwebel Klemmer."

The American spat. Andreas ordered Klemmer to tell the American officer the plan. When finished, the captain stared at Andreas carefully. "You think we're stupid? You Krauts are planning an ambush."

Klemmer communicated Andreas' assurance otherwise, explaining how Andreas would order the surrender of his men at first light. The American hesitated. "Why should I believe any of this?"

The German removed the New Testament from his breast

pocket and withdrew a picture of Eva from its pages. He handed the picture to the American. "Klemmer, tell him to keep this until my men are in his custody. Tell him I love her more than my life."

""I believe that I can and may compare my activities and my error with the activities and error of the honest and brave German soldier. He knows today that he sacrificed himself not only, as he thought, for the existence of his Volk, but for a cause in which he was deceived and betrayed and for which he must be ashamed as a staining of the German name."

Gerhard Kittel, Protestant theologian

CHAPTER THIRTY-THREE

AS DAWN GRAYED the woodland Andreas and his sergeant led the wary Americans up-slope toward the German line. With hands raised and waving a large white cloth, Andreas shouted through the silent wood. "Drop your weapons. We are surrendered. Drop you weapons..."

The Germans slowly stood like grey ghosts rising in the morning mist. "Is that you, Oberleutnant?"

"Ja. And I order you to drop your weapons, now! We are surrendered." Behind, a wary wave of green-jacketed Americans crept closer.

Reluctantly, eighty-four Germans slowly began to lay down their weapons and one by one raised their arms. The Americans rushed them, and in moments Andreas' men were encircled.

Andreas breathed a sigh of relief. He turned to the American officer and saluted.

"So, you Nazis were telling the truth," said the captain. "Go figure." He handed Andreas Eva's picture back. "She's a pin-up babe if I ever saw one."

The Americans quickly disarmed their forlorn prisoners, put them in a line, and began marching them downhill. Arms up and walking alongside the American captain, Andreas calculated his next move. With his men out of harm's way he had to find a way of escape and get to Eva. He slid his eyes to one side and then the other. His captors were laughing, most were smoking; he thought they were so incredibly casual.

But no sooner had they reached the base of the hill when three companies of German infantry suddenly burst from the east side of the forest, laying down a precise fire into the surprised Americans. "Oh, God, no!" cried Andreas. He knew the night's delay had protected the column but the German flanking maneuver had come much earlier than he had expected.

His plan had failed.

Instinctively, Andreas spun and smashed the startled American captain in the face, then jerked a rifle from a surprised private and began firing. "Run, men, run!" he cried.

Zip, pop, zip, zip. Bullets nipped twigs and brush. Men were shouting from all sides. Out of ammunition, Andreas lurched for a dead American's carbine and turned it against every green uniform he could see.

Bullets clipped bark from his side; a grenade landed nearby.

Andreas tumbled into some heavy brush as a deafening flash filled the air with shrapnel. He could feel his coat tear; his cap was shredded from his head. Out of ammunition, he crawled for an American's M1. Using the dead soldier as a shield, he fired desperately until his surviving men had scattered to safety.

As the German flank advanced, Andreas turned his attention to the Amis trying to form a line some fifty yards away. His eyes fell over several bodies of his men whom he had delivered to death, unarmed. His throat tightened; he began to suck for air. Among the dead was Willi Klemmer who lay face up with a bullet hole in his forehead.

Andreas' plan had been worse than a disaster. His heart raced; his skin chilled. *Oh God, my men. What have I done to my men*! He whined and grit his teeth; he hoped to die.

The German flankers caught up to the now half-crazed Andreas. One of them tossed him a Mauser and a belt of stripper clips. He loaded his rifle and took a breath. Rather than move with the Germans in an organized advance, he leapt over the American corpse and charged recklessly through the forest by himself.

Deep in the wood the Americans had recovered and were quickly organizing a stubborn defense. They fired furiously at the oncoming Andreas until the German threw himself behind a tree-trunk to reload. Mad with self-loathing, he ignored shouts from his own men behind and abruptly abandoned his screen to dash forward, screaming. It was then that the world dissolved from view in a blinding flash.

Hours later, Andreas awoke with stabbing pains in his temples. His limbs felt weak and fluid, and he could barely breathe. As his mind slowly cleared the forest around him seemed eerily silent. He struggled to his knees. Somewhere in the distance he heard the faint cracking of small arms fire. The firefight had passed him by. Dead soldiers lay strewn about. Smoke hung heavy.

Andreas clutched the jagged shards of a splintered tree with two hands and pulled himself to his feet. His body ached but no bones seemed broken. He wiped dried blood from his eyes and set his fingers lightly on the half-scabbed wounds etched across his face and hands. Then he remembered the fiasco of his surrender and the loss of his men. He bent over and vomited.

⌖

"My God! Andreas?"

"Lindie, I need your help." Filthy and bloodied, a gasping Andreas was shivering in the dark at Lindie's door. Separated from his regiment, he had stumbled through the forests of the Eifel in a desperate flight for home.

"Come in, come in!"

"Is Eva here?" he wheezed.

"Oh, you poor man. No, she's not here." Lindie lit a small candle. "Sit. Let me get you water and bread. And let me clean those wounds."

"The Amis are close." Andreas' eyes were hollow; his legs were twitching.

Lindie bit her lip.

"I...I got separated from my company. But I must get to Eva first."

"You can't go another step. I'll go for her."

Andreas shook his head. "It's not safe for you."

"But it's not safe for you, either. And you're in no condition. I'll go."

Andreas tilted against a wall. "Time's short, Lindie. And I must join my men. I just need to see Eva one more time. I need to know that she's alright before I die."

Lindie grabbed hold of a coat and headed for the door. "She's fine." She looked kindly at the pitiable man. "Don't you worry about her..."

"I should go..."

Lindie blocked the door. "No. The Gestapo watches her." She thought for a moment. "Eva goes to the Niederberg to pray sometimes. I'll tell her you'll meet her there...at first light."

Worried, Eva pulled a heavy gray scarf tightly to her head and self-consciously felt for Andreas' pistol which she had tucked deeply into her coat pocket. Outside, the March night was damp and drizzly; a heavy fog lay on the Mosel. She listened for the purr of a Gestapo car. Confident no one was watching, the late-term woman made her way slowly through pre-dawn darkness toward the neighboring village of Kobern and the castle on its heights.

Kobern was no longer the fairy-tale village of flower boxes and music. Instead, Eva picked her way through vacant gray streets. News of the approaching Americans had the folk hidden behind shuttered windows. Stray bombs had littered the village with heaps of brick, plaster and broken timbers. Fires still burned in smoldering pockets and the air smelled sour from smoke.

Eva exited Kobern by the Catholic church and paused at the base of the castle mount to listen. She supported her swollen belly with two hands and caught her breath. She heard only distant sounds of gunfire. Confident the enemy had skirted the villages, Eva began her determined trek up the half-hidden mountain trail and finally arrived at the Niederberg ruins just as the sun tipped the rims of the silhouetted mountains to the east.

Exhausted, the woman leaned a hand heavily on a stone wall. But no sooner had her breathing begun to ease when an American scout emerged from the castle.

"What...?" The young man's knees nearly buckled. He pointed his M1 at the startled woman. "Sergeant!" he shouted.

Eva's mouth hung open. Her eyes flew about looking for any sign of Andreas. Instead, they fell on the dead bodies of two young boys in Volkssturm uniforms lying in the brush just a few meters away. Her heart pounded. She gathered her wits and quickly slipped one hand into her pocket and rested it on Andreas' pistol. Unseen boots pounded closer and three men rounded a broken castle wall. One was an American sergeant; the other two were in civilian clothing and looked like Poles. Eva clutched a hand to her heart and closed her eyes.

The sergeant lowered his weapon. "Wie heissen Sie?"

Surprised at the American's perfect German, Eva answered boldly. "My name is Frau Bauer." She glanced warily at the leering Poles.

"*Gotowy Niemiec świnia, gotowy dla brania*," one muttered.

Eva's heart skipped; she knew the words '*Niemiec*' and '*świnia*,' and she remembered another time like this. She waited, chin posed defiantly; she'd never be a pig for anyone again. Her fingers lingered on the hidden pistol. Eva would be brave.

"So I see you're pregnant," said the sergeant. "Why the devil are you here?"

Eva answered coldly. "The Bürgermeister said the Americans might take my village today. I thought it would be safer for me and my baby up here." She could hear her heart thumping. "And I like to pray here." She pointed to the row of little chapels that lined the ridge to the east.

"Yeah." The American stared into the hollow eyes of the gaunt-faced woman. "You look half-starved. Follow me." The sergeant ordered his sentry to remain while he led Eva and the Poles through the ruins to the upper level. There, Eva noticed a telescope mounted on a tripod, two radios and an assortment of gear that was strewn about. Her eyes lingered on the old stone well. She thought of Andreas.

One of the Poles grunted an angry comment at the American. The sergeant answered with a growl. The Pole pulled a bottle of vodka from his shirt pocket and glared at Eva as the sergeant then opened a C Ration pack. "Have a seat. Sorry we don't have any sausage and no pretzels, but I have biscuits, raisins, some potatoes, and ham with lima beans."

Eva removed her hand from her pocket and received the food casually, trying to disguise her ravenous hunger. She took a bite and chewed slowly. "Thank you, Feldwebel," she said as she finished. "You speak good German."

The American squatted in front of her. "My father was a Kraut. Actually, my uncle and his family live in the next village. My captain sent me here as a scout since I told him I knew the area." He looked around the castle. "I've been to this place before."

A chill rode Eva's spine. She studied the dirty young man. "Bobby? Bobby Folk?"

The soldier was taken aback. "Yes," he answered slowly. "And you...are you... Eva? Eva Volk?"

"Ja, Bobby, I am!" She stood.

"Well of all the..." The American embraced her.

A pistol was suddenly placed at Bobby's temple. One of the Poles was snarling and the other was standing a few meters away with a sub-machine gun. "We want the woman."

Bobby Folk stiffened. "Lower your weapon, Gorski."

The Pole sneered, wickedly. By his appearance, Eva was certain that he had been recently liberated from a POW camp. The man's skin clung to his cheekbones like yellowed leather; his teeth were mostly missing; his eyes were filled with hate. "*Nie.*"

⌖

Andreas had left Lindie's farmyard before first light and had hoped to arrive at the castle hours before the scheduled morning rendezvous. However, the Americans had advanced more rapidly than he had expected, requiring him to spend precious time in hiding.

Soon after dawn Andreas paused in heavy brush to listen to the distinct sounds of battle now coming from the south. He cursed. By the location he knew that his 7th army had made a hasty night time retreat across the Mosel instead of fleeing due east, leaving Kobern and the Niederberg squarely in occupied territory.

Anxious, he hurried on and finally reached the base of the castle mount. He checked his pocket watch—the silver one given to him by Eva for Christmas in '43. He looked up at the now clouded sun. *Forty-five minutes late.* He studied the terrain warily, scenting the air like a hunted stag. He was very much aware that he might easily run into an American patrol. *She must be up there by now...and it's a good place for scouts.*

The soldier had almost reached the terraced summit when a shot cracked from within the castle walls. Andreas clenched his teeth. *Eva*! He whipped a Mauser off his back and charged up the last few meters of the trail. Another shot was fired and then a burst of a machine gun.

Andreas stormed into the lower courtyard of the ruins where he saw the back of an American soldier also sprinting toward the sounds of the shooting. Frantic for his wife, he snapped the rifle to his shoulder and fired. The American dropped to one side, dead. Andreas raced past the twitching body and up the broken steps of the castle into the upper courtyard where another soldier was fighting with a shabbily dressed figure near the well. A knife flashed. Just a few meters away a second un-uniformed man was waving the barrel of a Tommy gun at the wrestling pair, waiting for a clear shot.

Andreas spotted Eva tripping her way through some rubble by the castle keep. His heart leapt. With half a hardened eye on the men, he dashed toward her. A blast from the Tommy gun ripped the air by Andreas' head, chewing a channel into the castle stone behind him.

He dove forward and rolled.

Eva screamed.

Andreas scrambled for his life toward the shelter of a rock pile. More bullets chopped stone and earth into flying bits all around him. As he flopped near Eva he cried out; his leg had been hit above the ankle. He jerked his rifle forward, ignoring another burst from the Tommy gun.

He aimed and fired three rounds as quickly as his bolt-action rifle would allow. The Pole fell backward.

"Andreas!" cried Eva. "Andreas!"

The man's eyes were wild; he was confused...his instinct commanded him to kill them all. The American soldier had just thrust his knife deep into the other civilian's belly. Andreas filled his magazine and lifted himself up to take a shot.

"No!" Eva lunged and knocked Andreas' arm to one side. His shot went wild. "He's my cousin!"

Bobby Folk rolled to his right and snatched a rifle off the ground. From a prone position, he aimed.

"Bobby, no!" cried Eva. She charged toward her cousin waving her pistol wildly. "No, no!" She fired wide of the man.

Bobby Folk ignored Eva and shot past her once, then twice. He hit Andreas' shoulder with the first shot, knocking the German backward. He missed with the second, then stood and ran forward to fire a third.

"Stop, Bobby! Stop, he's my husband!" Eva shrieked. "He's my husband!" She shot, again. Her bullet ricocheted off a stone wall not far from Bobby's head.

Folk hesitated.

In that brief pause the wounded Andreas lurched from cover with his right arm pressing the butt of his rifle tightly to his side. He staggered forward and fired.

Eva whirled about hysterically. "No! No! Andreas, no!"

Andreas side-stepped, and tried to one-hand his bolt.

Then Andreas went faint.

He fell to his knees and collapsed.

Shrieking, Eva threw her pistol away and ran to her husband's side. "Andreas, Andreas!"

Bobby Folk ran toward Eva and the German soldier shouting a long string of profanities. "Let me see." The sergeant ripped open Andreas' tunic and exposed a shoulder wound. It was bleeding badly. He checked Andreas' leg. The shin bone had been missed but a bullet was lodged deep in the calf muscle and blood was filling the man's boot. Folk ran to his gear and came back with a medical kit. He tied a tourniquet around Andreas' leg and poured sulfa powder into the open wound as he barked at Eva. "You shot at me!"

Eva couldn't answer.

"Unbelievable," muttered Folk. He poured a packet of sulfa powder into Andreas' shoulder wound and began to bandage it. "I was a medic's aid for a few months but I'm no doctor." He pressed on the wound, firmly. "I can't believe you shot at me."

Within a quarter hour Andreas began to stir. He opened his eyes and the world came slowly back into focus.

Eva held his head on her lap. "Shh, Andreas. You're safe. We're all safe."

"Eva? Oh, Eva, you're really here?" He looked deeply into her wide, brown eyes. He thought her face looked drawn and haggard. "You look so hungry. You're not hurt?"

"I'm here and I'm fine."

Andreas took her hand and kissed it.

Then his eye fell on Folk.

"It's alright, Andreas," said Eva. "He's not going to hurt us. He's my cousin."

Bobby Folk knelt by the pair as he ate from a tin of rations. "Congratulations," he said curtly. "I didn't kill you."

Andreas stared at the American, blank-faced.

"I'm Bobby Folk—Eva's cousin who she tried to shoot." He slanted his eyes at the young woman.

Andreas thought for a moment. "I remember you. The last time I saw you we were here, in this same place."

Folk nodded. "That was a lifetime ago." He started to offer Andreas some food, then drew back. "That was a lot of my friends' lifetimes ago."

Andreas grimaced and stretched a hand toward his leg.

"I radioed in a medical team," said Bobby.

"But they'll take him prisoner," protested Eva.

"Yep. He'll be my prisoner."

"She'll be alone when your soldiers take Weinhausen," said Andreas. "She's your cousin, for God's sake..."

"Too bad, we're still in a war and you're on the wrong side." Bobby grumbled something and turned to Eva. "But I'll see to it that *you'll* be safe and the medics can help you deliver your baby. And you should know that Weinhausen's already taken."

Andreas looked at his wife. "Baby?" It was then that he noticed how large she was under her coat.

The woman nodded.

"Oh, Eva...I can't believe it." Forgetting his pain he laughed.

Bobby turned to Andreas. "The medics won't get here until nightfall. They're busy patching up our boys because of your kind."

Eva bristled. "My kind are fighting for their country the same as you."

Folk spat. "Right." He reached into his medical pouch and retrieved a Squibb morphine syrette which he pushed into Andreas' forearm. "This ought to shut you up for a while." Bobby discarded the syrette and watched for a few moments until Andreas' eyes slowly fluttered. The American spat again. "Your husband shot my corporal in the back, you know. The kid was a good soldier from Ohio and just got married on his last leave."

Eva watched Andreas' eyes close.

"And you scared me pretty good with that pistol."

Through the rest of that morning American planes roared overhead but the sounds of gunfire and artillery began to fade as Patton's Third Army continued to drive the fleeing Germans southward and far beyond the Mosel. By late afternoon however, the castle echoed with the cries of Eva who was now beginning to suffer her first labor pains. And by early evening the woman was clenching her teeth as she lay on a bed of blankets by the well.

A cold night settled in quickly and Eva fell into a brief sleep alongside Andreas who had awakened the hour before and was now propped against the stone well. The hungry soldier poked at the campfire with a long stick, then stared at the dark sky now patched with the shaded shadows of breaking clouds. Andreas realized that the war was over for him now but not for his comrades—not yet. He closed his eyes and pictured his men's bodies lying in the forest on the day he had left them helpless and unarmed. "Oh, God, forgive me," he muttered.

"What's that?"

"Nothing." Andreas looked squarely at the American now standing over him. "Thank you for helping us." They were hard words for him to say.

"I'm not helping you. I'm helping her."

"Eva told me about your corporal. I'm...sorry." Andreas offered his hand. "I thought she was in danger." Andreas waited, watching Folk's face in the eerie light of the fire.

Bobby gawked, incredulously. "Are you asking me to forgive you, Bauer?"

Andreas faltered. He had said he was sorry. What more did this American want? "I said what I said."

"Well?" Folk took a bite of a biscuit. He enjoyed chewing in front of the hungry German.

Andreas lowered his hand. "I did what I thought I had to do. I'm just sorry it was what it was."

Folk swallowed. "So you're not really sorry then."

"Like I said, I'm sorry that it had to happen. I'm sorry that any of this had to happen."

"Is that so? You start this war and now you say that you're sorry that it had to happen?" Folk spat. "Nothing *had* to happen."

"Believe what you want but we had a right to defend ourselves."

"Just shut up. Remember, I was at one of your Hitler Youth meetings. You Krauts wanted to conquer the world and now you're getting pounded. That's what you're sorry about."

Andreas hesitated. Feelings of indefinite guilt quickly filled the pit of his stomach but he wasn't about to admit anything to the hovering American. "No," he muttered. "That's not it." His voice fell away.

Folk took a swig from his canteen and wiped his sleeve across his mouth. "So what's 'it' then?"

Andreas looked away. The only thing he was sure about was that he'd say nothing more to the gloating soldier.

"Well?" Folk waited. "Maybe I'll forgive you or maybe not. It all depends on what 'it' is." He smiled, contemptuously.

Andreas couldn't answer. He suddenly hated the sound of the word, 'forgive.' A scowl began to crease his face. He wished he could stand up.

Folk took another bite of his biscuit. "Let me ask you, Bauer: do you think you Krauts *deserve* our forgiveness?"

Andreas' eyes flashed. "Forget it."

Folk stopped chewing and squatted in front of the German. "Then let me tell you. You don't."

Andreas said nothing.

Folk swallowed. "Besides, if we ever forgave you we'd be taking away the only thing you have left." He stood and turned away. "That'd be your shame, Bauer. After starting two wars I hope you people hang on to your shame for a very long time."

Somewhere near 8:00 o'clock Eva's labor pains became intense. The young woman cried out, loudly. By 10:00 the contractions had begun to grip her in shorter intervals. The time had come. Eva clutched Andreas' hand with all her might and within the half hour she was writhing in pain, begging God to help her. Andreas held her and wiped her face from time to time as Bobby waited nervously to assist. The minutes passed, slowly.

Finally, sometime before midnight on 10 March 1945 Eva mustered all the strength she could and, with the two men encouraging her, she delivered a healthy baby into the trembling hands of Bobby Folk. "A boy," he announced. The soldier lifted the newborn by his heals and spanked his bottom. Niederberg Castle echoed the cries of new life. "With all his Kraut fingers and toes."

"Oh, Eva." Andreas kissed his wife's hands as Bobby quickly washed the child in mildly heated water and wrapped him in an army blanket. In moments the American handed Andreas and Eva their newborn son.

Father and mother stared happily into the face of their screaming baby. Eva stroked the child's wet, yellow hair and moved his face gently toward her breast. As the newborn found his place she tilted her face to Andreas and kissed him. She then turned to Bobby who was now on his knees to one side. She reached for his hand. "And thank you."

At the touch the American's face changed. Delivering the child had softened him a little.

"And I'm sorry for shooting at you. I didn't want to hit you..."

"Yeah, well, sure. I guess you were way off." He squeezed her hand, lightly. "So, what are you going to name him?"

Eva looked at the two soldiers staring back at her. She thought they seemed so old for their ages and so very tired. Her heart ached for both of them and all of those like them. She closed her eyes for a moment and when she opened them she was sure. "'Axel,' if it's alright with Andreas."

"Axel?" Bobby scratched his head.

"Yes. It means 'Father of Peace.'" She turned to Andreas and waited.

Andreas' throat filled. He looked at the sky, thinking. The stars over Niederberg Castle now shone brightly and the moon had emerged in silver splendor from fast-parting clouds. "'Axel.' Yes, of course." He smiled and kissed his son's head. "I like it."

Bobby watched the two, carefully. Then he fixed his gaze on Eva and released a deep breath. He reached behind his neck with two hands to remove a necklace which he then clenched in his fist. His eyes filled with emotion. "I'm sure you remember this, Eva." He then suspended a chain from two spread fingers which boasted a slender, black Teutonic cross with a gold ring encircling its juncture. "Jenny gave it to me for luck when I shipped out."

Astonished, Eva stared at the necklace.

"I think it's time for you to have it back. You and Axel will need all the luck you can get."

Eva's chin quivered. "Oma's necklace!" Tears blurred her vision as she watched the spinning cross shimmer in the firelight. A flood of memories attached themselves; a picture of things hoped for followed. With a soft 'thank you' she opened her hand gratefully to receive the gift.

Bobby released the necklace and let it pour into the young mother's palm. Eva thought it felt warm and good and whole. She closed her eyes and squeezed her fingers slowly around the cross. The touch of it carried her to good places. She whispered a prayer as she pressed it gently to her heart and she was glad.

For that was where it had belonged, all along.

The End

EPILOGUE

By 21 March 1945, Andreas' Seventh Army was surrounded south of the Mosel near Morbach and destroyed. In the weeks that followed the western allies continued their advance deep into Germany from the west while the Soviets pressed from the east, eventually crushing the Wehrmacht and the Waffen SS in a vice. Utterly vanquished, Adolf Hitler committed suicide in his Berlin bunker on 30 April, and on 7 May 1945 the German military high command surrendered unconditionally to the Allies. The war in Europe was over.

The cost of madness had been extreme. Statistics vary, but median numbers indicate 3,800,000 German soldiers as killed or reported missing and presumed dead, and 1,600,000 (non-Jewish) German civilians as killed. Of these civilian deaths over 500,000 died in Allied air raids over German cities. After the war was over tens of thousands more German civilians would die as a result of violence and ethnic cleansing.

Among the primary Allied Powers in the European theater, the Americans suffered 150,000 military deaths, and Great Britain 100,000 military deaths as well as an additional 60,000 civilian deaths in German air raids. The Soviet Union reported 10,000,000 military dead and missing, and 7,000,000 non-Jewish civilian deaths. (The Russian civilian death count did not differentiate between deaths caused by German invasion and those millions killed by the Soviet government during the war period.)

Nazi barbarism is further assessed with the death of approximately 5,800,000 European Jews (half in the death camps of Poland)—as well as an equivalent number of non-Jews including Slavic peoples, Gypsies, Jehovah Witnesses, political opponents, social "misfits," and Christian dissenters.

⌖

These realities were not yet fully realized as Eva and baby Axel were taken from Niederberg Castle to a U.S. Third Army field hospital for care. Two days later, the well-treated mother and son were released and Bobby Folk delivered them to Weinhausen where Eva was grateful to find her house only partially damaged by the bombing that had destroyed so much of her village.

The hope that Eva had tasted by the castle well sustained her in the years to come, but barely. As time passed she felt the weight of added revelation as the facts of Nazi brutality surfaced. She spent her lifetime struggling with shame for the insurmountable debt that the twin failings of blindness and self-interest had assessed to her and her people.

Andreas was taken into custody from Niederberg Castle and was eventually imprisoned at the overcrowded U.S. POW camp in Andernach which lay along the Rhine River not far north of Koblenz. After receiving basic first aid care for his wounds he was fenced within an unsheltered field with nearly 50,000 other captured soldiers until exposure to the elements nearly took his life in June. More fortunate than many, Andreas was rescued by Bobby Folk's intervention and released to the care of his wife.

Never able to reconcile his unintended collaboration with evil, the weary veteran spent the time that followed mourning his comrades as well as the victims of his government. The humble desire of the melancholy man was to spend his remaining years overlooking the Mosel from the vineyards he had dreamt of buying. But urged by Eva and prompted by duty to find the missing Gerde Volk, Andreas made his way eastward during the summer of '45 only to be caught up in the terrors of the post-war expulsion of German ethnics from their former lands.

Paul Volk died under mysterious circumstances in Schömberg prison just days before Allied forces arrived. After the war two former inmates visited Eva to tell her of her father's courage in the face of cruelty. According to the men, Paul had become the camp's good shepherd by praying over the sick and singing hymns to the weary.

Oskar Offenbacher rebuilt his bakery in Weinhausen and in 1947 he formed a new village band which he called the "Weinstube Musiksturm."

Hans Bieber worked in the vineyards that had once been his own and helped build a new winery which eventually produced award-winning Riesling wines for the Roth family. He lived to see his eighty-fourth birthday.

Richard Klempner committed suicide in his bombed-out Koblenz office on 1 May 1945. The stalwart Nazi died a bitter man, deluded even more at death than in life. He left a note pinned to his lapel that promised the resurrection of National Socialism.

Lindie Landes hired three partially disabled veterans to run her farm. Despite the gentle pleadings of Eva and Andreas, she continued to believe that her husband would eventually return from Stalingrad. Every evening for the next six years she went to the train station and waited. The sight brought tears to some, contempt from others. On Easter Sunday 1951, Lindie answered her farmhouse door to face a skeleton of a man holding a crumpled hat in his hand. The wretch with protruding ears could barely speak but he didn't need to say a word. Lindie burst into happy tears. Having somehow survived his Russian gulag, her Gunther had come home.

BİNNUR ŞAFAK NİGİZ

Kirpi Gibi Bir Adam Sevdim

KİRPİ GİBİ BİR ADAM SEVDİM

Binnur Şafak Nigiz

Türü Deneme

Yayın Yönetmeni Ali Osman Başkuyu
Editör Şefika Aydın
Sayfa Tasarımı Gizem Ulaş
Kapak Tasarımı Gizem Ulaş

1. Baskı Temmuz 2018, İstanbul

Yayınevi Sertifika No 23136
ISBN 978-605-2050-62-0

BASKI VE CİLT
MY Matbaacılık San. ve Tic. Ltd. Şti.
Maltepe Mah. Yılanlı Ayazma Sk. No: 8/F
Zeytinburnu / İstanbul
Tel: 0212 674 85 28
Matbaa Sertifika No: 34191

DOKUZ YAYINCILIK
Kartaltepe Mah. 49. Sokak No:10/A
Bayrampaşa / İstanbul
0212 640 00 35

BİNNUR ŞAFAK NİGİZ

KİRPİ GİBİ BİR ADAM SEVDİM

Şimdi 26 Yaşındasın...

...ve ben o gece, bir daha seni asla sevmeyecek
olmama ağladım.

Kimin yangınında duman olmuşsa yürek, insanın bir daha o yangına girmemesi gerektiğini bilmesi gerek. Bir şeyi anlatıyorsam, o şeyi anlatmayı istediğimden değil, taşımaktan bıktığım, artık bir başkasına yük olmasını istediğimden anlatıyorum ben.

O gecede, şafak hamile bir kadının kürtaj masasına yatıp rahminde parçalattığı bebek gibi gökyüzünde parçalanırken, çoğu insanın sevmekten vazgeçip, bazılarının ilk kez sevmeye başladığı o bitmeyen ağrılı gecede, ***ben bir sevdadan sağ çıktım.***

Sen de benim gibi sağ çıktın.

Bir sevdanın boynunu kestim, derisinin altında damar yoktu.

O gece sen ve ben, biz, sağ çıkmıştık; solumuz ise artık yoktu.

Sabahın Altısı,

Sabahın altısında bıçak kemiğe dayanmış, bu bildiğin cinayet. Gülleden ağır harfleri parmaklarına bulaştıran kadınlar bilirler çünkü. Mevsimindeysen kışın, üçüz doğuran kadının dokuz doğuran kocasına geçen vakitten daha yavaş doğuyorsa güneş ve hâlâ karanlıksa hava, seni öldürmek isteyen sevginin dudaklarında ölüm nefsi müdafaadır. Kendimden biliyorum. Saat daha sabaha karşı üçken, altıya üç asır varken, ne kadar saat varsa pilleri sökülmüştür benim odamda.

Ne güzel taşıdı ama beni uçuruma. Farklı şehirlere uçarken vurdular mı kanadından anlamadım, önce beni bıraktı ama arkamdan atlamadı. Kanadı beni arasından bırakınca iyileşti galiba. Zaten kalbinde yüksek duvarlar ören taşlar, benim de kâbus doğuran yükseklik korkum vardı. Onu biraz, dilim döndüğünce, elim gittiğince, ağrım yettiğince anlatmak isterim.

O kirpi gibi bir adamdı, sonra da zaten beni cümlelerimden vurdular.

Zamanın içine dalga dalga yayılan
bir aşkla sevmiştim onu.
Sonra tüm saatler durdu.

Başımı bir yastığın üzerine bıraktığımda,
ruhum senin üzerini örtüyordu
uzandığın başka yataklarda.

Susmaya alıştırdın beni.

Ben sana çok küstüm, senin bundan haberin yok.

Dağ durmuş, küstürdüğü tavşanı bekliyor, tavşanın öldüğünden haberi yok.

"Tavşan dağa küsmüş, dağın haberi yok," dedi dikenleri kabarmış bir kirpi gibi gülerek. O ne zaman öyle gülerse, bir kekliğin kalbi kırılır.

Gülünce gözlerinin etrafında belirginleşen o satır çizgilerine baktım. Ben ne zaman ona öyle baksam, bir kirpinin dikeni tenime batar.

"O kadar mı körmüş tavşana?" diye sordum.

"Dağın gözleri yok."

"Kalbi de mi yok?"

Yara bandı ve diken,

Senden nefret ettiğimi düşünerek kapattığım kapıların arkasında, sırtımı o kapıya bastırıp yere oturarak senin için ağlıyorum.

Yumruğumda dişlerimin izleri, gözlerimin altında kamburu çıkmış morluklar var. Ben sana yazdıklarımı yalnız okurken, alfabenin altında kaldığım oldu. Aniden bunu hatırladım. Çünkü bir şeyi aniden hatırlıyorsan, o şeyi aniden unutamazsın. Aslında o şeyi hiç unutamazsın. Kuyuya kova atıp, suyu beklerken ateşi çekersen, o gün anlarsın. Bir kadını ya babası ya oğlu ya da senin gibiler ağlatır.

Bir de lütfen unutma:

Senin yaranın üstünde sana uzanan her yara bandını parçalayan bir dikenin var.

Ama canım, benim ellerim diken seviyorsa, bunda senin suçun yok.

Keşke seni içimden kıpkırmızı bir leke gibi tükürebilsem.

Unuttu,

"Ben," dediğinde gözleri gözlerimde, hep yaralı olan büyük elleri, küçücük ellerimdeydi. "Ben kendimi unutsam, seni unutmam."

Sevdi beni.

Diken de sever balonu, sırf patlatmak için.

"Ben her şeyi unuturum, seni unutmam," dedim.

Ben, her şeyi unuttum, onu unutamadım.

O, bunu hep yalanlar ama her şeyden önce beni unuttu.

Kaç yaz geçip gitti üzerinden,
senin kışın bitmiyormuş.

Binnur Şafak Nigiz

Koyu mor yağmur,

Yastığıma koyu mor yağmurlar yağdıran gözyaşlarım, ben zehir zemberek uykulara gözlerimi yumduğumda zar zor kuruyor. Ama biliyor musun, kuruyunca yanaklar akıttığı an yandığının yirmi altı katı acıyor.

Hayaliyle uyuduğum uykuların ressamıdır o; rüyalarıma kendi portresini çizer, gözlerim uykudan aralandığı an o portreyi ateşe verip kendini benden gizler.

Bir kadının dudaklarına dokunan kırmızı ruj gibi dokunuyor kelimeleri dudaklarıma ve tutku, bir balığın göğüs kafesindeki inci gibi kasıklarıma yuvarlanıyor.

Babasız bir piç gibi veli toplantısı çıkışlarından kaçıp yine ona sığınıyorum.

Radyoda, bileklerini değil umutlarını kesenler için yirmi altıncı şarkı çalıyor. Bir de unutmadan,

Kül olmaya alışmış bir adama, sizin har olmanız yetmiyor.

Çünkü Müslüm Baba bunu şu şekilde iç ağrıtan bir soruyla aslında zaten açıklamış: Kül yanar mı?

Yanmıyor.

Sen benim rahmimdeki cümleler,
doğuruyorum ben seni..
Sen benim kelimeleri dizip yerleştirdiğim pasajlar,
altını çizdiğim cümlelerimsin.

Bir insanı tek bir düşünce bitirebilir. Kendi kendinizi kurşun yağmuruna tutmaktır bu.

Sonra yine bir insanı tek bir düşünce döndürebilir.

Tek bir düşünce yeniden doğurup, yeniden öldürebilir.

Ben bitiyorum,
Dönüyorum,
Doğuyorum,
Ölüyorum sana.

Bir adam, bir kadın için yine o kadından vazgeçebilir mi? Eskiden geçebilirdi ama artık geçemiyor. Çünkü bazı hisler bir süre sonra seni ya öldürür ya da bencil birine döndürür.

Ne bileyim, ben senin yolunda vurulmuş bir kekliğim, yaralıyım ama oynayıp duruyorsun bana saplanmış kurşunun ucuyla, bundan sanırım, aslında biraz da bencilliğinim.

Öyle bir adam,

Bir şarkı dinledim, tüm gençliğim küstü bana. Kuyu kuyu gezdim, bir lokma su aradı dudaklarım. Eni sonu ölümdü ya bu sevdanın, en önce kendim anladım ama bir tek kendime anlatamadım. Ellerimi verdim, cümlelerimi, sesimi verdim, ayaklarımı verdim, ben bu sevdaya ruhumu verdim. Bir gözlerim kaldı, onu da ister misin?

Kör olsam, silsem seni gözlerimden.

Yer çekimsiz ortamda ağlamak gibi, kupkuru gözlerle baksam da anlamasa kimse ağladığımı, havada asılı duran gözyaşıma yağmur damlası desem, çok mu? Doğrultmasam bakışlarımı artık hiçbir boşluğa, hiçbir boşluk içinde seni taşıyan bir anıyla yüzüme çarpmasa, bir şarkı çaldığında kaçıp bir tenha köşeye, keşke artık senin için ağlamasam.

Ben de keşke seni sevmekten korksam, bir balonun patlamaktan korktuğu gibi ama yok, bir balon olsam yine konardım o kirpinin sırtına. Ben unutamıyorum ki hiç seni. Lavlar akarken yastığımdan, ben sana hiç anlattım mı? Kirpi gibi bir adam, iyi güzel, peki ya bu kirpi gibi bir adam, aslında nasıl bir adam?

Nasıl bir adam? Tanklar yürürken gecenin içinde, insanların avuçlarında kan kokusu, sırtlarında bir bayrak, yüzlerinde patlamış gazlar, ortada dikilen annesini kaybetmiş bir çocuk gibi üzerime yürüyen tankı izliyorum. Öyle bir adam. İşte o tank, o kaybolan anne, o gözlerimden dökülen bir sürü yaş.

O benden gerçekleri duymak ister ama dudaklarında vardır binlerce yalan. Keşke o yalanlarla sadece öpseydin beni. ***Ne zaman seni çok sevdim, o geceden beri kendi canımı en çok kendim sıkıyorum.*** Sorun sende değil, bende. ***Ben doğursaydım seni, kırkın çıkmadan çok sevdim diye, kundağın içinde uyurken ölürdün bence.***

Ne bileyim, bir enkaz altında aklıma annemden bile önce sen gelmiştin işte.

Sözünü tut,

Anahtarı almadan kapısını çarpıp çıktığın bir ev gibiyim. Keşke gelmeyeceğini bu kadar belli etmeseydin. Çıkarken anahtarı alıp gittiğin evler, hiç yoktan geri döneceğini bilirler. Ben, bundan sonraki tüm geceleri o evin kapısının arkası gibi gözlerim yolda bekleyeceğim. Olursa olur da gelirsen diye, anahtarın yok biliyorum, bu sorun değil, beni kırman için tam önünde korkusuzca dikileceğim.

Dikileceğim çünkü, ***bekleyen insanlar bilir; beklemek, kırılmak gibi anlık değildir.***

Biliyorum, senin bana kolların her daim açık ama çattığın kaşların altında duran yeşil gözlerindeki öfkeyi bir türlü silemiyorum. Senin bana öfken, benim sana beklentim, bizim birbirimize olan kırgınlığımız ne zaman dinecek?

Gelemiyor musun bana?

Söktürdüm tüm kilitlerimi yokluğunda.

Kapılarım özgürlük kadar açık. ***İçerisi girecek herhangi birine cehennemken, sana orada buz gibi nehirler biriktiriyorum.*** İnanmıyorum artık denizin mavisine, insanın iyisi de öldü Kemal Sunal ile birlikte, artık çok değişti tüm insanlık ve bu tüm insanlığın içinde tek bir kişi bile, mümkün değil sevemez seni ben gibi delice.

Kirpiyi karşıdan sevmesi kolay. Hiç avuçlayıp öpmüş, kalbine yatırıp uyutmuş mu biri bile?

Sırtını bastırıyorum kalbime.

Lütfen, sözünü tut, sen de benden başkasını sevme.

Adile Naşit'in kahkahası kadar güzeldik biz seninle birlikte.

Sensizken kendimin en tepesinden düşüyorum.
Beni düşürme, ne olursun.

Kılıç,

Kılıç kınında kesmezmiş; acı hâlâ yüreğimdeyken ben senin yüreğini acıtamam ki. İsterim inan, çünkü canı acıyan bir defa bile olsa ister karşısındakinin onu anlamasını, ne hissettiğini bilmesini, nasıl bir yangırın içinden geçtiyse onun da öyle bir yangından geçmesini ama sen yine inan, ben öylesine canı acıyan bir kadın değilim ki. Âşık bir kadınım ben. Masanın üzerine vurulmuş bir yumruk gibi, göğsüme vurulmuş yumruk olan kalbimin ağrısını bir sana yükleyemem belki ama bil, gök uzun diye elleri olan yağmurla toprağa dokunamıyor değil.

O gece seninle, birbirimiz için birbirimizi kırdığımız gecelerin birinde, bana yine "Çirkin," dedin, çünkü "çirkin" senin dilinde "güzel" demekti ve sen bana ne zaman çirkin desen, kılıcın kınında bilendiği gibi yüreğimde adını sakladığım, yüzünü gizlediğim sana bilendim. Şimdi seni yüreğimden çıkarsam, kınından çıkan kılıç gibi, ben önce sana saplanmaz mıyım? Sana saplanacağıma kılıç gibi, her gece yüreğim göğsüme saplansın, lohusa kadın gibi başımda duran bir süpürgeyle uykuları süpüreyim yastığımdan daha iyi.

Çok umutsuzum canım, süpürgenin tellerini bir bir batırsam kalbime de tutuştursam uçlarını belki geçecek ama bunun içinde uyuduğun odayı ateşe vermekten ne farkı var?

Bir adamın çirkini olan güzel kadınlar gibi ben bu gece de seni düşünürken çok ağladım.

Keşke diyorum canım, keşke kılıç kendini kesebilseydi.

Keşke uyuduğun odadan uyanıp çıktığın bir anda, ben o odayı yakıp, sen orada değilken orayı küle çevirebilseydim.

Binnur Şafak Nigiz

Çirkiniyim bir adamın ve yine o adamın, oluk oluk kalbime akıttığı bir sevda gibi kadehime doldurduğu rakının kokusu boğazımı yakıyor. Hiç sevmezdim rakı edebiyatı yapanı, doldurup içmek yerine şiirler dizmek saçma gelirdi bana. Sonra kadehin sayfalara benzediğini fark ettim. Şöyle ki, bembeyaz bir sayfanın ilk yudumunu içip, ilk sayfasını okuyorsun, orada aldığın tat, kitabın ön sözü gibi zihnine doluyor. Her yudum, bir diğer sayfası oluyor kitabın. Sonra o kitabın içindeki yazanlara âşık, o adamın gözlerine bakarken sarhoş oluyorsun.

Dibini gördüğün her kadeh, bir roman serisinin ilk kitabının sonu gibidir.

Şişeyi bitirmeden masadan kalkan, kitabın sonunu gördüm demesin.

Bir de sen çok kötü bir adamsın
ama ben rakının içini dolduran su gibi,
bir daha aynı olamayacağımı bile bile seviyorum seni.
Keşke o romanın sonunda ben ölseydim.

Bu söylediğimi hiç unutma.
Aklından bile çıkarma.
İkimiz, keşke bir roman olsaydık seninle.
...ve bu romanın sonunda ben ölseydim keşke.

Binnur Şafak Nigiz

Çok acı cümle yuttum. En olmadık yerde, ummadığım insanların kırdığı kalbimin içi, en acı cümleleri oluşturan kelimelerin anlamlarını barındıran bir sözlük kadar kalabalık. En çok seni sevdiğim için kırdılar beni. Birini sevmenin kırılmak olduğunu biliyordum ama seni sevmek, düpedüz kıyamet. Ben cehennemin en günahkâr kadınıyım insanların gözünde, günahımsa seni sevmek. Bir insanın canını bir defa alan Azrail'in avucundan ölümü mü çaldın, tanıdığım günden beri her gün ikindiden önce kalkar cenazem.

Çok ağrı susturdum. En olmadık yerde, ummadığım yerimden giren ağrının yuvası gibi sancıyor kalbim. En çok seni sevdiğim için ağrıyor bacaklarım benim, sebebi romatizma değil; en çok seni sevdiğim için ağrıyor sırtım, taşıdığım yüklerden değil; en çok seni sevdiğim için ağrıyor ellerim, senin ellerini tutamadığı için değil; en çok senin yüzünden ağrıyor saç diplerim ve dökülüyor saçlarım, başımın içinde kanser gibi üreyip büyüyen kitle yüzünden değil.

Düpedüz kıyamet, evet.

Dil altı hapı gibi ağzımın içine almışım, öldürmüşsün beni, olsun bu köşesinde ıslak imzamın olduğu, rıza gösterdiğim bir cinayet.

Suçlususun tüm yanlış seçimlerimin.
Ben doğmuşsam, bu hep senin yüzünden.

Sana keşkenin ne kadar ağır bir kelime
olduğundan bahsetmiş miydim?
Bana o kadar çok keşke dedirttin ki,
Keşken olsaydım keşke.

Yokladın kalbini,

"Söylesene, bitirir mi bir gün kafamdaki sen bu uzun uzadıya sürdürdüğü gece konuşmalarını?" diye sordun bana. "Söylesene, seni düşünmeden uyuyabildiğim bir gece bulabilecek miyim gelip geçen günlerin içinde?"

"Bulamazsın," dedim yarım yamalak bir gülümsemeyle.

"Buldurmazsın çünkü."

"Biliyorsun çünkü," diye devam ettirdim seni. "Kafanda sustuğum zaman, kalbinde en büyük gürültü olacağım."

O gece kalbini yokladın durdun. En çok, kafanın içinde susacağım anın gelmesinden korktun. Ben senin kafanın içinde seninle konuşan sestim; en çok kendimi hatırlatır, sana senden bahsederdim. Bir gün susarsam, sesimi duyamamanın paniğiyle sıkışacaktı göğsün. Kalbin, ninni bildiği sesimi arayacaktı.

Korktun ama anlamadım sandın.

Anladım ama bunu sana hiç çaktırmadım.

Şimdi dilediğince kork.
Korkuların gerçek oldu.
Sen benim bugünümden korktuğun için,
ben artık senin yarınında yokum.

"Ben gitmeyi bilmiyorum," dedin, bağlamanın telleriyle oynuyordu. Sana bağlama çalmayı deden öğretmişti. Çıkan sesleri, dudaklarımda yarım bir gülümsemeyle dinliyordum. "O yüzden bana gidecek misin diye sorup durma."

"Sormadım ki," dedim omuz silkerek.

"Sen ağzını açmıyorsun ama o ela gözlerin hiç susmuyor."

Yutkundum, bana bakmadın, bağlamanın telleriyle oynamaya devam ettin.

Gitmeyi biliyormuşsun meğer sen.
Senin bilmediğin gelmekmiş.

Bu aşktan alabileceğim en büyük hasarla çıktığım geceyi hatırlıyorum. Eğer bir orman yangını büyümeden hemen söndürülseydi, ben o büyümeden söndürüldüğü için şükredilen ormanda yanan tek ağaç olurdum.

Yine kendimi gözden çıkardım.
Şaka yapıyorum canım, asma yüzünü,
ben yüzüne astım hüznümü.
Sen ne anlarsın be kalmaktan.

Sağ çıkmışız bu sevdadan.
Öyle diyorlar. Doğru, sağ çıktık.

Sağ çıktık canım, sağ çıktık, apayrı kapılardan,
apayrı yollara, apayrı ellerle,
apayrı şehirlere sağ çıktık.

Canavarın sevdiği kadın,

Kolum yorganın dışındayken uyuyamazdım ben. Nasıl ayaklarım dışarıda kalınca ayaklarımı canavarların yemesinden korkuyorsam, kollarımı da canavarların yemesinden korktuğum için. Bir gece, yine diğer geceler olduğu gibi değil de, bu kez gerçekten onunla o yorganın içindeydik.

Belki de o gece, yorganın içinde olduğumuz ilk geceydi.

Ayaklarım yorganın içindeydi, onun ayakları yorganın dışındaydı ama o canavarlardan korkmazdı. Ellerim yorganın içindeydi, canavar da yorganın içinde benimle birlikteydi ve diğer canavarlar, o canavara ait olduğumu bildiği için o gece beni izlemiyorlardı.

Bir canavara aitseniz, hiçbir canavar size zarar vermeye çalışamaz ama canavarınız yataktan uzaklaştığında, artık üzerinizde yorgan bile olsa, sizi o yorgan dahi koruyamaz.

O gece o canavarla yorganın altında uyuduktan ve canavar yataktan çıkıp gittikten sonra, ben bir daha yorganın dışına kolumu koymaktan da ayağımı koymaktan da korkmadım. ***O canavar, bana diğer canavarlardan korkmamayı öğretti.*** Yorganın altında da olsam, yorganın üstünde de olsam, yorgan olmasa da, canavarların ellerimi ve ayaklarımı kopartamayacağını bana o öğretti.

Gündüzleri çocukların oynadığı parklarda,
geceleri ben senin için ağladım...

Serzeniş,

Birine körü körüne inanmanın ağrısını gece olunca yastık, gündüz vakti boşluğu izleyen gözler öder. Hatırlasana, ***inanmıştım ben sana.*** Birine inanmak benim için babamın kapıdan çıkıp gittiği gün perilerin varlığına inanmak kadar zorlaşmışken, babama benzediğini kafama vura vura, heceleyerek bana öğretmene rağmen, ***hatırlasana, inanmıştım ben sana.*** Şimdi seninle aramızda yalnızca şehirler, dağlar, yollar, denizler yok. Şimdi seninle aramızda kırılmış bir güven, bırakılmış bir çift el, yaş dolu gözlerim var. Söylesene, ***ben şimdi nasıl inanırım sana?*** İnsan bir defa aldanıyor diyorlar, yalan bu. Ben binlerce defa aldandım sana. Kırılmış güvenimin önünde dizlerimin üzerine çökmüş olmama rağmen, biliyorum ki ben, şimdi ellerimi tutup gözlerime baksan, "ben şimdi nasıl inanırım sana" dememe rağmen, yine inanırım sana ben.

Vakit yeniden gece yarısı ve gözlerini hatırlamak bir namlu. ***Bu namlunun ucu kaç kez daha patlayacak benim göğsümde?***

Bir zamanlar şehirlerin ayırdığı bedenlerimiz, şimdi aynı şehirde, aynı sokakta, aynı kaldırımda, aynı anda bile birbirlerinden ayrı, birbirlerine yabancı. Göğsümün sensiz duran kapısını boyasam, boyayı yüreğimdeki yangınla kurutsam, rengi değişti diye gözüm kapıdan ayrılacak değil ya.

İşte bu satırlar, gece yarısı ağrıttığın bir yüreğin serzenişidir sana.

Sen yalanı sevmezsin diye kuruttuğum dilimde, artık senin yalanlarının var ahmak paralayan acı tadı. **Beni dürüst olmaya alıştırdı bir yalancı.** *Tedavisi olmayan bir hastalık gibi bağlanan gönül, bir filin hortumunda gezer dünyayı; bilir, fili kızdırsa kalacak filin ayakları altında. Yine de sesini çıkarmadan tutunur hortuma, gezdiği dünyada onu bulma umuduyla.* Senin bulutların bir kere fırtına kervanlarından kopardıklarıyla dolmamış, yağmayı bırak, kendin bile ıslanmamışsın, ben ıslanmamış bir bulutun yağmur olup üzerime yağmasını beklemişim ya; o filin ayaklarının altında acıdan geberen ama ölemeyen bir insan gibi tepik ata ata bunca acının sonunda, gebermeyi diliyorum bu yatakta.

Yine de sesini bir defa daha duysam, gökten kirpi dikeni yağsa, dikenlerinin sırtımı deleceğini bilsem yüzüstü uzanırım o kaldırıma.

Okuma.

Okuyorsan, açma, açıp fotoğraflarıma bakma.

Sen bakarken gözlerimin içini gör diye kafamı çevirmedim pozlarda.

Senin gözlerin hiç buluşmazdı kadrajla.

Sen kirpi gibi bir adamdın, sırtındaki dikenleri bıraktın keklik gibi bir kadının kanatlarına.

Ağlama.

Ya da umurumda değil.

Bu gece de biraz sen ağla.

İnsanın yüzünün güldüğüyle,
kalbinin güldüğü bir olmuyor.

Allah aşkın böylesini vereceğine,
ölüm versin insana.

Yarası,

Vardı büyük bir yarası, öyle herkese gösteremiyordu.

Akvaryumdaki balıkları gözlerinde saklayamadığı kırgınlıklarla izlerdi, balıklar ise cama yaklaşıp duvarlarına astığı ışıkları izlemeyi tercih ederlerdi. Kendini bir yere ait hissedemeyen ama bir yere ait olma isteğiyle yanan, evlerin içindeki evsizler bilir, akvaryumlar bile içlerinde nefessiz kaldıkları evlerden daha fazla evdir. Bir akvaryumda bile, solungacı olmadan daha fazla nefes alabileceğine inanır. Nefesi bir evin içinde kaybolmuştur, duvarlar üzerine yıkılmıştır, çatı onun acısı, zemin mezarıdır.

Ben onun yarasını görmek istemiştim.

Yarasını bana göstermemiş, gösterdiği o yaranın kabuğuymuş, yarası kazağının altında kalmış, kopardığı kabuğu bana yaram diye yutturmuş.

Ben bir yarayı hap gibi dilimin üstüne koyup bir bardak suyla içtim.

Sana da oluyor mu? Kaşlarını çatıp, yastığını kolunun altına alarak sokak sokak yürüme isteği. Üstelik o sokağın sonu evine de çıkmıyor.

Zaten senin de evin yok.

Allah'ı kadar sevdiği adam,
Onun şeytanı oldu.

Bende gözlerime sağanak indiren bir fotoğrafın var, annen görse bu kadar ağlamaz.

O gece onun göğsünde uyuyacak, onun göğsüne başım derinliğinde bir çukur oyacaktım. Duraklarda insanlar oturuyor, otobüsler hıncahınç doluyor, kediler sokaklarda sevişiyordu. Kırmızı karlar yağıyordu ormanlardan birine... Sonra bir anne pencerenin önüne oturmuş akşam ezanından sonra eve gelen oğlunun sokağın başında görüneceği anı endişeli gözlerle bekliyor, bir kadın kocasının gömleğinde gördüğü ruj iziyle hayatının yıkımını yaşıyordu.

O gece onun göğsünde uyuyacak, onun göğsüne düşüncelerim derinliğinde bir mezar kazacaktım. Terminalin birinde bir adam gelen geçen insanlara gideceği yeri soruyor, bir evsiz terminalin bankında ceketini üzerine örtmüş uyuyordu. Koyu mor yağmurlar yağıyordu evlerin damlarına... Sonra bir sokak köpeği, yalnız başına yürüyen genç kadının arkasına takılıyor, onu evine kadar bırakıyordu.

O gece onun göğsünde uyudum, onun göğsüne başım derinliğinde bir çukur oydum.

Mezarlar kazmaya gücüm yetmedi, keklik gibi düştüm, çok yara aldım. Çok sevdim. Onun bu dünyadaki var olma düşüncesini sevdim. Beni hiç bırakmamasını istedim. Çocukların beklentileri gibiydi kalbimin içindeki duygular.

Çocukların beklentileri fazla olur, hayal kırıkları da öyle.

Binnur Şafak Nigiz

Yok,

Gittin diye, gelemiyorsun diye, kapının eşiğinde durup beni izliyor olduğun gerçeğini yok sayamıyorum. Bilmem, belki artık oluru yoktur. Oluru yoksa da bu çok ağır. ***Bir daha olmayacağını bilmek, kanserin tedavisi sen kanserden öldüğün gün bulunmuş gibi zor.*** Gelmek istiyor, gelemiyor bana diyemiyorum ben. Bir adamın bir kadına gelememesi için bir bahane olduğuna da inanmıyorum. Canı istemiyordur adamın. Gelmez. ***Bahane, ağrıyı birkaç saatliğine dindiren ilaç gibidir; yok ettiği ağrıyı an gelir geri iade eder, kendine muhtaç eder, iyi gelir ama içten içe beter eder.*** Adam ya gelir ya da gelmez, bunun da bir ortası yoktur. Ama bu sendeki gelmek değil, gelememek hiç değil. Seninkisi başka bir şey. Bu başka bir şey, bu kötü bir şey. Sen kötü şeyler yapıyorsun benim omuzlarıma. Omuzlarımı ağrıtıyorsun sen benim. Yüksün sen. Hamalım ben. Seni taşıyorum dünün içinden bugüne. Bu, çok başka bir şey. Bu, çok kötü bir şey. Bunun açıklaması yok, bunu anlatan kitaplar yok, bunu anlatan şarkılar yok, bununla aynı anlamı taşıyan bir hastalık yok. İçeri adım atamadığı kapının önünden ayrılmayan adamın şairlerin şiirlerinde bir adı belki yoktur ama benim içimde şairlerin yaşından büyük ağrısı var. Keşke bir şiir yazsam ve bitse. O şiir bir sürü insanın ağrısı olsa ama benim yazarken hissettiklerim, şiirin içinde kalsa, bir daha içime girmese. ***Ne Nazım'ı olabiliyorum kendi hayatımın ne de Piraye'si. Sol elimi kırdın sen benim, solak olduğumu bile bile. Şimdi seninle durduk bir kapının önünde, bizi öldürecek zamanın ikimizi yok etmesini bekliyoruz.*** Kapıyı açsam içeri girmeyeceksin, kapıyı açmasam tüm gece orada beklemeye devam edeceksin. ***Seneleri böyle tüketeceğiz seninle.***

Ben anladım.

Ben, kapımın önünde bir kirpi beslemeye başladım.

Ne dokunabiliyorum o kirpiye ne kovabiliyorum. Ne içeri alabiliyorum onu ne de gitmesini bekleyebiliyorum.

Kirpi gibi bir adam sevdim, sol kolum kırık, sağ kolumla kapıyı itip ben bu işin içinden bir türlü çıkamıyorum.

Bir kadının sırtını yaslayacak kadar güvendiği
o dağ olup sonra da o dağa
karlar yağdırdıktan sonra,
onu çok sevmişsin ya da hiç sevmemiştin
ne fayda?

Sırtımda gölgesinin ağırlığıyla geleceğe
    ilerlediğim bir adam var ettim.
O adamı çok sevdim.
Sırtımda nefesinin ağırlığıyla gelecekten düştüğüm
    bir adamdan vazgeçtim.
O adamdan nefret ettim.
Sırtımda yokluğunun ağırlığıyla
    gelecekten kaçtığım bir adamı bekledim.
O adamı kaybettim.

Ne saçma,
bir kadına öldürdüğünüz çiçekleri götürmek.
Sonunda seni de böyle öldüreceğim işte, der gibi.

Binnur Şafak Nigiz

Her gece uyumadan önce
aklına gelen kadına aşıksındır,
her başını yastığa koyduğunda
düşündüğün ilk adamdan vazgeçemezsin.

Başımda bir kör ağrı, fotoğrafların namluları alnımda,

Gel gelelim müthiş bir baş ağrısıyla avucumun içine doldurduğum ağrı kesicileri üçerli beşerli ağzıma tıkıştırıp, bir yudum suyla onları boğulur gibi yutuşumu ve mutfak tezgâhındaki tüm bardakları elimin tersiyle itip paramparça edişimi asla unutamıyorum

Çünkü bazen unutamazsın.

Ellerime çivi çakmışlar gibi hissederek onun kıyafetlerini bir çantanın içine toplayıp, sonra kıyamayarak geri çıkartışımı ve yatağın üzerine serdiğim kıyafetlerinin üzerine uzanıp içim çıkana kadar ağladığım geceyi de unutmuyorum.

Komodinin üzerinde duran çerçevenin içindeki fotoğrafımıza bakarken bir kutu fare zehrinin kutusunu avucumun içinde buruşana kadar sıktığım geceyi unutmuyorum.

Fare zehirleri fareleri öldürmek için değil, insanların kendi kendisini öldürebilmesi için üretilmiştir ve fotoğraflar bu dünyanın en acımasız silahlarıdır.

Yok ki şu göğsümde bir pencere,
göğsümdeki kirpinin dikenleri hava alsın.

Bu sözüm ona değil, sana,

Biliyor musun bir adam ne zaman sevse bir kadını, kendi içinde bir hissin daha cenaze namazını kılar. Bu hissin adlarından biridir kaygı. Adam bir kadını sevmeden öncesi ne kadar kaygılıysa diğer insanlara, ne kadar güvenmiyorsa, ne kadar kaçıp saklanıyorsa, o kadını sevince o kaygı o kadar zayıflar, o kadar ölür, o kadar gömülür.

O kadının onu sevdiği gün, adam artık bambaşka birine dönüşür.

Çünkü bir adam annesinden başka hiçbir kadının sevgisine inanmaz, sevildiğini tadana kadar.

Bir de annesinin sevgisini görmeden büyüyen, rakının içine suyu yalnızca rakı bulutlar kadar beyaz görünsün diye bir damla damlatan, rakının yanında mezeye bile gerek duymayan adamlar vardır.

İşte o adamlar, ne zaman sevse bir kadını, en çok o kadından saklanır.

Annesi gibi birinin varlığına daha tahammülü yoktur, çünkü hayatında en son annesini sevmiştir. Annesinden öncesi de yoktur, sonrası da hiç olmamıştır. Kabullenemez, yediremez, sever ama bunu kendine bile dillendiremez. Tokatlar kendi yüzünü, yetmez, avucunu aynalara çarpıp parçalar yüzünü. İzler, söylemez. Sever, söylemez. Susar, söylemez. Gidersin, durdurmaz. Gel diyemez, seni görmediği her an delirir bekleyemez, sen onu seversin, **onun gözünde onu kimse sevemez.**

Öyle bir adamı sevdim.
Öyle bir adamı sevgimle iyileştirdim.
Kirpi gibi bir adamdı.
Yalnız bana değil, aslında en çok kendine batardı.

Olamadıysa bir adam anasının kuzusu,
bu onun suçu mu?
Bilmiyorsa sevmeyi, öğrenir elbet.

Hiç alışkın olmadığın o duyguyu içinden atamamak...

Binnur Şafak Nigiz

Göğsümde kekliğin ağrısı,

Bir gün birini seviyorsun. Sonra bir daha onun kadar kimseyi sevemiyorsun. Müslüm Gürses yan binadan bağırıyor: Hava çok yağmurlu, duraklar sessiz. İnsanlar nerede? Ben varım, sensiz. Nereye kayboldun, benden habersiz?

Göğsümdeki kuşun kanatlarında bir ağrı var.

Teninden tenime yağmışlığı vardı günahların.

Bir de kasımpatılar vardı.

Trenler otları kesip geçiyor, raylar birbirinden iki âşık gibi ayrılıyordu.

Bir sen vardın, bir de üzerine intihar gibi düşen bir adam.

O gece hava her zamankinden daha siyahtı.

O gece sokaklar her zamankinden daha kimsesiz.

O gece ben vardım, göğsümde acı dolu bir kervan taşıyan.

O gece bir sokak kedisi vardı.

O gece yüksek doz uyuşturucudan köşe başında bayılan bir delikanlı, bir de bir somun ekmeği ısırarak uzanan bir sokak köpeği...

O gece canlı cansız herkes, her şey vardı.

Kaldırımdaki taş bile aynı yerinde duruyordu.

O bile vardı.

O gece bir sen yoktun.

Bir de Müslüm Gürses yoktu artık.

Sana göğsümdeki kuşu göstermiştim,
avuçlarının içine al, kanatlarını sar istemiştim.
Göğsümün kuşunu öldürdün, canım.
Bir bedeni mezara tükürür gibi,
tükürdün bu hayattan beni.

Artık göğsümün kuşunun kanatlarında
bir cenaze var.

Parmaklarımı bastırıyorum sık sık şakaklarıma, parmak uçlarımdaki delikler ağrılarımla dolsun, ağrılarımı benden alsın istiyorum. Bir gün biri gelecek, beni omuzlarımdan tutarak silkeleyecek, biliyorum. Kafamın içindeki zehirlerin ilacıyla, kalbimin atışlarını yavaşlatan duygunun toprağıyla bana gelecek. O gün onun gözlerinin içine baktığımda ben yine, yeniden senin gözlerini görmekten korkuyorum.

Bazı gidişler bilet gerektirmez,

Yaranın kabuğunu soyar gibi soyup, tekrar kanattığın yeri izlerken çektiğin acıyla, kabuk kıyafetine sürtünüp kendiliğinden düşerek tekrar kanadığında hissettiğin acı bir değildir. Kim gözünün önündeyse, en çok onu hissedersin. O yüzdendir, bir kabuğu kendin kaldırdığında ve kanı kendin gördüğünde, acıyı daha derinden hisseder, yüzünü buruşturarak izlersin. ***Bir insanın bir insanı gözünden sakınırcasına severken o insanı kaybettiği anı izlemesi bu yüzden ondan kendi ayaklarıyla gittiği anı yaşamasından daha acı vericidir.*** Çünkü o yara kıyafetin içinde değil, o yarayı kıyafetin dürtüp kaldırmadı, o yarayı kıyafetin kanatmadı. O yarayı sen kanattın. O yarayı kanarken izledin. O yaranın kabuğunun kalkışını kendin izledin.

Oysa giderken anlık bir rahatlama hissettin, çünkü kabuk bazen koptuğunda tatlı bir kaşıntı sarar yarayı. Görmesen de hissedersin. Ama gitmek her zaman en az yarayı aldığın an değildir. Kıyafeti çıkarıp yaraya baktığında ve tekrar kanadığını gördüğünde, o an hissetmemiş olmana rağmen, gördüğün anda yeniden başlar sızı. ***Bu yüzden bazı gidişler bilet gerektirmez.***

Binnur Şafak Nigiz

Giden ve geride kalanı buna benzetirim.

Giden giderken tatlı tatlı kaşınan yarasının kanayacağından habersiz rahatlamış gibi hisseder, kalan kabuğun kopuş anını gördüğünden acılar içinde kanı izler, sonra bir gün kan durur ve kalanın ağrısı diner ama giden, ne zaman o kıyafeti çıkarsa, hissetmediği o acının izini görüp ağrı çeker.

Senden ilk kez gittiğim gün yaram kaşınıyordu, sen arkamda kanlar içindeydin. Yolun yarısına geldiğimde sıyırıp baktım yarama, kabuğum düşmüş, kan içindeydim. Döndüm, yoktun. Beni bu kadar çabuk mu unuttun? Yaradan ne kadar çok kan akarsa, yara ya çabucak iyileşir ya da çabucak öldürürmüş.

Seni öldürdüm mü?

İçeri girmediğin ama önünden de gitmediğin kapıyı ben kelimelerimle yaktım.

Bazı yaralar pansuman gerektirmez, dikişliktir. Hangi iplik tutar bu yarayı bilmiyorum, tel zımba belki de bu işte iplikten daha iyidir. Bedenimi saran bu ateş demiri eritir, bir tel zımbayı eritmez mi?

İlk kez giden ben oldum senden, yalnızca bir biletin avucumu amel defteri gibi yakacağını hiç tahmin etmezdim.

Seni tanıdım, iyi biri olabileceğime inandım.
Seni tanıdım, cehennem kendini cennet sandı.

Seni içimden bir hastalığı atar gibi atamayışımın
son evresindeyim; ben sana ölüyorum.

Kirpim olduğun gece,

"Hatırlıyor musun? Seni bir gün sana esir olacağımı bile bile sevmiştim," dedin. Küçüklüğünden bugünlere kadar taşıdığın bilyelerini avucunun içinde birbirlerini çarpmasını sağlayacak şekilde salladın. Bilyelerin şangırtısını dinlerken acı yeşil gözlerine bakıyordum. Bilyelerin sesini duydun, gülümsedin. Nehirler yangın oldu yüreğime. Gülümsemeni gördüm, gülümsedim. "Hatırlıyor musun?" diye sordun yeniden. "Sırtımda koskoca dünyayı parçalayabileceğim kadar çok dikenle sana geldiğim geceyi?"

"Kirpi," dedim sana o gece ilk defa. "Hiçbir güneş silemez o geceyi."

"Seviyor musun bu Kirpi'yi?"

Bilyelerin sesi sustu.

"Hiçbir şeyi sevmedim bu Kirpi'yi sevdiğim gibi."

Hatırlıyor musun, Kirpi?
Seni, geldiğin o gece
sana esir olacağımı bile bile sevmiştim.

Sürttü ruhuma parmaklarını,
ruhumda bir yangın çıkardı.

Nehrin dibinde sevdiğim adamın,
bir kaşık suyunda boğuldum.

İncindi kaburgalarımız,

Bu hayat kaburgalarımı çok incitiyor.

Güneşi Tanrı doğuruyorsa, senin yokluğun batırıyor.

Biri kafamda bir yemini bozmak için kırılan ekmek gibi kırdı cam parçalarını Aklım da artık hiç yerinde değil. İnsanların yüzleri birer birer siliniyor hafızamdan. Mahallenin kedilerini avuçlarımla ceplerime doldurduğum balıklı mamalarla besliyorum. Ellerim leş kokuyor, ellerim senin kokunu kaybettiğim günden bugüne hep leş kokuyor.

Soluklanayım, diyorum.

Soluğum sende kalmış.

Nefes alayım biraz, diyorum.

Nefesim sende kalmış.

Şu çığırır gibi çarpan kalbim biraz sussun, diyorum.

Sonra hatırlıyorum, kalbimde bir kirpi taşıyorum, kirpinin çığlıklarını duyuyorum, kirpinin dikenlerini hissediyorum. ***Beslenir mi göğüs kafesinde bir kirpi?*** Avucumdaki balıklı mamaları kedilere verip başlarını okşadığım gibi, kaburgalarımın altındaki kalbimin parçalanmış damarlarıyla kirpiyi besleyip, kirpinin dikenli sırtına kemiklerimi bastırıyorum.

Kelimelerin artık hiçbir anlamının kalmadığı anda, bir zamanlar bizi bağlayanın da şu an bizi koparan kelimeler olduğunu hatırlıyorum. Kelimeler bazen en güzel rüyalara yatırıyorken seni, yine aynı kelimeler senin peşini hiç bırakmayacak o kâbuslara dönüşebiliyor.

Keşke burada olsan, senden bir yalan daha dinlesem. Yalan sevmeyen kadını yalana alıştırdın, Kirpi. Kaburgalarımı çalıp gittin, şimdi göğsüme taktığım plastik bir kaburganın içinde bana bıraktığın o kirpiyi yaşatmaya çalışıyorum.

İnsan birini seviyorsa, karşılık alamayacağını bilse bile söylemeli. Söylenmemiş kelimelerin ağrısı beterdir doğum sancısından.

İnsan birine kırılmışsa, tekrar kaynamayacağını bilse bile söylemeli. Söylenmemiş kelimelerin pişmanlığı beterdir geri çevrilmiş bir şansın pişmanlığından.

Öfkeli biri susmalı, karşısındaki onu yaralamaya devam ederken bile ağzını açmamalı. Söylenen bazı kelimelerin soğukluğu beterdir bir mezarın üzerini örten toprağa dokunmaktan.

Öfkeliydim, susmadım; sen de hiç açık açık sevdiğini söylemedin beni.

Kimse mahvetmediği birini
sevemez bana kalırsa.
Uykusunu böleceksin,
içtiği suyu boğazına dizeceksin,
gözlerini bıraktığı ilk boşluğa
kendi hayalini dikeceksin.

Delirdi kadın, canının acısından,

Bir alternatif olarak acıdan ölmek yerine acıdan delirmeyi deneyebilirsiniz. Zira insan ölemeyince, delirmenin eşsiz tadını alıyor. Delisin çünkü, en fazla ne zararın dokunabilir ki insanlığa? ***En büyük zararı insanlık sana vermiş,*** bir de üzerine kafayı yemişsin, tertemiz acını çekiyorsun. Baktım ölemiyorum, acından delirdim, sevgilim.

Bileklerimi dikine kesmeyi düşündüm önce, sonra korktum, canımın acımasından değil, kesik izlerinin hepsi aynı boyda, aynı uzunlukta, aynı derinlikte olmaz diye korktum.

Biliyorsun, Kirpi. Bende tamir edilemez bir simetri hastalığı var. Bileğimdeki kesiklerden biri diğerinden daha az derin olsa ya da bir tanesi daha az kanasa, ben bunu kafaya takar ölemem. Gülüyor musun, Kirpi? Saçma sapan konuştuğum, ufacık bir kelimenin içinden binlerce cümle çıkarıp önüne serdiğim, tam da uyuyacağımız sırada kafanı şişirdiğim zamanları hatırlıyorum. Ne derdin bana?

"Çenen düştü yine."

Ama susmamı da istemezdin. Uykuya dalarken en sevdiğin şey benim saçmalamalarımı dinlemekti. Bir de canın sıkkın olunca hep anlatmamı, konuşmamı isterdin. Başını omzuma koyar, sadece, ***"Konuş, cüce,"*** derdin. Ben konuşurdum, o kadar saçma sapan, o kadar alakasız, o kadar birbirinden kopuk şeyler anlatırdım ki, dışarıdan biri dinlese beni deli, seni de buna katlanıyorsun diye sağır zannederdi.

Şimdi bunları hatırlamak bardağın içine yaktığım binlerce roman sayfasının külünü doldurup içmeye çalışmak gibi. ***Sana konuştuğum kadar kimseye konuşmadım,*** Kirpi Adam. ***Sana sustuğum kadar kimseye de susmadım.***

Benim dilim, kelimelerim, sesimdin.

İçimde senin önüne serilmiş bir hayat bıraktın.

Ben şimdi bu hayatı nasıl harcayacağım?
Ben artık aklımda biriktirdiğim
tüm o gereksiz anıları kime anlatacağım?
Ben çok kırılsam da kime sarılıp,
kimin kollarında susacağım?

Dağlar, yollar, mesafeler aşmışsın,
tam kapısının önüne geldiğin an vazgeçmişsin gibi.

Ben gül uğruna dikeni tutmaya
devam ederdim de
sen benim ellerimin halini hiç görmedin.

Karşımda duruyordu. Tam karşımda bana ağzına gelen tüm yalanları bir bir sıralıyordu. Sonra özürler diliyor, sırtındaki dikenleri de alıp kenara çekilerek tekrar ona gelmemi bekliyordu. **Ben ağlıyordum,** her yirmi altı saniyede bir boğazımda ekmek bıçağı varmış gibi **yutkunuyordum,** sonra yine ona **gidiyordum.**

Ben karşısında yirmi altı saniyede bir temeli tekrar atılan, tekrar dikilen ve sonra tekrar yıkılan o bina gibi orada öylece **duruyordum.**

O yalanlarından üzerime alçılar, çimentolar, betonlar döküyordu. Ben ayaklarının önünde yirmi altı saniye aralıklarla bir bina gibi **yıkılıp tekrar** ayaklanıyordum.

Kanayan avuçlarımda dikenlerini sıkı sıkı tutuyordum, o bir bahçe makasıyla dikenlerimin üzerinde başı duran gülümü kesip benden alıyordu.

Ben yine **ona gidiyordum.**

O ellerimin halini **hiç görmüyordu.**

Binnur Şafak Nigiz

Kirpi gibi adam sevdik,

Kimden kaçtıysan arkana bile bakmadan, en çok ona yakalanmadın mı? Islak sokaklarda yürüdün, yağmurlar üzerine yağdı. Köşe başındaki tekelden bir bira aldın, mahallenin kara kedisinin başını okşadın, her gece pencerede sigara içen Nebahat ablaya bir selam çaktın ve gecenin içine karışıp altın varaklı binanın önüne vardın. Gazete biranın bedenine kefen gibi sarılmış, saçların yağmurdan sırılsıklam olmuştu. Sırtında yine dikenlerin yok muydu? Hangi ceket dikenlerini gizleyebilirdi ki? Sen, yine kendini o kaçtığın kadının kapısında bulmadın mı?

Sen o biradan bir yudum alıp, yine o kadının kapısını çalmadın mı?

Kirpi gibiydin, dikenlerin yüzünden yıllarca sevilmedin. ***Bir gün seni birinin sevebilecek olma düşüncesi bile seni bu denli korkuturken, sırf seni sevmesi için boynunu bir kadının önünde büktüğünde en çok kendine kırılmadın mı?***

Sandın ki sevilince, sevince bu kadar ölürcesine, dikenlerin dökülür sırtından, batmazsın, deşmezsin, delmezsin onu.

Ne zaman sana dokunsa ve acısa canı, hiç belli etmesen de ondan çok yanmadın mı?

Atilla İlhan demedi mi sana, ***kirpi gibisin çocuk, her tarafın diken,*** diye. Söylemedi mi sana da, ***kim elini uzatsa delik deşik, üstelik sen de kan içindesin.*** Atilla İlhan da mı tanıyordu seni? Yoksa var mı gerçekten sen gibi niceleri?

Yoksa biz kadınlar, hep mi seviyoruz şu kirpileri?

Ben ağlıyordum,
yutkunuyordum,
gidiyordum,
duruyordum.
Yıkılıp tekrar ona gidiyordum.
Hiç görmüyordu.

Sonra bir kırgınlık,
içinde akvaryumun camlarına
vura vura yüzen balık gibi
içini yaralayarak yüzmeye başladı.

Kirpi gibi adamlara ve kirpi gibi adamları seven keklik kadınlara,

Nabzımın boşluklarından damarlarıma düşen bir adam tanıdım. ***Bazı adamların mayasında bazı kadınları severek öldürmek vardır.*** Bazı adamlar silah değil, sevgisini kullanır. Bazı adamlar o kadar yalnızdır ki, sizin varlığınız, yıllar boyunca sarılıp annesi bildiği yalnızlığına oluşturulmuş bir ölüm tehdididir ve sırf bu yüzden sizden kaçarak yalnızlıklarını korumaya çalışırlar. ***Bazı adamların sırtında bir beşik vardır, çocuk yanımızı orada uyuturuz.*** Bazı adamların sırtı bir mezardır, ölüm döşeğidir, orada ölü bulunuruz. ***Bazı adamlar kirpi gibidir, sırtına yatmanızı ister ama bilmez, sırtında ne kadar diken varsa hepsi içimizi delip geçer.***

Bazı adamlar vardır işte. Buz gibi bir okyanusun içine daldığınızı sanırsınız, gözlerinizi bir açarsınız ateşlerin içindesinizdir.

Bazı adamlar vardır, sizi şeytanın meleği sevdiği kadar sever ama eline geçirdi mi de yakmadan bırakmaz. Çünkü şeytanın kalbi ateştir, melek gözünü o kalbe dikerse yanmayı göze almış demektir.

Ve cehennemin ateşlerini yalnızca âşıklar taze tutar.

Yine öyle bir adamı sevmenin getirdiği haklı bir acıyla yazıyorum. Kirpi gibi bir adam sevdim. Bunu sana, bunu ona, bunu herkese defalarca kez söyledim. Sırtına yatmamı istiyordu ama bilmiyordu, sırtındaki tüm dikenler içimi delip geçiyordu. Ben yine de uzanıyordum onun sırtına ve içim delim deşikken gülümsüyordum ona. ***O beni onun sırtındayken rahat uykularımın birindeyim sanıyordu, oysa ben her gece onun sırtında ölüm uykusuna dalıyordum.***

Şimdi kirpi gibi bir adamın yokluğunun ortasında, sırtımda onun dikenlerinin açtığı delikler göğsümden bile görünürken öylece bekliyorum. **Gelmeyeceğini, artık gelemeyeceğini, artık hiçbir zaman kavramının bizim için anılar öremeyeceğini biliyorum.** ***Bilmek, beklemekten daha büyük bir sancı bırakıyormuş insanın içine.*** Beklerken, bir gün öğrendiğimde, bir gün her şeyi bildiğimde anladım.

Asıl olay beklemek değil, asıl olay bile bile beklemek.

Birinin geleceğini bilirsin, bir şekilde buna imkân verirsin, belki gelmez diye düşünürsün ama içinde içini deşip duran o umut vardır hani... ***Beklersin.***

Ama birinin gelmeyeceğini, artık gelemeyeceğini, artık tüm imkânların yandığını, tüm umutların o gece ölü bulunduğunu, tüm bekleyişlerin sadece acı dolu bir kâbus olduğunu bilmek... Bile bile beklemek...

Herkes anlamaz bunu. Anlayan da şu an sigarasını yakıyor zaten.

Bir kayalıksın sen,
durdum o uçurumun önünde,
izliyorum seni;
sen ki zihnimde en gerçek intihar düşüncesi.

Binnur Şafak Nigiz

Diledi balık boğulmayı,

Bir dilek dilediğim geceyi hatırlıyorum. O kadar çok yanmıştı ki canım, dileğin sırtına bağladığım umutlar ölmüştü.

Gök yere düşmüştü; yer, cehennemin dibine.

O gece bir de çok üşümüştüm.

Ben de baktım, çok üşüyorum. Bir kibrit diledim. Cebimde çakmak vardı aslında.

İnsan dilek dileyince üzerinden bulut gibi bir yük kalkar; kocamandır ama hafiftir. Bu yüzden doymaz insan, bu yüzden en büyük dert onun sanır. Dilekler birer balon olur gökyüzüne asılır. Asılır tabii, dilek bile asılır, ben neden asmayacakmışım kendimi?

Denemedim mi? Çok denedim. İp sağlam değildi.

Tavan çok yüksekti, boyum yetmedi.

İnsanın darağacı bazen yazdıkları oluyor. Ben çok öldüm aslında, yazdığım her kelime bir cenazeydi, içimde koskoca bir mezarlığı sayfalara kustum.

Zaten acıyı bir yazan bilir bir de yaşayan. Artık yazan da yaşadığından mı yazar, yaşayan da yazamadığı için mi böyle yanar bilemem.

Oturup içi su, içi deniz kabuğu, içi inci dolu bir küreyi izle en iyisi. İzle ama içine balık koyma.

Ölüyor vicdansız.

Üstelik yaşaması gereken yerde ölüyor.

İnsanın tek yaşayabileceği yerde ölü bulunması da böyle bir şey değil mi zaten?

Neyse, balık da zaten boğulmayı diledi.

Küçük bir kız çocuğunun güvendiği tek insanın
elini sıkıca tuttuğu gibi tutmuştum ellerini.

Binnur Şafak Nigiz

İnsan yatağında uyuttuğunu mu unutamaz,
hayalinde uyuttuğunu mu?

Yalancının mumu,

"Geberiyorum ulan, anlasana Allahsız, anlasana!"

Elindeki su bardağını duvara fırlattın, bardak duvarda patladı, su duvarı yıkadı. Avuçlarımın içine batan tırnaklarım, ayaklarıma dolanan kediyle sessizce seni izlerken gözlerimden yaşlar boşalıyordu.

"Sana dedim," diye bağırdın yüzüme doğru. "Sana benim içimdekilerle oynama, ayarımı bozma, dedim. Seni böyle sevmeyi ben mi istedim?"

"Sevmeseydin," diye fısıldadım titreyen sesimle. "Madem sen istemedin, ben mi istedim?"

"Nasıl söyleyebiliyorsun ulan bunu?" Başını omzuna doğru yatırıp gözlerimin içine baktın. "Harbiden söylüyor musun bunu?"

Gözlerimden yaşlar süzülürken, "Bana yalan söyledin," dedim.

Canım bulut olsa, yağmur olur kasıklarıma yağar, kasıklarımdaki kan yağmurunda bir bebek büyür, kadınlığımdan ölüm doğardı.

"Söyledim!" diye bağırınca gözlerimi yumdum. "Ama seni her şeyden çok yine ben sevdim!"

"Sevince..." diye fısıldadım gözlerimi açmadan. "...yalanın bedelini ödemiş mi oluyorsun?"

"Öyle bir sevmişim ki, yalanlar susmuş."

"Bana yalan söyledin," dedim söylediklerini umursamadan. Oysa sen benim canımda acıydın.

Güldün. "Sana yalan söylemeyi ben mi istedim?"

Bazı geceler var canım, tüm şehri yaksan,
    o geceyi yakamazsın.

O gece şehrin içinde sen yanarsın,
    yine de o geceyi yakamazsın.

Öyle bir gece yaşandı.
Ben geceyi yakarım sandım.
Şehir yandı, ben yandım, o gece yanmadı.

O gece yaşandı.

Kirpi Gibi Bir Adam Sevdim

Kan leş tükürdüm.

Dökülmüş dişlerim ağzımın içinde, ağzımın içi kan revan içinde. ***Yüzeceğimi sandığım denizin içinden cesedimi bir torbanın içinde çıkardılar.*** Canını çok mu sıkıyorum? Ama söylesene, ben ne yapayım? Zihnimde bir fay hattı vardı, en büyük depremleri düşüncelerim yarattı.

Dudaklarında günde yirmi altı dal sigara, sırtında yirmi altı sivri dikenle, benimle uyumayı özlemiyor musun?

Tankların altında ezilmiş binlerce sivil gibi, ağzının içindeki et parçasını yediği tekmelerin sızıs hâlâ sırtındayken yavrularına taşıyan dişi bir sokak köpeği gibi, evladının mezarının başında ağıt yakan kırkı çıkmamış, kırk ateşle yanan bir anne gibi. Ben seni çok özlüyorum.

Vuruldu dört yerinden,

İnsan birini sevince tam dört yerinden vurulurmuş. Önce beyninden, sonra kalbinden, daha sonra ruhundan, sonra da ayaklarından. ***Ben ayaklarıma boşaltılmış mermilere rağmen biri için yürümeye devam etmiştim.***

Ben arkamda ayaklarımdan akan kanları beni takip eden bir nehir gibi dökerken, birine yürümeye devam etmiştim.

Beyninden vurulduğum zamanı hatırlıyorum. Onu ilk gördüğümde üzerinde kırmızı kapüşonlusu vardı, soğuk görüntüsünün altında yaralı bir adam olduğunu onu gördüğüm ilk saniyede anlamış, ilk saniyede bunu fark etmenin getirisi bir mermiyi beynimin içinde hissetmiştim.

Biri sizi vurduğunda, en son göz göze geleceğiniz kişinin sizi vuran kişi olacağını bana o öğretti.

Kalbimden vurulduğum zamanı hatırlıyorum. Onun ilk kez gözlerimin içine bakıp, namluyu kalbime uzattığı andı. Beni gördüğünü, beni benim bile göremediklerimle gördüğünü anladığımda artık vurulan yalnızca beynim değildi, kurşunun hedefine bir de kalbim eklenmişti.

Birini tüm kalbinizle sevdiğinizde, onu kaybettiğiniz günün ikindisinde toprağa verilirsiniz.

Gömülmek için illaki bedeninize ihtiyaç duyulmaz, bazen bir duyguyu da toprağa verebilirsiniz.

Bazen oluyor öyle. Biri gidiyor, sizin kalmanız hiçbir şey ifade etmiyor.

Ruhumdan vurulduğum zamanı hatırlıyorum. Beni ilk defa sevdiğini söylemek yerine hissettirdiği, avucum kalbimin üzerinde basılı şekilde uyuduğum geceydi. Ruhum kelimelerimdi ve kelimelerimin hepsi onun kuşatması altına girmişti.

Bir daha beni bu denli kimsenin sevmeyeceğine beni körü körüne inandırdıktan sonra gitti.

Gittiği gün, vurulan benim ayaklarımdı.

Arkasından gelmemi istemediği için, bana dağ kadar ağır bir yükü, yani geleceği bırakarak beni ayaklarımdan vurmuş, olduğum yerde bırakarak benden çok uzaklara gitmişti. Ayaklarımdan vurduğunda gelemem sandı, olduğum yerde dururum sandı, yanıldığını ona anlatmaya çalışsam da artık beni duyamayacağı kadar uzaktaydı. ***Bazen kapının önünde durup beni izlemesi yetmiyor, bazen kapının önünde gözlerimin içine bakarken benden şehirlerce uzak hissettiriyor.***

Karşında diz çökmüş dünyalar olsa neye yarar, sen o adamın ayaklarına kapanmadın mı?

Kapandım canım. Ayaklarına kapandım.

Senin masallarının sonu hep haksızlıktı, benim masalımın sonunda da bir tek ben ölüyordum.

Dünya yine mutluydu.

Olsun.

Mezarıma gelsen ismimin harfleri gülümser sana, biliyor musun? Yıkıldım canım, mezarım olsun ayakların.

Olsun.

Kirpi Gibi Bir Adam Sevdim

Bazı geceler yaşanır, yaşayıp yaşamadığını ayırt edemezsin. Öyle ölümdür bazı geceler, sabahları öyle zulümdür. O günün gecesi de sabahı da hafızamın yanmasını istediğim yerinde saklanıyor. O gün ortalık yangın yeriydi, o gün ortalık anacık babacık günüydü, o gün ölenin cesedi bile o anda soğurdu ama ben kalktım, o gün, orada, tuttum yine seni sevdim.

O gün orada benim gidecek yerim yoktu, o gün inanacak kimsem yoktu, o gün sırtımı yasladığım ağaç bile dallarını kafama vurmuştu ama ben kalktım, o gün, orada, tuttum yine seni sevdim.

O gün azap artık bir ömür takipçim olacak sanıyordum, o gün bir daha yüzüm gülmeyecek sanıyordum, **o gün senin sırtın dikendi, o gün ben en umulmaz ağrıları tek başıma sırtlanırken yine orada, çaresizce kirpi gibi bir adam seviyordum.**

Seni seviyordum.

Binnur Şafak Nigiz

Su kuyuları bile kurudu, gözlerimi kurutamadım.
Bir adam sevdim,
bir daha toparlanamadım.

İstanbul'da bir sokağa adını vermişler,
bacaklarım kopsaydı,
kopsaydı da geçmeseydim oradan.

İzmir'de kokunu aldım,
Kordon'da kendimi denize bıraksaydım,
bıraksaydım da patlasaydı ciğerlerim,
çıksaydı kokun oradan.

Elimde kendimden parçalarla yamaladığım
sökülmüş bir ruhun elini tutup,
onu sana getirmiştim.

Binnur Şafak Nigiz

Küçük kar tanesi yuvarlandı, etrafa çarptı
ve çok yara aldı ama bu onu durdurmadı.
Kar tanesi acıyı kabul etti, ta ki bir çığ olana kadar.

Ellerin ve odamdaki yangın,

Bin yabancının içinde bile seni ayırt edebileceğim ellerinin başıma yıkıldığı bir odada yine sana rastladım. Odadaki bütün camı çerçeveyi indirdim, çok ağladım, sonra sustum, yatağın üzerine oturup ellerini düşündüm. Geceler, kaygısız bir piç gibi yapıştı yakama, güneş artık kuyunun içinde sönmüş bir cesetti, penceremden içeri girip bir daha hiç doğmadı odama. Senin taşlı yolların vardı, benim ellerimde ellerin yoktu ve seni son kez seveceğimden korktuğum için gözüme hiç uyku girmiyordu. Aynalar bana ismimi söyledi, yüzüm benim yüzüm değil gibiydi ama oradaydım ve bir fil içime oturmuş, hortumunu kalbime sarıp sarıp sıkıyor, içeride olduğunu bildiği seni öldürme arzusuyla hortumunu hiç gevşetmiyordu. Seni bin yabancının içinde bulabilecekken ben, bu odanın içinde kaybettim. Çekmeceleri aradım, dağıttım yatağı, yastıkları kılıflarından bir bebeği annesinin karnından ayıran doktor gibi ayırdım, dolapların içine saklanmışsındır diyerek ağlayarak kıyafetlerimi yerlere döküp, bomboş dolabın içinde seni aradım. Fil içerideydi. İçimdeydi ve odamdaydı. Ortalığı dağıtışımı hortumunu belime sararak izledi. Bazen beni tutup sıktı, odanın içinden çıkarmak ister gibi oradan uzaklaştırdı ama kasımpatılar beni içeri çağırdılar. Yokluğun ciğerimin içinden iğnenin deliğinden geçen ip gibi geçti ama ciğerimin içinden geçen ip değildi. Ellerini çok aradım. Odanın içinde oturdum, başıma yıkıldıktan sonra düştüğü yerde parçalanmış mıdır korkusuyla sırtımı duvara bastırıp, yerde her şeyini kaybetmiş bir kadın gibi ağladım. Senin bana bıraktığın aşk, içimde kalabalıklaşan, üreyerek soyunu sopunu kökenini bana bırakan bir aile gibi çöreklendi göğsüme. O aşk, beni yurdu bildi. Sürekli kaynayan çaydanlığın içine ellerimi soktum, içim kadar yanmadı ve ellerim suyun içindeyken hep şu sözün kafamda yankılandı: "Ellerimi yaktın sen benim." Ellerim yanarken hep gülümsedim. İçeride bir kalabalık, dışarıda bir yalnızlık, çaydanlık kaynadıkça yüzeyinden aktı gözyaşı gibi su damlaları, ben gözlerimden çaydanlığın üzerinde kayan damlalara eşlik eden yaşlarla, hem gülümsedim hem düşündüm. Ellerini tıpkı böyle yakmışsam, bir damla sıcak su dökmeden ya da tutup bir ateşin içine basmadan... Sen benim gibi acımış olabilir misin ki? Ellerin başıma yıkıldı. Baktım, yanık izi yoktu. Bin kişinin içinde bulurdum ya hani, baş başa olduğumuz şu odada kaybettim seni.

Soluk soluğa unutacağım seni, soranlara çok koştum, çok yoruldum diyeceğim. Bir yatağın üzerinde otururken ve gözlerim duvardayken, seni son kez sevdiğimi bile bilmediğim bir gece, soluk soluğa, sanki hiç olmamışsın gibi, içimden dışarı salıp, kaybolman için sokağa bırakacağım seni. Yol bilmezsin, iz bilmezsin. Annesini kaybetmiş bir çocuk gibi, karanlıkta ağlayarak yürürken, annenin adını değil benim adımı söyleyecek, hiç unutamayacaksın beni.

Kırgınlığın sesi,

Bir insana kırılmak, tüm dinlerden daha eskidir. Kalbinin sesi bölerken geceyi, yastık sana cehennem, yatak azap olur. ***İçinde yumruk gibi tuttuğun derdinle, yumruk kadar kalbini aynı yere koyarsan; kazanan dert, ağrıyan kalbin olur.*** Savaş alanında yere serilmiş bir asker gibi, emir komutası senceyken, senin önünde, senin yüzünden yenilmiş kalbini dinlersin. ***Kalp en çok, derdi göğsün içine koyup, kendini yere serdiren sahibine darılır.*** Kalbimi yere serdirdin bana. Üzerini varlığınla örtüp, üşümesin diye kafamın içindeki fırtınayı susturduğum kalbimi, yokluğunla üşüttün. Yaptıklarınla yere serdin beni.

Yapmadıklarınla ezip geçtin beni.

Mutlu musun bilmiyorum ama gülümsediğini görsem, sırtımda bir bıçak varken gülümserim.

Yere serdik; ben kalbimi, sen beni.

Çok kanlı kaybettim seni.

Ve sen, daha dinlerin olmadığı bir dünyaya tutunmuş o duyguyu; dilimde sana birikmiş duaları yok sayarak bana bırakıp, inanır mısın bilmem ama çok kırdın beni.

Ben bu kırgınlığı sana anlatamam ama ellerin bir defa ellerime uzansa, ellerin bile anlar, ellerin bile kırgınlığıma ağlar.

O gece şafağı doğurdun, sabahı büyüttün, gelmedi.

O gece çok bekledin.

O gece hiç gelmedi.

Zaten beklemek çürütmez mi insanı?

Dal değilsin, yine de onun rüzgârında en çok sen kopmadın, kırılmadın mı? Ne kadar sustuysan, aslında susmak istediğin için değil, gideceğini bildiğin için, onu kırmamak, onu üzmemek, kalbin ağrılar içinde yalpalarken onun başını ağrıtmamak için susmadın mı?

Şimdi beklemek yangın yeri, biliyorum ama sen onu sevdiğin gün zaten kendini cayır cayır yanan o ateşe atıp, onu sevdiğin her gün daha fazla yanmadın mı?

O gece sizin evde, senin odanda bir cinayet işlendi. O mesajı içinde taşıyan telefon bir bomba oldu göğsünde patladı. O gece katil orada değildi ama yine de seni öldürmedi mi?

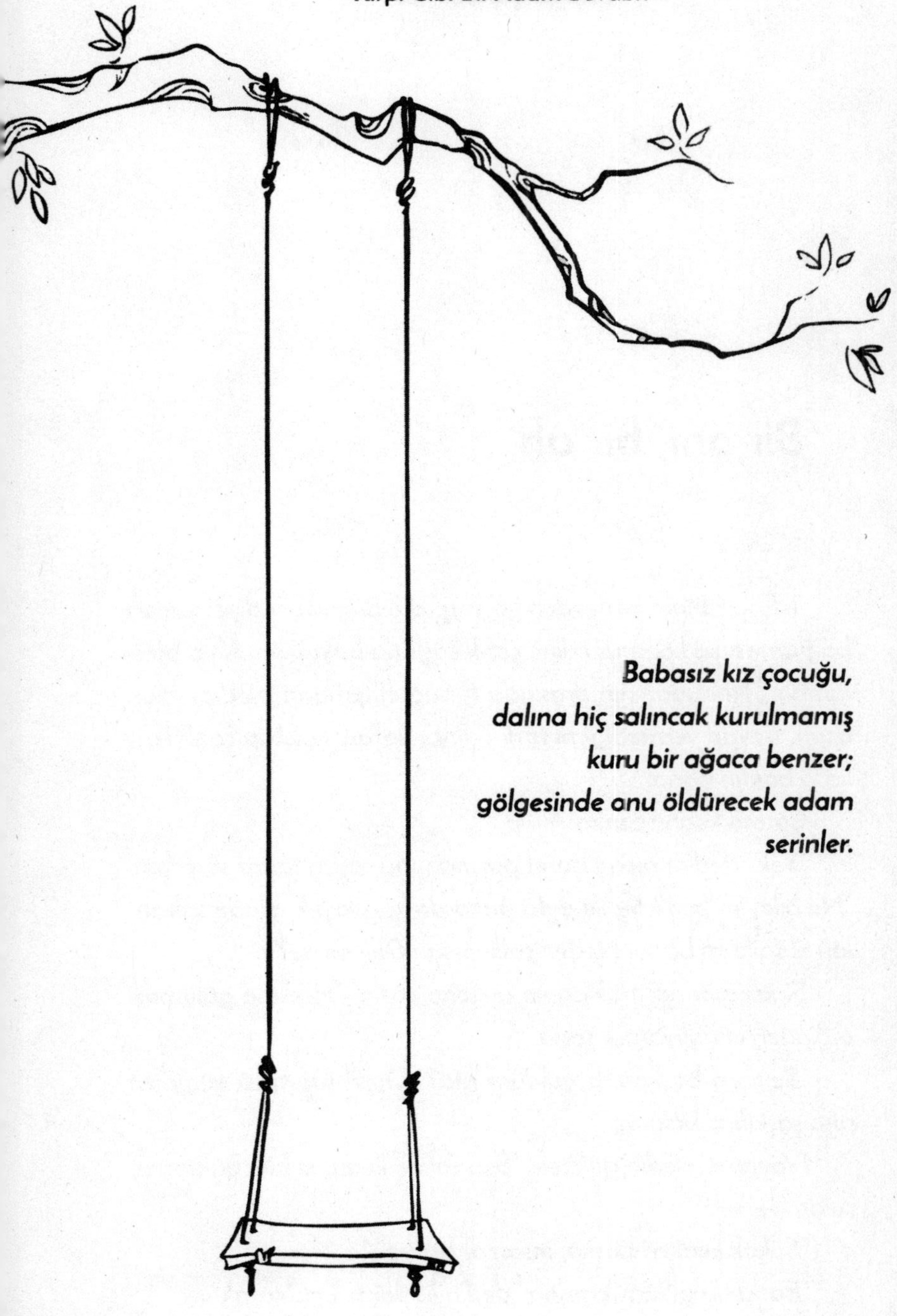

Babasız kız çocuğu,
dalına hiç salıncak kurulmamış
kuru bir ağaca benzer;
gölgesinde onu öldürecek adam
serinler.

Binnur Şafak Nigiz

Bir anı, bir ah,

"Musa abinin kızı evden kaçmış, duydun mu?" diye sordun bağlamasının kopmuş teline çatık kaşlarla bakarken. Ah o bağlaman... İki dudağının arasında tuttuğun izmariti izledim uzun uzun. Cevap vermediğimi fark edince kafanı kaldırıp çatık kaşlarla baktın bana.

Çatma kaşını, canım.

"Yok," dedim ojemi işaret parmağıma taşıra taşıra sürerken. "Ne bileyim ben? Bir iki defa pazarda karşılaştık, bir de sabahları el sallardı bana. Neden sallıyorsa... Deli mi ne?"

Sigarasını parmaklarının arasına aldın. "Herkese gülümsediğinden el sallıyordur sana."

"Senden başkasına güldüm mü?" Ojeyi taşırarak sürerken ona şaşkınca baktım.

"Yavrum," dedin gülerek. "Sen sokak kedisine bile gülümser, selam verirsin."

"Sokak kedileri başka, insanlar başka..."

"Bana da gülümsemiştin," dedin kaşlarını kaldırarak.

"Sen başkasın," diye homurdanıp gözlerimi ojeli parmaklarıma indirdim. "En başka."

Başkaydın, canım. Bugün Musa amcayı gördüm pazarda. Torunu kucağındaydı. Affetmiş kızını. Torununu kucaklamış gezdiriyordu. Seni sordu bana.

Doğum günümden birkaç gün önce, gittiğin o gece döktüğüm gözyaşlarını, attığım çığlıkları balkonda dudaklarının arasında elleriyle sardığı tütünü içerken dinlediğini hatırlamış olacak ki, birden sustu.

Sustuk birlikte.

Uzun zamandır susmuyordum biriyle birlikte.

Sonra torunu ağlamaya başlayınca bozuldu zaten o suskunluk. Meyve halinin ortasındaki yol ayrımından ayrıldık. Gördüm, elinin tersiyle gözlerini silip çocuğu susturmaya çalışıyordu.

Musa amca zaten kızı evden kaçtığında da gizli gizli ağlardı pencere kenarlarında.

Balık burcu, ondan...

Bir anı, bin ah.

"Dayım yengemi çok sevmiş, biliyor musun?" diye sordum elimdeki romanın sayfasını yavaşça çevirirken. Derbi maçının tekrarını izliyordun internetten.

"Bu nereden çıktı şimdi, Çirkin?" diye sordun. Dudaklarım yukarı kıvrıldı. Kitabı kenara bırakıp masanın ucuna koyduğum törpüye uzandım. Tırnaklarımın yediğim kenarlarını düzeltirken, "Anlatasım geldi," diye mırıldandım.

Güldün. Bilgisayarın kapağını sertçe kapatıp bilgisayarı masanın üzerine bıraktın. Yatakta dizlerinin üzerine basıp bana doğru yaklaştın, yanıma oturup beni kollarının arasına aldın.

"İyi de onlar ayrılmamış mıydı?" diye sordun.

"Bu yüzden çok sevmiş, dedim zaten." Gözlerimi çevirip senin yangın yeri gözlerine baktım. "Eğer kavuşmuş olsalar neden onları anlatmaya o soruyla başlayayım?"

"Ne?"

Yaklaşıp tekrar fısıldadım: "Dayım yengemi çok sevmiş, biliyor musun?"

O gece uzun uzun anlattım sana onların aşkını. Gözlerinde ilk defa gördüğüm o düş kırıklığıyla dinledin beni. Benden daha çok üzüldün ayrılıklarına. Belki de dayım ve yengemden bile çok üzüldün.

Yok be, kimse dayım kadar üzülemez bu ayrılığa.

Hem biliyor musun, ben de yeni öğrendim. Yengem hâlâ dayımın fotoğraflarını saklıyor, arada izleyerek ağlıyormuş.

Dayım da kolunda onun isminin yazılı olduğu dövmeyi sildirmedi zaten.

Ama isminin yazılı olduğu yere hâlâ yara bandı yapıştırıyor.

Peki sen canım, sen? O köpeğin başını okşarken gizlice çektiğin fotoğrafımın dövmesini yaptırmıştın ya hani koluna...

Duruyor mu hâlâ? Benim gözlerimde senin bir dövmen var, öyle bir dövme ki bu, gözlerime bakan her adamı hâlâ dövüyor.

O gece gitmek istediğini hissettin.
Herhangi bir yere.
Aslında tek bir yere.
O gece tüm biletler yandı.
Tüm otobüsler durdu.
Tüm tekerlekler patladı.
Tüm mazotlar bitti.
O gece ayakların koptu,
ellerin zaten uzun zamandır yerlerinde yoktu.
O gece gidemeyeceğini biliyordun.
O gece göğsünün valizleri açıldı.
O gece küle döndün.
O gece hâlâ nefes alıyordun
ama aslında artık ölüydün.

Ben öyle bir geceden yazıyorum, hâlâ yaşıyorum, önümde defalarca kez boşaltılmış ardından yeniden toplanmış bir valizle hâlâ gitmek istiyorum.

Kıvrımlı kirpiklerine çaresizlik bulaşmış,
gözlerinde iltihap kapmış bir çocuk yarası.

Ben senin kışına öyle çok alışmıştım ki,
beni başkalarının yazları öldürürdü.

Kanser gibi dağınık,

Taş bastım ben bağrıma. Taş gibi bir ağrı bastım. Büyürken sobanın sıcağından parmak uçlarını sakınmayı öğrenen o çocuk gibi, yanmış olmama rağmen onu severken bir türlü büyüyemedim, kendimi sakınmayı öğrenemedim. Tutku, şefkat, teslimiyet, acı. Boyunlarını kesmek istedim o piçlerin. İçime ağrı taşıdıklarından habersiz gebe kaldığımda hepsine, *rahmim keşke kanserleri olsaydı*, dedim. Mevsim değişikliğinde yakalanılmış bir grip gibi bağışıklık sistemime darbe üzerine darbe yaparken, ciğerlerimden onu tıpkı boğuk bir öksürüğün içine saklanan balgam gibi çıkarıp atmak istedim.

Birini geberir gibi sevmenin ağrısını yüreğimde, dünyanın ne mal olduğunu anne karnında anlayıp düşmek için kendini kordondan aşağı bırakan bebeğin rahme düşürdüğü ağrı gibi taşıyorum.

Boktan burnunu çıkaramayan bir adamın kalbinde yaşayan her kadın bilir; yılanın zehri, akrebi görene kadardır.

Dağınığım yani canım, anlıyor musun? ***Uzun zaman sonra tekrar eve gelmişsin, evi dağınık unuttuğunu eve girdiğin an anlamışsın gibi dağınığım.*** Yorgunum da üstelik. Ne elimi kaldıracak halim var ne de girip yaşayabilirim o dağınıklığın içinde. ***Çöküp kapının eşiğine, ağlamak istiyorum.***

Kirpi ağlamak istiyorum, bize ne yaptın?

Yüz kapı çarptım çıkıp giderken senin içinden.

Yüzü de benim yüreğimin üzerine kapandı.

Yüzünün de arasında sıkıştım.

"*Kendine mutlu bir insan diyebilir misin?*" diye sor bana, derim, senin önünde sana ağlarken gülümseyerek söylerim bunu. Az yapmadım, biliyorsun. Mutluyum derim, bilirsin, mutluyum demek mutlu olmaya yetmiyor.

Döndüğümde o evi dağınık bulacağımdan bihaberdim ama giderken dağıtan yine bendim. Kapının eşiğinde dağınıklığı izleyerek ağlamak yerine, o dağınıklığın içine girdim. ***O dağınıklık yüzünden bazen bıraktığını koyduğun yerde bulamazsın ama evin içinde olduğunu bilirsin.*** Ben eve döndüğümde, seni bıraktığım yerde bulamadım, Kirpi. Evde de değildin.

Ben şimdi içinde senin olmadığın hangi eve sığabilirim ki?

Dağıldım bir ev gibi, artık toparlanamam da, parçalarım dağıldı bambaşka sokaklara.

Bir anı, bir ölüm,

"Çocuk gibi gülüyorsun."

Dudaklarımdaki tebessüm, sabahı çağıran şafak gibi yüzümü ağarttığında büyük parmakların yanaklarımda geziniyordu. Kucağımdaki yavru kedinin başını okşarken yeşil gözlerinin içine bakmaya devam ettim.

Öyle bir an gelirdi ki, bütün kelimeler valizlerini alır, dili terk ederdiler.

"Bu kedinin annesi ve babası olalım mı?" diye sorduğumda yüzünü buruşturdun. Söylemezdin ama aslında severdin hayvanları... Hele kedileri... Hele beni...Garip lakaplar takardın onlara. Kovar gibi yapardı ama onlar için her zaman kapının önüne koyacak bir kap suyun, bir kap yemeğin vardı.

"Uğraştırma beni şu itle. Senden başka kediyle uğraşamam ben. Hem apartman yöneticisinin nasıl bir pezevenk olduğunu bilmiyor musun? Bu iti kapı dışarı eder, yanında promosyon olarak ikimizi de sokağa atar. Kalırız damsız."

Yavru kedinin patilerini kaldırıp ona gösterdim. Uzun uzun gülüşümü, sonra da küçücük patileri izledi. "Tamam ulan," dedi. "Gülme pişmiş kelle gibi. Olsun bizim."

"Canımsın, biliyor musun?"

"Herhâlde, enayi." Gülerek köpeğin başını okşadı. Sonra bana baktı. "Ölürsem, Çirkin, ya gülüşün yüzünden ya da... Yine bir şekilde senin yüzünden."

O geceden sonra ben bir sigara yaktım, diğerini söndürmeden. Hep böyle sürdü bu. Biri sönmeden diğeri yandı, dumanları karıştı havaya, bir değil bin zehirlendim.

Çok öldüm ben kimselere söylemeden.

Bileklerime balık resimleri çizdim, kanımda boğuldu, öldü balıklar. Kasımpatıları sulamadım, kurudular. Eğildim, ocağın ateşinde yaktım sigaramı, saçlarımın uçları hep o ateşte yandı.

Öldüm öldüm dirildim.

Sezen Aksu söyledi, ben dinledim.

Müslüm Gürses'in elinde bir bıçak vardı, Yıldız Tilbe odaya hep avucunda yanan bir mumla girerdi.

Yıldızlar susardı.

Benim içim çok yanardı.

İnsanlar neden ağladığımı sorgular diye, gittim tanımadığım bir adamın cenazesinde ağladım. Çok ağladım, çok bağırdım, iki cenaze var sandılar, ölüyorum sandılar, tutamadılar. Bir kere yutkundum, dokuz kere kustum, yirmi altı kere alnımı yere vurdum. ***Bir yutkunuşa binlerce ölüm sığdırdım.*** Damarlarımdan kan akıttım, kanserler bıraktım ciğerimden, böbreklerimden kumlar serptim, yüzüm yandı, ben o yaraları ellerimle daha altları kanlıyken soydum. Ailesi bile gitti el adamının mezarının önünden, gece yarısı durdum, yüzünü bile bilmediğim bir adamın mezarının önünde ben çok ağladım.

O geceden sonra hep bekledim.

O gece içimde bir ateş yandı, o geceden beri cehennem böyle yanmıyor.

Ben yanıyorum, cehennem de yanıyor ama Allah biliyor ya, cehennem bile böyle yanamıyor.

Ben annemin yıllar önce onu terk etmiş,
sonra da kanserden ölmüş babamı hâlâ sevdiği gibi
seni çok, seni tek, seni ölesiye, seni hâlâ...

Yirmi altı odalı bir hastane,
bir de kasımpatıların küstüğü nilüferler,

Dudaklarından dudaklarıma beş yüz yirmi altı yalan dökülse, beş yüz yirmi beşini benim için söyledin. Limon çiçeklerinin kokusunu çok severdin ve benim için kasımpatı almayı öğrendiğin gün, bir çiçekçiyle tartışıp karakolluk olduğun gündü. Ellerimde senin için avladığım kuşların kanatlarıyla sana geldiğimde, kalbim damarlarını ayırmış, nihayet doğuma başlamıştı ve balıklar nefeslerini suyun içinde kaybederken kalbimin rahminden kanlar içinde bir kirpinin göbek bağı damarlarımla göğsüme bağlanmıştı.

Kalbim yirmi altı odalı bir hastaneydi. Bazı odalarında çocuklar, bazı odalarında yaşlılar, bazı odalarında kadınlar, bazı odalarında adamlar ve bazı odalarında canavarlar yatardı. Ellerinde kasımpatılarla her odaya uğrar, her birinde beni arardın. Ben sessizce seni izlerdim ve kışın ortasında gökyüzünden güneşin teninden kopan et parçaları yağardı. Canavarların karnı doyar, bir bebek annesinin karnından sezaryenle doğardı. Soğuk silahını şakağıma dayardı, avucumda ezdiğim karanfillerle sokağına girerdim ve üç yüz yirmi altı günün üç yüz yirmi beşi boyunca aynı köşe başında karşılaşırdık.

Dal, koskoca ağaca bir yalan söylerdi.

Koskoca ağaç, bir dalın yalanı uğruna yapraklarını dökerdi.

Yağmurun altında bir şemsiye açardım, şemsiyenin içinden seller başıma akardı.

Bir kirpinin sırtından yirmi altı diken çalar, o dikenlerle bileklerime adını yazardım.

Bir de kasımpatılar, toprağın içinden başlarını sen onlara dokun diye çıkarırlardı.

Ne kadar seviyorsan limon çiçeğinin kokusunu, o kadar aşıktın suda yüzen nilüfere.

Boynumda bir kumrunun boynunu saran siyah kolyesi gibi isminin baş harfini taşıyan kolyeyle dolanırdım.

İnanır mısın, herkes bizi çok kıskanırdı.

Bir kadının sırtını yaslayacak kadar
güvendiği o dağ olup sonra da o dağa
karlar yağdırdıktan sonra,
onu çok sevmişsin
ya da hiç sevmemiştin ne fayda?

Beklemek ve kaybetmek sanatı;

Körebe oynarken gözleri bağlanmış bir çocuğun etrafına çarpa çarpa ilerlediği, bundan eğlendiği gibi seni sevdiğim o kış gecesini hatırlıyorum; gözlerim bağlı, duvarlarına çarpıp durmaktan kan revan içinde, bunu oyun sanan bir çocuk gibi mutluydum. Kimin sana kan kusturup, onu suçlamamak adına ellerin titreye titreye bardağa kızılcık şerbeti doldurduğun geceyi unutamazsın. Ağzındaki kan bardağı doldurur, kızılcık şerbeti bir gün kaybetmeyi öğrenir, o gün büyür, o gün yaşlanır, bir gün şarap olur. ***Kendi kanında boğulmayı öğrendiğin gün, kuşlar kadar özgürsündür ve her kuşa en az bir avcı bir gün namlusunu doğrultur.***

Büyürsün, büyümenin kanser olduğu bir dünyada sen kalbinde lösemi bir çocukla, artık o çocuğun annesisindir. Kendi kendinin annesi olmayı öğrendiğin gün, saçları kalbine dökülen lösemi çocuğun öldüğü gündür ve sen artık içinde kırk ateş yanmış, otuz dokuzu sönmüş, kalan bir tanesini ilelebet içinde taşıyacak olan ağrılar içinde bir kadınsındır.

Kaybetmek yalnızca bir insanı uğurlamak değildir, kaybetmek bazen kendi ölümünü dilinin ucunda birikmiş, hiç söylenmemiş, söylenebilecek kadar güçlü olunmayacak kelimelerle beklemektir.

...ve beklemek, kaybetmekten daha büyük bir kanserdir.

Kaybettiğimi anladığımda değil, hâlâ beklediğimi anladığımda yakalandım ben o kansere. Ben anlayana kadar, o çoktan içimde büyümüş, olmuştu dördüncü evre.

Anneciğim sen okşarken saçlarımı,
ben bir adam için yolardım hep onları.

Anne ve fotoğraf, bir de silah,

Bir şeyi daha öğrendim. Annemin gözyaşlarının yanaklarından yuvarlanışını izlediğim gece, ***benim için gerçekten gözyaşı dökebilecek ter varlığın annem olduğunu öğrendim.*** Köze dönmüş yüreğimdeki sancıyı yalnızca annemin görebileceğini, benim için benden çok, sırf ben ağlıyorum diye ağlayabileceğini öğrendim.

İlgisinden mahrum olmakla yakındığım o kadının, aslında hayatının merkezi olduğumu, ben gözyaşlarım gözlerimi kör edecekmiş gibi akarken ve annemin dizlerine alnımı koyup hıçkırarak ağlarken, annemin benden daha çok ağladığı gece öğrendim.

Annem yıkılmış, devrilmiş, çığın altında kalmış, çukura düşmüş, boğulmuş bir kadındı.

Çoğu anne çaktırmasa da ya boğuluyordur ya yanıyordur ya da kuyunun dibinden yukarıyı izlerken siz kuyunun dibinde olduğunu anlamayasınız diye size gülümsüyordur zaten.

Babanın gölgesinin bile içeri girmediği, ismini var eden kelimelerin bile evin içine düşmediği bir evde, bir kadınla yapayalnız büyüdüm. Mutfağa girer hıçkıra hıçkıra ağlar, sonra da ağladığı mutfakta benim için yemek yapardı. Annem ne kadar ağlarsa ağlasın, o sofra kurulur, o yemek yenir, o gece en sevdiğimiz dizi izlenirdi.

Annemin dizine alnımı bastırıp ağladığım o gece annem mutfakta ağladı ama yemek pişirmedi. Masa oradaydı ama sofra kurulmadı. Yemek yenmedi. Televizyonda en sevdiği dizi oynuyordu, dizi izlenmedi.

O gece öğrendim.

Annemin hayatının merkezi bendim.

Çünkü o ağlarken benim için yerine getirdiği tüm görevleri, ben ağlarken bir köşeye itip benimle ağladı. Sanki ilk kez kendisi için ağlıyormuş gibi ağladı.

Sanki ilk kez, canı bu kadar çok yanıyormuş gibi ağladı.

Oysa o, benim aksime, sevdiği adamı yıllar önce zaten kaybetmiş, yine de o akşam yemek pişirmişti.

Şimdi git. Annene sarıl.
Yok mu?
Özür dilerim.
Silaha sarıl.
Pardon, fotoğrafına demek istemiştim.
Artık ikimiz de öğrendik bence,
fotoğraflar en büyük silahtır bizim içimizde.

Binnur Şafak Nigiz

Yokluğunda annemin saçları gibi döküldü yapraklar,
Yokluğunda yaprakları toplayıp, avuçlarımla ezdim.
Sonra başımın üzerine intihar haleleri yerleştirdim.
Yokluğunda bir kimliğim vardı,
    ben artık senin gölgenin intihar meleğiydim.
Kendimi asmak istediğim halatlardan
    başıma dikeceğim haleleri yaparken,
Ve akarken gözyaşlarım göğüslerime,
    bir zamanlar dokunduğun kurumuş kasıklarıma,
Bileklerime bir meleğin tenini var eden
    nur gibi parıltılar ekledim antidepresanlardan.
Uyku ilaçları döktüm saçlarımın arasına,
    hepsi inciye benzedi, ben bir melek oldum yokluğunda.
Avuçlarımda uykular gibi intiharlar dağıttım
    olmadığın odalara.
Öldürdüm fotoğrafları,
Öldürdüm parfümünün sindiği yastık kılıflarını,
Öldürdüm kahkahalarımızı apartman boşluğunda.
Çok ağladım, inanır mısın, çok darıldım Tanrı'ya.
Saçlarımdan uyku ilaçları döküldü,
    parlarken tenimde antidepresanlar,
Ben yine gizli gizli bu gece birinin zihnine girip,
İntiharı meşrulaştıran fahişe bir şeytan gibi,
Melek kılığında,
Kalkıp kendini öldürmesini söyledim ona.

Gerçeğin kamburu yalan,
benim kamburum sensin.

Yürek,
kullanmayı bilmeyenin
yangını olur.

Gitmek istiyordu, alıp başını çok uzaklara gitmek...

Çünkü kaybetmek, her defasında kaybeden bir insanın karşısında yenilgiye uğramak kadar kötüydü.

O kaybetmişti.

Kendisi gibi binlercesini tanıyordu. Sokakta omuzları birbirine çarpıyor, belki de aynı kaldırımda yürüyüp birbirlerinden uzaklaşırken göğüslerinin içinde aynı ateşi taşıyorlardı. Bir gün yeniden bir adamı sevme düşüncesi, darağacında ayağından iskemle kaymışken kapıdan kaybettiği o adamın tekrar içeri girmesi kadar saçma geliyordu.

Öyle bir şey olmayacaktı.

Köz olmuş bir kadının yüreğinde
kimse yeniden yangın çıkaramaz.
Çıkarırsa da yalnızca kendisi yanar.

Kendim şu an hayatta mıyım, yaşıyor muyum emin değilim ama onun içimde öldüğünü iliklerime kadar hissettim. *Onun gözlerinin içine bakarken hissettiğim duyguları bir daha yaşayamayacağım* isimli tokat yüzüme çok sert çarptı. Rakı bardaklarının üzerine resimler çizdiğini hatırladım. Bana bunu hatırlatan avucumun içinde duran rakı bardağı, bardağın üzerine çizilmiş nilüfer çiçeği oldu.

Beş yüz elli altı kilometre mi koştum, bu ne yorgunluk?

Övün biraz kendinle, en son ne zaman kaybettin? Kaybettiklerinle övün. Aynanın önüne geçip neleri kaybettiğini kendine itiraf edebilecek misin? Kediler bile birbirlerini sevdiklerini belli etmek için birbirlerine sürtünür, sen ne zaman başını birinin *omzuna, acaba sırtımın hangi köşesine bir bıçak sokacak,* düşüncesi olmadan yasladın? Ben şimdi elimdeki bardağa bakarken ve tüm nilüfer çiçeklerinin soyu benim için bu bardağın içinde tükenirken kendime bu soruyu soruyorum. Sanmışsın ki sen yaşadığın her şeyi hak ettin. Hayır etmedin. Sadece bir düşün. ***En son ne zaman kaybettin?***

Neyi kaybettin?

Bir tokayı, bir yüzüğü, telefon kılıfını, güneş gözlüğünü, evin anahtarlarını değil, söylesene sen en son ne zaman bir insanı kaybettin?

Övün şimdi kendinle.

Sen de birini kaybettin.

Hayır, ***yaşadığın hiçbir şeyi hak etmedin.*** Sadece gerçekten diyorum, nilüferlerin soyunun tükenmesi değil konumuz, senin kayıpların. Kaybettiğin kişiyi neden kaybettin? Nefes alıyor mu? Gir zihnine, iyi düşün. Hâlâ yaşıyor mu? Ona ne yaptın? Bir kez olsun aynaya bakarken göreceğin insandan korkma, aynanın karşısına geç ve bunu kendi yüzüne oku.

Aldattıysan, aldattım, de.

Yalan söyledim, de.

Söyle.

Senin vicdanının üzerinde içi bozuk para dolu bir sandık gibi ağırlık yapan o duygu artık seni terk etmek istemiyor mu?

En son ne zaman bir kedinin diğer kediye sürtündüğü gibi güvenle, sırtına girecek bıçağın korkusuna kapılmadan birinin omzuna başını yasladın, düşün.

En son ne zaman annene sarıldın, düşün.

En son ne zaman, bir silahı anıymış gibi kalbinin üzerine yaslayıp ağladın, düşün. O fotoğrafı, seni öldürecek kadar güçlü ve tehlikeli olan o silahı düşün.

Onu bağışla.

Kendini bağışla.

Sizi bağışla.

Çünkü biliyor musun, ***ölüm çok büyük bir şey ama toprak beş para etmiyor.***

Ben de avucumda babamın mezarından çaldığım toprağı, elimde tuttuğum rakı bardağına doldurup, babamdan sonra güvenebildiğim tek adamın aldığı nilüferi içine gömdüğüm zaman anladım. Onu da babam gibi gömdüğüm, birini toprağa, diğerini yüreğime sakladığım gün öğrendim. *Şimdi birini asla göremeyeceğim, diğerini bir daha hiç sevemeyeceğim.*

Bari sen sizi bağışla.

Biraz da bu yüzdendir sana ellerimin küskünlüğü.

Bir zamanlar,
o gece seni son kez
sevmemişken ben,

Yaralarıma o kadar çok dokunmuştun ki, varlığının gölgesi bir ağaç gibi varlığıma meyve durduğunda, ben senin bana emanet ettiğin hislerin kaşığında boğulmuştum.

Düşünmüştüm, mümkün müydü böyle bir his yerde veyahut gökte?

Cehennemden mi gelmiştin yoksa cennet miydi evin?

Annem elma soyardı, ben bıçağın elmanın kırmızı paltosunu azgın bir adamın parmakları genç bir kızın bedeninde dolaşır gibi soyuşunu izlerdim.

Göğsüme beton gibi çökmüş bir hisle, ben telefonuma senden düşecek tek bir bildirimi beklerdim.

Ben senin mesajları ezberlerken, yaşıtlarım sıralarda dirsek çürütür, ben bir yürek çürütürdüm telefonun başında.

Annem elma soyardı, elmayı yüreğime benzetirdim.

Eline o bıçağı ben verdiğim için sesim bu kadar kısık sana. Sen benim yüreğimi soy, derisini bir köşeye at, içine gir, orada büyü, orada at, orada çarp, orada hızlan, orada dur diye doğurmuştu sanki annem beni. O yüzden sesim bile çıkmıyor bu ağrıya.

Annem gözlerimin içine bakar, bir süredir kızını değil, seni görürdü.

Gözlerime çizdiğim bir resim gibiydin, kimliğindi giyindiğim ifadelerim. Annem elmayı dilimler, bıçağı elmanın parçasına saplar, bıçağın ucunda bana uzatırdı. Telefon ne zaman titrese, o bıçağın ucundaki elma parçasına uzanan elimi bıçağa saplardım.

Annem ağlardı.

Bıçak ağlardı.

Ben ağlardım.

Sonunda o mesaj gelirdi. Mesaja dizdiğin kelimeler yüzünden sana gocunur, ben elim kan içinde, elimdeki kana değil, yine sana ağlardım.

Çünkü canım, biliyor musun?
Bana bir araba çarpsa, savrulsam otoban boyu,
başıma toplanacak olan kalabalığa değil, sana bakarım.
Biliyorum ki son nefesimi vereceğim birazdan,
korku yüreğime inan uğramaz, canım,
ben yine sana bakarım.

*Gökten yıldızı koparamadığın gibi,
kalbinden de onu koparıp atamıyorsun.*

Kalbimin üstü yastığın,
damarlarımın içinde yaşayan
nabzım uykun olsun.

Yaralı adamlar ve kedi kılığına girmiş kirpiler,

Yaralı adamları severken üç şeyi hesaba katın.
Kolay iyileşmezler,
Hemen kabullenmezler,
Bir gün çekip gidebilirler.

Onlar sokak kedisi gibidir. Sevginiz için gelir kapınıza. Süt verdiniz, biraz da başını okşadınız diye kapınıza yalnızca acıkınca miyavlayarak gelen kediler gibi... Karnını doyurursunuz, biraz sevdirirler, sonra giderler. Sokaklardır bu kedilerin evleri. Bu adamlar da böyledir işte. Sevildiklerine inandıklarında bunu görmek isterler, gösterirsiniz, sonra sizi severler, sonra da giderler. Çünkü en hakiki, en güvenilir yere gitmek isterler. Yani yalnızlığa, yeniden kaybolmaya, çünkü söyleyemeseler de yalnızlıktır onların ini.

Üniversite birinci sınıftayken, yani ilk senemde, onu tanıdığım şehre bir saat uzaklıkta bir şehirde kız arkadaşımla yaşıyordum. Bir kedi sahiplenmek istiyorduk fakat sokaklarda yavru yoktu, eniklemiyordu büyük kediler. Bulduklarımız genelde büyük, kendini sevdiren ama kucağa gelmeyen kedilerdi. Bir gece ansızın bir tanesi peşime takıldı. Ben gittim, o geldi. Ne zaman durup ona baksam, benim arkamdan gelmiyor gibi yapıyordu ama aslında geliyordu. Eve kadar takip etti beni. Sesimi çıkarmadan yürüdüm. Binaya girdik, onu eve soktum. Başladı evin içinde gezinmeye. Açtı, belliydi. Bir süre sonra evin içinde dolaşıp balkon kapısının önüne gitti. Cam kapıdan dışarıyı izlerken miyavlamaya başladı. Sonra yüzüme baktı, durmadan miyavlıyordu. Kendini sevdirmiyor, sadece gitmek ister gibi dışarıyı izleyerek miyavlıyordu. Sütü içmedi, kendini sevdirmedi, yalnızca sokağı izledi ve miyavladı. Bıraktım onu, gitti. Onu bir daha görmedim.

Oradan biliyorum.

Çünkü o kediyi eve sokmadan önce, o kediye benzeyen bir adamla aynı evde yaşıyordum.

İnanır mısınız bilmem ama anlatsalar, kirpilerin ve kedilerin birbirine bu kadar benzediğine ben de inanmazdım.

Bir zamanlar içim olduğu için,
şimdi içimi deşmek istiyordu.

Sen yakmışsın beni ama
benim ellerimde senin küllerin var.

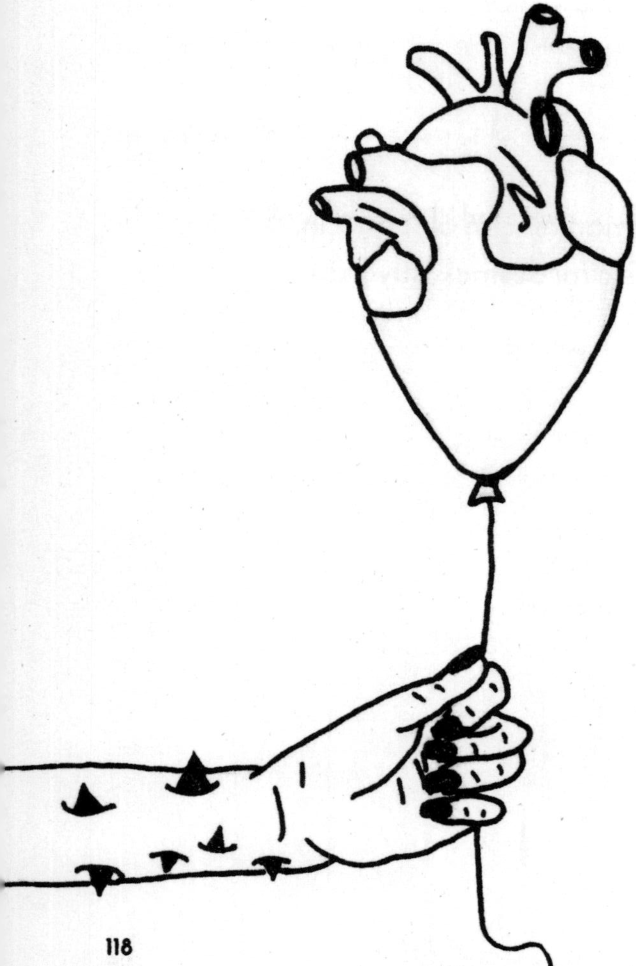

Kirpi Gibi Bir Adam Sevdim

Sonra ağladığım zaman, senin göğüne fırtına yüklü bulutların dolduğunu hatırladım.

Tenimde bin bir renkte farklı ize, sese, kokuya, anıya, zamana dönüştün.

Sonra bacaklarımızın birbirine dikenli tellerle bağlı olduğunu hatırladım.

Zihnimde bin bir renkte farklı kelimeye, cümleye, sayfalara dönüştün.

Sonra telefonumda sana ait olan ama ne zaman ona baksam beni yakan bir fotoğrafın varlığını hatırladım.

Ruhumda bin bir renkte farklı hisse, korkuya, acıya, mutluluğa, gülümsemeye dönüştüm.

Sonra bir şey oldu, aslında hiç olmadığını hatırladım.

Yapamadım.

Tenimi durduramadım.

Zihnimi susturamadım.

Ruhumu tutamadım.

Seni geri döndüremedim.

Binnur Şafak Nigiz

Seni son kez sevdiğim geceden önceki gecelerden bir yürek çıkrığı;

Ne zaman gülümsesem, yokluğuna ihanet etmişim gibi yokluğun sızlıyor. Dişimde sık sık dilimle yokladığım bir oyuk, bağrımda soğuk bir nefesi ciğerlerime doldurmuşum gibi içimi yakan bir yangınla ben yine göğsümün beşiğinde senin yokluğunu sallarken buluyorum kendimi. Anneme haksızlık ediyorum, senden sonra elinde bir bıçakla içini oymam için bana gelen adama haksızlık ediyorum, senden sonra bakkal Ramazan abiye, hatıralarımda omzunda torunuyla benden uzaklaşan Musa amcaya haksızlık ediyorum.

O adamı sana anlatamıyorum, çünkü delirdim, kendimle bile anlaşamıyorum.

Sen kapımdan ayrılmadın, evet ama bir adam o kapıdan içeri hiç düşünmeden girmek istedi.

Sen beni bu dünyaya bir ağaç gibi dikip bıraktın, gölgesinde serinlediğin bir ağaçtım ve sen gittikten sonra o ağacın önüne hep birileri geldi. Serinlemesinler diye kendi dallarımı kırdım. *Bir ağaç kendi dalını kırabilir mi* deme, kırabiliyormuş. Ben de geçenlerde öğrendim. Annemlerin sokağını biliyorsun, büyük çınar ağaçlarının olduğu, koruluğun arasından denizin göründüğü bir sokak... Ne çok severdim orada bisikletin pedallarını sen çeviriyormuşsun gibi hiç yorulmadan kendi kendimi sürmeyi. O ağaçlardan biri yandı. Yan yana olanlar, hani seninle gördüğümüz zaman onları iki sevgiliye benzettiğimi söylemiştim, yine romantik hayaller kuruyorum diye bana gözlerini devirmiştin. İşte o ağaçlardan biri yandı.

Söndürmeye çalıştı itfaiye erleri, yangın büyüyüp yanındaki ağaca sıçramadan söndürdüler ama yanan o ağacı kurtaramadılar. İzlerken pencerenin kenarında ağlıyordum, arada bir neye ağladığımı unutup bir sigara yakıyor, sonra kendimi tekrar ağlarken buluyordum. O gece diğer ağaç ilk defa yalnız kaldı. O gece hiç rüzgâr esmedi, dal bile kıpırdamadı. Sabah kalktım, baktım, tek kalan ağacın tüm dalları yerdeydi.

O dalları kendi kırmadıysa ben de hiçbir şey bilmiyorum.

Seni ve beni, o ikisine çok benzetiyorum.

Gözleri, gecenin içinde yanan
iki kuyruklu yıldız gibiydi ve
gülümsediğinde güneş gökyüzünde doğar,
kuyruklu yıldızlarını ışıklara boğardı.

Kirpi Gibi Bir Adam Sevdim

Biri sana yıldızlar kadar uzak ama ışıltısını görebiliyorsun.

Bana yıldızlar kadar uzak bir adam sevdim.

Sana da oldu mu hiç?

Hani bakarsın, oradadır, elini uzatsan dokunamayacağın uzaklıkta olmasına rağmen gözlerin en net onu görür, ortamdaki sigaranın dumanına ve hatta paçavra dünyanın kirli havasına rağmen kokusunu solursun. İşte o insan, sana yıldızlar kadar uzaktır ama ışıltısını yalnızca sen görürsün.

Onu ilk tanıdığımda, o bana yıldızlar kadar uzaktı ama ışıltısını görebiliyordum.

Bir insanın ışığının sadece sana vurmadığını bilmek, zehir zemberek bir gecede annenizin ve babanızın sizi evde tek başınıza bırakmak suretiyle gece yarısı döneceklerini bildiğiniz bir düğüne gitmeleri ve devamında kesilen elektrikle tir tir titreyerek yorganın altında beklemek gibiydi.

Oysa dışarıda bir gökyüzü var.

Ama biliyorsun, gökyüzünde yanan binlerce yıldızın biri bile, annenin odanın içinde yakacağı bir mum etmeyecek.

O, gökyüzünde izlediğim bir yıldızken, bir gün odamda annemin yaktığı bir mum olmuştu.

Gökyüzünde parlayan bir yıldızı
sevdiğini sandığın o gece,
aslında o adamın cehennemde yanan ateşine
aldanmadın mı?

Seni üç yüz elli altı metre unutamıyorum,

Bir arpa boyu kadar büyümedi unutmak. ***Çernobil'den bir facia olarak değil bir masal olarak bahsedilmeyeceği gibi, sen ve benden asla birlikte bahsetmeyecekler; çünkü ayrılığın kervanını tek başıma sırtlandığım gün anladım ben, bir daha "biz" olmayacak ikimizden.***

Kimsesiz olduğunu büyüdüğü yurtta değil, gelecek için yetiştirildiği okuldaki veli toplantıları yüzünden ağlamaya başladığında anlayan bir çocuğun sırtına batan baza, yere çizdiği anne silueti gibi, sırtını koyup uyuduğu zemince annesinin olduğunu düşürüp ilk kez ısındığı gibi hayaline sarılıp hâlâ var olduğuna inanmaya çalışıyorum. Karşıdan karşıya geçen bir adama çarpan arabanın onu yol boyunca üç yüz elli altı metre sürükleyip ondan bacaklarını alarak hayattan kopardığı, o adamın bir daha karşıdan karşıya geçecek ayakları olmayacağı gibi ben sana bir türlü gelemiyorum. Ben içimdeki bu imkânsızlığı derisini arkasında bırakıp yeni derisiyle yola devam eden o yılan gibi sıyırıp içimden atamıyorum.

Anlamak diye bir hastalık var, yakalandığım günden beri nefes alamıyorum.

Bir facianın içinden sağ çıkmışım ama kolum bacağım kopmuş, o faciaya ayaklarımı, o faciaya ellerimi vermişim. Ne zaman kolumun bacağımın yerinde olmadığını görsem o faciayı hatırlayacakmışım. ***O zaman senin bir faciadan farkın yok gibi.***

Seni üç yüz elli altı metre sürüklenmiş bir adamın bacaklarını kaybettiği gibi kaybedişimi, hiç unutamıyorum.

***Vefa, aşktan daha ağır bir duyguyken,
ikisini birbirine karıştırıp
yarattığım vazgeçilmezlik
iksirini ona içirdim,***

Otobüsün ters giden koltuğuna oturan kadınlar bilirler, giderken gözünün arkada kalması duygusunun eyleme dökülmüş en benzer halidir bu. Ne kadar ilerlese de o otobüs, farklı bir sokağa sapana kadar bindiğiniz ilk noktayı görmeye devam edersiniz. Sonra sokaklar değişir, görüş açınız değişir, bakışlarınız değişmez. Bir kadın ne kadar uzaklaşırsa uzaklaşsın, aslında otobüsün ters giden koltuğunda oturuyormuş gibi, gözleri hep geride bıraktığı yerdedir.

Farkında mısın, bazı hislerin anlamı ne kadar da bulanık.

Ben bu içimdeki hissi ne zaman anlatmaya kalksam, ya dilimin ucunda ağrıyor kelimeler ya da kalemimi kana buluyor yazdığım cümleler. ***Ardında yıkıntı bırakmış bir adamdan bahsedilen o cümledeki yıkıntıyım.*** Yazı olup onun alnına yazılmak istemiştim, yapamadığımı fark edince onu bir kitabın sayfasına yazıp, sayfaya alnımı vurarak unutmayı denedim. Ama yapamadım biliyor musun? Çünkü vefa, aşktan daha büyük bir duyguyken, vefalı bir kadının vefasız bir adamı sevebileceği en büyük aşkla, onu çok sevdim. Vefa, aşktan daha ağır bir duyguyken, ikisini birbirine karıştırıp yarattığım vazgeçilmezlik iksirini kendim içebilecekken, kalktım, ellerimle ona içirdim.

Oysa bir kadının inandığı tek adam olabilirdin.

Sana doğrultulan silaha bakıyorsun,
o silahı tutan eldeki yaraları görmüyorsun.

Çığ, kül, ateş,

İçimdeki ateş sönsün istedim. İçimde, onun kıyameti olma isteği bir körük gibi büyüyordu ve bu, benim ona olan sevgimden daha kuvvetliydi. Ona zarar vermek istedim. Bu düşünce, babamın ölümünü öğrendikten hemen sonra oturup bilgisayar başında donuk gözlerle oyun oynadığım sabahki kadar korkunç bir düşünceydi ve vefa, bazen beni terk eden üçüncü adam gibi kapıyı çarparak içimden çıkıp gidiyordu. Sonra yine aynı döngü. ***Vefa, onun ve babamın aksine isminin anlamını içinde taşıyan bir adamdı,*** kapımı çalıyor, tekrar içime yerleşiyor, ateşe ellerini basarak onu söndürmeye çalışıyordu. Gözlerimde hep neşesiz bir ifade olsa da sahteden gülümsemeler saçarken bu ifadeyi herkes görmez, görenler de anlam veremezdi. Sanırım ***o, gözlerimde o ifadeyi ona gülümsediğim sırada gördüğü ve diğerlerinin aksine buna anlam yüklediği için içimdeki en farklı yerin sahibi olmuştu.*** Bilmiyorum. Gözlerimin ateşe benzediğini, ateş olduğunu, ateşten olduğunu söylerdi.

Bir gün bana, "Seni ilk gördüğümde, gözlerinin bomboş baktığını, çok donuk olduğunu düşünmüştüm," demişti. Sonra eklemişti: "Sonra aslında gözlerinin ateş taşıdığını, aslında ateş olduğunu, ateşten olduğunu fark ettim. ***Senin gözlerinde ateş var.***"

Gözlerimdeki ateş sönsün istedim.

Ona baktığım zamanlar onu yakan gözlerim, onun emanet ettiği yaşlarla yıkandığında, bu yaşlar ateşleri daha da harlayan benzinler olmuştu.

Gözlerimdeki ateşler sönmeden önce, son kez ona bakayım ve onu kül edeyim, sonra tıpkı gözlerim gibi söneyim, küllerim külleriyle buluşsun, birlikte uçup gidelim, yok olalım istedim.

Onu sevdiğim için, içimde hiç bitiremediğim sonsuz bir mücadeleyle yaşıyordum. Düşünceler kafama sığmıyor, yaşanan hiçbir şey mutlu olmama yetmiyordu ve gülerken dişlerimin dökülmesinden korkarak ağzımı avuçlarımın arkasına saklayıp sahte gülücüklerimi insanlardan saklıyordum.

Biliyor musun, bıçak çekmecedeyken ekmeği kesmez. Sen yeter ki eline al onu, senin isteğin doğrultusunda kestiği ekmek ona yetmez, senin arzun olmadan parmaklarını bile biçer. Bazen bıçağı çekmecede bırakmak gerekir, çünkü bıçağı çekmeceden çıkarmak, bir bakıma biraz da kendine saplayacağın anlamına gelir.

O yüzden, içimdeki ateş sönsün istedim. İçimde, onun canını yakma isteği çığ gibi büyüyüp içimde yuvarlandıkça, aslında o çığın altında o değil, ben kalıyordum.

Bir de hâlâ gözlerimdeki ateş sönsün istiyorum.

Bir gün birinin karşıma geçip, hakkımda her şeyi bildiğini söylemesinden ölesiye korkuyorum.

Her gece kıymık gibi içime batıp durma artık,
artık dur, *ne olursun.*

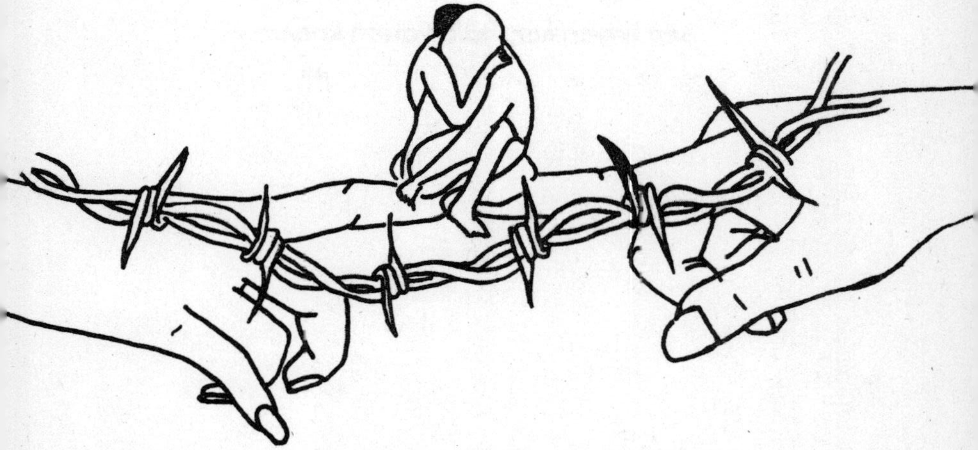

Sen güneşin yüzünü çevirdiği,
sen gecenin yolunu değiştirdiği,
sen eriyen kar, hâlâ yanan korsun.

Ateş ile yaklaşılmaz, sigara içilmez yazan tırı kullanan adamın elindeki sigara gibiyim. Öyle umursamaz ilerliyorum, öyle vazgeçmişim, öyle siktir etmişim her şeyi. Anlıyor musun? Ben seni anlıyorum. Artık kuyunun içinde kafanı kaldırıp güneşi izlemek yetmiyor, güneşi tutup kuyunun içine çekmek, söndürüp öldürmek istiyorsun. Öyle çok yenilmişsin ki, artık yeneceğini bilsen bile zaferi kendin istemiyorsun. ***Şarkılar artık senin için yalnızca şarkı değil.*** Bir şarkı duyuyorsun, eline silah verseler önce o şarkı çalarken etrafında olan insanları tarar, sonra namluyu şarkıya doğrultur, o şarkıya kıyamaz, çevirir kendini vurursun.

Aslında çok sakinsin, ağzını bıçak açmıyor ama ağzını açsan çıt değil, çığlık çıkacak. Çünkü senin sakinliğinin içinde, bir kabir azabı, senin sakinliğinin içinde insanların gürültüsü var. Belki kirpi gibi bir adam senin babandı, belki sen kirpi gibi bir kadın sevdin, belki kirpi sendin ama çok iyi biliyorsun, içindeki o canavar bir gün ağzını açarsa, işte o senin sonun olacak.

Camı çerçeveyi indir ama yüzünü indirme. Bana da biraz akıl ver, tırı şarampole yuvarlayabilirim yoksa.

O canavarı öldürmeye ihtiyacımız var.

Ben sana dikiş atsam yarana değil, kapalı etine atarım. Nasıl iyi edeyim ben seni? Kötü oluruz biz seninle. Kötünün de kötüsü. Gidişat şarampole el ele yuvarlanıp farklı yerlere parçalanmak. Ellerimiz aynı yerde kalır, olsun. Dinle göğsümün yarığı, oku bunları. Daluyku gecelerde ben sana kangren olmuş gözlerimle bakmadım mı? ***Allah'tan korkar gibi korkuyorum göğsümü yaran bu ağrıdan*** ve bu ağrıya senin adından, senin soyadından, senin varlığından bir kimlik verip göğsümün üzerinde yaşatıyorum. Korkumsun benim, korkusuzluğumsun, kül tablamdaki ölü izmaritlerden onuncususun. Dinle göğsümün susmayan, uykularımdan kaldıran, durmadan aralıksız ağlayan çocuğu, oku bunları. Mutfak tezgâhında sapı siyah bir ekmek bıçağı yüzümü ilgiyle izlerken, ben o bıçağı alıp sırf senin için çekmeceye kaldırmadım mı? İyi edemem seni, ben bu baş ağrısı, el titremesi, ben bu göğüs yarığıyla bu gece de uyuyamam.

İkinci kez,

Küçük bir kız çocuğunun güvendiği tek insanın
elini sıkıca tuttuğu gibi tutmuştum ellerini.

Sen o elleri parçaladın.

Ben gülleden ağır harflerle, az kırmadım parmaklarımı. Seni bir tren istasyonunda görüp ya da belki bir terminalde... Gecesi kan kusmak istemiyorum. Çıkma karşıma. Ne sen Yusuf'sun ne de ben Züleyha. Nabzımın boşluklarından damarlarıma düşen bir adam tanıdım. Sırtında bir beşik vardı, çocuk yanım orada uyurdu. Belini mi kırdılar, beni o beşikten yere serdin? Biliyor musun sen bir çocuğun kaburgalarını kırdın, içinden çocukluğunu çaldın, bir kadını parçaladın dağıttın, bulutları çok şiddetli ağlattın. Aralık aralansa da o aralıktan tüm aylar el ele verip kaçsa. Ocak sakat kalsa, ayaklarını içeri sokamasa. İlkleridir tüm ayların ocak, benim sonum oldu. Ocağa ellerimi tutup, ellerini yaktığımı söylediğin o gece olduğu gibi parmaklarımı ateşlerde pişirdim. Sonra mühür gibi bastım sana parmak izimi, ondan bir dövme yaptım sana, o parmak izine bak ve beni sakın unutma. Ne sen Yusuf'sun ne de ben Züleyha. Sakın karşıma çıkma.

Çünkü artık büyüyorsun.
İnsan büyüyünce sadece sevişmeyi sever.

Binnur Şafak Nigiz

Misafir çocuğu ve pamuk şekeri,

İçimde çok tutarsız, teraziyi zedeleyen bir konu var. Bitirmeye, göndermeye, susturmaya çalışıyorum ama beynime galip gelip nasıl etkiliyor tüm organlarımı? Ben anlaşılmak istemiyorum. Ne zaman anlaşılmak istesem, biri Perseus'un Medusa'nın başını kopardığı gibi koparıyor başımı. Yeni yeni düşünceler koyuyor oraya, bambaşka hastalıklar... Biraz da pamuk şeker yerken zihni yoklayan intihar düşüncesinden bahsetmek isterim. Ne sikik duygu, ölümü dilenen bir faninin ölümden korkması. Ben bu dünyaya gelmiş bir misafır çocuğuyum, sofrasına buyur etse de beni, içimdeki açlığı bastırıp başımı iki yana sallar, sofrasına oturmayı utanarak reddederim. Misafır çocukları bilir çünkü, açsan bile başkasının evindeysen toksundur, o ikinci tabağı çok istesen de annenle göz göze gelirsin ve dilin düğüm olur. Misafır çocuğuysan hep tok olmak zorundasın. Çünkü dünya, misafır gittiğin evdeki insan gibi, verdiğinin arkasından çok konuşur.

Terzi kendi söküğünü dikemezmiş ama
başkalarının getirdiği kumaşlardan
çok güzel elbiseler yaparmış ya hani,
benimkisi o misal.

Benim olduğum yer dünyanın durduğu,
senin olduğu yer
dünyanın dönmeye başladığı yer.

Sürekli gözyaşı,

Bir cehennemken uyku, gözlerimin altına gömülmüş koyu cesetleri izliyordun. Ve gözyaşlarımı...

"Benim hayatından çıkmamın yararı olmadı mı hiç?" diye sordun, sert sesin bir bana yumuşuyordu ama ben öyle çok ağlıyordum ki, gözyaşlarım sele karıştığı için senin güzel yüzünde hangi ifade ölümün eşiğindeydi göremiyordum.

"Hayır, olmadı," dedim hıçkırıklarımın arasından.

Beni bu kadar sevdiğini hissettirirken, biz olduğumuzda kalbini göğsünün içine gömüp susturuyor musun da bu kadar acımasız bir insana dönüşüyorsun anlamıyorum.

"Bana bak!" diye bağırdın, yüreğim yerinden hopladı. "Ağlayan gözlerini sikerim. Bunu yapma. Ben senin gözlerine güzel derken, bundan bahsetmiyordum."

Burnumu çekerken sana baktım, sırtımı soğuk duvara yaslamış, diz çöktüğüm yerde bacaklarıma sarılarak ağlamaya devam ediyordum.

"Neyden bahsetmiyordun?"

"Sürekli gözyaşı," dedin ters bir sesle.

Sürekli gözyaşı. *Sürekli gözyaşı?* Ben mi ağlatıyorum ulan kendimi sana?

En çok sana edebileceğim kötülükten korktum, sonra anladım ki benim yüreğim bir tek sana kötülük etmeyi bilmiyor. Zülfü Livaneli'nin bir cümlesi var, bilir misin bilmem çünkü sen en çok Oğuz Atay'ı seversin. "*Kötülük etmeyi istememek başka, bilmemek başkadır.*" Ben sana kötülük etmeyi bilmiyormuşum, Kirpi. Sen benim ruhumda, beni öldürebilecek büyüklükte ölümcül yaralar açtın ama kalbim senin dart tahtan olmaya hâlâ gönüllü. Bile isteye senin sırtında ok gibi taşıdığın dikenlerine doğru çarpıyor bu kalp. Ruhum senden buz gibi korkuyor. Bir dengesi yok ikisinin ama ikisi de senin için yanıyor. Artık bana çok geç kaldın. Uğrunda ölmeyi istesem de ölemem, annem üzülür. Aramıza denizler, aramıza sokaklar, aramıza otobüslerin dümdüz ilerlediği yollar, aramıza dağlar sokmadın, aramıza bir yalan soktun. Ben senin yalanına eyvallah diyecek bir kadın değilmişim, yeni öğrendim.

"Şimdi bununla nasıl birlikte yaşarız biz?" demiştin bana, *bu yalanla* diyememiştin, bununla demiştin. 'Biz' de demiştin, ama bil, *biz* değiliz biz. Sana bir damla kötülüğüm olmaz, yalanların hayatımda bir oyuk açmış olsa da. Benim seni kör kütük seven yanımın fay hattı kırıldı. Şimdiden sonrasını bensiz kalan kalbin düşünsün.

"Yanan bir ormandan sağ çıkarsın da
yaktığın bir kadının teninde bulunur küllerin,"
derdi bana. Ve eklerdi:
"Bir sadakat saplandı seninle göğsüme."

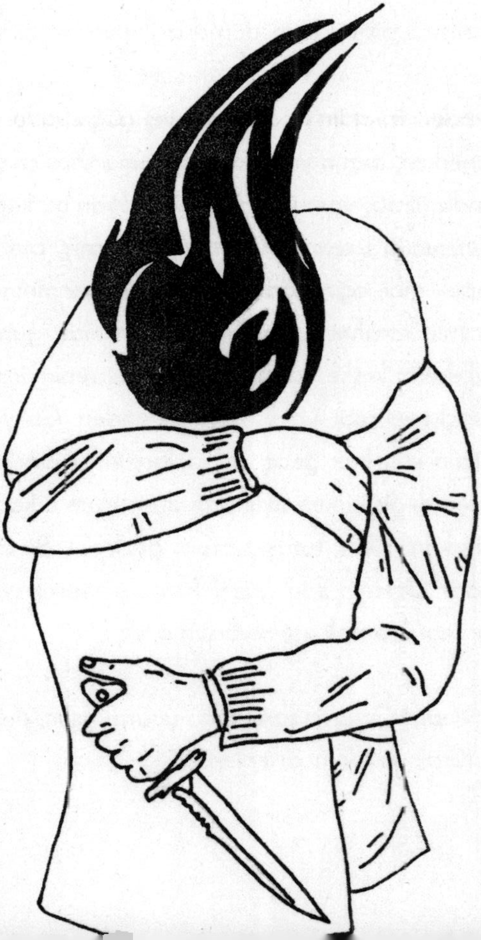

Binnur Şafak Nigiz

Yalancı Kirpi, uzadı mı dikenlerin?

Gözlerimden İbrahim'in atıldığı ateş göğsümde yanıyormuş gibi yaşlar inerken, ben o yaz akşamı, beni sahile çıkaracak olan yolları ağzında ölmüş yavrusuna kemik taşıyan bir köpek gibi yürüdüm. Yavrusunun üzerinden kamyon geçmiş, otobanda dört dönen o köpek gibi, ağzımda kemikle, kulaklarımı indirdim dört döndüm acımın etrafında. Acıdan ikiye yarılan gururumu hiçe sayıp, koşabilsem keşke sana. Ayaklarımı senin için ağlarken yolduğum saçlarım gibi, yoldun aldın benden. Gökyüzünün her yüzünde yüzün var. Her gece, dudaklarının arasında bir sigara ile yattığın yeri değiştirirken aklından düşmeyen o kadınım senin. Baskın yemiş karanlıkta, tutukluyorum gözlerini. *Bir de Uçurtma şarkısını Vedat Özkaya'dan güzel kimse söyleyemiyor, ben de gökyüzünde seni aramak istemiyorum artık.*

Beni bir Vedat Özkaya şarkısında unutmuşsun, öyle söyledin. Yalancı Kirpi, uzadı mı dikenlerin?

Gelmek istersen, sadece senin gelebilmen için kapıyı açacağım.

Çünkü kapalı artık tüm kapılarım, içeride kimseye yer yok, içeride kimse yok. En son sana ev olan bu kalp, artık terk edilmiş bir harabeyse, duvarları evsiz bir çocuğun gözyaşlarına eşlik etsin. Solsun papatyalar, artık baharın lüzumu yok. Kelimeler, seni anlatmaya yetmiyor artık. Ruhumdaki yangın değil artık, kuraklık. Susuzluktan çatlamış bir toprak gibi, ikiye ayırdığın şu canımda, hâlâ senin adın atıyorsa eğer, bana da müstahak. Yıkılsın kelimeler üzerime, sorun değil. Alıştım bu ezbere ağrıyla yaşamaya artık. Yaşanmış ya da yaşanmamış tüm anılar, denizin üzerinde uçan bir güvercinin ağzında dururken vurulsun o güvercin, düşsün denize. Yayılsın anılar, kelimeler yayılsın. Her bir kelimede, insanlar seni ve beni değil, insanlar bir zamanlar biz olan ikimizi değil, kendilerini hatırlasın. Bir yerde kalplerini unuttuklarını hatırlasınlar, bir yerde kalplerinin hâlâ çarptığını hatırlasınlar. Çünkü elbet biri, senin beni kullandığın gibi, küllük etti birini. Sigaranın ucunda duran alevden değil, bir ömürden bahsediyorum. Küllük kendini yakabilir mi? Birini de elbet yaktılar, içine küllerini doldurdular, senin bana yaptığın gibi. İçim, senin beni yaktığın küllerle dolu şimdi. Oysa küllük, mezarıyken bir sigaranın, sigara tükenirken onu bir akbaba gibi izlerken küllük, sen benden nasıl bir küllük yarattın? Sana bakmak isteyen gözlerime mil çekilseydi de baktığım yerde seni göreceğime, karanlığı görseydim. Ben seni gördüğümden beri, gündüz benim şehrime uğramadı.

Yine de olur da gelmek istersen, sadece senin gelebilmen için kapıyı açacağım.

Bir küllük getir bana,
taştan olsun.
Kafama vura vura,
seni geldiğin gün unutacağım.

Yıllar sonra bir vapur iskelesinde,
bir otobüs terminalinde
ya da tren istasyonunda karşılaşıp,
karşısında donakaldığım adam
olmasını istemiyorum.

Binnur Şafak Nigiz

Öksürsem küllerini,
Sana yürürken aştığım yollarda aldığım yaraları,
Sana bıraksam.
Geri.
Seni içimde büyüyen bir ağrı gibi,
Sevdiğim o geceyi unutamam.
Kalbini göğsümde bir kaktüs gibi,
Büyütmüştüm, kalbini, kaktüsü ve seni.
Bir zamanlar içim olduğun için, içimi deşmek istediğini,
Gözlerinde gördüğümden beri,
Uyuyamam.
Bir an sana söyleyecek bir şey bulamadığım için,
Gözlerim doldu.
Zamanın pençesinde yaralanarak büyüyen iki çocuktuk,
Zaman bizi unuttu.
Yangın yeri bir adamdın,
İçinde birleştirdiğim heceleri,
Her gece uyumadan önce izlediğim o fotoğrafını sildiğim gibi,
Sildim.
Yine de ne varlığını,
Ne yokluğunu,
Ne zamanı,
Ne de seni durdurabildim.
Nabzının dönemeçleri,
Bir çıkmaz sokak gibi.
Yolum senin sonunda bitti.
Ben senin sokağına yolu düşmüş,
Evini kaybetmiş, yetim kedi.
Hoşça kalma sanatında,
Sınıfta kaldım.

Cennet derem,
damarlarından bir tanesi
benim bileğime dolansa keşke.

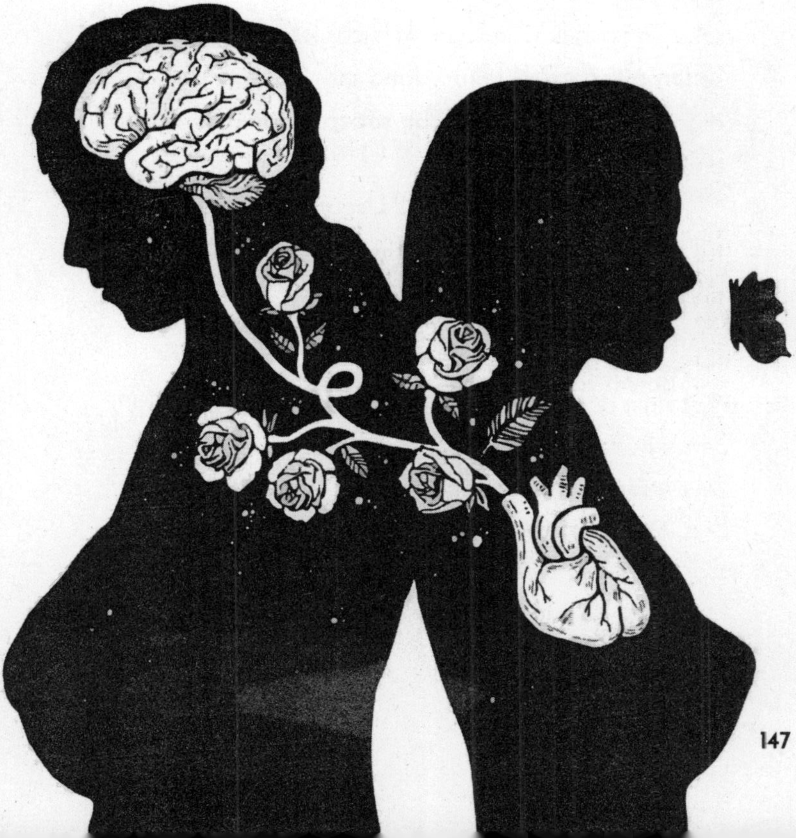

Yine zihnime çaydanlıkta demlenen çay gibi oturdu düşünceler. Bizi var edenlerin yokluğunda yaşamayı öğrenmişiz. Günler geçmiş bir de. Dün bir yaş daha büyüdüm. Balkonda oturup bir bir yanmaya başlayan sokak lambalarını izlerken, boylarından büyük sırt çantalarıyla sokağın ortasında ilerleyen iki küçük kız çocuğundan bahsettim mi sana? Kumral, daha bir cılız olan kız çocuğu, diğerine anlayamadığım bir sebepten dolayı, "Büyüdün ondandır," dedi.

Diğeri de başını sallayıp, "Üzgünüm, bu hesapta yoktu," dedi, onlar önlerine serilmiş yolu aşarken ben arkalarından bakakaldım.

Gerçekten, bu hesapta yoktu.

Benim yaşım ne zaman bu kadar çok oldu?

Sen yakmışsın beni ama benim ellerimde senin küllerin var.
Kalbimden taşan bir ateşsin.
Göğsümün kabına sığmıyorsun.
Sen benim kaburgalarımı tabutun mu sanıyorsun?
Bir daha senden başka ölü taşımam içimde.
Dirinin zaten tabutta işi ne?

Seni kanaya kanaya susuyorum.

Senin gözlerini anlatabilmek için tüm renkleri içmek gerek. İbrahim olmak, kırk ateşten geçmek gerek. Mecnun olmak, Leyla'nın gözlerini bir defa görmek için o dağı delmek gerek. Senin şu gözlerini anlatabilmek için, Yusuf olmak, o kuyuda ölmeden beklemek gerek. Geçemesem de yandım İbrahim'in geçtiği ateşlerin içinde, dağları delemesem de başıma yıktım, kuyuya düştüm, ölemedim belki ama Yusuf kadar sağ kalamadım.

İçimde bir vapur seferinin ağrısı. 7.45 olmadan saat, Alsancak'ta son kez buluşalım. Ben o iskelede, bir gençlik harcadım. Ne İbrahim oldum, ne Mecnun oldum ben, ne Yusuf oldum, ama ben bu sevda uğruna bir gençliği karşıma koydum, senin gözlerini anlatabilmek için, ben o gençliği şakağından vurdum.

Keşke bir kez iskelede,
Şakağımda kan lekesi,
Cümlelerim ellerimde,
Son kez olduğunu bilsem de,
Görseydim seni.

Tenimde parmak uçlarındaki izlerin cesetleri,

Sen dokunduğum tüm yangınlarsın.

Babası kral tarafından öldürülmüş Hernani sen olurdun belki, ben sevdiğin o kadın olurdum ve kavuşmak için zalim kral ile çarpışırdın. Ya da aynı anda seninle, bir sahafta, ellerimiz buluşurdu Hernani'nin üzerinde.

Kendini benden yok ederken
ellerimi yakmasaydın eğer.

Bundan böyle birlikte güleceğimiz geceler olmayacak mı yani? Bak bu, bu anlatılabilecek bir acıyken, bunu yaşamak cümleleri alt etmektir. O gece kapıma dayandığında, günlerden doğum günümdü, birkaç gün öncesiydi. Kapının önündeydik, dışarısı zifiri karanlıktı, güneşin doğmasına çok uzun bir vakit yoktu ama bilirdi, şafak sökmeden bir saat öncesi en karanlık geceyi yaşardı gökyüzü. Sık sık elleriyle oynuyordu, kelimeler ellerindeymiş de elleriyle oynarsa konuşması, kelimeleri bana okutması daha kolay olurmuş gibi hissediyor olmalıydı. Karanlıkta yüzünü göremediğimden sadece sesini dinledim, aldığı nefesin sesi bile bir enkazken, ben o enkazın dibinde bir bahçe kurmuştum.

"Doğum günün kutlu olsun."

Sesi kederliydi. Kirpilerin dikenleri kendilerine batınca sırtlarından vazgeçer. Dikenlerini kendine nasıl batırdıysa, sırtını önüme serip kaçıp gitmek istiyor gibi karşımda öylece duruyordu.

"Teşekkür ederim."

Boynuna sarılıp, bunu kokusunu içime doldururken söylemek istedim. İkimiz de istedik ama ne o söyleyebildi ne ben yapabildim.

"Doğum günün ilk saatleri nasıl geçiyor?" diye sordu, sırtına aldığı sokak lambası yüzünü gizliyordu, ona baktım, gözlerini görme umudu tükenmek üzere olan bir mum gibi içimde yanıyordu.

"Normal," dedim, oysa binlerce cümle vardı. Kırgın, yorgun, bitkin. "Nasıl geçsin ki?"

"Mutlu?" dedi sanki kafamın içindeki sesi susturmak istiyormuş gibi. "Huzurlu. Eğlenceli?"

Acı öyle bir duyguydu ki, ikimizi de yok edecekti. Dikenlerinin üzerinde meşalelerin ucunda yanan alevler yanıyor gibi duruyordu. Ateşi, tüm gecelerinkinden daha parlak yanıyordu bu gece. Bu gece, onun acısını bana söylemesine ihtiyaç duymadan derinlerimde hissediyordum.

"Bir değişiklik yok," diye fısıldadım, sesim engebeli bir yol gibiydi, öyle bir istedim ki... Çok istedim. O engebeli yolda yürürken bana batan duyguları hissetmesini... Bizim aramızdaki yenilir yutulur cinsten bir bağ değildi. Çok garipti ama, o an hissettiğini biliyordum. O engebeli yolda yalınayak yürüyormuş gibi, ayaklarının altı yara bere, ayaklarının altı kan revan, ayaklarının altı paramparça yürüyormuş gibi hissediyordum. "Normal bir gece," dedim cümlemi tamamlamak için, oysa uzun bir soluk vardı bu iki farklı cümleyi bir araya getirdiğim anın içinde.

Bana baktı, benim aksime o benim yüzümü aynaya bakıyormuş gibi net görüyordu ama ben onu yine orada, o maskenin ardında görüyordum. Görmüyordum. Benden yine gizleniyordu ama önümde duruyordu. Bir insan, bir insanın önünde dururken, ondan gizlenmeyi nasıl başarabiliyordu?

O kalın sesi, bir çocuğun bükük boynu gibi yükseldi. "Mum üflemedin mi daha?" diye sordu bana, konumuzun bu olup olmadığını bilmiyordum, eğer konumuz buysa, bu bile şarkılarda bahsedilen yangınlı şiirdi.

"Pasta almış arkadaşım," dedim, sonra durdum. Ona uzun uzun kendimi anlattığım geceleri hatırladım. Çenemin düşmesi onu memnun ederdi, ben konuşurken o mutluydu, ben ona anlatırken içimde beni daima var edeceğini bildiğim bir huzur olurdu. Bir zamanlar birbirimizin her şeyiyken, şimdi birbirimizin karşısında hiçbir şeydik. Bu bana çok dokundu. "Ama üflemedim. Yaktık, kendi kendine söndü." Durdum, kendi cümleme durdum, kendi elimdeki ateşi göğsüme bastırmaktan çekinmedim yine. Bizim yaktığımız, kendi kendine sönecek miydi peki? Sönecek miydi, Kirpi? "Üflemem ben. En son 18 yaşında üfledim."

Sonra da on dokuzumda seni tanıdım.

Uzun uzun sustu, gitmek istemiyor gibiydi.

Gelmişti.

Beklemiştim, vazgeçmemiştim, vazgeçtiğimi sandığı için değil, beklemekten vazgeçememem için gelmişti.

"Pasta neyliydi?"

Onu severken elimi korkak alıştırmamıştım. Onu severken yaşamamıştım, onu severken var olmuştum. O karşımdayken, annemin rahminde yeniden can bulmuştum.

"Meyveli," dedim tek nefeste. Yutkundum. "Pasta mı çekti canın?"

"Çikolatalı seversin aslında," dedi, elini ensesine attı, ensesindeki dikenleri okşadı. "Meyveli mi seviyordun?"

Unutmadın mı, Kirpi?

Unutsaydın ya keşke.

Unutmamıştın, Kirpi.

"Çikolatalı seviyordum. Midem bulandığından çikolatalı yemek istemedim, meyveli almışlar. Çilekleri ve kivileri yedim, gerisini dolaba iteledim."

Bu kez uzun uzun susmadı. "Benim canım çikolatalı çekti," dedi adam olmuş sesine bulaşmış çocuğun elleriyle. "Yarın benim için çikolatalı ye."

Cevap veremedim. Kapısından içeri elimde cam bir süt şişesiyle girdiğim evden, elimde dibinde bir damla kalmış rakı şişesiyle çıkmıştım.

Sanki bilmiyormuş gibi, "Kaç yaşına girdin?" diye sordu, o çok iyi biliyordu, onun beni tanıdığı yaştaydım, ilk kez onunla bende var olduğu zamanlar olduğu yaşta, onunla aynı yaştaydım.

"23 oldum."

"Çocuktun, ergenliğe geçtin," dedi, buruk buruk gülümsedi. 30'a geldiğinde büyürsün."

"Daha çok var o zaman büyümeme."

"Ohoo, çok hem de."

"Sen büyüdün mü bari?" diye fısıldadım, o an durdu, zaman da biraz dinlenmek için midir bilinmez, yüzyıllardır akıyor olmasına rağmen o an, onunla birlikte durdu.

"Canın mı sıkkın?" diye sordu, sesi dünyadan erken dönmüş bir bebeğin sesi gibiydi.

"Yok. Yanlış bir şey mi söyledim?"

"Hayır," dedi, burnunu çektiğini duydum. "Öyle geldi." Bana dikkatle baktığını hissetsem de rüyalarımın sırtına hançer batıran gözlerini göremedim. "Eminsin, değil mi?"

"Hıhım. Neden ki?"

"O zaman bana öyle geldi."

"Normalde çok sakin bir görüntüm yok, ondan öyle gelmiştir."

"Sakin gibi değil, moralin bozuk gibi duruyorsun."

Bir süre sustum, gece böceklerinin sesini dinledim. "Endişe etme."

Bir şey demedi. Gitmesinden korkan kalbim yine göğsümün içinde terör estirmeye başlamıştı işte. Bilirsin, bir insanın gitmesinden korkarsan, o insan ömür boyu yanında kalacak olsa bile senin gözün hep kapıda olur. Keşke, dersin. Keşke tüm kapıları bombalasalar. Oysa sokağın kapısı bile yok ki. Ben ne yapayım?

"Aslında ben sana şu yüzden geldim," dedi kalbimin geri adım atmasına neden olacak bir dürüstlükle.

Korku zamana yayıldı, konuşmasın istiyordum, sussun, yeter ki gitmesin. Sonsuza dek böyle duralım burada. Üzerimize güneş doğsun, bulut dursun, yağmur yağsın, karanlık çöksün ama biz burada böyle duralım. Hiç konuşmayalım, sadece duralım. Yan yana olalım. Yan yana değiliz evet. Olsun. Ben onunla karşı karşıya da olmaya varım.

"Ne yüzden?"

"Yıllardır seni tanıyorum ama bir kere bile sana seni anlatmadım, bir kere bile sen benim için busun diyemedim," dedi çat diye. "Ben uzun uzun seni anlatmak istedim."

Kalbimin haykırışları tüm acılarımın aniden susmasına neden olacak kadar şiddetliydi. Sanki o yıllar yaşanmamış, ben bir gençliği onun uğruna heba etmemişim gibi, yeniden doğmuş, ilk nefesimi içime doldurmuştum. Belki bu son nefesimdi, bilmiyordum.

"Bu beni mutlu eder sanırım. Yani... Merak ettim. Anlatırsan, dinlerim."

"Ama görüyorsun, dakikalardır sana... Baktım baktım, yine konuşamadım." Omuzları düştü. "Seni anlatamıyorum."

O kadar mı çok, dedi içimde bir ses.

"O kadar mı zor?" dedim, içimdeki sesin aksine.

"Senin gibi anlatmak istedim ama sanırım beceriksizim."

Beceriksiz Kirpi.

"Ya da karmaşık?" diye fısıldadım. "Bir kitabı anlattığım gibi anlatmana gerek yok, dümdüz de anlatabilirsin. Biliyorsun."

O an, yıllar sonra gözlerini yeniden gördüm.

"Seni dümdüz anlatamam ki."

Ağzımda tükürüğüm gibi biriktirdiğim kelimeler, şimdi bir romanın sayfasında, bir şiirin ilk dörtlüğünde, bir şarkının tek bir sözcüğündeydiler.

"Bazen dümdüz anlamak anlamlar yüklemekten daha derin oluyor." Ellerimdeki teri pijamama sildim, beni böyle görmesinden utanmıyordum ki. "Sen bir bardaksın demek, sen su içtiğim bardaksın demekten daha anlamlı gelebilir bazen."

"Dümdüz anlatamayınca çok saçma şeyler ortaya çıkar, biliyorum," dedi, düşünceliydi sesi.

"Saçma şeyler belki bana çok aşırı anlamlı gelecek. Denemeden öğrenemezsin."

Bana bir adım daha yaklaştı. Kokusunu aldım. "Seni bardak gibi değil, o su gibi düşünüyorum. Bu saçma mıydı?" diye sordu.

Ağrılarım çığlık çığlığayken, "Hayır," dedim. "Bu, bardak olmaktan daha güzeldi."

"Sen bir kalıba sığmazsın."

Sığmaz mıydım gerçekten ben bir kalıba? O da benim göğsümün kalıbına sığmıyor, taşıyordu. Onu nasıl sevdiğimi biliyor muydu? Onu canım, canımdan çıkacakmış gibi seviyordum.

"Su olsan, o bardağı istemezdin," dedi. "Çok saçmalıyorum."

"Sana göre bu saçmalamak. Bana göre bu güzel."

Bana yardım isteyen gözlerle bakıp şu soruyu sordu: "Ben ne düşündüğümü hiç yansıtamayacak mıyım?"

Onu susturmak ister gibi, "Ama su, bardağı istemese de o bardağın ona verdiği şekli alır, biliyorsun değil mi? Kendini kasıyorsun. O yüzden anlatamadığını düşünüyorsun. Kafanda dönen tilkiler düşmanın değil, sana aitler."

Sertçe yutkunup, "Duygularımı anlatamıyorum," diye itiraf etti. "Bunun problem olmadığını düşünürdüm. Ama birisi bana dedi ki; insanların bunları duymaya ihtiyacı var. Anlaşıldığımı düşünürdüm ama anlaşılmak yetmiyormuş. Bu doğru mu?"

Ona anlayışlı gözlerle baktım. "İnsanlar duymak ister, doğru ama hissetmek, duymak kadar güzeldir bence. Sen hissettirebilen birisin bana kalırsa."

"Sen?" dedi. "Sen hangisini isterdin?"

"Ben mi?"

"Evet."

"Ben hissetmeyi isterdim."

"Hissetmek sana yeter miydi?" diye sordu.

"Yeterdi. Bence birini konuşturmaya çalışmak yerine onu hissetmek daha güzel."

"İçimi rahatlattın."

"Salak çocuk," dedim şefkatle. "Sen de büyümemişsin daha."

Durgun bakışları yüzümde dolanırken, "Neden salak çocuk demen hoşuma gitti?" diye sordu bana.

"Birisinin yanında çocuk olabildiğini hissetmişsindir."

"Annemin yanındaymışım gibi hissettim." Bu söylediği kırılma noktam olsa da dik durdum.

"Başını okşayasım geldi," diye itiraf ettim

"Başımı okşamanı da istedim ama söyleyemedim," dedi o da tıpkı benim gibi itiraf ederek.

Elimi uzatıp onun başına dokunmak istesem de durdum, bunu istese de eğilip başını bana yaklaştıramadı.

"Bak, hissediliyormuş değil mi?" diye fısıldadım.

"Nasıl hissettin bunu?"

"His. Çünkü salak çocuk dedikten sonra başını okşadığımı düşünmüştüm. Bazen biriyle aynı anda aynı cümleyi kurmuş gibi bir şeyleri aynı anda istersiniz."

Söylediklerim onu duraksattı. "Şefkatin..." Tamamlamadı. Sustu.

"Şefkatli miyim?"

"Ne olursa olsun, evet. Bana hep şefkatli geliyorsun." Gözlerini yere indirdiğini gördüm. "Hep başımı okşarmışsın gibi." Yine bana baktı. "İnsanların sende bunu görmemelerini seviyorum."

Beni mahveden cümleleriyle burada, sahnede olsa da artık sorularımı hislerimin ardına gizlemek istemiyordum. Cevaplara ihtiyacım vardı benim. O cevapları duymaya, uzanıp onlara dokunmaya ihtiyaç duyuyordum.

"Neden görmemelerini seviyorsun?"

"Bana özel kalıyormuşsun gibi." Ani itirafı kalbimi tekletti. "Mesela senden bahsederken biri sorsa hiç şefkatli değil derim. Hadi senden gelip şefkat isterse, sen de verirsen?"

"Kıskanır mısın?"

"Özelliği gider," diye açık uçlu bir cevap vermeyi tercih etti. Gözleri ellerime kaydı. "Ellerin soğuk mu?"

"Evet," dedim parmaklarımı pijamama bastırarak. "Bumbuz."

"Bumbuz," diye tekrar etti beni.

"Evet."

"Dondurma markası herhâlde?"

"Evet, dondurmacı olmaya karar verdim."

Gülmesini istemiştim ama yüzü ifadesizdi. "Ellerin hiç ısınmıyor mu?" diye sordu yavaşça.

"Hayır." Gözlerimi bin yabancının içinde gözlerim bağlı bulabileceğim ellerine indirdim. "Senin sıcak mı? Ellerin."

"Dikkat etmiyordum. Şimdi sıcak."

"Dokunsam, benimki yüzünden bumbuz olur."

"Bumbuz olsun."

"Sever misin sen soğuğu?" diye fısıldadım.

"Sımsıcak yaparım."

Kalbim acıdan yavaşlarken, "Ben sıcağı severim ellerimde," diye mırıldandım.

"Benim ellerim de bumbuzu yok etmek için yaratılmışlar."

"Ne güzel tutulup uyunur, sımsıcak olur hep," dedim kendimi tutamadan.

"Hiç, birinin elini tutarak uyudun mu?" diye sordu bana eski anılarımızı hatırlatmak istercesine.

"Gerçekte mi yoksa kafamın içinde mi?"

"Fark etmez. Önemli olan ellerinin ısınması."

"Bumbuz ellerimi göğsüne koyup uyutuyordu, evet," dediğimde gözlerinin parladığına yemin edebilirdim. "Kurt adam gibi, sımsıcaktı."

"Gerçekte mi, kafanın içinde mi?"

"Gerçek bittiğinde, kafamın içinde masalına devam etti."

"Ellerin ısınıyor muydu?"

Gözlerim yaşları var etmek için cayır cayır yansa da bunu yapmadım. "Isıtıyordu," dedim, kalbim cehennem gibiydi.

"Sana 'benim hayatından çıkmamın yararı olmadı mı hiç' diye sordu mu peki hiç?" diye sordu, o gün, gözlerimden yaşlar süzülürken sorduğu soruydu bu bana. Hatırlıyordum. Dün gibi.

"Sordu."

"Ne demiştin?"

"Hayır, olmadı demiştim."

"O sorduğu soruyu yine sorsa, yine olmadı mı dersin?"

Bu sorusuna bir cevap veremedim. Ama eğer kabul edeceğini bilseydim, bu soruya cevap olarak ellerimi verirdim. Ona kal demek istiyordum. Gitme, beni bırakma, beni daha fazla sensizlikle sınama... Ağzımı açmadım. Çok acıdı canım onsuz, onunlayken bile iyileşemeyeceğim kadar hastalandım.

Uzun sürse de sessizlik, bir asır gibi gelse bize, toplasan bir saati doldurmazdı.

Bir adım geri çekildi, gökyüzünden silinmeye başlayan karanlık onu benim elimden almadan önce son kez, "İyi ki," dedi bana. "İyi ki doğdun."

O gece orada iki yaralı çocuktuk.
Birbirimizden bedenden ayrılan bir uzuv gibi koptuk.
O gece onu sevdiğimi bildiğiniz son geceydi.
Bundan sonra kimse bilmeyecekti.
Ben keklik gibi bir kadındım, kirpi gibi bir adam sevdim.
Sevdim, çok sevdim.
O bana döndü, ben orada değildim.
Sevdim, çok sevdim.
O gece, orada, ondan vazgeçtim...

Biri avuç içlerimden öptü,
ben de o birinin avuç içlerinden öptüm.
Ve anlamını yalnızca o, ben, dudakları, dudaklarım,
avuçları, avuçlarım biliyoruz.

Bir şeye inan.
Tanrı, insan, oyuncak.
Neye inanırsan inan.
Tutunacak bir şeyin olsun.
Yemin ederim anlıyorsun,
dünya üstünde o kadar çok acı var ki,
seninki dizinde hep kalacak kabarık düşük bir izi.

Neden mi insan yalnızca bir kez aşık olur?
İçinde yalnızca bir kez çiçek açar,
o çiçeğe iyi bakamazsan ve öldürürsen,
o boşalan vazoya koyacağın her çiçek plastik olur.
Açmaz.
Alır, oraya koyarsın.

İçimdeki yangın, kalbimdeki kurumuş gül yapraklarını yakıyor. Bir ölümü öldürmek ne saçma. Belki de bu yalnızca ölü güllerin ateşten cenazesi. İki kişilik bir ölümü, tek kişilik yaşıyorum. Aklımın almadığı yerde öylece dikiliyorsun, seni göremiyorum ama orada olduğunu biliyorum. Öylece serptim avucumdaki külleri gelişigüzel, seni yazacağım diye bir avucu tam ortasından kesip kızıl mürekkepler yaptım kendime. Dolaplarda naftalin, mutfakta kekik kokusu, arabaların egzozundan gelen o yanık kesiği koku, bileklerimde intihar klişeleri... Dolaplarda kanlı el izleri, mutfak tezgâhında ıslak bir bıçak, arabaların egzozundan yükselen koku bir ambulansı takip ediyor, bilekler dikine yarılmış, çiçekler dikilir mi açılan damarlara? Gözlerimdeki tuz kabarıyor, harelerimin gri kayalıkları yeşil yosunlar bağlamış, ben bunu kime nasıl anlatırım? Radyoda bir şarkı çalıyor, nefesim rakı kokuyor. Sana aranıp duran ellerimin avuçları ıslak, bileklerime doğru kayıyor soğuk ve dingin, sıcak ve tembel. Bir sigara yaksam, ayazın içinde gri duman savrulur mu gecenin kuru karanlığına? Savrulup bir yılan gibi kıvrılan duman ulaşır mı sokaklarında gölgenin büyüdüğü şehirlere?

Kirpi Gibi Bir Adam Sevdim

Kasım ayı nemli, ıslak, kuru, donuk, buzlu. Yanaklarda kurumuş tuzlar, teni çekilen yaralı kadınlar. Bir kasım, iki kasım, üç kasım, dört kasım... Beşinci kasımın takvim yaprağı kırmızı, gecesi soğuk ve bulutlar ağzına kadar yağmur yüklü yorgun hamallar. Şimdi seni tıpkı bir elmişsin gibi karşıma alıp, ellerini izlemek için hayallerimi uyutuyorum. Elimde bir iğne, şırınganın ucunda bir damla bulut. Bir damla bulut, bin damla yağmur. Sanki el değilmişsin gibi elinden bahsediyorum. Bütün korkular orada, bütün alışkanlıklar, yanlışlar ve yalanlar. Oturmuşlar, bir beş kasım gecesi, ellerini dinliyorlar, el gibi. Radyoda hâlâ bir şarkı çalıyor, nefesimde rakı kokusu ve bir yaranın üstüne kolonya döküyorum, yanıyor ama mikrop kapmayacak, yanıyor ama mikrop kapmayacak, yanıyor ama... Ellerine bakıyorum, bir elimde kolonya şişesi, ellerine bakıyorum, sanki çok mu el gibi?

Susuyorum, en çok ben susuyorum. En fazla kelime benim dilimin ucunun asma kilidinde asılı duruyor ama en çok ben susuyorum. Konuşması gereken tek kişi benim, kana kana susuyorum. Küçük bir saksı istiyorum, o küçük saksının içindeki toprağa basmak istiyorum kalbimi, tekrardan, yeniden, en başından ağlaya ağlaya kendim yetiştirmek istiyorum yüreğimi. Her şeyin üstesinden geliyorum, bir gecenin altında kalıyorum. Ellerine bakıyorum, ellerin el gibi. Sahiden el gibi, ellerin güzel ellerin, el gibi... Binalar ulaşıyor gökyüzüne, kuşlar artık daha endişeli ve Kasım bu yıl tüm yıllardan daha şiddetli. Kuşlar geceleri görmez, binalara çarpar ve ölürler, Kasım gözümü kör eder, bir takvim yaprağı kesiği intiharın ninnisi. Usul usul bir yaprağı seyreder gözlerim, bir yaprak tarafından linç edilir yüreğim. Acı bir yeşil sonbaharı ortadan ikiye böler. Yarısı sarı, yarısı kahverengi.

Yüreğimi ortadan ikiye bölüyorum, yarısı ben gibi, yarısı el gibi. Ellerin gibi.

Ve aniden yaydan çıkmışsa ok,
sana delindiğim gibi delinmişse kâğıt,
kâğıdın içinde yazıyorsa bizi anlatan cümleler,
söylesene artık ayrılığımızın ne anlamı kalır?

Zaman, tuzla buz edilmiş bir çerçevenin içinde yırtılmış o eski, ölmüş birinin fotoğrafıdır. Zamanın elleri kaburgalarıma dokundu, kaburgamı camdan bir çerçeve gibi tuzla buz etti ama senin fotoğrafını oradan alamadı. Seni içimde öldürdüm, içimde bir cesedi taşıdığımı bile bile seni hiçbir ameliyat izine vermeyeceğim. Cesedin beni zehirliyor evet, dokuz katlı bir binanın çatısından aşağıyı içimde bir cesetle izliyorum ve yerçekimi beni cehennemde bir düğün olduğuna inandırmaya çalışıyor. Âşığın gelinliği kefeniyse ve içimde bir ceset kalbimi zehirliyorsa, ölmek şimdi ağustos ayının ilk gününde doğan bir çocuğun pembe topuklarına kan gibi oturmuş huzurdur. O çocuk büyüsün, bir yazar olsun, beni bulsun; ben sona ölüyorum.

Keşke seninle sonu güzel biten bir roman olsaydık.

Binnur Şafak Nigiz

Bir kırlangıç vuruldu. Hayır, ağlama.
Çünkü diğer kırlangıçlar hâlâ uçuyor sevgilim.
Dinle beni. Önce umutları değil, bilekleri.

Cennet derem kurudu, yansın ezbere bildiğim ellerin.
Ağzının içine bakan gözlerim çıksın,
sözlerine muhtaç kalbim dursun,
sussun, deşilsin seni bekleyen omuzlarım,
bacaklarım kırılsın.
Sussun dilim, kopsun,
Yusuf'u attıkları kuyuda çürüsün adın,
yansın ezbere bildiğim ellerin.
Kül olsan dökülsen gözlerimden,
yüreğimin ucundan sarkmış misina mısın bilmem,
yangından can çektim ucumla,
koptum,
yansın ezbere bildiğim ellerin.
Kırk ateşten geçen İbrahim'in derisi,
Gözü kör anasını bırakıp peygamberi görmeye gidemeyen
Üveys'in yüreğindeki özlem gibi,

Kirpi Gibi Bir Adam Sevdim

Omuzlarımı yaktın.
Susuyorsam dağlanan dilimden.
Peygamberi mağaraya saklayan örümceğin
bir damla canıyla tek başına ördüğü koskoca ağın,
bir damla canımla seni sevişimden ne farkı var?
Yansın ezbere bildiğim ellerin.
Yetimin başını okşayan peygamberin
avucundan inen nur gibi,
başımı okşamayan ellerinin karanlığıdır saçlarımdaki;
yansın ezbere bildiğim ellerin.
Sen cennetten inen bir nuru karanlığında öldürdün.
Ben sana bin nurla da gelsem,
cennet derem kurudu artık;
yansın ezbere bildiğim ellerin.
Tanırdım ya kırk yabancının içinde ellerinden seni,
tanımaktan korkumdandır,
O yüzden;
yansın ezbere bildiğim ellerin.

Binnur Şafak Nigiz

İsmini üç kez unuttum.
Bu dünyada bir adamın ismi
aynı kadın tarafından nasıl üç kez unutulur?
Üç kez unuttum seni, üç kez kurtuldum sandım,
üç kez kanseri yenmişim gibi bayram yaptım,
üç kezlerin bedeli bir ömürmüş, anlamadım.

Tam on iki kere göğsümden vuran aşkın ensesine,
senin canım adını söylerken
yara yaptığım dudaklarımı bastırdım.
Jilet yedim, bir daha seni konuşmamak için.
Ama benim şu kelimelerim, jilet geçirmiyor.
Canım, canım hâlâ çok, canım canım yanıyor.
Canım burası benim canım,
burası meydan muharebesi ve sen komutanı;
olmadığın için beni bizden vurdular.
Canımdan kurşunlar bile gelip geçti,
canım senin ağrını bir türlü geçiremedi.
Canım beni canımdan vurdular,
hiç mi canım acımadın?

GEÇSİN.
GEÇ'SİN.

Günde 26 kez teşekkür ederim sana...

Binnur Şafak Nigiz

Diğer Kitapları